T0029489

ART BY
Therese Andreasen

Everyone is talking about Maxym M. Martineau's

BEAST CHARMER SERIES

"Keep an eye on Maxym M. Martineau. If I'm not mistaken, we have a bona fide genius in our midst."

—**Darynda Jones**, *New York Times* bestselling author

"Original, breathtaking, absolutely fabulous."

—**C. L. Wilson**, *New York Times* and *USA Today* bestselling author

"A fresh new fantasy. Left me with a happy sigh and a fervent wish for a beast of my own. Highly recommend!"

—**Jeffe Kennedy**, RITA Award–winning author

"Maxym Martineau weaves an irresistible blend of adventure, magic, and romance. A unique world full of danger and intrigue and a delightful ensemble of characters will leave fans of fantasy romance breathlessly awaiting more. Prepare to be charmed!"

—**Amanda Bouchet**, *USA Today* bestselling author of the Kingmaker Chronicles

"*Kingdom of Exiles* captivated me with its distinctive fantasy world of exiled Charmers, enchanted beasts, and alluring assassins. A fantastic tale of magic, romance, and adventure—I can't wait to read more."

—**L. Penelope**, award-winning author of *Song of Blood & Stone*

"A strong female lead and a band of lovable assassins? Count me in! I cannot wait to see what more Maxym has to offer."

—**Alexa Martin**, author of *Intercepted*

SHADOWS OF THE LOST

MAXYM M. MARTINEAU

Cover Design by Regina Wamba
Cover images by artem/Adobe Stock, drutska/Adobe Stock, SasinParaska/Adobe Stock, Azure/Adobe Stock, Liliia/Adobe Stock
Map illustration by Travis Hasenour
History of Lendria illustration by Laura Boren/Sourcebooks
Front and Back portraits by Therese Andreasen
Custom Beastiary illustrations by Aud Koch
Additional stock images © Daria Ustiugova/Shutterstock, Vera Petruk/Shutterstock, Anton Tokarev/Shutterstock

Published by Sourcebooks Casablanca, an imprint of Sourcebooks
P.O. Box 4410, Naperville, Illinois 60567-4410
(630) 961-3900
sourcebooks.com

Cataloging-in-Publication Data is on file with the Library of Congress.

Printed and bound in the United States of America.
VP 10 9 8 7 6 5 4 3 2 1

Oslo's Ruins
LENDRIA
HIREATH
Midnight Jester
Kitska Forest
Devil's Hollow
CRUOR
Penumbra Glades
Nepheste's Ruins

Glacial Springs
Silvis's Ruins
Luma Lake
WILHEIM
The Gaping Wound
Tyrus's Ruins
Eastrend
Lightwood Forest
Ortega Key
Kings Isle
Yuna's Ruins
Queens Isle

A HISTORY OF
LENDRIA
1 THE FIRST WAR
2 Many beasts die and become monsters of the Kitska Forest
3 ZANE RISES from the dead as the first assassin
4 Cruor founded
5 HIREATH ESTABLISHED
6 WAR WITH RHYNE
7 FROZEN PRINCE OF LENDRIA, AKA NOC, DIES
8 Noc raised as undead
9 War with Rhyne ceases
10 NOC BECOMES GUILD MASTER OF CRUOR
11 NOC ACCEPTS BOUNTY on exiled Charmer Leena Edenfrell
12 Leena gifts Noc, Kost, Calem and Ozias with beasts
13 LEENA IS TAKEN HOSTAGE by the Charmers Council
14 CRUOR BATTLES HIREATH, frees Leena
17 NOC FALLS PREY TO OATH'S MAGIC
18 Attempts to murder Leena

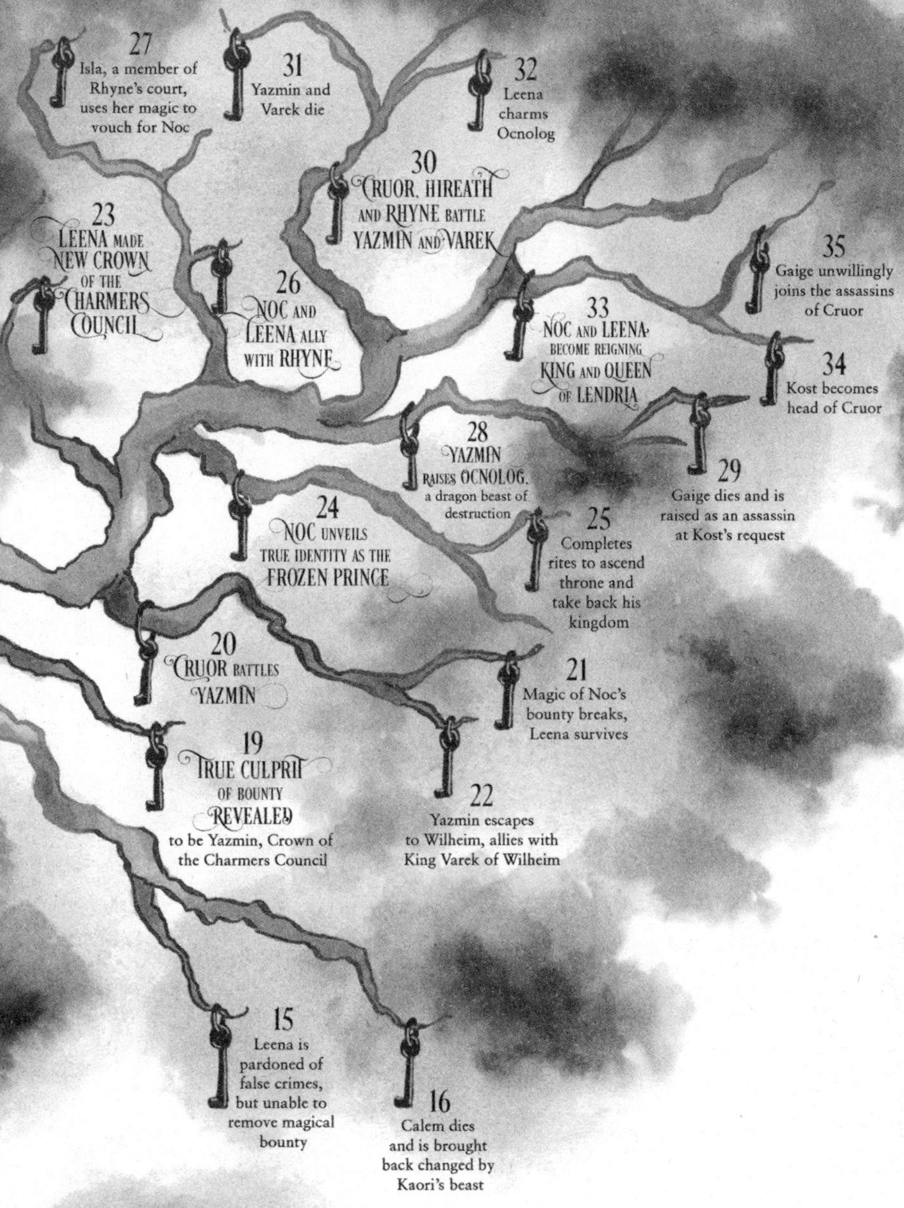

BEST READ FROM

ROOTS TO BRANCHES

ONE

KOST

I couldn't bear to look at him. Not for more than a few moments.

Shadows writhed around Gaige, slithering between the cushions and coiling around his legs with abandon. He had no desire to control them. To harness his newfound power as an undying assassin and form weapons out of the darkness. Instead, he let them run wild as if they were beasts he didn't have the power to charm. His resistance was what had brought me to this quiet alcove. There wasn't another assassin in sight—rare for the size of our manor and the number of members we housed. The only group I'd passed on my way to the library had been huddled around the coffee table in the parlor, trying to distract themselves with a game of Klimkota. But try as they might, the bright, gem-colored pieces and tiered board could only hold their attention for so long. Gaige's shadows wreathing the open doorway to the library were impossible to ignore.

And so were the guild members' whispered concerns.

"What's going to happen to him?"

"I heard he's refusing to train."

"Maybe he should go back to Hireath. He doesn't want to be here, not really."

Hireath. When Ocnolog, a legendary dragon beast, rose from

his underground tomb, he'd destroyed the peaceful beast charmer city. Gone were the elaborate houses built high in the trees. The breathtaking keep that'd been carved out of an alabaster mountain near the falls had been reduced to rubble. The gargantuan tree housing the library—burned to ash. Ocnolog had leveled it all. Set it ablaze and never looked back. There was nothing left but debris, charred trees, and scorched grass. Fortunately, we'd evacuated everyone before he'd awoken. While many used the newfound peace between Wilheim, the capital city of Lendria, and the Charmers to find homes elsewhere, Hireath was still a sacred site. The Charmers Council would not rest until it was restored to its former glory.

Most of the Charmers Council.

"What do you want?" Gaige asked, pulling me from my thoughts.

I'd never heard a more loaded question. There was a veritable number of things I desired from Gaige, but only one wish came to mind in that moment: control. No, safety. I wanted him *safe*.

"Why aren't you training?" My gaze cut to the window behind him, overlooking the back lawns of Cruor. There, my second-in-command, Ozias, and third-in-command, Calem, were running drills with some of the newer members. Gaige hadn't trained once since his transition from living to undead, from beast charmer to assassin. It'd been over a month, and while I could afford him some leniency to mourn his former life, it was time he started training in earnest.

"Because I don't want to." Gaige didn't bother to look up from his book, instead turning a page painstakingly slowly, as if he enjoyed the gentle scrape of parchment on parchment.

"That's hardly a reason." I brushed my hands along my vest before crossing my arms. "You *must* train."

"I *mustn't* do anything."

Clenching my teeth, I fought back an exasperated huff. "Gaige. This isn't negotiable. You're not in control."

He snapped his book shut and chucked it across the library. It careened past shelves loaded with worn tomes and headed straight for the low-hanging, candlelit chandelier dangling above one of the heavy wooden tables. Just before it hit its mark, shadows leapt from the crevices of the room and snared the book.

"That looks like control to me." His rich baritone was edged with resentment and something sharp. And I knew that unnamed emotion, the one that felt so much like hatred and disgust, was aimed directly at me.

I opened my mouth to respond when his shadows quivered as if they'd been electrified. They shifted to menacing spires and speared the book, slicing clean through the pages and binding. A flurry of torn parchment churned in the dark chaos of his power until the tendrils finally dissipated, leaving nothing but a pile of shredded pages behind.

My stomach knotted several times over. "I see you and I have different definitions of control."

Gaige's jaw tightened, and he looked away.

Learning to wield the shadows was a necessity. If they grew without restraint, uncontained and ravenous, they'd devour their host and pull him or her deep into the shadow realm, never to be seen again. I'd only witnessed such a fate once before. Even then, Talmage, a previous guild master of Cruor, had killed the assassin before the darkness could engulf him entirely. The power behind those virulent ink-black tendrils had been otherworldly.

And Gaige's shadows were nearly as disastrous.

"You cannot prolong this any longer. You are undead. You walk with the shadows. This is your life now, chosen or not, and it's time to lead it."

He shot up from his seat, fists clenched by his side. *Gloved* fists. "I did *not* choose this life, Kost. I'm dealing with the wretched hand I've been dealt, and I'll do whatever I damn well please with it."

My brows shot up, and I stepped forward, going toe-to-toe with the man I'd once thought I might love. "Wretched? Is that what you think of this place? Of your brethren? Calem? Ozias? *Me*?"

His nostrils flared as heat colored his eyes a dangerous shade of steel. He raised his right hand between us and yanked the glove off. I cringed. His faded Charmer's symbol never ceased to rack my body with guilt. Before, the inked marking had been a vibrant, citrine tree full of life. Now...it was nothing more than a smeared, charcoal etching. A permanent reminder of the beast realm and all the beloved creatures he could no longer access.

All because of me.

"How many times, Kost?" His voice was barely a whisper, but it simmered with so much fury it felt as though he'd shouted. "How many times do we have to have this conversation? You will never comprehend what I lost the day I died."

He stared at me for moments on end, waiting for me to break. And I almost did. I almost slumped to the bay window bench and buried my head in my hands. I was so desperate to end this agony for the both of us. I wanted to stop fighting. I wanted things to just be easy, for once. I wanted things to go back to the way they were before he'd met his demise in the Kitska Forest, and yet I was ashamed to even think that. Those were the very words that had been uttered to me when I'd been raised and subsequently left by someone I loved.

Slowly, I exhaled and willed my frustration to flee. I would not do that to Gaige. I would not leave him to face this fate alone. I'd known that begging Noc, the former guild master of Cruor, to raise Gaige would have consequences. I'd known it'd likely make it impossible for him to call on his Charmer magic ever again. And still I pushed for it to happen, selfishly wanting him to live. His fate was my responsibility.

I couldn't break; I needed to be strong for him. Cold, even, if that's what it took to help him find his way.

"I'm not here to discuss what you lost, Gaige. I'm here to help you forge a new path forward, even if you didn't want it to begin with." I stepped around him, nearing the window and gazing at the silhouettes of training assassins in the faded, heather-purple light of dusk. Swallowing thickly, I tugged at the hem of my vest. "I can train you privately, if you'd prefer. I am at your disposal."

Gaige blinked, and for a moment, there was a sliver of the man I used to know. A surprised curl to his lips. A mischievous glint to his eyes. He seemed to recognize his inadvertent reaction, though, and squashed it immediately.

"There was a time I would have taken you up on that offer. For something else, of course," he said. My ears burned with his insinuation—so at odds with the suffocating weight of despair in my chest. Slowly, he regloved his hand. "But not anymore."

"Someone else then." I hated the way my voice came out shaky and weak. "I don't care who trains you, just get it done. That's an order from your guild master."

He chuckled, a dark, nasty sound. "And just how are you going to enforce that? You're my guild master in name only. I won't be doing your bidding."

"I only have so much patience, Gaige. If you continue to bait me..."

"Oh, come on." Gaige pushed past me as a whirlwind of shadows encircled him. "Don't you have better things to do? Go run the guild. I promise I'll, I don't know, not destroy a book next time." He toed the shredded pile of parchment and binding for effect, and then let the swirling tendrils swallow him whole. So dark and all-consuming were his shadows that I couldn't even track his movements. One moment he was there and the next he was gone, whisked away to gods only knew where.

I stormed down one of the aisles until I found a shelf heavy with tomes against the back wall. With far more force than necessary, I tugged a muted-yellow book by the binding, and the hidden door leading to the guild master's private study swung open. I stepped through and slammed it shut behind me. The telltale, muffled thud of books falling followed, but I didn't bother to reopen the passage and clean up the mess I'd made.

With the books or Gaige?

Exhaling tightly, I pushed that thought away and sank into the ornate, stuffed chair behind the desk, turning my attention back to the work that always awaited me. I grazed a few pieces of parchment. Bounties. A dull ache simmered behind my eyes, and I rubbed my temples. Becoming Cruor's new guild master was an expected development. Noc couldn't possibly be both king and guild master, and as his second-in-command, it was only logical for me to take over.

Yet, both Noc and Leena—Crown of the Charmers Council, Queen of Lendria, and a sister to me despite our initial rocky beginning—had been somewhat resistant to the idea. They wanted me to remain in Wilheim with them as their adviser. While the idea of dissecting political agendas and helping to strategize the well-being of an entire nation had its appeal, there were things here that needed a close eye. One thing—person—in particular, but he wasn't exactly easy to watch. For the time being, the work that came with being guild master was a wonderful distraction. But even with ample jobs and responsibilities before me, I still couldn't find the will to focus on my duties.

A whisper of shadows swirled in the corner, and I stilled. Tendrils pulled from every hidden crevice in the office, and they interwove in indistinct patterns until knitting together in the shape of a man. Noc. He craned his neck from side to side before tucking his hands in the pockets of his fitted trousers. He didn't wear a crown, but the royal insignia, a griffin, was embroidered on the chest of his tunic. It should have been a bold silver, but the shadows washed out all color. Even the crystalline-blue of his eyes.

"Your Majesty," I said, burying my frustrations with Gaige in a smile. It was genuine, at least. Seeing my friend would always bring me joy. Shadow walking meant we could visit each other whenever we desired, despite the distance between Cruor and Wilheim. It was a small boon in an otherwise unfortunate predicament. I'd never expected the guild to feel so empty without him.

He scoffed, and the shadows about his jaw fluttered in response. "Not you, too. Calem already says it every chance he gets."

"He does it precisely because it elicits a rise out of you." I leaned back in the chair, allowing my muscles to mold into the worn fabric. It'd only been a week since Noc and Leena's wedding and subsequent crowning ceremony. And Calem, who was undoubtedly causing a ruckus somewhere within the guild, made it a point to refer to Noc as "king" whenever the opportunity arose.

"Yeah, well..." He glanced about the room, as if taking in the familiar surroundings of his former office. "I'll have to come up with something equally irritating to call him."

"Good luck with that." I braced my elbows on the desk. "How's everything going?"

"We're making progress. Trade has officially reopened with Rhyne, so we should see an increased shipment of goods in the coming weeks."

"That's good. Is Rhyne in need of any assistance with their

borders? I'm sure we can afford to send a few members if necessary." I shuffled the parchment before me, eyeing requests and the details of the bounties.

"Not necessary." Noc ghosted his hand along the bookshelves lining the wall as he moved toward the desk. Shadows dissipated and appeared with every subtle shift as he toyed with the bindings. "If anything, we need the help in Hireath."

A nagging sensation trickled down my spine, and I pursed my lips. "Gaige hasn't been back yet."

"I know." Noc came to a halt across from me, eyes cast downward. "Kaori and Raven have been asking about him. They're handling the rebuilding effort just fine, but they worry. We all do." Of course the members of the Charmers Council were asking about Gaige. He'd been a residing member for decades. Kaori and Raven were his closest friends. Yet, he'd cut off contact with them and refused to discuss his home altogether.

"He won't train. Not with me, not with Ozias, not with anyone." I stood and began to pace as the study walls closed in around me. Ozias was an expert at teaching members of Cruor to control the shadows. Even so, he couldn't coax Gaige to learn.

And that was a dangerous thing.

"I don't know what to do," I said.

"How close is he?" Noc's question was barely audible, but it rang through my mind with the force of a gong.

"Too close." I stopped and removed my glasses, pinching the bridge of my nose. Then I extracted a small, mulberry cloth from my breast pocket and polished the lenses. "I don't think he has much time left."

Noc strode toward me and placed his hands on my shoulders. The lack of true contact was apparent, but the icy familiarity of those dark tendrils soothed my frayed nerves. "He'll come around. He has to."

Or he won't, and we'll lose him to the shadows. The unspoken truth of Gaige's future hung heavy in the air, and I clenched my jaw.

Noc let his hands fall to his sides. "Leena and I leave tomorrow for Rhyne. When we return, we'll stop through Cruor on our way to Hireath. If he hasn't figured it out by then, she'll knock some sense into him."

With a quiet sigh, I replaced my glasses. "I hope she's successful."

"She will be." Noc tipped his chin ever so slightly, peering at me for a long moment before frowning. "I hate to leave so abruptly but..."

"Go." I waved him off as I returned to the desk. I slid into the chair and grabbed the nearest quill and inkwell. "I need to evaluate these contracts and determine who would be best suited for the jobs."

"Maybe Gaige needs an assignment. Purpose will help." Shadows gathered around Noc, temporarily darkening the room. He hesitated for a breath, half his body already lost to the shadow realm and other still firmly planted in my study.

"We won't lose him, Kost."

But as I nodded in answer and Noc disappeared, I couldn't help but feel like we'd lost Gaige already. The man we knew before had died. This new person was shrouded in a sinister darkness. No matter how much I wanted to try to pierce that veil, I wasn't sure he'd let me.

One way or another, the shadows would come calling. And the only person who could stop them was Gaige.

Two

GAIGE

The Kitska Forest felt like home. It shouldn't have, but it did.

I lingered on the fringe of the tree line and watched as Calem and Ozias ran their brethren through a series of drills. With my senses heightened by death, the forceful grunts and exhales coming from the assassins as they physically attacked one another were easy to discern. Calem was shirtless—he was always shirtless during training, it seemed—and his bronzed skin was somehow aglow despite the lack of direct sunlight. His thick, blond hair was tied up in a loose bun that threatened to topple over as he swirled out of Ozias's grasp.

Ozias laughed—a deep sound that was incredibly pleasing to the ear—and craned his neck from side to side as he repositioned himself before Calem. Sweat plastered his white work shirt to his dark skin, and he gave his large biceps a flex as if to remind Calem that he could pulverize him at any given moment.

But Calem was faster and much too cocky for that. They both backstepped into a void of darkness and continued their sparring in the shadow realm—a veil between this world and death that only the undead could see. The rest of the group ceased their training to watch, and I could hardly blame them. As much as I despised this new life, the skill they exuded was still admirable.

It was hard to tell whether the dark tendrils swirling about me were of my own making or a result of the strange magic that seemed to pulsate from deep within the wood. Pinesco pods—with their eerie, eyelike pattern—rattled from the treetops in the faint breeze, so much like the unsettling, raspy exhale of a fearsome beast.

But I knew all the monsters in this place. And I was the worst one.

How self-deprecating. Sighing, I folded my arms across my chest and leaned against the nearest trunk. Rough bark scraped against the exposed portion of my arm, but I didn't flinch. These days, the only thing that gave me pause was the notion that I was expected to do something with these forsaken shadows...and Kost.

My throat tightened. He was so damn infuriating. Yes, we'd rectified things to a certain extent, but that didn't mean I was in a rush to follow him around again. I couldn't look at him without anger building inside me. I didn't know how to forgive him. And I couldn't pinpoint why. I'd more or less accepted Noc and Leena's role in my resurrection. They'd both known about the risk. Of what it might do to my powers, but Kost?

A phantom burn spasmed from the back of my gloved hand—where my emblem used to be—and the shadows around me jolted. Being a Charmer was everything to me. Discovering rare creatures, studying their unique habits and ways, befriending them and enjoying their everlasting affection... I'd lost it all. Charmer magic was not compatible with the dark magic of the undead.

Maybe I'd forgiven Noc and Leena because it wasn't their idea to bring me back. It was Kost's. And maybe it burned all the more because there was still a small sliver of hope inside me, desperately begging for me to acknowledge it. Because on the rare chance I found respite in my dreams, they were always about my old life. About him.

And with that image teasing my waking moments, tinged by

shrouding darkness, it was impossible to forgive—or to move on. I was still so *angry*, and that only made the shadows worse.

The heady, soulful groan of a door to the beast realm opening rushed through the quiet evening, and I straightened as my hand immediately went to the bronze key dangling about my neck. Calem and Ozias had finished their shadow drills, and they'd brandished their own keys to summon the magical beasts Leena had gifted them when they'd first met.

A sour taste crept up the back of my tongue, and I let my hand fall away from my key. The keys were meant for non-Charmers, in case one of my kind—one of my *former* kind—decided to offer a beast to someone they found worthy. I would've required hundreds of keys to summon all my beasts like I used to. Instead, I only had one. As much as I cherished the one creature I had left, the key was a reminder of everything I'd lost.

Ozias's Laharock, Jax, appeared and rammed his thick, dragon-like skull into Ozias's chest before extending his long neck to the dusk sky. Stars were just beginning to dot the darkening night, and he stared up at them with a look of peace. One that was swiftly interrupted when Calem's rambunctious beast, an Effreft named Effie, soared through the air and let out a series of sharp but happy trills. She had the build of a small dog and the head of an eagle. Flapping her wings vigorously, she dusted the earth beneath her with a fine powder that glittered like diamonds. Tiny white flowers instantly bloomed around the feet of the small gathering who remained, and a joyful swell of laughter bubbled around them.

I hadn't summoned Okean in days. Lithe and aqua-blue, my legendary feline was a sight to behold. His power to summon and control water had a unique way of both invigorating and calming me at the same time. And yet I hesitated to call him. I knew in my bones he'd come without fail, but I feared my shadows would haunt him.

He wasn't like Effie and Jax. Okean had lived with me for decades, and he'd witnessed my death. I wasn't the same person he loved before, and I wasn't sure I'd ever be. What if he didn't like what I'd become? I didn't. And if he rejected me or feared me...I wouldn't be able to take it. No, Okean was better off lounging in the beast realm, enjoying the company of all the beasts I had to abruptly leave behind.

Not all. Heavy footsteps thudded at my back as twigs snapped beneath the weight of massive paws. I tilted my head ever so slightly until I caught sight of a bear-shaped outline the size of an elephant bull. Boo lumbered forward, a faint mist curling from his snout, and he chuffed in acknowledgment at my shadows before coming to a halt by my side.

"Hey, Boo."

A warm growl simmered from the back of the Gigloam's throat. Like me, Boo was undead. Nearly all the beasts that'd aided their Charmers during the centuries-old war that split our continent into factions had died in the battle against Wilheim. But just as the assassins rose for the very first time back then, so too did the beasts. They'd been wild and untamable, and as a result, lived in the secluded Kitksa Forest where they were deemed monsters.

Until I came along and tamed one. More or less.

Patting Boo's thick neck, I worked my fingers through his tough, matted fur. Gigloams were supposed to have lustrous, mossy-green coats. Boo's was dull and looked more like aged seaweed. Death had amplified his characteristics in a way that made him seem more gruesome, more fiendish than he really was. The bone helm that protruded over his skull had yellowed and cracked in places, and the moon etched onto it was at three-quarters; his stag-like antlers were jagged and sharp, as if they'd been snapped in half. At first glance, his muddy-red eyes appeared soulless. But that was far, far from the truth.

Snorting, my Kitska beast shoved his nose into my shoulder, and I stumbled to the side.

"What?" I asked, swatting him gently.

He sank to his haunches with a heavy thud, and the ground trembled. Shaking his head vigorously up and down, he grunted as the tops of his antlers tore through the low-hanging branches.

"That doesn't help me," I said, unable to keep my lips from tipping upward.

His gaze wandered to the open clearing where Jax and Effie played. Jax had a way to go before fully growing into his dragon-like body but was large enough to withstand a playful blow from Boo in case it packed too much…oomph. His gleaming red scales, trimmed in gold, were near impenetrable—even for Boo's claws.

Maybe not his teeth, though. I gave my creature a sidelong glance, debating whether or not to encourage him to join in on the games, when a heinous, earsplitting cry shook the trees on the other side of the clearing. Everything around us fell silent. The assassins in the field went stock-still, and their beasts huddled close as they targeted an indistinct spot in the darkened wood. Even the wind died, save an eerie whisper of air that stank of death and decay. Boo stiffened, his thick hackles standing on end, and he peeled back his maw in a menacing growl. After a moment, he slowly got to his feet and began summoning moonlight between his antlers.

"Hold on." I grabbed his snout and pulled his head downward. The three-quarter moon could allow him to manifest a dangerous amount of power. "There's no need to blast one of your brethren into oblivion. Come on."

Without hesitation, he sank to one knee, and I climbed atop

his back. The moment I was situated, he barreled forward across the clearing, just as Calem and Ozias called forth shadows from the depths of the forest. In the time it took me to breathe, they'd turned those wispy tendrils into glittering blades as real and as solid as the earth beneath my feet. It was the type of control every assassin trained to achieve.

"Wait!" I shouted, urging Boo forward. He came to an abrupt halt when we reached the group, and I slid off his back to stride toward my own newfound brethren. "It's probably just confused. Let me take care of it."

"Did you call it? Is it one of yours?" Calem looked back and forth between Boo and me, and while he let his hand fall lax by his side, the blades he'd summoned remained suspended in the air by his waist. His muted-red eyes were ringed in mercury, and that dangerous hue widened a fraction. One wrong move, and Calem would shift into a monstrous beast that rivaled even the undead creatures in the Kitska Forest. His condition was a by-product of almost dying and subsequently being saved by a legendary feline, and it was incredibly hard to control.

"No," I said. Another hair-raising call shook the treetops.

Ozias turned to the small group of members they'd been training. "Get inside. Someone tell Kost." They nodded in unison as they eagerly raced back to the manor, faint shadows clinging to their heels.

Irritation flickered to life in my gut. "It's fine. There's no need to involve him."

"He's our guild master. There's every reason to involve him." Calem beckoned to Effie, and she circled above his head once before perching on his shoulder. Jax, too, moved in close. At a moment's notice, he'd be able to summon a wall of lava rock that could act as a barrier to protect us from whatever monster was rampaging in the wood.

"It's just a Kitska beast. I can handle it." I strode forward, gait stiff, and Boo followed. A breath later, Calem let out an exasperated sigh, and he and Ozias fell in line behind me with their own very-much-alive beasts.

"How can we help?" Ozias asked as we neared the tree line.

"I don't know yet. I..." A deafening howl cut me off, followed by a cascading series of harrowing screeches. Not one, but three, creatures emerged from the dark. They were the size of large wolves with humped backs and bony, protruding spines that ended in arrowhead tails. Their bat-like heads riveted at odd angles, and whiskers sprung from their pointed ears and trailed the length of their body like thin fingers.

"What in the actual fuck are those?" Calem pulled Effie off his shoulder and settled her on Jax's back before crouching into his heels. The blades hovering about his waist quivered.

One beast snarled in answer, and it took a few predatory steps forward. The tufted, gray fur covering its body shifted to black alligator hide along its legs, and massive talons left canyons in the soft grass beneath its feet.

"Mizobats." At least they had been before death and the Kitska Forest had twisted them and made them untamable for any normal Charmer. A chill settled deep in my bones. "No one make any sudden movements."

Even Boo heeded my warning, his breath no more than a shallow exhale against my neck. The Mizobats chittered among each other, their back-and-forth resembling that of insect mandibles clicking together. They sniffed the air in unison. With milky eyes, they were almost entirely blind; but their sense of smell and otherworldly hearing—coupled with their tentacle whiskers that could feel even the slightest shift in the wind—made them adept hunters.

"Gaige?" Ozias's lips barely parted, but the sound of his

question might as well have been a bullhorn to the Mizobats. Their ears flicked to attention. One by one, they peeled back their lips in a menacing snarl.

Edging forward, I drew their focus to me. "Easy, there." Shadows began to gather near my fingertips. The slithering tendrils wrapped my wrists and snaked through the air in the direction of the Kitska beasts. My newfound power would never put a living creature at ease, but the undead monsters of the forest were much more familiar with the dark.

At least that was the case with Boo and a handful of others I'd encountered.

"We're not going to hurt you." I inched even closer, and I presented the back of my hand to the nearest Mizobat. "You're safe."

The leader slowly brought its scrunched nose to my knuckles. The Mizobat inhaled deeply, savoring my scent for a few seconds before exhaling. A moment passed as I let it assess me—assess all of us—without moving. I couldn't see Ozias or Calem behind me, but death had heightened my senses to a degree that was almost unbearable. I could hear their erratic heartbeats, their shallow breaths.

Muscles loosening, the other Mizobats approached me and gave me a good sniff.

"See?" I rotated my palm up. Shadows knit together in a small sphere that hovered for a moment before collapsing and dispersing through my fingers. "We're the same."

The beast sat on their haunches, curiously eyeing the wisps, and were all but tamed when a sudden influx of shadows exploded around us. They rushed upward to blanket out the sky before smothering us in a maelstrom of wild darkness. My mind went blank at the sudden display of power. I hadn't sensed anyone else, and yet now we were surrounded. How? Why? One moment I'd been exerting control over my shadows, luring the Kitska beasts in, and then *this.*

It was as if those inky tendrils had bloomed from the very earth beneath our feet. As if my lure had summoned them and not the creatures. But as wild and violent as they were—and I knew my own power had a tendency to lash out—they didn't feel like my shadows. They couldn't be. Maybe a newer assassin lost control. Maybe...

A sharp wail pulled my focus, and I whirled in place. "Ozias! Calem!"

They didn't answer.

"Boo!" I tried again.

In the sheer chaos, I heard the frantic cry of Effie and an uneasy warble from Jax. Ozias and Calem were shouting, too, but the whistling of the shadows—like a screeching void that sucked up all sounds—deafened everything.

A sudden white light ruptured the dark for a split second, and I caught sight of Boo. But as the beam of moonlight faded from between his antlers, the tendrils formed as quickly as they'd dispersed and obstructed him from view.

Gritting my teeth, I dared to take a few steps into the storm. Shadows eviscerated my clothes, slicing clean through to my skin and exposing raw flesh and blood. They cut with the efficiency of a freshly sharpened blade, and I buckled to the ground as one tendril sliced me from forehead to chin, just narrowly missing my eye. Yelling, I clamped my hands over my face and prayed—begged—for the shadows to stop.

And then they did.

They disappeared with such abruptness that, if not for the heady ringing in my ears and blood weeping from countless wounds, I wouldn't have believed they'd existed at all.

Letting my hands fall away, I blinked. My eye burned and I sucked in a sharp breath as I rotated so I could see Calem and Ozias.

"Effie!" Calem cried. Like me, he was covered head to toe in gashes, but he paid little mind to his injuries. His hands were shaking over his badly mangled beast, and she whimpered in response. Her mint-green feathers were a muddy red, but she was breathing, if erratically.

"Get her to the realm! Jax, too," I shouted, glancing at Ozias's beast. For the most part, his Laharock had faired the best out of all of us. Those gleaming-red scales had protected Jax from the brunt of the attack, but there were a few places where the plates had been pried almost clean off. Still, the beast realm would heal both Effie and Jax in time.

Ozias wiped blood from a deep wound across his lips and nodded. They gripped their bronze keys tight, and the signature groan of the realm door opening crested over the now-quiet lawns. I scoured the clearing, hoping to find the one responsible for unleashing the onslaught of shadows. A retreating shadow darted into the woods, pausing only for a moment at the threshold of the tree line. It lingered as if it were watching, and then suddenly it was gone. Before I could investigate, a belabored chuff rooted my place.

Boo was slumped to his haunches and bleeding profusely. Unlike Calem and Ozias's beasts, Boo couldn't return to the realm, which meant that the lacerations lining his rib cage would need immediate medical attention. Fortunately, the infirmary would have adequate materials to treat his wounds. He would survive.

"Thank the gods," I muttered, finally allowing myself a sigh of relief. But just as we were regaining our bearings, so too were the Mizobats. Somehow, the shadows had all but glossed over them. They had a few nicks marring their hides. Nothing overly serious, but certainly enough for them to think we'd attacked them. And judging by their challenging, predatory shrieks and quivering whiskers, they were no longer interested in being tamed.

"Get back!" I yelled to Calem and Ozias, scrambling to my feet. "GET BACK!"

The Mizobats lunged forward—two immediately breaking off and heading for Boo—while the leader raced straight to me. Calem and Ozias were shouting, each still in the process of safely ensuring their beasts made it home. Boo howled in rage as the other Mizobats sank their fangs into his hind quarters.

A shield. Form a shield! I crossed my arms and braced for the hit while calling on my power. I tried to focus. Tried to pull darkness from the surrounding night and bend it to my will. I tried—

A maelstrom of charcoal shadows manifested before my eyes, just in time for the Mizobat's massive talons to clash against an ink-black rapier.

A rapier? Oh. *Oh.* Relief and frustration and anger coalesced inside me as the tendrils peeled back like a cloak falling to the ground, and a man emerged. Kost. The muscles of his exposed forearms strained as he held his weapon steady. His jaw was set, ice-green eyes hard and wild. The tendons down his neck jumped, but he didn't budge as the Mizobat tried to bury him with its weight.

Without meeting my gaze, he bit out an order. "Get inside. Now." Then, a little louder, "Calem, Ozias—take care of the ones on Boo." With Effie and Jax safe, they leapt into action, calling on their own shadows to wrangle the monsters swarming my Gigloam.

"I'm not going inside. I can help."

Kost did an impressive sweeping motion that dislodged the beast's talons from the blade, and he angled the tip directly at the creature's jugular. The Mizobat hissed and crouched low. Its tentacle whiskers lashed wildly around us as it determined where and how to strike.

"Go inside," Kost seethed as he sidestepped me, blocking the Mizobat from my view.

My stomach hardened, and I pushed to my feet. The shadows I hadn't been able to summon to protect myself began to gather around my hands, and the Mizobat roared in response.

"Gaige!" Kost shouted, his stare darting from me to the enraged monster. "You've done *enough*."

I flinched, and the brewing anger in me died. A cold, defeated emotion settled over me instead, and I let my face go blank. Of course he blamed me. I could argue and try to tell him that I hadn't done this. I'd only attempted to tame the Mizobats with a shadow lure—something I'd made a point to perfect in order to help these poor monsters. The violent tendrils that'd birthed from the ground itself? I didn't do that. I couldn't...

My fingers trembled. At least, I hadn't *meant* to. It didn't feel like I did. Still, the way Kost looked at me now told me everything I needed to know. He believed I'd caused this. It's not like I expected anything different from him. I knew I was a burden. I heard everything the members said about me. It shouldn't have hurt to discover Kost felt the same.

"Boo needs you. No one else here knows how to treat a beast. Now, go."

At least *someone* needed me. I turned my back on Kost, ignoring the small, insistent part of me that begged me to stay. Not because I wanted to defy him, but because I wanted to make sure he would be okay. But the larger, dominating voice—the one full of resentment and anger—won out and I walked away from Kost. Again.

Ozias and Calem had managed to chase off the other Mizobats, and they'd ushered Boo to the deck surrounding Cruor. I rushed to my injured beast and ran my fingers over his coat, counting the number of wounds and gauging their depth. Once I'd started my assessment, Ozias and Calem left without a word to join Kost.

He would be fine. He'd always be fine without me.

And so I slipped inside to gather supplies from the medical wing to do the one thing I couldn't mess up: care for a beast.

THREE

KOST

"Tell me exactly what happened."

Ozias, Calem, Gaige, and I were under a makeshift canopy Ozias had set up for Boo. He crouched before Boo's head, gently rubbing his snout as Gaige attended to the wounds on his rib cage. After threading a suture needle, Gaige began methodically stitching Boo's abdomen together. Calem leaned against the railing of the deck and crossed his ankles. He met my hard gaze for a beat, then quickly glanced at Ozias.

"Well?" I prompted.

After another shared look, Ozias cleared his throat. "It wasn't a big deal." Gaige paused for a moment, as if the response had taken him aback, but he recovered quickly and continued to work in silence. I narrowed my eyes.

"You really shouldn't worry so much." Calem rolled his head from side to side. "Honestly, this isn't the first time a Kitska monster has stumbled onto our lawns."

"It's the first time *this* has happened." I gestured wide to include all of them. Calem was covered in blood, and there was a network of lashes across Ozias's arms and Gaige's back. Not to mention Boo's severe injuries. My family would heal fast enough. The undead could recover from almost anything. Beneath the slick layer of red on Calem's chest, I could already see tendons sewing together and skin re-forming as the minutes passed. But Boo? My eyes cut to the Kitska beast, then to Gaige.

"You were lucky," I said. "This could've been much worse."

"What could've been? Boo's injuries?" Gaige's answer was terse. He set the needle down and dug his fingers into a clay jar, scooping out a hefty amount of salve. Gingerly, he slathered it against his beast's hide. Boo let out a sigh of relief and dropped his head into Ozias's hands. His eyes slipped closed, and within a matter of moments he was snoring. Gaige wiped away the last remnants of ointment on his trousers. "Or maybe you were referring to me?"

For a moment, I didn't respond. I hadn't meant to insinuate anything, but the truth was undeniable. Gaige wasn't in control. I was in my study when this whole debacle started, and I'd thought everything was fine. I'd watched from my window as Gaige, so confidently and calmly, approached the Kitska beasts. And they'd responded beautifully, only for a sudden influx of shadows to destroy the budding trust he'd built.

Ozias stood. "I don't think that's what he—"

"You start training in the morning. That's an order," I said, ignoring Ozias's attempt to smooth things over. Whether or not I hurt Gaige with my assessment was irrelevant. The only thing that mattered was ensuring something like this never happened again.

Gaige glowered at me. "You're good at giving those lately."

"It's for your own safety," I said. My chest tightened as I fought to keep my voice flat. I didn't understand how he could continue to fight me on this. There was absolutely no point in denying what he was any longer. But every time I let my emotions get the better of me, I ended up saying something I didn't mean. Facts, even when cold and harsh, were easier—safer. "Keep acting this way, and you'll die. No one here can save you but you."

Gaige launched to his feet and met me head-on. "At least this time if I die, you won't be able to bring me back."

"Is that what this is all about?" Shadows furled around me, moving at a breakneck pace until a slender rapier took shape in my hand. Gripping it tight, I raised it between us. "I promised to end your life at any point if you requested it. Are you ready?"

Heat simmered in his steel-blue glare, and the muscles along his jaw twitched. He inched ever so slightly closer, resting his cheek against my blade. And then an achingly familiar emotion filled his eyes: anguish. I could hardly unpack the weight of his pain, and it hit me with enough force to take wind from my lungs. Something broke in my chest, and I let the rapier disappear as my shoulders slackened. I'd just decided to stand by him, and now I was threatening him. Even if it was an oath I'd promised to uphold.

Even if I knew I could never follow through on such a promise.

His lips quivered, and he squeezed his eyes shut. He inhaled deeply, and when he met my gaze again, all expression was wiped clean from his face.

Without a word, Gaige turned and walked away. The door closed softly behind him, and I deflated entirely. How did he continue to do this to me? There was nothing left between us, that much was evident. Yet every hard look from him was like a blade to the gut, constantly twisting deeper so I was forced to remember why, exactly, it hurt so bad. All because I'd let him slip past my defenses and entertained the ridiculous notion that we could've actually been something...*more*.

Sliding my hand beneath my glasses, I pinched my nose. "Tell me what really happened."

"I mean, what we told you is the gist of it." Calem pushed off the railing and quietly stepped around Boo. "One minute everything was fine, and the next it wasn't. There's not much to tell."

"Did he summon those shadows?" I let my hand fall away and slowly walked toward the porch. My brothers fell in line beside me, worry lines framing their eyes. Gaige was important to all of us, not just me.

"I don't think he would deliberately." Ozias rubbed the back of his neck.

"Let me rephrase: did either of you summon those shadows?" They didn't respond, which was answer enough. Sighing, I took the steps to the back door and paused for a moment. I'd hoped being beneath the same roof with Gaige would make things easier. I'd hoped he'd come around and see that our life, *my* life, wasn't as cursed as he believed it to be. So far, all it was doing was hurting us both. "The new recruits had already returned to the manor at that point. So, it stands to reason that if you didn't summon the shadows, then it must've been him." Tilting my head upward, I scanned the rows of windows until I spotted Gaige's on the second story. "And if he's summoning shadows against his will with that much violence..." I didn't need to finish that thought. "Do what you can to get him to train."

I let the door softly click closed behind me as I made my way inside. My sour mood was more pervasive than Gaige's shadows, and the assassins all but faded away as I moved through the halls. When I finally reached my quarters, I quickly locked the door—futile, considering who resided here, but somehow still reassuring—and breathed a weighted sigh. The rich mahogany bed edged in bronze dominated my vision. I wasn't convinced sleep would truly cure the bone-deep exhaustion, but it would at least put the day's events temporarily behind me. Slipping out of my shoes, I set them neatly by the oil-rubbed armoire. Then, I unbuttoned my ebony vest and finally freed myself of my long-sleeved tunic.

A phantom pain rippled from the decades-old scar over my

chest. Instinctively, my fingers traced the twisting path, as if the fatal wound were a whorling pattern on a wooden table. *Jude.* A brackish taste flooded my tongue, and I jerked my hand away. It'd been years since I'd even thought of my former lover, but the memories of him—of the pain he'd inflicted—were becoming more insistent. It was as if Gaige's presence caused them to resurface, as if I needed to relive that agony in order to better understand him.

"Don't be ridiculous," I muttered. Sinking to the mahogany bed, I touched the bronze key resting against my sternum. I told myself that I'd elected to wear my key for security purposes. Kaori, Calem's mentor and a member of the Charmers Council, had gifted us all with mage-crafted, indestructible necklaces where we attached our beasts' keys. It was practical. Safe. And it had absolutely nothing to do with the absurd notion that Gaige also wore his about his neck. Wrapping my fingers in the chain, I held the key in my palm and thought only of Felicks, my Poi fox beast.

Warmth blossomed from the pendant and purled through my limb as the groan of hinges filled my room. Felicks appeared not a moment later. Leaping into my lap, he placed his paw on my chest and gave each cheek a single lick.

"Hello, Felicks." I stroked the length of his spine, marveling at the snow-white color of his fur and the sable stripe running from his crown to the tip of his tail. The amethyst orb nestled between his massive ears clouded for a moment, and as the fog cleared, a series of still pictures filled my mind. His ability to predict the future for up to two minutes at a time, and consequently share that vision with me, was an invaluable asset. For now, though, he only foresaw a good scratch beneath the chin, followed by a nap against my chest.

Chuckling, I obliged and ran my fingers along his maw. "When are you going to show me something I don't already know?"

Of course, it was fairly obvious to assume that my gentle

creature would enjoy a good scratch, and yet the more time I spent with Felicks, the more in tune with his power I became. Sometimes, even when he wasn't around, I'd experience a strange moment of precognition. Almost as if my surroundings had slowed, but my actions, my vision, kept moving in real time. It's how I'd made it in time during the Mizobat attack. It was as if I'd known they'd attack before the creatures even did.

Glancing down at my beast, I let out a quiet hum. I'd been consistently summoning him from day one, which meant he could now remain in our world for considerable amounts of time. Days, even. No doubt that only deepened our bond and made it easier for him to share visions with me. I wondered if, somehow, he was showing me what he could from the beast realm.

Felicks tilted his head to get a better angle, and then batted my hand away. He pranced to the center of bed, circling once before promptly sitting atop the pewter duvet. With his tail twitching over the damask pattern, he pinned me with an unblinking, impatient stare.

"*Tsk.* You're impatient tonight." Placing my glasses on the nightstand, I slipped into bed. Felicks let out a quiet but happy bark as he snuggled in the crook of my arm with his head atop my chest. His eyes slid closed.

"Can you show me anything else?" I murmured. "Anything more than the immediate future. I..." I gently rubbed his ears and along his orb, and his breathing deepened. "I don't know what I'm doing, Felicks. I don't know how to make things better."

But as the minutes passed and my beast fell into a deep slumber, the visions stopped altogether. And while I hadn't expected his power to suddenly expand in such an unprecedented way, I couldn't help but feel utterly defeated. I'd helped countless assassins adjust to their new lives. I'd been the target of so many emotions—rage, misery, indifference. I'd weathered it all, and yet somehow, with

Gaige it was different. It was the opposite of manageable, and I couldn't escape it.

Perhaps it was so difficult to navigate this situation because I was the guild master. I'd been the second-in-command for so long that I assumed I'd be prepared for the role of leader. Yet, as I lay there staring at the ceiling, mindlessly petting Felicks, I knew the responsibility I felt, the guilt, went beyond the position I held at Cruor.

No, this was unique to Gaige. This was why I'd chosen never to fall in love again. Not that I had fallen in love with him, of course, but this burn was so similar to the pain I felt because of Jude that it was hard to not liken my previous experience to this.

This was a predicament of my own making, and I had to fix it. No matter what that outcome entailed.

FOUR

GAIGE

I absolutely loathed my room. Everything in Cruor was far too… heavy. Tables crafted from solid wood and squared off in a precise, efficient style—dark stains as far as the eye could see. There were enough wrought-iron accents to convince me that one of their leaders had stake in an iron mine at some point in their past. When I'd first caught a glimpse of this place, it'd held an air of mystery and intrigue, and I'd found the low lighting and dark palette alluring. If a building could possibly smolder, Cruor positively did. But now…I just missed home.

Rolling to my side on the four-poster bed, I pulled the woven sheets tight around me. It was impossible not to stare at the damning pair of gloves resting on the bedside table. I placed them there each night, and I'd slip them on again the moment I rose. I hadn't taken to sleeping with them on yet, but the possibility was always there.

Pale, ivory light slanted through the thick pleated curtains, and for a moment, I could almost pretend I was back in Hireath. There, the moonlight had bounced across the alabaster tiles in my room, bathing everything in a pleasant glow. There was space to move, to think, to breathe. It was like living in a cloud, complete with airy drapery and soft hues to accent the white oak furnishings. The steady roar from the waterfall was a constant backdrop, and the absence of it now was deafening.

But it was gone, decimated by Ocnolog, and I didn't have the strength to face my people—my friends—and rebuild the home I'd once loved.

Plus, I had my own share of problems I needed to sort out first.

I bit out a wordless curse and yanked the spare pillow over my face. The old me would've leapt at the opportunity to learn a new skill, especially one as useful as bending shadows to my will. But wielding them with purpose would be an acceptance of my fate, and while I knew I couldn't change my situation, I wasn't sure I was ready to let go of the life I used to have. But perhaps more importantly—and more paralyzing—I was afraid of the dark stealing what little solace I'd found in taming the Kitska beasts. This magic was all-consuming. No other member of Cruor, or even Charmers for that matter, could tame the monsters in the cursed wood. It was an ability unique to me. My Charmer's lure—the very magic we used to tame wild beasts—was tainted but still alive within my veins. If I lost that talent, too...

As if on cue, a distant, warbling howl sounded in the night. Others might have found the errant cries startling, but there was something peaceful about the bestial calls. They were a reminder of home, and they had a way of soothing my senses. My limbs grew heavy as my thoughts slowly faded away, and I welcomed the promise of sleep. Just as my consciousness was about to succumb, an errant shiver coursed over my body. I pulled the blankets tighter. Moments later, though, the insistent, prickling sensation was back.

I pulled the pillow off my face, expecting to find I'd somehow untucked myself, and froze.

A vast and endless expanse of gray stretched out before me. Thin smoke carpeted the floor, and it curled and churned as if a breeze were ushering it forward. Yet, there wasn't a whisper of wind to be found. Or any sound, for that matter.

"Calem? Ozias?" I sat upright and gripped the edge of the bed tightly. "Kost?"

No one answered, but I wasn't convinced they could hear me. The void had swallowed my call the moment it left my lips. A quiet ringing started in my ears, and my breath quickened. Immediately, my hand went to Okean's key. I'd expected to feel a pulse, like a warm heartbeat, signaling my connection to my beast was intact. Instead, the key was ice-cold against my skin. My stomach hardened. Where was I, even? Could I summon my beast in this state? What dangers would he face?

Relax. You're dreaming. My cantering heart slowed. I was no stranger to lucid dreams, but this was beyond any I'd experienced before. I could taste the minerals in the air, feel the soft kiss of mist. But everything from my room, save the bed where I waited, had disappeared. Dreaming was the most plausible explanation. Cautiously, I uncurled my fingers and once again studied the quiet abyss.

With a slow, steady movement, I grazed the top of the mist with my foot. It furled outward, revealing a bed of smooth, ebony river stones. After a moment, the smoky tendrils lazily re-formed and obscured the earth.

"Joy," I murmured. "What lovely inner mess am I about to unpack?" Since my transformation, I'd been plagued with nights like this. The good dreams, the ones about my past, always ended up hurting the most because they ended when I woke. They were worse than the nightmares. Exhaling deeply, I stood only for the bed to vanish in a puff of smoke.

Please let there be monsters. Anything to jolt me awake.

Since there was no discernable direction but forward, I took a few measured steps into the mist. As soon as I moved, the fog rushed upward like a waterfall careening toward the sky. A bed of sable stones stretched out before me in a slender, straight path leading into the horizon. Craning my neck, I glanced behind me. The path abruptly stopped a few inches from my heels.

"Forward it is." There was no sense in fighting it. The sooner I got this over with, the sooner I would wake. Still rushing ever upward, the walls of mist showered me in a faint vapor as I walked. Gooseflesh rippled across my bare chest and arms, and I frowned. Kost had mentioned that the undead were rarely bothered by the cold. I wasn't exactly *bothered*, but... A particularly chilly stone rolled along the arch of my foot, and a shiver shot down my spine. Something was different about this place.

Just more proof you're dreaming. Shaking my head, I kept walking. Minutes ticked by in mind-numbing silence. Where were the terrifying demons? The heart-wrenching flashbacks? Hireath on fire? I'd grown accustomed to those images, and yet this total absence of, well, *everything* was somehow more unsettling.

Or more peaceful. That thought stopped me in my tracks. Again, I looked behind me to find the ever-present mist had eaten away at the path, making it look as though I'd hardly moved at all. There was nothing but emptiness around me, and that lack of judgment, of fear, was startling. Agony had become part of me, etched so deeply into my bones that I could never escape the pain or despair. But here, I was weightless. Here, I was free.

It was as if that realization broke the muffled silence. Something fractured in the distance, and suddenly I was enveloped in the sounds of night. The soft, questioning hoots from owls, the faint chirp of crickets on repeat. Even a breeze toying with leaves. Outlines took shape in the fog on either side of the path. Dark, blurry shapes—unformed but recognizable—bled against the gray backdrop. A thicket of trees surrounded me, but they thinned in the distance.

It wasn't anywhere I recognized, and that only filled me with a deeper sense of serenity. A slow, relaxed smile pulled at my lips.

Finally. Starting up again, I dragged my fingers through the fog walls. Mist swirled outward at my touch, dispersing, and re-forming as I continued onward. With every deep breath, the faint mineral taste of the air sharpened to something familiar—salt. Soon, the trees gave way to large boulders, and just out of sight, rushing water crashed against something solid. The path beneath my feet widened until it pooled outward onto a black, sandy beach. A full moon sat heavy over ink-black water, and jagged sawtooth rocks pierced the surface. Angry waves crested against the boulders, and the white, churning foam spilled over their porous surface before rushing up the sand. Frigid water circled my ankles and soaked my linen pants, but the icy sensation couldn't damper the sense of wonder in me.

The veil of fog had vanished here, revealing a crystal-clear night dotted with millions of burning stars. It was unlike any place I'd ever seen, and I never wanted to leave.

As I stared at the raging ocean before me, I spied a sphere of whirling darkness hovering above the water. Shadows. Even here, I couldn't escape them. But maybe here I could control them. Raising my hand toward the orb, I focused on the snarling, writhing tendrils. And then I beckoned to them with the slightest curl of my fingers.

The orb went still. Satisfaction bloomed in my chest, and I tried to force them to disappear. But instead of fleeing and leaving me in peace to enjoy my foreign surroundings, they exploded. In a virulent frenzy, they multiplied until they blanketed the night sky and extinguished all light. A piercing whistling shredded my ears, and I slapped my hands against the side of my head and winced. Pressure built in my chest, and I struggled to breathe. Fear gutted me as the shadows cocooned me in a wild tornado. I couldn't control them. Not in real life, and not in my dreams.

So this is *a nightmare*. Squirming my eyes shut, I screamed at the top of my lungs. Fire burned my throat as I pushed myself louder and louder. I needed to wake up. I *had* to wake up. But when I opened my eyes, I was still lost in the flurry of darkness. It was so similar to the maelstrom I'd endured earlier that a disastrous, small doubt crept from the recesses of my mind. One I refused to examine. Trembling, I reached toward the tendrils.

Another hand shot out of the shadows and snared my wrist. I choked on my scream and stumbled backward, but the iron grip kept me from tumbling into the oblivion. Calluses scratched against my skin as they dragged along my pitiful Charmer's emblem. The nails were chewed to the quick, and where wrinkles should have been, lines of dried blood ringed the knuckles. The hand jerked my wrist upward, as if bringing it in for closer inspection, though I couldn't glimpse a body.

Until suddenly there was a pair of haunting, faded-blue eyes staring first at my emblem, and then at me. A burning, crimson ring encircled their pupils, and my body filled with an unbearable sense of dread. Warning bells clashes in my mind.

Danger. I was in danger.

Yanking my hand out of the stranger's grip, I fell back into the snarling shadows. They sliced against me like they'd done earlier on Cruor's lawns, and blood welled along the cuts. I couldn't tell if I was falling or if the rushing sound in my ears was the raging tendrils lashing out. All I knew was that I didn't care, so long as that gaze wasn't boring into my soul any longer.

Squeezing my eyes shut, I pressed my chin to my chest. "Wake up. This is just a dream. Wake up!"

The shadows howled in response. There was no end to this nightmare. No end to the darkness. No end—

A pair of hands gripped my shoulders tight, and I let out a

bloodcurdling scream. I clawed at them frantically, trying in vain to pry them from my body.

"Gaige!"

The hands dug deeper, cupping beneath my bones and rooting me in place. And still, I raked my nails along the skin on their forearms. Blood trails followed in my wake, but my assailant didn't budge.

"Gaige, snap out of it!"

A flicker of awareness triggered in my mind. That voice was familiar. I cut a quick glance to the hands on my shoulders. The nails were neatly trimmed and pristinely cleaned. No dried blood to be found, save where I'd ravaged the skin around their wrists. The shadows around me faltered.

"Please, Gaige." Soft. Broken. *Broken? Why?* My body went limp with fatigue, and I gave up trying to fight. My bedroom slammed back into view so abruptly that my stomach dropped, and I keeled over the edge of my bed to vomit in the bin. My vision swam in circles, black dots dancing across my eyes, until everything slowly steadied. Breathing deeply through my nose, I focused on the pair of bare feet before me. Then, I pushed myself into an upright position.

Face ghostly pale and eyes wide, Kost stood before me. His hair was ruffled, spectacles missing. Judging by his lack of shirt and loose, wrinkled pants, I'd somehow roused him from sleep. Deep gouges lined his wrists, as if a deranged beast had attacked his forearms in desperation.

"Are you all right? What happened?" he asked.

"I'm fine." The words burned against my vocal cords, and I rubbed my throat. "What happened to you?"

"What happened to me?" He blinked. Slowly. "You happened. Look." He nodded at my chest. With an absent hand, I brushed my palm down my sternum, expecting to wipe away beads of sweat.

That dream had been all too real. No doubt I'd been screaming in my sleep, sweating through the sheets...

My breath hitched as I glanced at the red sheen of blood across my fingertips. Launching from the bed, I crossed the room in three quick strides to stand before the floor-length mirror. At least a dozen cuts stretched across my exposed skin. Of course, they were already rapidly resealing before my eyes, but there was no erasing the smeared trails and splatters of left behind blood. I caught a small rivulet on my shaking fingers and stared at it. Real. It was all real. Even though I'd been dreaming, I'd lashed out in the world around me. Ringing crested in my ears, and I sank to the floor in a heap.

Kost was at my side in less than a breath. He crouched before me and placed his hands on my shoulders, right where they'd been when he'd pulled me out of my nightmare.

"Gaige," Kost murmured. "It's okay."

"It's not," I croaked.

He gave me a gentle squeeze. "You lost control in your sleep. It's not...uncommon. But it's imperative you train in the morning. Do you understand? You cannot risk yourself or anyone else any longer." With a careful, precise touch, he grazed one of the now-healing wounds on my arm. I shivered but didn't dare argue. I know I'd been dreaming but... It had felt so, so *real*. And if Kost witnessed my shadows wreaking havoc on the manor... If they alerted him to come here...

Everything really was my fault. A deep ache simmered in my skull. I hadn't meant for this to happen. Not earlier with the Mizobats, and certainly not in my dreams. Those vicious, black tendrils hadn't even felt like my shadows. Their power, their energy was so unfamiliar to me. But maybe that was what happened when they grew stronger than their host. They were becoming a force I didn't recognize, and one I couldn't control.

"I didn't... I..." Words failed me entirely. For a long moment, I stared at the space where his fingers rested against my skin. Part of me wanted to fall into that touch, to let myself completely break so he could help me put myself back together again. But even now, physically depleted and mentally spent, I couldn't bring myself to forget about our past, even for a night. There was still an indignant glimmer of anger that refused to be squelched, and I brushed his hand away. His lips thinned, but he didn't reach for me again. Which was an unnecessary knife to an already bleeding heart, but I couldn't have it both ways.

We stood, tension wrapping us in an uncomfortable silence. I broke it with a half-hearted wave over my shoulder. "Let me sleep. I'll train with Ozias and Calem tomorrow."

He stiffened, and then his expression went blank. "Of course. Good night." Without another word, he exited my room and closed the door behind him.

Grabbing a damp towel from the attached washroom, I quickly wiped dried blood off my chest and arms. Then, I removed my pants, pausing when I grazed the cold hems near my feet. Frowning, I inspected the peculiar wet spots on either leg. So consumed by the sight and sensation of blood against my skin, I hadn't noticed the damp press of linen against my calves.

Rolling the fabric between my forefinger and thumb, I half expected my fingers to come away a faint reddish pink with diluted blood from a wound I'd missed. Instead, they came up clean.

Water?

A chill spider-walked down my spine. I'd stood in the ocean in my dreams, the cool waves crashing against my ankles and climbing my calves. My pulse thundered in my veins as I slowly brought the hem to my nose and inhaled deeply. The brackish scent of salt hit me hard and fast, and I dropped the pants on the floor.

No. No, no, no. Sweat. It's sweat. I jerked back and bumped into the frame of the bed. Nothing else had been real. It was just a dream. The shadows were here in Cruor. *My* shadows. And I wasn't the only one who'd been hurt. Kost had been bleeding. No doubt others had suffered the consequences of my inaction.

If it were sweat, it would be elsewhere, too. I swiped at the backs of my knees, my thighs, my waist. Nothing.

You're panicking for no reason.

Closing my eyes, I forced out several slow breaths. Once I wrangled my nerves, I let my shoulders roll back and tipped my head to the ceiling, stretching my neck. There was no sense in focusing on the sweat-soaked fabric. It was a natural reaction to the extreme fear I felt in my dreams and the exertion I so obviously experienced by summoning my shadows. But as I returned to bed, my gaze went straight to my gloves. Quickly, I slipped them on and once again pulled the sheets tight around me. As I lay there, staring at the ceiling and counting down the seconds until morning, I couldn't shake the feeling that I had actually walked across a distant ocean shore. Or that I'd awoken something dangerous. Something with burning, hollow eyes that were now pinpointed on me.

FIVE

LEENA

Late night over the open ocean was spectacular. The choppy waters were ink-black and jagged like glass, and the moonlight bounced off the sea to shower our ship in a cool glow. We were traveling to Rhyne to finalize peace negotiations and reopen trade routes, which meant we'd be away from home for some time. There was still so much to do in Wilheim and Hireath—in all of Lendria, for that matter—but a small part of me was thrilled to be traveling again. I'd spent my life roaming the lands in search of magical creatures, and the prospect of encountering new beasts was an undeniable thrill. Even if that wasn't the purpose for our venture. Leaning against the ship's railing, I inhaled deeply and savored the taste of salt on the back of my tongue.

"You should try to sleep." Noc's lips ghosted against the back of my ear as he braced his hands on either side of me. The subtle weight of his chest against my back was tantalizing. "We arrive at Rhyne tomorrow morning."

"I know." I placed my hands on top of his and twined our fingers together. "The crown never rests, it seems."

He chuckled. "You've only been queen for a minute and already you're complaining?"

"Not complaining, just eagerly awaiting the day we get to rest." I turned around to stare up at Noc. Gently, I grazed the crescent-moon scar along his cheekbone. "When things settle, I'm demanding we take a week solely to ourselves. Deal?"

He planted a gentle kiss on my fingertips. "Deal. We'll put Kost in charge. He'll reform every inefficient practice far faster than we could, anyway."

"While I appreciate the honest assessment of my abilities, I'm going to have to decline." Kost's voice drifted over us, and I startled in Noc's embrace. Peeking my head around his shoulder, I spied Kost lingering in the open doorway to the quarters Noc and I shared, nothing more than a shadowy form that wavered in the ocean breeze.

Noc slid his arm to my waist as he faced his brother. "Something happen?"

Kost hesitated. Just a fraction. Just long enough for me to catch the tightening of his shoulders, even with the fluid nature of his shadow form. Noc had visited him just a few days ago, and already he'd felt the need to seek us out. The only reason he could even pinpoint us on this ship was because of his close tie to Noc and knowledge of our travel route. He also knew just how important this meeting with Rhyne was. He never would have come if something hadn't pushed him to do so, let alone at this late-night hour.

"It's Gaige. He's..." He shook his head once. I'd never known Kost to be at a loss for words. There was so much in that little pause. Guilt. Responsibility. Longing. Finally, he continued. "I'm exhausting all possibilities."

I didn't miss how he didn't directly answer Noc's question. As if answering would somehow cause more grief. For him or Gaige, I didn't know.

Noc seemed to notice it, too, and he frowned. "Has he gotten worse?"

"Possibly. It's hard to say." Again, he seemed to dance around the truth. But before Noc could pry further, Kost looked at me. "I was hoping you could help."

"Me?" Instinctively, my hand went to my bestiary. The subtle warmth that pulsed from the leather binding signaled my connection to the beast realm. I had magic, sure. But not the kind Noc, Kost, and Gaige shared. What I knew about the shadows was limited to what they showed me.

Kost shifted, and his body temporarily blurred to a mass of dark wisps. "I know there isn't a beast out there that could reverse his condition. I imagine that would've been the first thing Gaige tried."

"There isn't. I looked, too." I looked away, unable to hold Kost's gaze much longer. The guilt there was a mirror to the snaking, twisting feeling in my gut. After all, I was the Crown of the Charmers Council. I'd been there when Gaige died and allowed Noc to raise him, even though I knew how difficult it would be for Gaige. I was just as responsible, and I wanted nothing more than for my friend to find peace.

"I assumed as much. But I wonder if we could approach the problem differently." Kost began to pace, his footfalls making no sound against the wooden planks of the ship. "What Gaige misses is connection. If we could find a way to give that back to him, maybe..." He fell silent. He didn't *need* to say more for us to understand.

"Connection?" Noc mused as he tipped his head to the sky in thought. "How could a beast give him that? He already has Okean."

I shook my head. "He had hundreds of beasts. The ability to summon Okean is a fleeting reprieve, one that I imagine is painful in its own right. Every time Gaige summons him, I have no doubt he's reminded of all the others who can't come to his side."

"Exactly." Kost's brows pulled together as he tried to piece together a solution. Then, he halted. "Is there a beast that can grant him passage to the beast realm? A Telesávra, perhaps?"

My stomach knotted, and it had nothing to do with the unsteady waters. "No. I'm not sure there is—"

"Please." He'd crossed the hull to stand directly in front of me. Between the shadows and the soft lighting of the night, I hadn't gotten a good look at Kost. But now, with him just inches from me, I could see the worried lines framing his eyes, the haggardness and anxiety in his gaze. His unkempt hair and wrinkled attire. It wrecked me to my core, and I reached out to grab his hand. My fingers met cool tendrils that refused to hold their shape, but I didn't pull away.

"Okay, Kost. I'll see what I can find." It felt like a shallow promise. I wanted to offer something more substantial. A solution perfectly suited to Gaige's needs. And yet as I pictured the pages of my bestiary, nothing immediately came to mind. I would have to look elsewhere, search other texts and consult other Charmers to see if anything could be done. In the past, I would've gone straight to Gaige. But if he hadn't found an answer, I wasn't sure where to turn. But I would try. I wouldn't give up on him.

"Make sure he trains." Noc's voice was low, remorseful. "Even if you can't see the progress, every little bit helps."

"Thank you." Kost's answer was more of an exhale, and I watched as he practically deflated. How long had he been running himself ragged? How many hours had he spent searching for answers, likely unbeknownst to everyone around him? I wouldn't let him endure this alone. Not anymore.

"Get some rest," I said. He nodded and then disappeared, no more than a shadow fleeing into the ocean waters.

"We might have to delay our vacation," Noc murmured as he pulled me in close.

"I know." It was all I could manage, but I didn't need to say more. Instead, we simply held each other and stared silently at the horizon, neither of us willing to speak into existence the grim future that Gaige—and Kost, so desperate to help that he was tearing himself to pieces in the process—might be facing.

SIX

KOST

The early morning air was quiet, save the gentle harmony of birdcalls trilling from the branches of the forest. A soft, golden-yellow light, trimmed in a burnt ocher, rose from above the treetops and settled over the lush lawns behind Cruor. There wasn't a cloud to be found in the sky. It was the type of morning I savored. Under normal circumstances, I would've slipped into the kitchen to brew a steaming mug of coffee, selected a book from the library, and then reclined in one of the slatted chairs on the deck.

But not today. Leaning forward, I pressed my forearms into the railing and clasped my hands together. A short distance away, Calem, Ozias, and Gaige were locked in a heated discussion—more like an argument—as Gaige failed to complete the simplest of drills for wielding the shadows. It'd been a week since his disastrous nightmare, and he'd yet to show any marked improvement. They'd spend the morning working with shadows and the evenings running physical drills. He exceeded there, much to my surprise. Most Charmers rarely trained in physical combat and relied entirely on their beasts for protection. But Gaige had always been a quick study, and apparently this wasn't his first foray in hand-to-hand combat. Still, while it helped to strengthen the vessel responsible for summoning the shadows, controlling them was another matter entirely.

Control was exactly what he needed. Jaw clenched, I studied the wild, black spires twisting around him. Even now, days later, I couldn't shake the memory of that night. I'd awoken to concerned shouts from my brethren, only to emerge from my room and find those erratic, thrashing tendrils raging through the halls. Calem and Ozias were there, too. They'd jumped into action without waiting for my command, rushing into the snarling dark to yank our unsuspecting family out of their rooms and into safety outside the manor. Again, Gaige's shadows had responded in violence, and each person who surfaced from the abyss was covered in shallow cuts.

The sight had wrecked me, and in an instant, my own shadows snarled to life. They'd coated me in protective armor as I strode headlong into the darkness. Gaige's shadows howled in response, barreling into me in an attempt to thrust me out. By the time I'd made it to his room, my muscles burned from exertion, but I'd spent decades finessing my magic. It would take more than erratic, uncontained shadows to break me.

But what I'd found in his quarters was another thing entirely, and I came to an immediate standstill. It was like walking into the eye of the storm. Sable tendrils crawled across the ceiling and floor like smoke escaping from a fire. In the center of his bed was a cocoon of shadows that had obscured Gaige entirely. He was in a casket of his own making, and it was so similar to what happened with Noc when he'd been controlled by Yazmin, the former Crown of the Charmers Council, that my limbs went numb. I hadn't been able to breach the shield Noc had created around him and Leena as he'd threatened to end her life. Ozias, Calem, and I had stood on the outside, helpless, as we prayed they'd both survive. Somehow, Leena had saved him. She'd broken through the hold on his mind, and the shadows dispersed.

And I'd had to do the same for Gaige. Coating my hands in shadows, I'd driven them deep into the interlocking thicket of tendrils surrounding his body. Sweat had trickled down my neck as I ripped them apart like stitching from fabric. I didn't know how long it'd taken for me to finally break through. All I knew was my fingers were raw and trembling, and then suddenly I'd felt his shoulders and anchored myself to him.

"Morning," someone said tightly. Lost in my reverie, replaying events I hoped I'd never have to relive, I hadn't noticed the three assassins who'd joined me on the deck to watch the early morning training.

"Emelia," I said in greeting. My gaze flicked from her to her twin brother, Iov. They shared the same widows' peaks, sepia-toned skin, dark eyes, and full lips, but their similarities stopped there. Where Emelia prided herself on structure and discipline, Iov was more like a young Calem in the making. And Astrid... My gaze flicked to the woman standing between them, her teakwood eyes a bit bleary given the hour and her normally spiked hair unkempt—but she looked happy. Her death had brought her back to Emelia and Iov, and it was clear there was no place she'd rather be than with her childhood friends. They were all holding coffee, and Emelia handed me the extra mug she carried. Steam curled upward to tease my nose and brought with it the rich scent of vanilla.

"Thank you." I cupped it between my hands as I straightened. "Though I doubt you sought me out to bring me coffee. Were there more attacks?"

In the week that Gaige had been training, Kitska beasts had begun prowling the borders of our home. There'd yet to be a life-threatening injury to any of our sentries, though several had returned battered and bruised. After the second incursion, I'd doubled up patrol and mandated hourly check-ins. Emelia was responsible for running the guard and kept me filled in. I prayed she hadn't come to tell me that our efforts were proving futile.

"No, thankfully." A loose strand of glossy, black hair fell across Emelia's cheek, and she tucked it behind her ear. "It's something else."

My shoulders tensed. "What do you mean?"

"Well, it's not really in our purview..." She cut a furtive glance at Calem, Ozias, and Gaige.

"We caught wind of some monster attacks, away from Cruor." Iov gently blew over his coffee before taking a quick gulp. "Just something we overheard while getting drinks at Midnight Jester last night. Could just be travelers telling stories, but..."

I sipped my coffee slowly. "What was the nature of the attacks? Were the Kitska beasts provoked?"

"It didn't sound like it," Emelia said, hedging her words. She shifted from one foot to the next, her gaze momentarily flitting to where Boo slept nestled against the porch. He hadn't moved since Gaige stitched him up, but his consistent, soft snores were reassuring enough.

"And the travelers weren't exactly in the best shape when they stumbled into Midnight Jester," Astrid said. She met my stare with a level of boldness and resilience I'd grown to respect. New as she was to her lifestyle as an undead assassin, there wasn't much that fazed her, and I valued her straightforward manner.

Iov drained the last of his coffee. "Lots of serious wounds. Honestly, I'm surprised they even made it to the tavern in one piece."

The coffee turned to ash against my tongue, and I set my drink on the railing of the deck. Gaige had managed to subdue a number of the undead beasts, like Boo, but there were still countless creatures living in the Kitska Forest. "What direction did they come from?"

"South of here, along the path to Moeras. We're not sure where the attack happened, but we assumed you'd want to know." Emelia's gaze softened as she once again looked to the training grounds. I followed her stare, and the already building tension between my shoulder blades ratcheted higher, forming an endless knot I didn't have the dexterity to loosen. Gaige had called forth a handful of shadows, and they hovered above his palm, quivering with frenetic energy. But before he could mold them into anything tangible, the tendrils caved in on themselves and slithered through his fingertips to the grass. They fled to the forest, and he bit back a curse.

I watched as they dispersed into the dark wood, and a sickening realization formed: if Gaige was inadvertently releasing his magic into his surroundings, as he'd done during his nightmare, then there was no telling who—or in this case, what—he was affecting. He was riling the Kitska beasts with his irrepressible power, and if we didn't find a way to contain his abilities quickly, there would inevitably be more casualties.

My stomach plummeted to the ground. I didn't want that to be the truth. I was afraid of what something like that would do to Gaige. That he might actually ask me to fulfill my oath to end his life. I couldn't... My fingers trembled as my vision blurred.

Emelia cleared her through. "Kost?"

Her voice did nothing to slow the chaotic spiraling of my thoughts. Training wasn't helping. Everyone progressed differently, but even those slow to grasp the shadows should've been able to at least contain their powers by now. But Gaige... He was an emotional outburst away from bringing Kitska beasts right back to our doorstep.

Or, apparently, to someone else's.

I took a deep, shuttering breath, and Felicks's key shifted against my sternum. I'd never wanted to predict the future more than in that moment.

"Kost." Softer this time. Emelia placed her hand on my forearm, and that touch grounded me. Reminded me that I had a duty, as guild master, to protect the assassins of Cruor. I needed them safe as much as I needed Gaige in control. Even if I didn't want to believe that he was responsible for… I could hardly bring myself to think it. But I had to. I *had* to. Regardless of how I felt about him, I couldn't fall prey to willful denial, not if I wanted to keep those I cared for out of harm's reach.

"You're positive they were not regular beasts?" It was a mad hope, one that I knew wouldn't last. But I had to ask. Normal beasts rarely—if ever—attacked people unprompted. In the decades I'd lived on Lendria, I could count on one hand the number of beasts I witnessed before meeting Leena. Still, if there was a chance they were acting out over their monstrous counterparts, then maybe Gaige's shadows had nothing to do with. Maybe he wasn't luring them here and riling them with his uncontained power. Maybe…

"The descriptions the travelers gave seemed…" Emelia faltered.

Her inability to find words was answer enough, but Astrid didn't hold back. "Horrific. The stuff of nightmares."

"Understood. Thank you for informing me. I'll handle it," I said. Straightening, I hid away all my emotions. My brethren needed to believe that I would protect them no matter the cost. And I would.

But I would also protect Gaige. Even if he resisted. Even if he was unwilling to face the truth.

"I need to speak with Calem, Ozias, and Gaige," I said.

"Of course." Emelia dipped her chin quickly and turned on her heels, Iov and Astrid in her wake. As I descended the steps onto the lawns, Gaige once again summoned and failed to control a ball of shadows, and he tossed his hands to the sky in defeat.

"That's okay. No one starts off perfect," Ozias said, clapping a thick hand against Gaige's back.

"Unless you're me," Calem said with a grin. "I was born perfect."

Ozias rolled his eyes. "Don't let him fool you."

"Not likely," Gaige muttered.

"Maybe you need to try a defensive tactic," Calem said as he rubbed his thumb along his jaw. "Most of us start with blades because they're smaller and require less finesse. But a shield is just a whole mess of shadows grouped together."

Ozias raised a brow as he grinned. "When did you become the teacher? It's not a bad idea, though."

"Told you, I'm perfect." He grinned and then angled his right arm over his chest. With no more than a thought, shadows rushed to his frame and coated his forearm in a shield just wider than his limb and long enough to hide his fingers. "Try this."

Ozias stepped away from Gaige and nodded. "Go ahead."

I slowed my pace, eyes locked on Gaige's form. He mimicked Calem's stance and summoned shadows to his fingers. They slithered across his knuckles and gathered in his palm before coating his forearm. It was more like a vambrance than a shield, but it was the first time I'd seen him summon anything other than a writhing ball of tendrils. I froze, too afraid that any movement would break his concentration. His shadows trembled likes muscles pushed beyond the point of exhaustion, and Gaige frowned at the flimsy creation. All at once they collapsed, and he groaned.

"It's no use." Sweat clung to the collar of his pewter tunic, and he pushed the cuffs of his three-quarter sleeves past his elbows.

"That was good!" Calem clapped his hands together.

"You're not giving yourself enough credit," Ozias added.

"Why would I? I can't get them to hold any shape to save my life. Literally." His shoulders slumped. "Remember the Mizobats? I couldn't protect myself then."

Irritation flared within me, and I grimaced. "And that's exactly why you should continue to practice." In a few quick strides, I joined them and folded my arms across my chest. "We can't afford any more incidents."

Gaige narrowed his eyes. "Thank you for that obvious reminder."

"He's making progress. It just takes time," Ozias said. "This is my thing, Kost. I can help." His warm, dark gaze was gentle, but firm.

I wanted to believe him. There was something to be said for his skill as a trainer. New recruits mastered control over the shadows much faster under his guidance than they ever did under my direction. But I'd been silently watching their daily sessions, hoping to spy even the smallest sliver of improvement. I had no doubt Gaige understood Ozias's teachings. His mind was a magnificent thing, but his efforts, the execution of his drills, felt forced.

There was effort, certainly. And conceptually, I assumed he understood. He never questioned Ozias or Calem about the process of summoning the shadows. Where he faltered was the execution. It was shaky at best, as if he were afraid of what would happen if it solidified into something tangible and real. I knew he never would've chosen this life for himself—and that was why he'd refrained from training until now—but his hesitation to fully commit was still apparent. He needed motivation. What that looked like, though, I didn't know.

"We don't have time." Normally, I wouldn't interfere with Ozias's methods. There was a chance he could still help Gaige and find that drive that was missing. But Gaige was my responsibility, and I couldn't seem to keep myself away.

Calem let out an exaggerated sigh. "You're always so dramatic. He hasn't lost control in a week."

"He's hardly gained any, either." I said.

“As inspiring as always.” Gaige glowered.

“Incentive will help.” Or at least I hoped it would. “Pack your things. We leave in an hour.”

Ozias frowned. “What? Why?”

“Better question—where?” Calem chimed in.

“Whatever it is, I’ll pass. I’m not interested. We can pick this up when you get back.” Turning on his heels, Gaige started toward the edge of the Kitska Forest. He spent the majority of his time there, searching for undead beasts in the hopes of offering them some reprieve. But each moment he lingered in those dark woods was another moment he could inadvertently release his disastrous shadows and rile the monsters. I needed him to join us both to help assess whether we could tame the rampaging Kitska monsters in the south and to keep him from upsetting more creatures—especially if we weren’t around to subdue them.

“There have been reports of Kitska beasts attacking in Penumbra Glades, just outside of Moeras,” I said to his back, and he stilled. “I assumed you’d want the opportunity to handle the issue.”

Silence stretched between us as the early morning sun crept higher into the sky. I hadn’t entertained the notion that he might decline the journey, and suddenly a new sense of unease stirred in my chest. I could pass it off as uncertainty regarding his power and what he’d do if we weren’t present, but I knew it was more than that, even if I didn’t dare voice it.

Gaige cast me one sidelong look over his shoulder. “I’ll gather my things. Someone will need to check in on Boo while we’re gone. He can’t make the journey in his current state.” As he shifted directions and disappeared into Cruor, Calem and Ozias rounded on me.

“You cannot be serious,” Calem said. The mercury line around his irises flared as he clenched his jaw. “He’s not ready for something like that.”

“I hate to admit it, but I agree with Calem.” Ozias brushed a thick hand over his head. "His shadows are still heavily influenced by his emotions."

"I know that, but perhaps some purpose will help him focus." My mind rewound to the conversation I had with Noc when he appeared in my office to check in on our situation. Perhaps his suggestion would prove fruitful. "We're running out of options, and we need to keep Gaige's mind occupied. An idle mind is what concerns me."

Or a dreaming mind. I pushed that thought aside and turned toward the manor, Calem and Ozias close behind. They didn't argue any further, but their unspoken feelings were palpable. They were scared. Not of Gaige, but for him. They knew—or rather, didn't know—what would happen if the shadows engulfed our newfound family member. While I couldn't begin to fathom what kind of fate that would entail, I did know one thing for certain: I would do anything and everything to stop it.

No matter the cost.

SEVEN

GAIGE

Every reverberating hoofbeat of our Zeelahs was harsh against the heavy silence. I didn't have to be a scholar to know that the strained muscles of my brethren's necks, pursed lips, and white-knuckle grips on their reins were out of the ordinary. And I *was* a scholar.

Of course, our surroundings didn't help, either. The dense thicket of trees crowded the narrow path, forcing us to travel in tandem. Mangled roots covered in moss puckered through the soft dirt, and our mounts carefully picked their way forward. The morganite stubs nestled between their ears offered a faint, peachy glow that helped them see in the low light of the woods. Roughly twenty hands tall with deerlike frames, it wasn't exactly easy for Zeelahs to navigate the terrain, but they were hardy. A few errant nicks and bumps from thorn-laden vines and dead branches wouldn't bother them. Travel to Penumbra Glades would be slow. We had no idea what manner of Kitska beasts attacked the travelers or if they were the type to migrate. I needed to study the path, search for them with my magic, and see if any trails cropped up. Finding and soothing the distressed Kitska beasts was my only priority, regardless of how much time it took.

Still... My gaze traveled to Calem's back. It was almost impossible for him to remain quiet for this long. Shifting in my saddle, I shot a cursory glance behind me. Ozias patted the tan and white hide of his mare as he urged her along. His lips stretched into a smile, but it didn't quite reach his eyes. I nodded before righting myself and giving in to the silence. Ahead of Calem, Kost led the caravan. He never once looked back.

Not that it matters. My leather gloves squeaked as I clutched the reins tighter. They were all on edge, and I could only assume it was because of me. We'd departed from Cruor a few hours ago, and already they were acting like I was bound to explode.

Why bring me along, then? I chewed on the inside of my cheek. No doubt Kost was worried about the shadows that'd lashed out during my dream state. It would make sense to keep me close, to monitor the behavior of my power and keep the rest of the members of Cruor safe from any more unexpected outbursts. It's what I would've done. Even so, the thought of being carted around just so I could be watched soured my tongue.

I bit back a huff of annoyance. They'd all stressed the importance of mastering the shadows, even Noc and Leena. The moment they'd insinuated I could get lost in the shadow realm permanently, I took to the library and scoured the shelves for any credible information pertaining to such a fate. There were a handful of documented cases of assassins disappearing from our world, and it was after months—a few even making it to a year—of failed training. I'd only been recently turned. Even though my shadows behaved differently than a few others who'd recently been raised, I still had time. But the pressure to become something I reviled, something that completely eradicated my Charmer powers, only made me want to delay further. If not for Leena, I wouldn't even have Okean. This was not the life I chose, but the path ahead of me would be my own.

We rode uninterrupted until early evening when a small, oblong clearing on the shoulder of the path came into view. Only then did Kost glance behind him to signal to his brothers that we'd be peeling off. One by one, we followed his lead and steered our Zeelahs toward a line of trees mostly unmarred by vines. Dismounting, I looped the leather reins loosely around the trunk, giving it a tug to secure the knot. Calem and Ozias immediately fell into routine, as they seamlessly began setting up camp. Ozias erected two tents before I could blink, and Calem paused only for a brief moment to receive some direction from Kost I couldn't decipher. With a tight nod, he summoned his shadows and disappeared into the wood.

"Start a fire," Kost said to me as he tended to the mounts, siphoning water from a pouch into tin bowls at their feet. "Calem will be back soon with food."

"Right." I crossed to the tree line and crouched. Brittle branches, twigs, and moss littered the forest floor, and I snared the driest wood I could find. The intense overgrowth from the leaves and pinesco pods above locked in moisture, making it difficult to secure logs that weren't rotted from the inside out. But building a fire was something I could do, and even if it was a simple task, I wanted to prove to them that I could handle myself.

A twig snapped in the distance, and I glanced up. Crickets chirped in the air as the evening set in, and the soft hoot of an owl met my ears. Between the increasingly dim lighting and the density of the forest, there wasn't much to see. Still, I squinted into the tangled tree limbs and undergrowth. I hadn't sensed a Kitska beast nearby, but some creatures were excellent at evading attention. When nothing stirred, I went back to searching for tinder. If there were really a threat in the woods, the fowl and insects would fall silent.

As I snared a decent-size stick, a branch overhead creaked as if it were bearing too much weight. I jerked my head upward, but again, there was nothing to be found, and the sounds of the forest continued on. Unease settled in my gut, and I stilled. I'd heard something, and yet... My gaze bounced from branch to branch until I spied a peculiar dark spot in the tree next to me. My eyes narrowed. The lighting in the woods was poor, but I should've been able to see the outline of the branches in the very least. Instead, it was simply an onyx void.

The hairs on the back of my neck stood on end. A *moving* void.

The edges of the abyss were writhing, collapsing and re-forming to loosely maintain the veil of darkness.

Shadows. My heart hammered against my rib cage. Was I sleeping again? When had I dozed? My fingers trembled, and inky tendrils began to form in my palm. They slithered around my wrist and skittered up my forearm, but as erratic and uncontrolled as their movement was, they still looked—*felt*—different than what I spied in the treetops.

Before I could investigate further, a body emerged from the abyss and rocketed toward me. Carried by the shadows, they were on me in an instant. I screamed as something—someone—slammed into me, and I careened into the clearing where Ozias and Kost were still setting up camp. I tumbled across the earth until I smacked into a jutted tree root. Wood splintered around me, and I dug my hands into the dirt for purchase.

"We're under attack!" I shouted, quickly searching for Ozias and Kost. Ozias stood there, slack-jawed with hands limp by his side, while Kost grimaced. Gaze hard, he folded his arms across his chest.

"Remember your training," he said.

"What?" I scrambled to my feet. The shrouded person was on the move, stalking toward me like a predator toying with its prey. "What's going on?" The shadows around my hands quivered, and I shot a bewildered look at them.

"Focus on your stance. Center yourself," Ozias called. His initial shock had been replaced with a grim determination as his gaze flickered between me and the attacker.

A jet-black blade careened toward my face and then peeled off at the last moment. Strands of freshly cut hair fell to my shoulder, and I fingered the space where my locks used to be as I whirled to face the assailant.

"Pay attention." His voice was guttural and dark, almost feral. The shadows around his eyes parted for a moment to reveal muted-red irises ringed in mercury. Calem.

Confusion shifted to rage in a second, and my nostrils flared. "What the hell are you doing?"

"Trimming some of that hair back. I'll keep at it 'til you and Ozias share the same style if you don't stop me." It was meant as a jest, but I couldn't ignore the challenge in his stare. Leave it to Calem to turn everything into a battle. He sent a series of shadow blades aimed straight for my head, and I threw my arms up to protect my face. The shadows around my arms exploded, knitting together in two horribly formed shields with far too many cracks, but they deflected several blades while the others mysteriously changed trajectories and burrowed into the soft bark of the tree at my back. The weapons dispersed almost instantly, but not before Calem could attack again.

Another volley of blades, another round of hits. Within minutes, the malformed shields I'd managed to summon were gone. Calem had crouched low to the ground, his hands lazily toying with blades as he waited for me to find my balance.

Not a single weapon had hit its mark. Calem was better than that. Horrifically so. He lived for the hunt, which meant he'd been tailoring his attacks, pulling back when he knew I wouldn't be able to deflect them.

"Nice work." His grin was borderline unsettling, but he'd paused his assault. For now.

Slowly, I straightened. "Are you done yet?"

"Nope." He slowly lifted his palms upward, and the shadows around him snarled in response. With ease, more blades manifested by his side, and he angled their deadly points in my direction.

"Let's limit it to five, Calem. You keep calling off the extras, anyway," Ozias shouted.

My gaze swiveled to Kost and Ozias. Neither of them had moved, but Ozias had turned his focus to Calem. Kost continued to study me as if I were a puzzle in need of solving.

Realization hit hard and fast, and I nearly broke my teeth I clenched my jaw so hard. "You told him to do this."

"Correct." He clasped his hands together. "The threat of blades seemed to trigger you into summoning your shadows. Harness that."

The remaining shadows clinging to my frame sharpened. "You could warn me next time we're about to train."

Kost lifted a single shoulder. "You couldn't protect yourself when the Mizobats attacked, and already you've done better here. I'll take progress however we can get it."

I hated that he was right. I was a burden when it came to that attack, but here at least I'd defended myself. Somewhat. "This *exercise* is over."

Kost's lips thinned. "Not yet. You've continued to pull back from your training prematurely. Push your limits."

"Push my limits?" I wanted to punch him square in the face. Vaguely, I wondered if that effort would appease him. "All I do is push myself." Sort of. Of course I didn't want to accidentally harm anyone with my wayward shadows, but I knew I'd put off training for far too long. I'd resisted, and I hurt people. A small part of me knew that was the undeniable truth. And yet...

No. I pushed myself in ways Kost didn't understand. Could never understand. I *liked* who I was before. Now, I was something else.

"Let's see it then," Calem called, giving me forewarning where none was warranted. He could've just struck, and I doubt I would've responded in time. Instead, I glanced his way just as he flicked his wrists and sent more blades careening toward me.

Heat boiled to a head in my core, and power surged through my chest down to my fingertips. *Push. Push. Push.* If anyone pushed here, it was Kost. He pushed me into this life, he pushed me away from him. Violent and wild, my shadows burst forth and surged across the field. They moved with a ferocity that matched my own ire, racing with unparalleled speed and darting erratically like a creature attempting to strike fear into its mark. They intercepted Calem's attack, obliterating his shadows into harmless wisps before slamming into him with the force of a beast. Calem's back cracked against the earth, and he howled in answer. He was on his feet in seconds, shadows racing over his body and stone-like scales forming and receding along his exposed forearms. Mercury flooded his stare.

Tendrils spired around me, there but not really within my grasp. I knew that look in Calem's eyes. He was about to shift into a creature I wasn't sure I could stop. He despised losing above all else, and his bloodlust had only increased with his added bestial power.

"Calem," Ozias warned. He inched in the direction of his brother.

"I'm fine," Calem snarled. "This will only take a minute."

"Focus on what they taught you this morning," Kost called, voice sharp. His gaze darted between me and Calem. "Stop his attack, and then we'll be done."

Visions of the last time my shadows writhed beyond my control flooded into my mind. The network of bleeding cuts across Kost's hands. The gashes on my chest. Gods only knew if I'd wounded someone else; I hadn't asked, and no one had told me otherwise. I'd already stomached enough guilt. I didn't want to hear the truth if I had.

Calem barked out a laugh. "Incoming." He lunged, shadows wrapping around his feet to thrust him forward with otherworldly speed.

All at once, my shadows stilled of their own accord. They towered around me like obsidian stalagmites, seemingly immovable. Face stricken, I placed a shaky hand on the nearest one. It was as if I'd freed a monster. My touch sent them barreling across the ground like a stampede. Their forms were far from solid, but I swore I heard the gnashing of teething and harrowing, guttural snarls. They ripped through the earth, leaving canyons of dirt in their wake, and were on Calem in a breath. They barreled into him and coiled around his limbs, rendering him immobile, before suddenly flinging him into a boulder. The smack of his head against the stone rang heavy in the clearing, and as his body slumped to the earth, a streak of blood trailed after him.

"Calem!" Ozias screamed.

No. No, no, no. I was running before I could think. My shadows were still circling him, their movements erratic but deadly. A handful of tendrils reared back and knitted together into a devastatingly sharp blade. Slowly, it poised itself over Calem.

I thrust my hands outward, trying in vain to regain control. *Come on. Come on!* But the shadows didn't respond. They continued to close in on their prey, writhing as they prepared to strike. Everything slowed then. I felt the shadows move before they did. Felt the release of tension, the thrust of power, as that blade careened toward my slumped friend. He wouldn't survive. It was a terrible sense of knowing that settled like a fog over my mind.

I'd killed Calem.

Me.

And then as my shadows moved, Kost appeared. I don't know how he managed to get there so fast. It was as if he were somehow a few seconds ahead of the rest of us, acting before even my shadows decided to strike. He threw himself over Calem and enclosed them in a dome of onyx just as my blade sliced the air. When the tip met Kost's shield, a piercing whistle erupted in the clearing, and I watched in horror as my weapon pushed through.

No. Not Kost, too.

There was still too much left to be said. Staggering, I threw my hands wide and imagined clawing my shadows apart. I wanted to rip them into docile shreds, to send them fluttering in the wind and leave my friends unharmed. Because if I killed them…

The whistling faded in time for a strangled grunt to fill the void. My heart hammered against my throat.

Who…

My shadows returned to me and writhed like a nest of vipers at my feet before suddenly shooting in the woods beyond my reach. Gone. Just like before.

I hadn't succeeded. I'd sworn for a moment that I had. I thought I'd wrenched back some semblance of control, forced them to disperse, but apparently even that was too much for me to accomplish.

But then, the remnants of Kost's dome dissipated, and he sank to the ground with an obvious exhale.

Breathing. My eyes cut to Calem. The rise and fall of his chest was steady. Relief slammed into me, and I rushed to them with Ozias right by my side. By the time we reached them, Calem was already blinking and rubbing the back of his head. His fingers came away red, and he winced. Then, his brows drew together as he spied Kost before him.

"What happened?" he asked.

"I..." I couldn't find the words. Kost tensed and then bit out a sharp curse. His hand went to his shoulder blade. A clean rip from the base of his neck to the top of his rib cage dominated my vision. My shadow weapon had cut through his defenses and sliced open his skin. Deep.

But didn't kill him. Maybe I *had* found a way to pull back, if only a little. It was a small victory, but I hardly felt victorious.

Kost's voice was sharp enough to pierce a Laharock hide. "Gaige lost control."

Rather, I'd nearly killed him. Both of them. He didn't need to obscure the truth for my sake. My emotions had gotten the better of me, and my shadows didn't hesitate to react to my anger. It didn't matter that I hadn't intended for any of this to happen. It still happened just the same.

Calem leapt to his feet. His eyes met mine and he grinned, as if his life hadn't just hung in the balance of my unpredictable power. "It'll get easier. I promise."

Kost stood slowly. "That's enough training for tonight." Then, to Calem, "Are you sure you're all right?"

"Please. I had Gaige right where I wanted him." Nothing apparently shook Calem's resolve. Just mine. He waved Kost off as he started toward camp. "I do need some fresh clothes, though." His tunic was in tattered shreds, and a few cuts were visible beneath them. The wounds were already healing, though, and he wiped away smeared blood with his shirt.

Kost's stride was stiff beside him, his own cut quickly healing with each measured breath. I could hardly bring myself to look at him. "Likewise."

Calem craned his head over his shoulder to look at me. "You actually detected my presence, though, which is progress."

The tension between my shoulders loosened a fraction. "I did?"

Right now, I'd take any win. Any sign that we were moving forward so nothing like this ever happened again.

"Well, sort of anyway." He shrugged.

We came to the camp and Calem grabbed his bag. He rummaged through clothing as he slumped to the ground. Ozias sat beside him on a log, his thick hands clasped together before him. Concern was still evident in his deep brown eyes, but the veins tracking his arms were no longer popping through his skin.

His caterpillar-thick brows scrunched together as he glanced at me. "Did you see him?"

"No, I only saw a void."

Ozias smiled. "That's good! We can all see each other when we move through the realm. You're almost there." A small bubble of relief formed in my chest.

And then Kost popped it.

"You should have mastered that skill already." Kost removed his glasses and polished the lenses with tense fingers. His words were frosty—rightfully so, given I'd just run a shadow blade into his back. I didn't even have it in me to be frustrated with his response. So instead, I said nothing. My mind was a swirling mess. There were a few moments of control nestled in the absolute shitstorm I'd just manifested, but I couldn't bring myself to accept praise for something so small when everything else was so obviously bad.

As the rest of them set about preparing dinner, I simply stared at my hands. My *gloved* hands. Even on a base level, I was hiding. Hiding from the truth of my existence, burying it beneath leather as if that would somehow lessen the ache of that horrid reminder on the back of my hand. I couldn't face what I'd lost. I couldn't face what I was supposed to be now. I'd pushed for solutions in the beginning, when I spent days in the library searching for answers. The only difference was, I hadn't pushed to get better at being undead.

I'd pushed for a cure. I wanted a way out. And when I couldn't find one… I gave up.

I never even tried to control the power I'd inherited. Not really.

Tears pricked the back of my eyes. If my inaction meant nearly killing someone I loved… Not loved, but… If it meant almost killing Kost…

He was right. He was always right.

Without bothering to say good night, I slipped into the tent Ozias had kindly set up for me and fell upon the makeshift bed. My fingers trembled as I curled into a ball and squeezed my eyes shut against a burn of tears I refused to give myself the relief of shedding.

I didn't care if I slept or not.

EIGHT

KOST

Weak light filtered through the canvas of my tent, signaling the morning's arrival. With a forceful exhale, I pulled back the thin blanket I'd packed, pleased to finally be traveling in more temperate weather. The undead had a high tolerance for cold, but I much preferred the crisp, spring air and gentle warmth from the sun.

After dressing quickly, I stepped out into the quiet morning, only to falter at the edge of my tent. Gaige was already awake, sitting on a dying tree stump and tending to a small fire. Judging by the ashy color of the coals, it'd been burning for some time. An unpleasant tingling crawled over my skin, but I kept my expression carefully blank.

"Couldn't sleep?" I sat on a smooth boulder across from him. A gentle breeze ruffled the flames, and they snarled for a moment before dying back down.

Gaige poked the logs with a slender stick. "I slept some." The bags around his eyes, however, contradicted that statement. His gaze was bleary, his hair a bit frazzled. With his elbows braced on his knees, he rolled his neck from shoulder to shoulder. He dragged his gaze from the flames to me. "Does everyone in Cruor get up at such a ridiculous hour?"

"Clearly not." I jerked my thumb to the tent at my back. Ozias's steady snore ebbed and flowed with the cadence of ocean waves. "He won't wake up until midmorning at the earliest unless someone rouses him. Calem on the other hand..." I tipped my chin toward his tent. The flaps were tied back to reveal an empty interior, save a saddlebag he'd propped up like a pillow. "He always rises with the sun."

"I assumed it was just to find us breakfast."

"It's always been that way. Maybe someday he'll tell you about it."

Gaige rolled the firestick between his gloved hands. "I thought the dead didn't talk about their past."

A familiar pang prickled from the scar above my heart. "That's why I said 'maybe.'" I hadn't touched the decades-old wound, but somehow, Gaige's tired gaze slanted to my chest just the same. I wasn't exactly eager to discuss my former life, either. Everyone at Cruor had died for a reason. Sometimes, those reasons were better left buried.

Braiding my fingers together, I ignored the weight of his stare and returned to more important matters. "Did you have another nightmare?"

"Not this time. I think yesterday's events were chilling enough to put my mind in a stupor." He turned his focus back to the flames. "I could've killed you."

His words were incredibly soft, and I stilled. "But you didn't."

"I..." He let his words fall away and didn't bother to offer anything else.

"We'll keep working." I shifted closer to the fire. Closer to him. "The other time you lost control, during your nightmare... What happened?"

Slowly, as if some invisible force were tugging at a string

attached to the crown of his head, he raised his chin to meet my gaze. "It was just a dream. Lots of shadows and a man."

I frowned. "A man? Anyone you recognize?"

"I only really saw his eyes and hands. Next thing I knew, you were shaking me awake. Why?"

The final log on the fire crumbled, showering the air with sparks. Tracking one of the errant, fluttering embers, I let out a tight sigh. "We don't really know what happens to those lost in the realm."

"But I wasn't lost. You found me lying in bed."

"True." I removed my spectacles and studied the crystal-clear lenses. "All logic indicates that you were merely experiencing a bad dream. Still..." I replaced my glasses and stood. "You must take your training seriously. We were able to rescue those nearest your room when the incident occurred, and we were fortunate that their injuries were minor. The same goes for yesterday's incident. Next time, we might not be so lucky."

"You act like I think this is some sort of game." He tossed the stick into the fire with more force than necessary. Heat simmered behind his glare, chasing away some of the exhaustion from his expression. "I don't *enjoy* hurting people. That pastime is better suited for you and the rest of your assassins."

The muscles between my shoulder blades tensed. "I don't enjoy hurting people."

"Physically or emotionally?" Shaking his head, he let out a bitter laugh. I couldn't help but feel like it was masking something else. Like this emotion was easier to display than whatever agony lay beneath. "Regardless, you're pretty damn good at it."

"Do you think I wanted this fate for myself?" I kept my tone careful, even. I'd given in to my frustrations too many times when it came to Gaige. He had a way of getting under my skin like no one had before. Yet I could withstand the majority of his insults and his insatiable bitterness, because deep down I was afraid. I was afraid that if I reacted too strongly, too harshly, I'd burn him so badly that I'd never feel the sting of his hatred again. Only his indifference.

And that would be a hundred times worse.

He shrugged tightly. "I wouldn't know. You've never—"

A loud curse from Ozias cut off our conversation, and he stumbled out of his tent. Bleary-eyed and shirtless, he blinked at us several times before letting out a deep groan.

"Just a dream." He dragged a hand over his face. "Damn, that felt real."

"I know the feeling," Gaige muttered.

Stifling a yawn, Ozias nodded. "Guess I'm up. Calem already on breakfast?"

Kost lifted a shoulder. "I assume so. Haven't seen him."

"I spotted some mushrooms along the path just before we hit the clearing. I'll grab those to go with whatever he's hunting." With another belabored yawn, he cut across the clearing in the direction of the path, stumbling as he went.

"He won't be himself 'til he has coffee." I glanced around until I found his percolator. He'd prepped it the night before, so I gently propped it near the coals before returning to my seat.

"He and I have that in common," Gaige mused. Whether by design or not, Ozias had effortlessly cut the tension between us, returning things to an almost-normalcy I'd been craving.

"I think we all do. Actually, I'm not certain if Calem actually enjoys it or if he only drinks it—"

A thunderous crash, followed by a startled, distant scream, reverberated through the forest. Both Gaige and I pivoted toward the sound. Birds scattered overhead in a frantic flurry, and smaller, harmless creatures barreled past our camp before diving back into the woods. With frenzied whinnies, our Zeelahs tugged on their knotted reins.

"Ozias or Calem?" Gaige asked.

"I don't know." The forest had fallen unnaturally quiet. "Are there Kitska beasts about?"

Gaige absently touched the back of his hand where his symbol used to be. Shadows began to leak from his frame and slither through the grass at his feet. "Likely. I haven't sensed any nearby creatures, but..."

Another frightened yelp, much closer than before, split the air. Calem rocketed from the tree line and nearly crashed right into us. His golden hair was undone and wild with twigs and leaves. Minor scratches lined his arms, as if he'd torn through the forest without care for the barbed vines. Face parchment-pale and eyes wide, he came to a halt before us. "We're going to die."

I'd known Calem for as long as he'd been raised. I'd never seen him like this. "What happened?"

"We have to get out. We have to leave *now*." He pushed past us and rushed toward the Zeelahs.

"Wait." I snared his wrist and tugged him gently to a stop. "Ozias isn't here. We can't leave him."

"Let go of me!" Calem clawed at my grip, leaving raised marks along my skin. "I swear to gods if you don't let me go, I will shift and bite your hand off."

"Calem." I placed my free hand over his. "Tell us what happened."

Beads of sweat lined his hairline, and a violent tremor rattled his body. Straining against my hold, he turned his bulging stare on me. There wasn't an ounce of mercury to be seen. A quiet ringing crested in my ears. Calem was scared. No, *terrified*. Almost as if bespelled into abject fear.

"Please," he begged.

Without letting go of him, I jerked my chin toward Gaige. "What could cause this?"

Gaige's hand had flown to Okean's key, and he gripped the pendant tight. "There's no way of knowing what kind of beasts lurk in the Kitska Forest. So many creatures from all over our world died here, and they simply remained. Native or not."

A twig snapped in the forest, and Calem flinched. He tried again to wrench himself free. "It's coming."

"Ozias!" I shouted at the top of my lungs, praying he hadn't gone too far. A strange, prickling sensation skittered through my mind, followed by a jumbled flash of images that were near impossible to decipher. But the overwhelming sense of dread was something I couldn't mistake.

Felicks?

The key dangling about my neck seemed to burn at the thought.

A hysterical laugh bubbled from Calem's lips. "We're going to die. It's finally going to happen."

Gaige crouched before Calem. "Tell me what you saw."

A mess of shadows bloomed to life around us, and Ozias bolted from the shadow realm. His chest heaved as scoured the area. "What happened?"

"We don't know. We'll figure it out as we go. Get the Zeelahs." I let go of Calem and turned to our frightened mounts. Between his reaction and that strange, preternatural sense of…something, I knew we had to flee.

A branch splintered in the wood, and Calem's erratic laughter died. Slowly, he raised his chin to stare out into nothing. "Too late. It's here."

I felt it before I saw it. A frigid, bone-deep cold slammed into my body at the same time a musty, mothball-like odor filled my nose. All sounds disappeared into a vacuum, save the crunching of leaves and twigs coming from the forest. A pain burned through my lungs as my legs turned to lead, black spots dancing across my vision. I couldn't breathe. Couldn't think. All I could do was watch and wait. It was as if the approach itself were meant to instill terror. None of us could move. With, every passing second, every uneven, ragged breath, we knew we were one step closer to death.

The Kitska monster emerged with the calm surety of a predator. Covered in a thick, feathery hide, the beast was the size of a large hound with the body of a fox. Ivory antlers grew from the crown of its owl-like head. With an elongated, flexible neck, it swiveled its head to skewer us with three endless, glowing, violet eyes.

The moment I met its stare was the moment every horrifying memory coalesced in me at once. The chalky skin and blue-tinged lips of my mother as a sickness claimed her life. Jude's scream as he'd been attacked and thrown to the ground. The cool sting of a blade above my heart, followed by the sticky warmth of my own blood. The weeks it took me to die, and the horrendous, soul-consuming fear of being alone in the end. But the worst image wasn't something in my past, but a deep-seated fear I hoped never came to fruition: Gaige lost to the shadows, screaming as his mind was ripped to shreds.

I crumbled to my knees. *Death would be better than this.*

The creature sauntered forward, its talons digging through the soft earth with ease. The visions played on repeat in my mind, and I began to shake uncontrollably. In my peripheral, Calem and Ozias were doing the same, but Gaige had tucked his chin to his shoulder. He dared to look my direction for a second and silently mouthed something to me.

Not silently. A blip of awareness managed to make its way through the onslaught of horrifying visages. The tendons along

Gaige's neck were strained, his veins bulging. His throat bobbed as his lips moved, as if he were shouting.

Shouting.

"Kost!" His voice broke the void, and suddenly our surroundings slammed back into focus. "Summon Felicks!"

The pain in my chest sharpened. *No.* I couldn't bring my beast to endure this horror. We were about to be slaughtered, and none of us could do anything to stop it. I knew it like a truth seeded deep in my bones. This horrifying creature had immobilized us with its stare, and there was no escaping the presence of death that surrounded it. I wouldn't condemn Felicks to the same fate. I shook my head once, unable to muster words.

"Trust me. It's the only way." Fingers trembling, he tapped the key dangling between his collarbones before pointing to mine. "Do it."

Between us, Calem and Ozias were speechless. Tears bisected their cheeks as they stared at the looming monster. Calem held his stomach tightly and rocked on his heels. Lips parted and face stricken, Ozias had grasped either side of his head. Every fiber of my being rioted at the idea of summoning Felicks, but Gaige seemed so sure. I knew he'd never condemn my beast to death. He'd never condemn any beast to death. I had to believe in him. I had to trust that this was the only way to save us.

Wrapping my fingers around Felicks's key, I centered myself with a shaky, long breath. Heat immediately bloomed from the metal, and with the flux of his power, the cold abated. Wondrous, effervescent light glowed around us as the beast realm door swung open, and Felicks appeared. Hackles standing on end, he positioned himself before me and growled at the impending monster.

The creature shifted its focus to my Poi, and the desperation and fear that filled the air faltered.

A low, threatening growl simmered from the back of Felicks's throat. The monster cocked its head in response and let out a questioning hoot. Despite his diminutive stature, Felicks squared up to the monster without a trace of hesitation, lips peeled back in a snarl. He took several definitive steps forward.

The monster responded by ducking its head several times before kneeling to the ground in a strange bow. All three eyes remained locked on Felicks. Felicks yipped, and the orb atop his head clouded as a new future brewed. Seconds ticked by, each one somehow longer than the last. My breath hitched as I waited for him to share the visions of our impending deaths.

But they never came.

Instead, Felicks showed me a series of images where we all survived—and Gaige standing before the Kitska monster with a shadow lure cupped between his hands.

My gaze cut to Gaige as the scent of mothballs disappeared from the air. His body practically deflated in a sudden show of relief, and he slowly approached the monster. Felicks went with him, sticking close to his ankles with a focus he normally reserved for tracking his next meal, but the hackles along his neck had gone down.

"It's all right," Gaige murmured, as he bowed deeply before the beast. The creature looked up, first glancing at Felicks before extending its neck to inspect Gaige more closely. When it pulled back, Gaige righted himself and gestured to my Poi. "This is Felicks. Would you like to join us?"

And then the monster did perhaps the most peculiar thing I'd ever seen. Crouching on all fours, it raised its rear to the air and wagged its fox-like tail with exuberance. A trill of excited birdcalls escaped its beak as it targeted Felicks with what I could only assume was a playful stare. With that, the last trickling of fear in my gut died. Standing, I brushed my hands along my clothes and eyed the curious creature. Calem and Ozias blinked as their trembling subsided, their confused glances hopping from person to beast until they too halted on the now amicable Kitska monster.

Gaige chuckled and cupped his hands before him, summoning a small orb of shadows. It hung above his palm for a moment before dripping between his fingers to crawl through the air in the direction of the beast. "This is my scent. I can't send you to the beast realm anymore, but you can stay with me."

Sniffing at the wispy tendrils, the beast bobbed its head toward Felicks and hooted.

"He belongs to Kost," Gaige said, pointing to me. "But he summons Felicks daily. You'll be able to see him regularly."

Bounding in a sudden show of excitement, the monster circled the pair. As Gaige let his shadows disperse, a pleased grin toying with his lips, Felicks leapt after the monster. They darted back and forth across the clearing, my beast yipping like a young kit and the creature letting out a strange amalgamation of a high-pitched bird squawk and a bark.

"Thank the gods for Felicks." Gaige turned to us as he tugged on his gloves, ensuring they were still in place. "Without him, we would have died."

"I felt like I did," Ozias mumbled as he rubbed his hands along his biceps. "What was that?" There was still an air of disbelief to his words. I could hardly blame him.

Gaige grimaced. "Foxels are harbingers of death. They typically only leave their dens to hunt small game, which they do by immobilizing their prey with gripping fear. If you avoid eye contact, you have a chance to flee. Otherwise"—he nodded to where we'd frozen before the beast—"well…you experienced that firsthand."

"Is it even safe to keep him around?" Calem asked.

Gaige frowned. "Yes."

Ozias shifted uncomfortably from one foot to the next. "Are you sure?"

"If Gaige says it's safe, then it's safe." I blew out a tight breath. My visions had been so visceral, so raw, and yet Gaige had been the one to come up with a solution. He'd been smart enough to avoid the Foxel's gaze and save us all. The least we could do was trust him.

The gratitude on Gaige's face was palpable. So much so that I had to look away.

Calem tracked the rambunctious beasts zooming through the grass. "What are they doing? I've never seen Felicks act this way, not even when Effie tries to play with him."

"Poi and Foxels have a special bond." Gaige's smile returned. "In fact, the only way to charm...*tame*"—he corrected himself, and his expression tightened—"a non-Kitska Foxel is with the help of a Poi. Foxels won't harm them under any circumstances, and they often form lifelong friendships with one lucky Poi in particular. In this case, Felicks."

My brows inched toward my hairline. "Lifelong?"

"Yes. While I'm confident I can keep him in line, I believe I'll always be second to Felicks in the eyes of...Rook?" He waved at the pair, failing to snare the attention of either creature. "How does Rook sound? Do you like that?"

Rook's only acknowledgment was a joyous squeal, but that was enough for Gaige. His grin deepened in earnest, and he made his way back to the fire. He moved aside the percolator, now thoroughly brewed, and stacked tinder carefully atop the still-warm coals. They caught quickly, but the heat couldn't chase away the chill creeping down my spine. I believed that Gaige had made the right decision and that we were no longer in danger, but there was still the matter of how Rook found us.

"You said Foxels rarely leave their dens," I began, treading lightly both with my words and my gait as I rounded the hungry flames. Ozias and Calem said nothing, but while the stench of death and aura of fear had dispersed, the coiled tension racking their shoulders remained. "Why did Rook attack, then?"

"Calem likely stumbled into his territory." Gaige poked at the fire. "They are normally passive and avoid conflict, so you must have been closer to his home than you realized."

"I didn't notice anything," Calem hedged.

Gaige lifted a shoulder. "It's hard to tell anything apart in the Kitska Forest unless you know what you're looking for."

"And the Mizobats?" My voice was soft, but I knew he'd heard it by the way he flinched. "Would you say their attack was abnormal as well?"

Abandoning the fire, he skewered me with a hard stare. "What are you insinuating?"

"I'm addressing facts." I fiddled with the cuffs of my sleeves, rolling them slightly so I had reason to look at my hands instead of Gaige. "There's a link we're missing."

"And that link is me?" Gaige's lips thinned.

"You lost control of your shadows in front of the Mizobats, and they attacked. Later that same evening, your shadows escaped again during your dreams." I forced myself to meet his terse scowl. "A week later, we received word of beasts attacking travelers on normally safe routes. And now, after losing control while training with Calem, this."

"*This* was not my fault. If you recall, I'm the one who told you to summon Felicks. If not for me, we'd be dead."

If not for your powers, this never would have occurred. I curbed the thought before it could escape my lips. I didn't believe in coincidences, and every sign indicated that Gaige was the source of the attacks. While I'd never hesitated to deliver harsh truths before, something about Gaige's wild, pleading stare made it impossible to utter those words. He *needed* the appearance of Rook to be Calem's fault. He was losing faith, losing his grip on...well, himself. We'd only just convinced him to train, and it was vital that he continued to do so.

"Let's break down camp and keep moving. I doubt Rook was the monster responsible for the attacks, as those victims are very much still alive."

Without waiting for him to respond, I returned to my tent, allowing the flaps to close behind me. For now, at least, we were all intact. But as I gathered my things and caught sight of Gaige's silhouette through the canvas, I couldn't help but worry that the wavering shape of his form had nothing to do with the barrier of fabric between us and everything to do with his ravenous power.

NINE

GAIGE

I didn't think it was possible for my brain to ache, but it did. The consistent, nagging throb behind my eyes was a pulse steadier than my heartbeat, and I wanted nothing more than to sleep and rid myself of the wretched feeling. But I couldn't. After my botched training with Calem, I'd gone to bed in fit of frustration, only to once again find my feet on that distant, foreign beach. I'd told Kost my dreams had been uneventful, but I'd stretched the truth. The only difference was that this time, when the swirling, black mass of shadows called to me from the ocean waters, I picked up a jagged stone and smashed it into my temple.

Only to wake up to another nightmare—possibly one I'd summoned—in the form of a Foxel. Rook. Now, bounding alongside my Zeelah with his tongue lolling out the side of his maw, he hardly seemed like a threat. We'd already been traveling for hours in the direction of Penumbra Glades without incident. The stench of death had abated the moment Felicks snared the Foxel's attention. The only thing Rook was liable to do at this point was trip one of our mounts.

"Hey, watch it," Calem barked as Rook darted in front of his stallion in an attempt to get closer to Kost. Or rather, Felicks, who was perched behind his master on their Zeelah's behind, ears twitching as he studied Rook. Kost didn't bother glancing over his shoulder, and instead sucked his teeth as he urged his mount ahead.

"He really loves Felicks," Ozias said. The path through the Kitska Forest had widened just enough for him to guide his mare beside me, and he watched Rook with a rapt curiosity I usually only saw in Charmers. "You think he'll get along with Boo?"

Boo. He'd grown surprisingly attached to me, and I hated leaving him behind. But Iov was more than eager to take up the duty of caring for his wounds and feeding him. Boo had won over every assassin within Cruor's walls, but none more than Iov. The number of apples and honey that man fed my beast was probably the reason for Boo's increase in weight.

"I'm sure he'll enjoy having a regular playmate around."

Ozias's wide smile nearly touched his ears. "Good. I figured since we hadn't seen Okean in a bit that those two didn't get along."

My gloved fingers found the key dangling around my neck before I realized I'd released the reins. A trickle of warmth simmered from the point of contact, and with it came a sinking, twisting feeling in my gut. Okean would've loved to spend time with Boo and Rook. He was equally as playful but summoning him would mean showing him the part of me that I despised. And if I lost control of my shadows while he was outside of the beast realm, if something happened to him...I'd lose the only part of my past I still truly had.

Swallowing thickly, I abandoned the key and urged my mount forward. Once things were calmer—once I was calmer—I'd call on Okean.

The rest of the day was spent in tension-filled silence. Occasionally Calem or Ozias would attempt to break the quiet, but after failing to engage Kost or me, they eventually gave up. Without a doubt, this wasn't the type of journey they were used to, but I simply couldn't muster the energy to participate in innocent banter. As for Kost, his serious facade was a shield we didn't have the means to pierce. I wasn't even sure I wanted to.

When night fell and we made camp, he did finally speak, but only to issue orders and note that there would be no training after this morning's *debacle*. My jaw ached from my unending teeth grinding, but a tiny part of me was glad to forgo another round of failed exercises, at least for the night. But when it came time to stow away in my tent and sink beneath the blankets, I couldn't bring myself to sleep. That horrifying, burning gaze, rimmed in fiery crimson, stared back at me each time I closed my eyes. It was as if I were being examined, the contents of my life carefully pored over and considered, leaving no stone unturned. I couldn't escape it, and I knew if I slept, I'd meet those eyes again.

Blasted nightmares. When we returned to Cruor, I'd seek out the closest healer and ask for a sleeping draught potent enough to blank out dreams. For now, I was resigned to long nights and even longer days.

Which is why when we arrived at Moeras, the small trading town built on platforms above the unstable marshes of Penumbra Glades, I barely had the wherewithal to determine the hazy, evening fog from the murky earth beneath my Zeelah's hooves. It'd crept in slowly, snaking around the roots of trees, and thickened once we finally broke free from the Kitska Forest into the open flats marking the glades. Riddled with the scent of salt and earth, a quiet breeze rustled the thigh-high cattails around us. There wasn't much to take in. The expanse was vast and plain, the same vegetation on repeat until it came flush with the sea.

The town, at least, was a welcomed sight among the swaying plants. The entrance was marked by a simple tower with a polished, jade-green bell quietly hanging in the belfry. Wooden stilt houses with gabled roofs sat above the glades, connected by plank bridges.

Kost brought his Zeelah to a halt. A curiously tense muscle strained along his neck. "Moeras."

Calem guided his mount beside Kost, and then stretched his hands to the sky. "Been awhile since you've been back."

If I hadn't grown accustomed to studying Kost—or at least, I *used* to take an interest in his expressions and physique—I wouldn't have noticed the near-imperceptible flinch. "I was here when Noc died."

I raised a careful brow, looking first at Ozias—who was of course unsurprised by this tidbit—before clearing my throat. "Noc died here?"

For the first time since my *incident* with Rook, Kost met my gaze. "Yes. Just beyond this town during a battle with Rhyne."

"I wasn't referring to that." Calem dropped his hands on his thighs, the loud slap an exasperated, resounding thing.

This time, Kost's flinch was entirely, perhaps intentionally, obvious. Snapping his attention to Calem, he leveled him with a cold look. "I know." Then, without glancing in our direction, he said, "Follow this path. The first establishment you will encounter is the stable. House the Zeelahs, and I'll meet you at the inn within the hour." He dismounted swiftly, batting away the cattails that smacked against his legs.

"Where are you going?" The question was out before I realized, and I silently hated myself for my morbid curiosity. I was *done* with Kost. He was the guild master of Cruor. For all I knew, he had business to attend to that was beyond my purview. Why did I care at all?

He didn't look my way. "I'll join you shortly." Stepping into the shadows, he moved quickly down the path and into town, turning behind the first set of buildings and disappearing from our view. Beside me, Rook let out a questioning hoot. He nodded his head fervently in the direction of Kost before rubbing against my leg with the artistry of a cat.

"It's all right. Felicks will be back." I let out a tight sigh. "Though you should wait for us in the woods."

"What? Why?" Ozias asked.

"I could stable him with the Zeelahs, but I doubt Rook would do well with that. If anything, it'd make him anxious, and the last thing we want is him prowling the town without us in light of recent events." I looked down at my Kitska beast. A gentle whine sounded from the back of his throat. He shoved his snout against my trousers, and I gave him a reassuring pat. "You're safer out here. We'll come as soon as we can."

Rook let out a resigned huff, but he turned and trotted toward the tree line, glancing back several times before finally slinking away.

Calem snorted. "That was a pout if I've ever seen one."

"Most definitely." A smile tugged at my lips, and I righted myself in my saddle. "We should go before he tries to tail us into town."

"If you say so." Ozias looked after Rook; a crease of worry etched into his forehead. After a beat, he pushed ahead of us and snagged Kost's lingering mount. "C'mon, let's get settled."

We quickly deposited our Zeelahs at the stable and climbed a short flight of wooden stairs onto the raised stilts of Moeras. The vibrational hum of cicadas filled the air, drowning out all other sounds save the occasional greetings of inhabitants we passed on the creaking plank bridges. We strolled by house after house of riotous color. Teal with gold accents. Burnt sienna. Smoldering red. Emerald green. It was as if the residents knew their surroundings were bland, and they made up for it by decorating their homes in earnest. There was something pleasing about the inconsistent color schemes, the raucous clashing of a violet cottage next to a sunflower bungalow.

"It's no wonder Kost is such a stickler for colors," Calem muttered. He adjusted the packs dangling from his shoulders, hoisting them higher up.

"What do you mean?" I asked.

"Never mind him," Ozias said, offering a rare glare toward his brother. Calem shrugged, leaving Ozias to answer with an exaggerated eye roll. Their nonverbal language, perfected over the years, was bizarrely entertaining to watch—and not at all subtle.

"Wait, is this where Kost is from?" I asked, piecing together Calem's comments like a puzzle.

"He rarely talks about it," Calem said.

"Which means we shouldn't be. C'mon, there's the inn," Ozias continued before I could interject, and he hooked a right toward a large, single-story building with three dominating gables. While the paint colors were understated, the wooden pillars holding up the building were something else entirely. Intricate, hand-carved patterns read like stories, depicting wars of old and even creatures I'd never glimpsed. I wanted to jump from the bridge and battle against the cattails just to run my hands over the wood, to feel the beasts' forms, the breaths in their chests. But Calem nudged me forward, and I had to abandon the works of art for a simple door and a hanging, iron sign that read *The Wooden Flower.*

Ozias pushed through first and approached a middle-aged man bent over a desk. He rolled a toothpick between his teeth as he scratched our names into his guest book, then fished a handful of rusted keys from a hidden drawer.

"This way," he said with a wave, coming around the table to escort us down a nearby hallway. "The right wing is where you'll be staying. Tavern is in the middle, behind where you checked in.

Lucinda, she's our cook, is known for her venison. You ought to try some if you're hungry." After passing several heavy wooden doors, he came to a stop before one labeled *Marigold*. "The next three are yours, too. Cornflower, Lavender, Rose." He handed us our keys one by one, giving Kost's extra key to Ozias. "And there's a bard who plays in the evenings. Lots of folks come in to see him."

"Thanks," Ozias said with a grin. "Appreciate it."

"Let me know if you need anything." He tipped his chin in parting and then left, whistling a quiet tune as he went.

Once our overly friendly attendant was out of earshot, Ozias handed us each a key. "Take a breather while you can." He unlocked his door and stepped into his room letting it click firmly closed behind him. Calem didn't hesitate, jostling the iron handle of Cornflower until the key slid into place. His door swung shut just as I opened mine. I came to an abrupt halt at the threshold of Lavender as the inn's name rang through my mind.

"Gods." The Wooden Flower was, in fact, full of flowers—wooden and alive. Almost every square inch of my quarters was coated in a shade of pale purple, down to the hand-carved wooden frame of my bed. A deep, lustrous green accented the decor like the vines and leaves that accompanied the flowers draped from the ceiling rafters. The air was perfumed with the thick scent of lavender, and while I'd always been indifferent to flowers, it was impossible not to admire the beauty of it all.

"How do they even manage this?" I mused, reaching my fingertips toward the ceiling to graze one of the lowest velvet petals. In all my years of travel, I'd never once visited Moeras. The marshlands of Penumbra Glades had never been appealing to me, but now a growing bud of intrigue had bloomed in my mind, and the desire to learn more—to see more—took hold of me with a force I'd all but forgotten.

Reaching for my necklace, I gripped Okean's key tightly. It was a familiar pull, not quite as strong as the drive I'd felt for discovering new beasts, but something similar. It was an echo of what I used to feel. Of who I used to be.

All this time, I'd been trying so hard to hold on to my past that I'd resisted training, searched for Kitska beasts in the woods, researched cures... All the while, I'd walled off the one part of me that I'd been trying so hard to find. I was so afraid to lose it that I'd forgotten it made me who I was today. Okean was part of that. He was all I had left. And it was better to live with the pain, the reminder, of what I'd lost than never see him again.

The only person rejecting my fate was me. Not Okean. Not Kost. Not the rest of my brethren at Cruor. Now I had to learn to live with it, too.

With a shaky breath, I closed my eyes. The heat of Okean's and my bond ignited with intensity, and I focused on the power I used to wield so easily. A grating, rich intonation met my ears as the beast realm door opened. A pleased yowl crested above the groaning hinges, and Okean bounded out of a pillar of soft, white light. The door closed with his entrance, the magic in his key receding to a gentle flicker of warmth, and my feline beast sank to his haunches.

His liquid-blue coat shimmered as if he'd just emerged from water, and his finned tail flicked back and forth as he studied me. Jeweled eyes, more stunning than any sapphire, stared at me with a strange mixture of joy and annoyance. With a jerk of his head, he averted his gaze and pretended to scour the ceiling.

"Are you pouting?" I crouched before him and offered my hand.

Instead of ramming his head into my palm—begging me to run my fingers over his finned whiskers and scratch beneath his jaw—he batted me away with an oversized paw. A sharp hiss escaped from his maw.

A hollow, deep pain invaded my chest, and I withdrew my hand. "I'm sorry, Okean."

He didn't acknowledge me.

"Okay, fine." I sank to the floor and propped my elbows on my knees. "I'm sorry I haven't called on you. I just..." I looked away from his frame. Everything about him was agonizingly beautiful. He was a constant reminder of the potential I used to have, but he was also *here*. I could've lost my ability to see him like I had the rest of my beasts, but by the grace of the gods—and Leena's quick thinking to use a Charmer's key to bind him to me—I could still summon him.

And I loved him dearly.

"I'm a mess." I dropped my head into my hands. The warm leather gloves obscuring my symbol smelled of oak and hide, and I dug my fingers into my forehead. "I don't know who I am anymore."

But it was more than that. I was afraid like I'd never been afraid before. The dark, twisting shadows that I'd begun to wield didn't scare me, but their power, what they did to *my* Charmer magic, horrified me. They'd blanketed out a part of my soul and stripped me of my power to summon beasts. I'd become something else entirely, and I didn't know how to take the next step forward. And I'd always known how to do that before.

A weak sob racked my shoulders just as something heady and solid rammed into my chest. Okean had knocked away my hands and was attempting—poorly—to clamber into my lap. His weight was crushing, but I didn't care. In that moment, the only thing I wanted was to hang on to the one thing, the one beast, that made me, me. Wrapping my arms around his broad body, I buried my face in his hide. He plopped his head on top of mine as a deep purr hummed from the back of his throat, sending gentle vibrations down my spine. Silent tears dripped from my eyes.

"I just didn't want you to get lost in the dark with me."

It was a fear so great I hadn't dared voice it before. But it was always there, lurking in the recesses of my brain and growing stronger with every passing day. If I failed and the shadows consumed me, trapping me in an endless existence in the shadow realm, what would that do to Okean? Would he be safe in the beast realm? Or worse, what if he were by my side when it happened? Would he fall into the darkness, too?

Okean didn't move. He weathered it all—my tears, my fears, everything. And I knew in my soul he'd follow me into the shadows if he had to. Just like I knew I'd do everything possible to keep that from happening.

TEN

KOST

The people of Moeras didn't bury their dead. They burned them atop cedar beds and covered their ashes in salt. The only reminders the townsfolk kept of those who'd passed were wooden lilies. Handcrafted and painted a soft white, they dangled from the main bridge stretching across the largest portion of the marsh. They danced with the wind, colliding together and releasing a pleasing reverberation like wooden chimes. The tradition had started with the first founders of the town, and as such, there were many—but my gaze settled on only one. Jude's. I hadn't been the one to hang it, but I'd watched from the shadows as someone else did. And his name was still etched on the stem, a taunting reminder of a past I'd thought I'd laid to rest.

But as I stood among the dangling tokens of the dead, that decades-old pain throbbed from the scar above my heart. Rubbing my chest, I glared at the homage to Jude. To the person who'd stolen my life in more ways than one and abandoned me when I needed him most. And despite it all, I'd found my way here. The moment we'd set foot in Moeras, the ghost of my past snared me and dragged me back.

"*Tsk.*" I turned abruptly, knocking several of the lilies with my shoulders, and the cresting mellow tones of wood on wood did nothing to abate my sour mood. For the first time in a long time, I wanted to train like Calem, sparring until my breath gave out and my knees caved. I wanted to feel nothing but the burn in my lungs, the very real, very corporeal pain of pushing my body beyond its limits.

The desire filled me to the brim, and I stormed to the Wooden Flower. Using my shadows to sense where my brothers were, I turned down their hall and sharply rapped on each of their doors.

"Let's go," I said without waiting to greet them. I could hear them moving, feel Calem's surprise in the way he vaulted through the shadows to his door and Ozias's flicker of concern. From Gaige, I felt nothing. My feet were rooted to the ground outside as I poked at his shadows, trying to sense anything at all. A quiet ring filled my ears, and an uncomfortable tingle prickled over my skin.

Seeing Jude's flower dredged up more than I cared to admit. About him, about Gaige, about me. It was better for me to simply be Gaige's guild master. No matter what was previously between us—which was nothing more than a dream, a ghost of what could have been—I had to stay the course. Anything else opened the door for heartache, and I couldn't do that again.

Gaige opened his door and glanced at Ozias and Calem as they joined me in the hall. Tilting his head slightly, he met my stare. "Where are we going?"

"To the fields to train. Now."

In a matter of minutes, we were approaching the murky salt marsh, our boots squelching in the uneven muck. With Moeras at our backs and the endless, cattail-ridden expanse before us, there was plenty of room for us to practice—without inciting any major damage. Pausing at a hollowed-out log teeming with moss and toadstools, I unbuttoned my vest and tossed it haphazardly across the wood.

Calem's eyes were wide. "What are you doing?"

"Training," I ground out. Rolling my cuffs up above my elbows, I strode out into the glade.

"Yeah, but..." He fidgeted, bouncing from one foot to the next. "Are we sparring?"

"I'm not doing that again. Not with you," Gaige muttered as he shot Calem a furtive glance.

"You're sparring with *me*." Turning to face him, I dug the balls of my feet into the soft earth. I couldn't let him train with Calem or Ozias to that extent again. I had full faith they were capable of taking care of themselves, but I was their leader. And if Gaige were to accidentally harm one of them under my guidance, then their pain would become my burden, too.

And a smaller, more irrational part of me simply wanted Gaige to understand my frustration. Which was futile and utter nonsense, given I'd never spoken to him about everything I was feeling. I couldn't.

Shock plastered Gaige's expression as his mouth fell open. He recovered quickly, slamming his jaw shut and removing his light jacket to toss it beside my vest. Like me, he rolled his black sleeves over his forearms.

"What is even happening right now?" Calem asked more to himself than anyone in particular.

"Kost," Ozias tried, his voice soft, "you sure about this?"

"Yes. I'll limit myself like Calem did," I said. My pulse thrummed in anticipation, and for a moment I reveled in it. It was such a base feeling. Something tangible and authentic and so very, very straightforward. Whereas everything with Gaige... Convoluted and messy.

Ozias studied me for a long moment. He knew something was wrong. I could see it in the way his breath caught in his chest as his brows crawled together. Still, he didn't argue. He shook his head once before turning to Gaige.

"You good to do this?" he asked.

Gaige rolled his lips together. "I'm not sure. What if..."

"You'll be fine." I couldn't help the strain of my voice. All I wanted was to forget about the wooden flowers dangling within eyesight beneath the main bridge. I couldn't read their names from here, but I knew Jude's was there. Just as I knew things between Gaige and me could never be.

Gaige blinked, but then nodded. "All right."

With one last belabored look in my direction and some wordless muttering even I couldn't parse, Ozias sighed and folded his arms across his chest. "Let's keep the shadow work to a minimum after what happened in the woods. Gaige, focus on using your power to help you keep your footing and move swiftly rather than form blades or shields."

"I should've brought snacks." Calem leaned back on his heels as he cradled the back of his head with his hands. A grin split his face in half. "I haven't seen Kost spar in ages."

I ignored him entirely, focusing only on Gaige. On the uncertain way he carried himself. On his twitching, gloved hands. "Are you ready?"

He stilled. "Let's get this over with."

He'd barely finished speaking before I was on him. In the span it took him to breathe, I'd summoned my shadows and wrapped them around my feet and ankles, making it easier for me to speed across the uneven ground. He failed to track my movements, so when I appeared behind him, he turned a half second too late.

"Find your stance." I gripped his elbows and pulled him lower, knocking him off-balance. He stumbled over a log before catching himself. Already I was gone, sinking into the shadow realm and circling him as he scoured the swaying cattails. The last time I'd touched Gaige had been to pull him out of a violent dream. It had been devastating to see him so broken and alone.

My mind was a colossal mess when it came to him. One moment I cared and the next I pretended that I didn't. I hated the way he looked at me, and I hated myself for knowing the reason he was pulling away was because of me. I hated that I had to do it to protect myself. I hated it all. My thoughts never rested, and I just wanted to be done with these swirling emotions. I wasn't strong enough to handle this again.

It was better to wall myself off than fall in love and risk being left all over again.

"Try to find a disturbance in the air," Ozias called. "Something that isn't quite right, something that requires a second look."

Gaige settled into the balls of his feet and steadied his breathing. I moved to his side before he could detect me and slipped out of the realm.

"Better." One word, spoken above the shelf of his ear.

So close.

He startled but leaned away without losing his footing. Shadows curled around his ankles and tethered him to the earth, offering him stability where he'd previously had none. They disappeared as quickly as they'd formed, and he leapt back just out of my reach.

"This is like some bizarre game of tag," Calem whined. "Throw some punches!"

"He doesn't need that." Shadows flung to my limbs, hiding them from view. "He needs control. Finesse. A wild punch solves nothing." A thin tendril snaked through the grass to stretch itself taut behind Gaige. So focused on me, he hadn't bothered to reassess his surroundings.

"And awareness." The words left my mouth right as he backstepped over my solidified thread, and he fell on his rear into the soft loam of the marsh.

"Lovely," Gaige growled as he clambered to his feet. Mud soaked his trousers and dribbled across his boots. "What do I have to do to end this?"

I considered Calem's jest. "Land one blow. Tag me, if you will."

"Fine." Gaige lunged forward with a sudden, impressive display of shadows at his heels. I jumped to the side, narrowly missing his surprise attack, and wheeled around in time to find he hadn't stopped. He'd simply course corrected and was already within arm's reach yet again. I darted backward, allowing my shadows to carry my feet over the rougher terrain that Gaige's tendrils couldn't quite traverse. He barreled through the mess of cattails and broken logs and filth until he had to pause for breath.

"Nice work!" Ozias shouted.

"Stay light on your feet. You're tearing apart everything in your path," Calem added.

"This is ridiculous," Gaige sputtered. "How long do you intend to keep this up?"

"As long as it takes," I said. I launched toward him and cut around his body, crouching low and jabbing at the back of his knees. He keeled and hit the ground with a loud curse. Flailing wide with one arm, he attempted to smack my shoulder and missed. I was already several feet away, waiting for him to regain his composure. With mud splattered across his cheeks, he glared up at me through his disheveled locks. Shadows began to pool beneath his feet.

And then they swallowed him whole. One moment he was before me, bruised and covered in muck, and the next he was behind me. He brought his fist to my side, nearly connecting with my kidney, and I fell to the earth to avoid being struck. I hit the ground and rolled, swiping his feet out from under him. Cicadas took flight in a flurry as his back cracked against the earth.

He screamed, more in frustration than pain, and shadows immediately wreathed his ankles. Within seconds he was on his feet again. I charged after him as Ozias barked techniques, and Gaige managed to control his tendrils just long enough to sidestep my advance. Rather than swing around, I ran headlong into the shadow realm.

And Gaige followed.

Our surroundings trembled with the addition of his snarling, barely contained tendrils. I spun on my heels to face him, blocking his wild punch and sidestepping as he tumbled to the ground. All around us the erratic strands of darkness spired. Stepping into the shadow realm was like pulling a veil over our world. It was still there, we just looked and moved through it differently. But when Gaige's shadows added to mine, everything blurred out of focus. Hesitating, I glanced at the space where Ozias and Calem had been not a second before.

And then Gaige knocked me off my feet and pinned me to the ground. The action dislodged my glasses, and they arced through the air until they toppled onto a jagged stone. The splinter of glass was unmistakable, but Gaige's attention was fully on me. With his legs on either side of my hips, he settled his full weight against my hips. His breath was hot against my skin as he fought to catch his breath, arched over me.

"Got you." He smirked. Okean's bronze key slipped free of his collar, dangling from its chain to ghost the base of my throat, light as a kiss. I could hardly think straight. Gaige's sheer presence, the *heat* it inspired low in my gut, made me both want to wrap him in my arms and disappear into the safety of the shadows. And yet, we were already in the shadow realm, and I had nowhere to run.

So I looked anywhere else but at him. "The realm. Something's not right."

"How so?" He barely glanced at the snarling, black void that had encompassed us, brilliant eyes locked on my face. On my mouth? Surely not.

I forced myself to focus. "Can you see Ozias? Or Calem?"

"No." He frowned and finally looked up from me.

"That's not right." I blew out a breath, painfully aware that his thighs were still pressed against my hips, his weight still bearing me down against the soft earth. I couldn't remember ever being this close to him, in such a compromising position, no less. It had been literal decades since I'd felt this way, and the rising heat was making me increasingly flustered. Each second that passed was a dangerous game that was both thrilling and terrifying. I wanted him close. I wanted him gone. I wanted to stay exactly as we were, and yet never revisit it again.

Unable to take any more conflicting emotions, I attempted to sit up and put some much-needed distance between us. As I pressed my hand into the soft loam of the earth, it gave way beneath my grasp and I toppled back to the marsh. Gaige, too, was thrown off, and his knees slipped out beneath him, bringing his body flush with mine, hip to hip, chest to chest.

For a moment, neither of us moved. I felt his chest expand against mine, the heat of his shocked breath against my neck. A shiver raced over my skin.

Gods, I didn't want to care, but I did. Why did I let my emotions get tangled up with him? A tightness invaded my throat, and I swallowed thickly as I kept myself completely still. I would not react. I would not do something that would only hurt me more in the end. Slowly, Gaige braced himself on either side of my body. I hated the way it felt cold when his weight shifted away, but I refused to let it show.

He didn't pull away entirely, though, and instead studied me with a look I wasn't sure I'd ever be able to unpack. Slowly, he dusted his gloved fingers beneath my eyes, swiping away beads of muddy water.

The twisting pressure in my heart was unbearable, and my world narrowed to that strange look in his eyes.

"Your ears are pink," he said quietly.

Heat traveled to my cheeks, and I looked away to see that the shadows had disappeared. So wrapped up in the weight of him, I hadn't noticed the sudden return of the cicadas, or the startled shouting of Calem and Ozias as they blundered about the marsh calling our names. The stench of salt and grime did nothing to chase away the tantalizing scent of cedar and pears clinging to Gaige's collar. He'd invaded all of my senses, rendered me useless and compromised. And of course, that was the exact moment Calem pushed through the cattails to find us still tangled up together.

He took one look at us and burst out laughing. Hands on his knees, he keeled over as he called to Ozias between sharp, uneven inhales. "I found them."

Before Gaige could move off me, Ozias was there, too. His expression shifted from worry to embarrassment in one second flat, and he gripped the back of his neck as he stared at the evening sky. "We thought we lost you guys."

"Nope. We're fine." Voice airy and full of nonchalance, Gaige was anything but perturbed. He stood easily, brushing the dirt and grime from his shirt as best he could. I envied the way he unabashedly regarded his friends. Meanwhile, I scrambled to my feet with much less grace.

"Good work." I made a beeline for the log and snagged my vest, avoiding eye contact with Ozias or Calem as I viciously fought to regain control of myself. "Let's freshen up and then meet in the tavern for a meal."

Calem bounded toward me and draped a lazy arm across my shoulders. "Wait, I want to hear all about what happened in the realm. How much *training* did you actually accomplish?"

"I feel rather trained," Gaige added, a flicker of humor coloring his response. I'd forgotten how much I'd missed his incessant banter.

"Enough." I didn't trust myself to say more. I didn't know what to say. I could deny—and I would—that anything romantic happened between Gaige and me. But his look, the way his breath instantly fell into sync with mine, the feel of warm leather against my cheeks… I didn't dare unpack it. I brushed Calem's arm off and called to my shadows. They covered me in an instant, and I relished in the cool kiss of the wisps against my burning skin. "Be at the tavern in thirty minutes." I stepped into darkness, knowing full well that they could still see me striding across the marsh, but feeling better under its cover nonetheless.

For the first time in the decades of my shared history with Calem and Ozias, they arrived before me at the tavern and were already seated. I hadn't sensed Gaige when I left my room, but I wasn't sure if that meant anything anymore. He wasn't at the table my brothers had picked, and a cursory glance around the establishment revealed nothing, save that we were in for a loud evening.

Townsfolk clamored into the Wooden Flower, vying for tables and chairs as they shouted drink orders above the growing ruckus. Unlike Ortega Key, the seaside town I'd visited with my brothers when we first searched for beasts with Leena, Moeras didn't have a separate tavern from the inn. The draw to the marshland wasn't large enough to warrant individual structures, and thus all the locals always ended up here.

Including you. I flinched at the errant thought and pushed it to the side. Weaving around bodies, I took the chair beside Ozias. Fortunately, they'd chosen a table somewhat removed from the more boisterous sections of the establishment, and Ozias had propped his chair in such a way that his broad shoulders leaned against the wall. His rich, brown eyes were light, and he watched the happy patrons with a wide smile. But across from him, Calem only regarded me.

The smirk on his face told me what he was going to say, so I interjected before he had the chance to speak.

"Nothing happened between Gaige and me. He lost control of his shadows, struck me, and I knocked him off-balance. Startling him must have been enough to pull us out of the realm."

Calem's answering grin was annoyingly devilish. "I was only going to say that you look weird without glasses."

"Yes, well." My hand instinctively went to push my frames up my nose, but I halted midair. "I'll replace them soon enough."

"I think you look fine." Ozias's smile was much less mocking, but there was a hint of a tease in the way his eyes crinkled at the corners. "Though I do think it's strange you wear them to begin with."

"I've been saying that from the beginning!" Calem threw up his hands in mock exasperation. "We have perfect—no, more than perfect—vision. What happens if you get punched in the face?" He paused for a beat, his lips twisting impossibly further. "Again?"

Struck, but semantics. He didn't need to know everything. "Then I'll obviously be fine, as having them removed in the heat of battle has no detriment on my ability to see."

A barmaid with coppery skin and jet-black hair sidled up to our table. "Sorry about the wait. Can I get you something to drink? Or are you waiting on someone…?" She jerked her head to the side, indicating the empty chair across from me.

"No need to wait, I'm here," Gaige called as he dodged a

particularly drunk woman. Briskly, he pulled out the chair and took his seat. "Sorry about that. Lost track of time."

"So it seems." It physically pained me to be late, and while I couldn't instill that same level of punctuality in my family, I'd learned to plan for such things. Glancing past him, I studied the overflowing flowers hanging from the rafters. A single pot closest to the bar held a cluster of bright-red tubular buds surrounded by dark-green leaves. *Nordus lesta*. A smile tugged at my lips. "We'll each take a glass of Anahel's Craft."

A surprised look came over her expression, but it shifted quickly to one of delight. "Of course! I'll be right back." She left swiftly, her long, glossy hair swishing behind her.

"What on earth did you just order for us?" Calem asked, tracking her progression as she navigated the floor.

"The Anahel family is practiced in the art of making gin. Each year, they distill a small amount specially made with rare botanicals. To add to the allure, they don't advertise the cut." I pointed to the red blooms dangling above the bartender. "Unless you know what you're looking for. That signifies the ingredient used in this year's batch. It's a favorite of mine."

Gaige stared at the *Nordus lesta* with a tantalizing sense of curiosity, and all at once I was transported back to Cruor's library, to the first night I'd spent reading books with him while we searched for a cure to Noc's former curse. Gaige had lazily trailed the whorls of the wooden tabletop while studying me with that same level of interest, and my breath had caught in my chest, just as it was now. His soft, brown hair framed his face and skated along his shoulders, just begging my fingers to touch it. I could still feel the heat of his breath on my neck, and for a moment, I wondered what those parted lips would feel like against my skin.

"Fine by me so long as it goes down smooth," Calem said,

breaking Gaige's unintentional hold over me. I glanced toward my brother and nodded. I didn't trust my voice to not betray my uncharacteristically wild emotions. Neither Gaige nor my brothers seemed to notice my prolonged stare, and Ozias was quick to return to more demanding matters.

"You did well today, Gaige." He leaned forward and clasped his hands together on the table. "The better you get at calling on your shadows, the faster you'll be able to react."

Gaige flashed him a genuine grin. "Thanks."

"But I am curious to know what happened." Calem gave me a sidelong look. "We really couldn't find you."

Calem's comment was the douse of cool water I needed, and those perilous desires vanished. "I couldn't detect you two, either. It seems Gaige's shadows were able to blanket out the world entirely."

"It's been like that recently. In the beginning, it was a bit clearer, but now it's mostly just shadows upon shadows." Gaige frowned at his own words.

An uneasy feeling stirred in my gut. Gaige was exhibiting dangerous abilities that I didn't know how to handle. There wasn't anyone else at the guild whose shadows behaved the way that his did. If we didn't figure out why, I wasn't convinced we'd be able to keep his power from growing beyond all measure—and taking him with it.

Calem and Ozias's gaze were heavy on me as I exhaled quietly. "We'll need to work on that, too."

Gaige met my stare as the barmaid returned. With careful hands, she delicately placed a glass before us one by one. She stared at me expectantly until I brought it to my lips. With a deep inhale, I savored the fragrant aroma of botanicals before finally allowing the clear liquid to grace my tongue. Elegant and dry, it coursed over my taste buds with ease, leaving behind a pleasing mixture of lemon and spice.

“Thank you. It’s wonderful.” I sat the glass down, signifying I approved of the drink, and she beamed. Calem, Ozias, and Gaige did the same.

“Holy shit, that’s good,” Calem said to his glass. Ozias nodded his agreement as he gently cradled it between his hands. Like me, Gaige breathed deeply before sipping, and his eyes lit up brighter than the night stars. *So much curiosity*. His appetite for the world had been voracious once. I wanted nothing more than for it to be that way again.

The barmaid’s tinkling giggle at Calem’s reaction pulled my focus, and she took our food orders before once again disappearing into the crowd.

“So… How did you know about the gin?” Gaige fingered his tumbler. Again, I caught that flicker of interest, of wonder, in his stare. He made me want to share things like this—things about my past—that I’d never wanted to share before. Even though I knew deep down that he didn’t care, that he had no desire to reignite anything with me, I couldn’t help myself.

“I moved here when I was young.” I took a long sip and welcomed the courage that came with the sultry flavor. “And stayed here until I died.”

Calem and Ozias shifted in their seats, neither one of them daring to speak. They knew the story of my past. It’d taken me decades to share it with them, but they knew. Gaige was already privy to more about me than most of the guild, and he’d only just been raised. Still, neither of my brothers interrupted. Sharing details about our past was always a delicate subject, and as a courtesy, we gave each other the space to speak when the occasion arose.

Gaige raised a brow. “Are we here to exact revenge under the guise of monster attacks?”

A small chuckle loosened itself from somewhere deep in my

chest. Gaige's surprised stare riveted to my lips, and heat simmered along the tops of my ears. "No. Rest assured, this was many years ago. Some might recognize me, but those responsible for my death are long gone."

In one way or another. Jude's flower bloomed in my mind, but I banished the image with a single shake of my head. He hadn't killed me. Well, he hadn't *physically* killed me.

"How did you die?" Gaige's voice was soft, but it struck with the force of lightning, and I stiffened in my chair. Ozias and Calem looked as though they wished they could become part of the wall. They'd pressed against it to give us space, and they had tipped their heads toward each other as they passed the time with useless conversation. But I knew they were listening. They'd twitched at Gaige's question, too.

I took another pull from my glass. How much to tell? It's not that my death was anything spectacular to begin with. It's just that there were exactly three people who knew about it—Noc, Calem, and Ozias. If I shared this piece of my history with Gaige, I'd no doubt invest even more of myself in him. He'd already made it abundantly clear that there was no future for us, so what was the point of offering him any part of my past?

"Slowly and painfully," I hedged, ignoring the weight of his stare and instead rubbing my fingers over my breast pocket. It wasn't a lie. My death *had* been slow. It was the reason I still carried the scar on my chest.

He set his drink down and cupped his chin with his hand. "Riveting. You're such an eloquent storyteller. Care to elaborate?"

There was something in his words that gave me pause. He knew that the dead didn't unbury their past. He was prodding, certainly, but even the teasing air to his tone felt hollow, as if he were masking another emotion that he didn't want me to decipher. I didn't understand his angle. What did he stand to gain by having this conversation? Even worse, why was I falling prey to his tactics?

Before I could fashion a response, the bard appeared in the center of the room. Strumming a polished lute decorated with vines and roses, he twirled in place and began to sing. His baritone voice—detailing a parable about the true nature of monsters—rang out loud and clear above the now subdued conversations of the tavern.

Being here in the Wooden Flower, sitting across from a man I appreciated—fine, desired—sent me reeling back into the past. So when I looked around again, I didn't see Gaige but Jude in all his roguish beauty. His eyes were the color of good whiskey, his deep-bronze skin tanned from his work in the sun. The nicks on his fingers—a constant, given he was the town's herbologist and responsible for securing the rare flowers that went into making Anahel's Craft—told a story of passion and love. I'd admired every single imperfection. But most of all, I'd yearned for his lopsided smile and sharp tongue.

Until one night his penchant for twisting words led him to cheat the wrong traveler in a game of cards. I'd been sitting with him in this very tavern, listening to this very tune, when Jude swept his winnings from the table with a mocking grin. And I'd been there as we walked home, drunk from gin and the high of winning a large sum guaranteed to buy us a cottage of our own, when the traveler and his men jumped us.

"Kost," Ozias said gently, nudging my arm. The memory fled, and I blinked an errant tear free of my lashes. I caught it with the back of my hand before rubbing both eyes, feigning exhaustion. I doubted it fooled anyone, but they kept their words to themselves. Ozias's brows inched together, and his lips were downturned. Across from him, Calem stared at the table, not an ounce of humor to be found.

"Sorry, I shouldn't have asked," Gaige mumbled, averting his gaze.

I brushed it off with a wave. "It's fine."

The bard's song came to an end, and he gave the crowd a final flourish before the cheers erupted around us. Maneuvering between bodies, the barmaid returned with our platters trailing up her arms.

"It's a bit rowdy tonight," she said, voice loud enough to carry over the patrons. "Fewer folks are spending time outside lately."

Unease prickled my senses, and I accepted my braised venison and leeks. "We heard about the attacks."

A grim expression filled her dark eyes. "My father was attacked not two nights ago. He managed to get away, but..." She sighed as she dished out the rest of our meals and then wrapped her arms around her stomach. "Our healer left to acquire more medicine. I just hope it doesn't happen again."

"Where did they occur?" Gaige asked.

"Past the stables where we farm." She shivered but shook it off with a smile. "You have nothing to fear, though. We're patrolling the area, and attacks are rare. Something must've spooked the monster." A local shouted her name, and she pivoted, tilting her ear to the sound. "Enjoy the food." Rolling her eyes, she spun around to attend to a group of men a few tables away.

Gaige frowned at his soup. "We should check it out and see if we can determine what kind of beast it was."

"In the morning." I picked up my knife and sliced into the meat. "We'll rotate shifts tonight to keep watch over the town to be safe."

"How sure are we that they'll be back?" Calem asked around a mouthful of bread.

"We can't even be certain they were the same beasts that attacked the travelers who made it to Midnight Jester." Gaige listlessly stirred his spoon. Dumplings, scallops, and an assortment of veggies formed a whirlpool in the light broth.

"Well, it didn't sound like there was an incident last night." Ozias skewered roasted green beans with his fork and pointed them at Gaige. "Everything will be okay. We'll figure it out."

"We just need to find out why they're attacking in the first place," he said quietly.

The unspoken fear, the truth, hung heavy in the air between us, transforming the pleasant atmosphere into something stiff and uncomfortable. We all suspected Gaige was responsible, even if he wasn't fully willing to admit it to himself. Perhaps facing reality on his own would help usher him toward control.

Or it would break him and cause even more chaos. My food was becoming more unappealing by the minute, and it had nothing to do with the excellent flavor. We spent the rest of the meal in silence, each of us mulling over our thoughts between forced bites and long sips of alcohol. Calem excused himself first, not even bothering with the troupe of women who'd stationed themselves nearby. They'd been throwing not-so-subtle glances his direction all evening, but he made for his room with a mumbled good night. Ozias did the same, placing a gentle hand on my shoulder before giving it a squeeze.

Gaige watched them go with tired eyes. "Am I really so difficult to be around?"

"No, quite the contrary." I pushed my plate to the side, unable to stomach another bite and instead opting for more gin. "They care for you, Gaige. They're worried, and they don't know what to do."

"I wasn't talking about them."

My spine tensed. "What are you insinuating?"

A defeated sigh escaped his parted lips, and he drained the last of Anahel's Craft. "I don't understand you."

"Then the feeling is mutual." I didn't dare move. Didn't dare pull my gaze off him. I studied every inch of his expression for a sign, for some indicator as to where this was going. But the only thing I saw was bone-deep exhaustion.

"You were upset earlier, at least when we started training." He dragged his gaze upward, meeting my stare. "It was...different. I've never seen you like that."

It was more hurt than anger but explaining that to him would only open the door for more questions. Questions I didn't want to answer. "I apologize for that. I let my emotions get the better of me."

"I just want to know why." There was a question hidden in the depths of his steely, guarded look, but I wasn't entirely sure what it was. Being with him was like walking along the edge of a blade. I could tell him the truth, share more of my past with him and see where we landed. Or I could shut him down and protect this feeble heart in my chest. No matter which way I swayed, I was bound to get cut.

"Being back here is difficult for me. There's a lot of history wrapped up in Moeras, and I let it affect me more than it should have." I had one good swallow left in my glass, and I contemplated finishing the drink now or waiting to see if this conversation turned more hazardous. Perhaps it would require another round altogether.

He leaned closer across the table, his gloved fingers gently nudging the iron candle fixture in the center. "Then you understand why I can't go back to Hireath."

I chewed on this for a moment, letting his words settle deep into my mind. Hireath no doubt was an immense source of pain for him. A place tied to a power he no longer possessed. Yet if my time in Moeras was teaching me anything, it was that bandaging a wound that deep before it was lanced only allowed for it to fester. Maybe the best thing for Gaige was to face the pain, to find some salve associated with his past so he could finally, finally come to grips with his future. It would be difficult. Immeasurably so. I was only facing my past after decades of time, but Gaige didn't have that same luxury. He needed to act now.

I finished my drink and set the glass down gently. "Even so, you should go back."

He revolted so suddenly, so harshly, that it was as if he'd been struck by an invisible beast. Gone was the question in his probing stare, and in its place was nothing more than a look of pure indignation.

Hands gripping to fists, his lips peeled back in a grimace. "Of course you want me to leave, too."

I frowned. "What? I don't think you're—"

"Enough." He stood quickly, the chair scooching out behind him. "I'm tired, Kost. Leave me out of your rotations tonight. Or were you even planning on asking me to help to begin with?"

My retort died in my throat. I *hadn't* intended to ask him, and he read it plain as day on my face. Not because I didn't think he was capable, but because I could see what his powers were doing to him. He was a ragged, sleep-deprived mess. Above all else, he needed to rest. If he continued to push himself without giving his body and mind the recovery it needed, he'd have an even more difficult time harnessing the shadows. But before I could explain any of that to him, he left, forcefully parting his way through the crowd to retreat to his room. I stood without thinking and took one step to follow, only to stop at the edge of the table. I'd grown familiar with the sight of his back, with his agitated gait. And we'd both excelled at walking away.

Perhaps it was time to let it simply *be*. As I sank back to my chair and stared at my empty tumbler, I felt myself fall off the edge of the blade. It was an endless, tumbling descent that left me raw and weak. I'd suffered so many wounds in my life, both in this one and the one before I died, and none had left me more battered and bruised than this. I'd lost, and I was letting us be lost at the same time. Somehow, I knew in my core that no one could ever live up to Gaige, and letting him slip through my fingers now was better than letting it happen in the future.

Still, it cut like I knew it would. Deep.

ELEVEN

GAIGE

The slender, oblong parcel resting on my nightstand taunted me. Wrapped in sepia parchment and tied with simple twine, it was unassuming enough. The pair of spectacles inside, the ones I'd rushed to find in the small window of opportunity before dinner, were meant to be an olive branch. Now I only wanted to use them as kindling for the unlit fire in my room. But the weather was tepid and there was no need for flames, so I chucked the package at the wall instead. The soft thud as it hit the rug-strewn floor was anything but satisfying.

I was just so *tired*. Physically, emotionally, mentally. Maybe if I hadn't deprived myself of sleep for the past day, I would've given Kost the chance to explain—or better yet, to backtrack. But hearing him confirm my exact fear, knowing that he wanted me gone, too… I was tired of being a burden. All I did was hurt or scare the people I cared about, and it seemed like the only thing they wanted was to rid themselves of me.

Wrapped up in swirling doubt, I didn't bother to remove my clothes before falling into bed. I didn't bother to try to stave off sleep, either. I didn't have any fight left. All I'd needed was some reassurance. Some belief that I was making progress, and some faith that these attacks weren't because of me. Not a single one of them had offered to nip that fear in the bud. Instead, they'd let it sit over us while we ate and then ran away.

And then Kost pushed *me* away.

I couldn't do it anymore. So I slept. And I didn't flinch when the world turned into a gray waterfall of mist and shadow, and I once again found my feet on the ebony path of smooth river stones. Without hesitating, I strode forward, determined to face this nightmare head-on. I'd been paralyzed by fear the first time. The second time, I'd forced myself to wake before the stranger could trap me in their clutches. But this time, I'd confront them. I'd make the nightmare end once and for all. I couldn't control the shadows in my reality, but I would control this.

As determination flooded my body, ink-black tendrils swarmed to me in earnest. They answered my bidding and encircled my fingers before racing ahead of me to cut through the gray expanse like rivers of black. The surrounding, misty vapor had chilled me before, but now all I felt was heat. Every step I took fueled the growing anger in me. No one understood what it was like. No one even *tried*. Fire pumped through my veins, and I moved forward with a purpose I hadn't felt in ages.

Trees blurred behind the gray veil of mist, until it suddenly cleared when I reached the black, sandy beach. I strode straight to the ocean's edge. Like before, a pregnant moon sat low over the horizon, showering the ink-black water in a luminous glow. Sawtooth rocks formed pillars in the sea, and hovering above the choppy waters was a snarling, swirling orb of shadows.

"Come to me." The orb went still in response, just like before, but this time I wasn't filled with dread. I was brimming with anticipation. And it knew. Or rather, the person lingering inside that cocoon knew. Because instead of rushing over me in a frenzy, the floating sphere moved toward me with controlled slowness. When it reached an arm's length away, the shadows once again revealed the stranger I'd met during my first nightmare. A man with faded-blue eyes rimmed in crimson. A man who looked like me.

His hair—*my* hair—was unkempt and greasy. Dirt and grime were smeared across his forehead and cheekbones, and the beard clinging to his jaw threatened to tangle with his locks. We shared the same build, the same wild shadows. They continued to rush over him like hungry beasts and kept him suspended in the air. Occasionally, a tendril would go as far as to nick his skin, but he didn't react. He seemed impervious to it all, and his wounds healed in seconds. Each time his blood was spilt, the shadows quivered and spired higher still, giving the impression he was standing among daggers.

A cold heaviness settled over me. This man *was* me. He was everything I was bound to become.

"You've returned." His voice seemed hoarse from misuse, and he rubbed one of his marred hands along the exposed, pale skin of his neck.

"So… Are you meant to be me?" Some kind of dream creation of my subconscious mind? His clothes were more filth than fabric, but despite his obvious disheveled experience, he didn't exude an ounce of discomfort. If anything, he appeared strangely…confident.

"I am the Lost." His shadows inched him closer. "And the Lost are me."

Well, I supposed that was true. All I felt was lost.

"Riddles in my dreams. Lovely." I let out an exasperated sigh.

The man shook his head once. "Not a riddle. Not a dream."

"Right, well, can you tell me what I'm supposed to get out of this?" I gestured wide to include the raging ocean and mist-filled expanse at my back. His eyes tracked my movements, and all at once I'd realized he'd yet to blink. The chill I'd been missing earlier attacked my bones, and I shivered.

"Get?" Again, the tendrils around his body pushed him forward. "What do you want?"

"I want to control the shadows, like you." I nodded to the spires forming around him, and he chuckled darkly.

"No, you don't."

"Yes, I do!" My hands formed neat fists by my side.

In a rush he was on me, only a breath away, his shadows licking my skin. "No, you don't." Without pulling back, he whispered into my ear, "You want them gone." And then he gripped my hand so tightly that pain shot through my tendons. With a deliberate tap, he pointed to the Charmer's emblem hidden beneath my glove.

"No." My denial was equally quiet and full of none of the confidence he wielded.

He sighed, a raspy, horrific sound like a rake being dragged over stone. "I know. I was like you once." He released my hand. "And soon, you will be me."

"What is that supposed to mean?"

One of his tendrils snaked out of his aura and reared back. It struck hard and fast with the precision of a viper, leaving a slit across my cheek. The tang of copper filled my nostrils.

"I'll let you in on a secret. You cannot control what does not want to be tamed. You should know that better than anyone else, Charmer," he said. Slowly, he dragged one of his fingers along the cut his shadow made, and he brought my blood to his lips. His eyes slipped closed.

Fingers trembling, I wiped away the rest as my skin began to heal. "What's going to happen to me?"

When he opened his eyes again, the whites had gone bloodshot, and an eerie smile claimed his lips. "Are you ready to find out?"

Deep, rumbling bells rang somewhere in the distance, and suddenly everything was too loud—the crashing waves like piercing cymbals, the building crescendo of roaring insects, even the slither of shadows now more like the sharp, hair-raising scrape of metal on metal. Again the bells tolled, and with that unsettling intonation the ground shook. Fractures split the beach and a void opened beneath us as black sand poured into the abyss. Only his shadows kept me from suffering the same fate, but I wasn't sure what was worse—him or the fall.

With the flick of his wrist, one shadow formed a deadly spear, and he poised it above my throat. I swallowed, feeling the bite of it against my skin and the subsequent heat of my blood. But before he could curl his fingers and command his weapon, the bell rang again, and this time his shadows shuddered. An electrical current surged through the tendrils, and they released me into the void. A scream ripped through my lungs as I tumbled downward. Wind whistled by my ears and the world swam out of focus, until the bells sounded again and I shot out of bed.

Chest heaving, I gripped my nightstand for purchase and allowed myself a minute to acclimate. I was still in the Lavender room. The same velvet petals hung over my head, and Kost's damn glasses were still angrily intact in their package on the floor. As my heartbeat returned to an acceptable pace, I began to pick up on the sounds of the surrounding inn, and once again my pulse skyrocketed.

Horror-filled screams rose above the constant toll of a bell. Something was wrong. I burst into the hall to collide with a frantic throng of people all running in opposite directions. I spied the barmaid at the end of the hall, trying to convince patrons to remain in their rooms and board up their doors and windows. I made it to her in the span of a breath.

"What's going on?"

Her body trembled in response, but she managed one shaky word. "Monsters."

The bell tolled again and then was abruptly cut off, followed by a resounding boom. I felt the reverberation in the ground as it traveled up my feet and through to my hands. Without seeing it, I knew. Something had brought the tower down.

"Keep everyone indoors," I said to the barmaid before turning on my heels and speeding down the hall. I couldn't sense Kost, Calem, or Ozias's shadows, which meant they were already outside dealing with the possible threat. I needed to get to them. Fast. My training with Kost surfaced in my mind, and I focused on my shadows as I ran. Not for protection, not for defense, but for movement. Something simple, something that wouldn't accidentally hurt anyone. With the curl of my fingers, I beckoned them to me—and to my surprise, they came. They snaked around buildings and wrapped themselves around my ankles. I didn't have time to marvel at the sensation, at the swell of relief in my chest. I just kept running. Aided by their power, I was at the edge of the town in seconds, and I faltered at the sight.

The splintered structure of the tower lay in a heap, the bell cracked and sinking into the soft mud of the earth. Ozias stood at the mouth of a bridge practically pushing locals into a nearby cottage. Down on the marsh, Calem and Kost stood back-to-back, each one holding glittering, ink-black weapons as they stared down a gaggle of Slimacks.

Slimacks? They were supposed to be solitary creatures, and yet here they were, acting as a pack. Furthermore, they weren't undead monsters. They were true, living *beasts*. Their wormlike, fleshy bodies were pink and still coated in a thick mucous membrane. If they'd been touched by death, Kitska beasts like Boo and Rook, I would've known. But these beasts... They seemed perfectly normal—attack aside. Each one moved across the earth on four, squatty legs as they kept their bloated bellies elevated above the marsh. It was absurd to see them above the earth and rampaging like this. They preferred to live underground and would press their legs flush with their bodies as they chowed through even the densest dirt to burrow deeper and deeper.

And they hated sound. My gaze cut to the toppled bell. How? They were strong beasts, but they didn't have the critical thinking skills to dissemble a tower. At the cacophonous intonations, they should have just fled or burrowed beneath the earth to escape the reverberations. Yet the structure had been cleaved in half with the precision of a massive blade—something else Slimacks couldn't do. Among the wreckage, an ink-black tendril darted between fractured pieces of wood before slithering through the marsh. When it reached the forest edge, a pleased, collective sigh seemed to rise from the darkness itself.

And then a massive Slimack came barreling from the depths of the forest. Unlike the others, this one's hide had been leeched of color and it was easily double in size. With uncanny speed, it unhinged its jaw and tore through the earth to dive beneath the surface. I watched in horror as a mound of dirt followed in its wake, and it circled behind the normally docile beasts to erupt from the dirt. The guttural cry raised every hair on the back of my neck. The Slimacks shuttered in response and resumed their attack, driven by the undead Kitska beast at their backs.

My stomach roiled violently as a chill swept down my spine. Shadows. Even now, I could see them ringing the Kitska Slimack. I'd trained with Kost and then dreamt of the Lost. And I knew in my bones that my companions would suspect my powers were responsible. Even now, presented with what I knew about Slimacks' natures…it was hard not to blame myself.

A pained shout from Calem spurred me into motion, and I left my fear and doubt on the bridge. I joined Kost and Calem at the same time Ozias did, and the four of us put our backs together as we faced the cavernous, open maws of the Slimacks. Instead of teeth, hundreds of writhing, barbed tentacles slipped over each other, prepared to trap and consume anything within reach.

"What do we do?" Shadow blades hung in the space around Calem, quivering with anticipation as they waited for him to execute an order. His mercury eyes were full of malice, and he crouched low to the ground as scales formed and receded across the skin of his arms.

"Sound will drive them back." I cut a glance again at the broken bell and suppressed a shiver. Had I caused this? Still, the Slimacks shouldn't have attacked. They lived harmoniously with people, their excrement fertilizing the soil and creating a nutrient-rich base for plants. They ate dirt, for gods' sakes. Again, my gaze found the monster lingering in the back. Waiting for the opportunity to strike. Even it shouldn't be acting this way. But those dark tendrils had propelled it forward as if it were doing the bidding of something—someone—else. "Ozias, get the bell." Kost held his glittering rapier steady.

"On it." He vaulted toward the tower with the help of his shadows, reaching the structure in no time. But his sudden departure alerted two of the Slimacks, and they peeled off after him.

Kost glared at the Slimacks prepared to intercept Ozias, but we'd have to trust that he could handle them. For the moment they'd left, the ground beneath our feet had begun to move. Earth and muck and cattails spilled over one another until two more Slimacks appeared to replace the ones after Ozias. There was no telling how many more lingered beneath the surface.

"Calem, shift. Now," Kost commanded.

Calem didn't need any further prompting, and in the span of a breath, he shed his human form in favor of the monster in his veins. Stone-like scales pushed through his skin, and he fell on all fours, massive claws cutting through the loam like knives through butter. A ferocious growl rumbled from deep in his chest as he sauntered forward. Glistening fangs caught in the moonlight, and he stood tall before the threat, a monstrous hound with mercury eyes. Tipping his head to the night sky, he let out a harrowing howl that sent goose-flesh rippling down my arms.

Frantic, wet hisses engulfed us as the Slimacks quivered, and they rammed their bodies into one another as they failed to shake the sound. But rather than flee, they lunged. Their mucous bodies slipped over Calem's tough hide, and they wrapped around him like cobras until he kneeled to the ground. He was left prone to a single, larger Slimack that had abandoned its legs and was slithering toward him, mouth open, at an unearthly speed.

"Kost! It'll swallow him whole!" The monster's mouth grew impossibly wider as it moved, opening large enough to inhale Calem and the creature's fellow Slimacks. But Kost was faster, darting forward with the help of his shadows. As he moved, his rapier grew longer, deadlier, and with one clean sweep, he arced it high and brought it down behind the base of the creature's head. Black blood splattered our forms and flooded into the glades. Kost turned to rush to Calem's side, only to have his feet swept out from under him. The Slimack he'd thought he'd murdered had spun around, revealing that its rear—complete with the same gaping maw as its head—was just as deadly.

"They regenerate! Severing the head won't do anything." I thrusted my hands outward and begged the shadows to come to my aid. *Please.* I closed my eyes and thought of the cool, gray expanse from my dreams. *Please.* The feel of ebony sand and the sight of jagged, sawtooth rocks. *Please.* The swirling, angry orb of shadows that had calmed and crossed the waters at my beckoning. *Please.* I imagined a faded-blue stare rimmed in crimson.

Power surged through to my fingertips as I peeled open my eyes. Shadows, virulent and angry, spiraled around me and I forced them to listen. To obey. They writhed as if they'd been electrocuted, but still rushed forward to pry the Slimacks off Calem's back and thrust away the one looming over Kost. My vision quaked as an invisible weight settled on my shoulders. I tried to push against it, to stand tall, but my knees buckled as my breath turned ragged and sweat dampened my brow.

You cannot control what does not want to be tamed.

The shadows deserted me in a rush, leaving me raw and vulnerable. At least Calem and Kost were safe. They'd righted themselves and come to my side, just as the Slimacks regrouped and once again encircled us like the prey we shouldn't have been. The first one lunged and Calem responded, leaping into the air to crash into it with enough force to knock the creature unconscious. But the others didn't falter, and they converged in a rush. Calem tore into their slimy bodies, leaving deep gashes in his wake as he tried to claw his way out of their deadly embrace. Yet those barbed tentacles were impossible to track, and they began to work their way beneath his scales and lift them off one by one. Howling, he tore into the meat of their stomachs, and blood slicker than oil, fragrant with the stench of rotten fish, surrounded us.

Three more charged toward Kost and me. Rapier held high, he waited for them to strike. They reared back with lethal purpose, but as they cracked open their gaping maws and lunged, a rock wall with molten-lava veins erupted before us. They crashed into the jagged surface, and I couldn't separate their pained hisses from the sizzle of burning flesh. I tracked the vein of lava through the marsh to see Ozias protected behind a barrier of his own with an enraged Jax by his side. The cracked bell hung from his powerful jaws, waiting to be struck. But it was as if the creatures knew, because more and more Slimacks were rupturing through the soil and attacking Ozias.

I touched my gloved finger to my key. "Help them."

The groaning hinges of the beast realm door crested over the cries of the Slimacks, and they writhed at the uncomfortable sound. It didn't compare to Okean's roar, though, and he landed in our world a snarling, howling ball of rage. He didn't even wait for my command. Water surged from his jaws as he targeted the Slimacks attacking Ozias and Jax. The powerful torrent careened them into the woods, and he jerked left and right to target each new monster breaching the earth's surface.

A wayward Slimack sped through the air and slammed into the rock wall protecting Kost and me. Rubble shattered around it from the impact, and Calem bounded toward us. Black blood stained his fangs, and he was coated in slime. A few scales had gone missing, revealing soft hide beneath and wounds of his own.

And then an eerie sound, like a hard swallow magnified for all to hear, turned my blood to ice. Time slowed as I dared to look at the Slimacks. They'd all halted in their attack to eat. They were scooping up particles of Jax's wall and ingesting them, lava and all.

Wide eyed and frozen, Kost stared at the writhing ground before us. "Will that kill them?"

I barely found my voice. "No. They can stomach *anything*. And they take on the properties of what they consume until they eat again."

Before our eyes, their once pallid, pink skin shifted black and hardened like coals. Faint lines of red tracked the surface and pulsed in time with their heartbeats. Calem had managed to take down a few by skewering their inner organs directly. Now...

Standing, I ran toward Ozias, Okean, and Jax with Calem and Kost on my heals. "Sound the bell!"

All around us, the beasts lunged. We were tackled to the ground, the Slimacks' rough hides now tearing into our skin. I lost sight of everything beneath the weight of thrashing monsters. A torrent of water smacked into the Slimack directly atop me, but another simply replaced it. Calem was howling, Ozias was screaming—there were so many sounds and none of them good. Kost yelled something over the cascading roll of hisses, but I couldn't quite grasp it.

Until finally, the bone-deep reverberation of the bell. The toll rolled over us with the force of a tidal wave. The monsters retracted in on themselves, forming tight balls and hissing loudly as they tried to block out the sound. I craned my neck in time to see Ozias had fashioned a hammer out of the shadows. His muscles bulged and contracted as he struck the bell with enough force to widen the crack. The toll cascaded over us, and some of the smaller Slimacks finally retreated. Only the larger ones, hardened by Jax's rock wall, remained. And the monstrous Kitska Slimack lingering on the fringe of it all. For a moment, I was free. I scooted backward through the muck, sliding away from the now-quivering Slimack that had previously pinned me.

Ozias slammed the bell again, this time fully cracking the metal and breaking it in two. A few creatures peeled away, but with the bell now shattered, I wasn't sure there was anything strong enough to derail the remaining Slimacks. Especially not the undead one. It slammed into me and my breath left my lungs in a rush. I tried in vain to keep its yawning maw away from my head. Barbed tentacles slashed against my skin, and I tasted my own blood.

You caused this. I sank further into the earth beneath the weight of the monster I'd summoned. Okean had either given up on his water assault or needed to recharge, because he'd thrown himself at the Slimack and was violently clawing to try to pry the creature off me. But the Slimack's lethal rear end reacted, and before I could warn Okean, tentacles had sunk into his hind quarters and were dragging him back.

"No!" I flailed against the monster. I couldn't lose Okean. I *wouldn't*. Tears stung my eyes as I tried in vain to summon my shadows. Faint wisps, weak and intangible, slipped through my fingers. Why did they fail me when I needed them most? Why couldn't I protect the ones I loved? A wordless, defeated screech burned my throat raw as I watched Okean slide dangerously closer to the monster's vast maw. I couldn't save anyone. And I'd never be able to.

I locked eyes with Okean, prepared to hold his gaze until the very end, when a frigid cold settled over the glades, followed by a musty, mothball odor. Everything stilled, save the twisting tentacles of the Slimacks that seemed to have minds of their own. The only sounds that remained were their eerie, slippery caress, the rustling of cattails in the breeze, and the definitive padding of hurried footfalls.

Relief hit hard and fast, and I stopped fighting against the monster. "Only the Slimacks!"

Rook's answering call, the strange amalgamation of a hoot and a bark, was all the assurance I needed. He was by my side soon enough, and he stared down the pack of Slimacks with burning, violet eyes. They shriveled under the weight of my Foxel's power, succumbing to fear and rendering themselves immobile—save their tentacles. One of which snagged along my trousers and left a gash in my thigh.

And then the monster vomited. Fluorescent green poison splattered over my open wound and seeped deep into the exposed tissue. All at once, pain fired through me with the force of a thousand blades, cutting my insides with every damn heartbeat. I screamed so loudly that the Slimack on top of me actually flinched, despite being gripped by terror. My bones cooked from the heat burning its way through me, and I writhed in place on the ground. Frantic shouts barely pierced the veil of my agony—Kost, Ozias. The worried caterwauls of Jax, Okean, and Rook. A gut-wrenching howl from Calem. Until finally, sweet relief came in the form of darkness, and I lost consciousness.

TWELVE

KOST

Time slowed as I watched Gaige's head slump against the marshy loam. Muck and filth splattered the sides of his face, but he didn't move to wipe away the grime. His eyes had rolled to the back of his head, and his body had gone dangerously limp. Everyone had sprung into motion—Ozias and Calem chasing off or eliminating the last of the Slimacks. Okean and Rook sliding across the slippery terrain as they raced toward Gaige. Jax following close behind, erecting a precautionary rock wall to protect them. I hesitated only for a moment. I still couldn't wrap my mind around what had happened. One moment Rook had immobilized the Slimacks, and the next Gaige had been writhing in pain with bile on his leg.

And now, this. Panic exploded in me, and I tore through the marsh to kneel beside him. "Gaige."

No response.

"Gaige." I shook him gently. Then, roughly. My fingers turned bone-white against his shoulders. "Wake up."

When he didn't respond, I released him and immediately touched the bronze key around my neck. The beast realm door groaned open, and Felicks rushed outward.

"Heal him. Quickly." I pointed at Gaige's torn trousers. There, a gash marred the skin of his inner thigh—and it was already festering. The green bile had quickly sunk into the meat of his leg, leaving behind a grotesque shimmer that turned my stomach. His skin wasn't stitching itself back together.

Felicks poised himself above the wound and inhaled deeply. Any second now and he'd lick the length of the gash, delivering a saliva capable of healing injuries. But instead, his hackles stood on end, and he peeled back his lips to hiss at Gaige's leg. Gingerly, he backstepped from the wound until he was safely at my side.

"What's wrong?" My hands went still as I eyed the laceration.

Felicks's orb clouded in response. The wait for his vision to solidify felt like eons, each second scraping by and pushing my adrenaline to new heights. All at once I was reminded of the time Gaige had died. It hadn't been so different from this. I'd seen the vision from Felicks and bolted to Gaige's side, but I'd arrived too late. My beast couldn't do anything then, either. Spots danced across my vision as my breathing came quick. He was going to die. Again. But this time, I wouldn't be able to raise him. This time, I *had* been here, and I'd still failed him. I'd failed him in so many ways. I hadn't helped him with his shadows. I hadn't made him feel welcome in my home. I didn't get the chance to tell him...

My beast's vision forced its way into my mind. Within the next two minutes, Effie would be here, and we'd be readying our Zeelahs to return to Cruor. Gaige was still incapacitated, but not dead.

Relief sang through me, and I sagged into the earth, only to launch to my feet a breath later. "Calem!"

Calem's ears flicked to attention at my call, and he charged toward us. Ozias ran behind him, casting one last look at our surroundings to ensure we'd taken care of the last of the Slimacks.

As Calem skidded to a halt before me, he shifted back into his human form. Blood and muck glistened against his naked skin. "What happened?"

"Summon Effie. Now."

Unlike his clothes, his key still dangled from the cord about his neck. Nothing bestial could destroy it, thanks to the magic of the tree from whence it was plucked. Touching his key, he opened the beast realm door and allowed Effie to soar into our world. With a trilling, happy birdcall, she circled us twice before settling on his shoulder. Her inquisitive, pale-pink eyes traveled over the scene stretched out before her. Then, her head riveted to Gaige.

"The wound." I indicated to his leg. "Felicks showed me a vision of her pouring her magic over it. I think…I think it will stave off the infection long enough for us to get him to Cruor."

Calem's face was grim, but he nodded once. "You heard him, Effie."

She needed no additional prompting. With a quick beat of her powerful wings, she took to the air and hovered above Gaige. Glimmering, magical dust fell from her wings like the first snowflakes of winter. They lazily drifted to his leg and covered the wound in a thin blanket of gossamer particles. When the first layers began to dissolve, Effie returned to Calem and knocked her beak against his chin.

"Good girl," he mumbled, scratching the soft spot of her chest.

Ozias had reached us just as Effie had begun to use her magic, and he'd remained tight-lipped until now. "Is he going to be okay?"

"I don't know. But we need to leave. Quickly." Thankfully, neither of them argued. They both sent their beasts home to the safety of the realm and took off. Ozias headed for the stables to gather our Zeelahs while Calem slipped into the shadows and raced back to the Wooden Flower to retrieve our things. And I waited. Heart pounding. Gaze locked on Gaige's impossibly still body. Grateful that at least his condition wasn't worsening—for now.

I'd lost count of how many times I'd fantasized about feeling the weight of Gaige against my chest—but not like this. Limp and unconscious, he bobbed against my sternum in time with my Zeelah's sprinting gait. His ashen face and ragged breathing, occasionally punctuated by a mumble from his fevered dreams, wrecked me entirely. He'd started to deteriorate, and I feared Effie's magic was fading faster than we had time to heal him. We were only minutes from home, but days away from the Slimack attack, and Gaige was dangerously weak in my arms. I'd held him dead before. I wasn't ready to do it again.

A murder of crows cawed angrily as we disturbed their slumber. They took flight in a hurry and chased us down the path. A soft bark from Felicks pulled my focus. I'd never sent him back to the realm, instead allowing him to ride atop Rook's back as we barreled toward Cruor. Every two minutes he shared another vision with me. And every two minutes I allowed myself one quick breath of relief at the sight of Gaige still alive in my arms. But the moment the vision faded, my anxiety spiraled, and I found myself counting down the seconds until Felicks would show me the future again. I could feel my connection to him weakening, though. I'd never kept Felicks out of the realm this long before, and there was a strained tension like a pinched nerve that was growing sharper and sharper with every passing breath. Soon, I would have to send him back to recuperate. Soon, I wouldn't know what the future would hold for Gaige.

"Kost!" Ozias shouted. I glanced over my shoulder at him and Calem. With the jerk of his chin, Ozias nodded toward the treetops where our sentries typically patrolled. Emelia and Iov were racing through the branches overhead, worried gazes locked on Gaige.

"Kaori? Raven?" I asked, gripping Gaige tighter.

Emelia careened from one branch to the next, never missing a beat. "Already in the hospital wing."

"Alert them of our arrival." I dug my heels into my Zeelah, and she whinnied in response. Sweat had long since formed and dried against her neck and chest. We'd only paused once in our journey, and it'd been brief. Just long enough for Calem to shadow walk to Hireath and find Kaori. We needed their help. Our resident healer was knowledgeable, but beast wounds required an entirely different skill set.

"On it," Iov shouted back. He and his sister cut through the trees faster than we could round the bend, and they were gone from our view within seconds. On my right, Rook kept close to my mount and vaulted over thorn-laden vines with practiced, sure footing. To my left, Okean. His hide was full of shallow cuts from errant barbs from the forest, but he never yowled. Their muscles must have ached, but they didn't falter. We only slowed when we came to the winnow point just outside of Cruor's territory.

Shadows gathered beneath our feet and surged around us like roaring rivers, thrusting us forward without us having to move at all. As quickly as they'd appeared, the tendrils dispersed in a burst. The void deposited us outside the mangled iron fencing surrounding Cruor, and we sped through the open gates riddled with moss and vines. Ozias and Calem dismounted first and rushed to my side. Gently, I eased Gaige down to their waiting arms.

We left our mounts outside and threw open the double doors into the foyer. The assassins lingering there were stricken with concern. We moved past them to take the stairs up to the second story, Rook, Okean, and Felicks on our heels. I barely remember crossing the loft and pushing open the doors into the medical wing. Bleach and lemon stung my nose as polished silver instruments winked at us from open wooden shelves. A row of unoccupied cots stretched across the floor, but the room was far from empty. Three women stood stock-still by the nearest cot, their eyes locked on Gaige.

Gripping the metal railings, I nodded to the stark white sheets. "Here."

Ozias and Calem gently laid down Gaige before backing away to make room for our healer, Uma. Dressed in a long-sleeved gown with gloves secured over her hands, she fixed a cloth mask over her mouth and nose. She had decades' worth of knowledge when it came to herbal remedies and procedures, but that didn't quell the roiling fear in my gut. Especially when her soft periwinkle-blue gaze snapped to mine with fervor. Creases lined the space between her brows, along her forehead. Creases of doubt.

Fortunately, she wasn't alone.

"You idiot," Raven bit out, but there wasn't a trace of anger in her words. She moved to the foot of the bed and placed her palms flat on either side of Gaige's feet. Her hair, a brilliant shade of crushed copper, fell in front of her saffron-colored eyes. Stunning ink whorls covered her warm, tawny skin, and she dug her sharp nails into the sheets.

Wordlessly, Ozias came to her side and draped an arm around her shoulders. She trembled beneath his touch, but didn't retreat like she used to.

The third woman, Kaori, moved to Gaige's head. "What happened?" With gentle, delicate fingers, she wiped sweat from his brow. Ever the picture of quiet sophistication and strength, Kaori's dark, oval eyes were inquisitive and sharp, even when full of concern for her longtime friend. Glossy, ebony hair spilled over her pale skin, and she brushed it off her shoulder.

"It was a Slimack," I said, my knuckles turning bone-white as I gripped the cot harder. Beside me, Felicks rubbed against my leg—a small sign of comfort. I recounted the events as best I could, occasionally allowing Calem or Ozias to interrupt and clarify details I may have missed.

"Felicks wouldn't attempt to heal it," I said in a whisper, dropping my eyes to the beast winding between my ankles.

"It would've killed him," Raven said, voice dangerously low and full of an emotion I didn't want to name. "Slimack bile is capable of disintegrating anything. They vomit on things occasionally to break down denser material for consumption."

"What about mimko extract?" Ozias asked. He glanced down at Raven before looking to Uma. "We used it on Gaige before, when he'd been poisoned by a Yimlet."

I'd almost forgotten about that injury—it'd felt like years ago when Yazmin had attacked her people and upturned our world. Gaige had been struck by a creature that'd left a weeping wound across his abdomen. Uma and Ozias had been able to eradicate the poison spreading through his veins and stitch him up, although the scar was still there. But that wound had been fresh—this was nearly two days' old. The Slimack's bile wasn't even present on the surface anymore. All we were left with was an elongated gash on Gaige's thigh that wouldn't close and a network of ivy-green veins spiderwebbing across his body.

As if echoing my thoughts, Kaori shook her head. "This…this is too deep." A single wrinkle formed between her manicured brows. "We can use Stella's saliva."

Calem blanched. "Gaige is already having enough trouble controlling his shadows. I'm worried what that would do to him." Kaori looked up at him, a flicker of unspoken understanding passing between them. Stella was Kaori's Ossillix, legendary feline—and the very beast responsible for Calem's still-beating heart. He'd fallen in our first battle against Hireath, and she'd saved him. She'd also given him a wild, hair-trigger monster that was almost impossible to control. Wresting the beast in his veins into some semblance of submission had taken an enormous amount of work, and it was something he still actively practiced.

Calem was right—it was the last thing Gaige needed.

"Well..." Uma gently prodded at the opening in his thigh, and ivy liquid, so dark it bordered on black, squelched onto the cot. "We can always drain him."

"Drain him?" My grip grew impossibly tighter.

She nodded. "Honestly, I think the only reason he's still alive is because of our restorative powers. That's slowing the poison's spread, but it's not killing it. If it reaches his heart..." Suddenly, she tore his tunic away, scattering buttons and thread across the tile floor. Ringing louder than the bell outside Moeras erupted in my ears. Ivy sludge had tracked all the way up his stomach and wrapped his ribs. His skin was paper-white, blanched and sweaty, and the poison pulsed in his veins with every ragged inhale, worming closer to his heart.

Kaori considered this for a breath before giving a definitive nod. "Thankfully, he's unconscious. We'll need to start immediately."

"He's dying," I trembled, "and you're talking about carving him open?"

Raven didn't look at me. "We'll need buckets to catch the blood."

"Will that get all of it out? How can we be sure?" Ozias asked, as if this weren't the absolute most horrendous decision in all of Lendria.

"Someone will have to act as a blood donor, and we'll add mimko extract to help purge any remnants. It's the only way to flush it out entirely," Uma said. She was already rummaging through shelves and cupboards to acquire a plethora of gleaming tools. She set them on a tray and wheeled it over before taking a pair of scissors to Gaige's clothes.

The quiet snip of shears slicing through fabric filled my ears. "I'll do it."

"That's probably for the best." Kaori gestured to an empty cot, and Calem quickly pushed it closer to Gaige's bed. "In a way, you share the same blood, thanks to Noc. And the same magic."

The notion that we were about to slice him open from head to toe still rattled me, but we didn't have time to think of another solution. Uma had already secured a large, clear beaker with tubing on either side, and she'd placed it on the bedside table between my cot and Gaige's. Tearing off my tunic, I climbed onto the bed. Crisp sheets crinkled beneath my weight, and I held out my arm.

"Do it."

Grabbing a piece of Gaige's torn shirt, Uma tied a tight bandage around my bicep. Then, with a practiced jab, she stuck a needle into the crook of my inner elbow. Not a breath later, she carefully glided a slender tube into my open vein, and blood began to ooze toward the beaker.

"Ozias, the extract," Uma murmured without looking up from my arm. He snagged a small green vial from one of the open shelves and, at her behest, uncorked the stopper. I gagged at the pungent, acrid aroma of spice and fermented vegetables. Uma shot me a threatening glare, rendering me immobile while she taped the tubing into place and removed the bandage on my bicep. My insides twisted into knots as my throat bobbed, and tears stung the back of my eyes.

Ozias dumped the entirety of the extract into the beaker between Gaige and me, and the fetid scent only worsened. Our beasts sneezed and pawed at their noses before padding across the room to curl up together against the farthest wall. Despite their distance, their gazes were intent, and I knew without a shadow of a doubt that they'd remain here until Gaige awoke.

"Disgusting," Calem muttered, his face parchment-pale. Raven had pinched her nose and was staring at the nauseating container housing my blood and the extract in wide-eyed horror. Ozias, Uma, and Kaori apparently had iron senses. None of them flinched, and Uma had already moved on to Gaige's arm. Once she'd fastened his tube in place, she checked to ensure the beaker was high enough for gravity to aid in the transfusion. The moment my blood started to flow into Gaige's arm, she dusted her hands over him.

"Now for the hard part," she said.

I would have traded a year in an enclosed space with no fresh air and nothing except mimko extract instead of what I witnessed next. I'd seen lacerations before. The sight of blood and gore hardly fazed me. But watching Uma swiftly lance Gaige's inner arm from wrist to shoulder tore at my insides in ways I never anticipated. The urge to protect him, to leap from the cot and wrench the blade from her hands, was so visceral I hardly recognized it. Rationally, I knew she was helping. But I hated the wet kiss of the blade against his skin. The sudden gush of blood as it poured from his wound and splattered against the metal bucket.

Kaori had inched closer to watch, and she frowned at Gaige's wound. "We'll need to do more."

"What?" The alarm must have sounded in my voice, because Ozias sidled closer and placed a gentle hand on my shoulder. "What's wrong?"

"It's worse than we thought." Kaori pushed up the sleeves of her flowy tunic. She nodded to Uma, who moved the full bucket to the side and replaced it with an empty one. "The poison has thickened his blood, making it impossible for it to flow freely. We'll have to force it out." With deft fingers, she clamped her hands down on either side of Gaige's upper arm and squeezed.

Thickened globs of green-black poison squelched out and dribbled to the floor, followed by another rush of blood. My vision swam, and I pressed my head flat against the pillow. There were too many smells clashing with each other. The sharp lemon of the room, the metallic tang of blood, the fetid extract, all compounded by the sickening hint of rotting flesh.

Calem excused himself, and I heard him vomit just outside the double doors. Raven was quick to follow, her gait stiff and awkward as she speed-walked out of the room. Part of me wished I could've done the same, but I was tethered to Gaige—and not just because of the tubing between us. Nothing could have pried me from his side in that moment. I needed to know he would make it through this. I needed to know that we weren't slicing into him for nothing.

I just need him. A shiver raced over my body. Whether it was due to the lack of blood or the unrelenting compulsion to ensure he was safe, I couldn't say; but that soft acknowledgment was far too dangerous. So I buried it deep and forced myself to focus on the sounds of the bloodletting and prayed that maybe, one day, I'd be strong enough to utter those words to him in person.

And that he'd live long enough to hear them.

Kaori, Ozias, and Uma worked for hours, each one taking turns wringing the poison from Gaige's arm like a soaked rag. Finally, when his blood ran clean, I signaled to Felicks and had him seal the wound on Gaige's thigh and arm. He obliged, and then I sent him back to the beast realm for some much-needed rest. The medical room was a war zone, complete with sloshing buckets of blood tinged a strange green color. Drenched towels littered the floor where they'd attempted to mop up messes along the way, but the repulsive odor of it all still hung in the air.

After draping a fresh sheet over Gaige to hide his bare skin, Kaori left in search of Raven. Uma, too, excused herself, stating she'd return shortly and not to mess with the tubing. It'd still be hours yet before I'd passed enough blood to Gaige for him to regain consciousness, so Ozias made a quick break for the kitchen and returned with food and water.

We ate in silence as I stared at Gaige. Damp curls clung to the muscles of his neck, but thankfully the veins were free of poison, their color now their normal blue-green hue. A sheen of sweat glistened against his pale skin, but there was a pallid pink tinge to his cheeks. With each predictable rise and fall of his chest, my own breathing normalized. I hadn't realized how shallow my inhalations had become, how much tension I'd been holding in my lungs throughout the entire process. Exhaling deeply, I felt every muscle in my rib cage loosen a fraction.

"He'll be okay," Ozias finally said. He'd been watching me carefully, only choosing to speak once our plates were clear.

"I believe that now," I murmured. I went to adjust my glasses and faltered. I still hadn't replaced them. Fortunately, I had a spare set in my room. "I'm just glad that's over with."

Ozias rolled his head from side to side, stretching the space between his shoulders. "What about you?"

"I'm fine." I settled deeper into the cot, and the exhaustion I'd been fighting hit me with the force of a beast. Weights tugged at my eyelids, but I forced myself to stay awake a little longer. To keep Gaige in my sights just a bit more, just in case. "I'm just fatigued from all this. We haven't slept in days."

"That's not what I meant." Ozias reclined in his chair, and the wood creaked beneath his weight. Like me, he'd forgone sleep to ensure Gaige was safe. There were bags beneath his warm, brown eyes, but the weariness in his stare felt different somehow, like a parent who was stuck watching their child endure far too much hardship. Too much pain.

"What is it, then?"

"I'm just ready for you two to quit dancing around each other with blades in one hand and roses in the other. You don't need either of them."

I blinked, the action like sandpaper scraping against my eyes. "What is that supposed to mean?"

Ozias sighed and stood slowly, giving my leg a parting squeeze. "Maybe my analogy is off—you know I'm not great with words—but you're supposed to be the smart one. Figure it out." With that he exited through the doors out into the halls of Cruor. I glanced at the sleeping forms of Okean and Rook as I considered Ozias's words.

Blades and roses. My focus shifted to Gaige. Sleep teased my senses as I turned on my side, careful to keep my arm propped up in a way that my blood continued to flow. With my hand dangling off the edge of the cot, I could almost graze Gaige's fingertips. His *ungloved* fingers. I burned to feel his hand in mine, but I didn't dare bridge that gap. Instead, I called on my shadows and allowed them to curl in my palm. It was a poor substitute for what I really desired, and the normally soothing feel of their icy touch only irritated me. Without much thought from me, the tendrils shifted between a glittering, ink-black blade and a budding rose. Truly, I wanted Gaige to have both. Yet as I mulled over Ozias's words, I closed my eyes and let the shadows disperse. I knew he was right—I didn't need either. All I needed was his hand in mine, and that was the very thing I couldn't allow myself to have.

THIRTEEN

GAIGE

For the first time since being raised, I slept without dreaming. I didn't know how long I'd been out, just that my body ached from the kind of rigidity that comes with being sedentary for far too long. My eyes peeled open with the stiffness of salt-ridden sheets, becoming more fluid after several forceful blinks. The room was dark, save for a few candles scattered about the space. Their pale, orange glow illuminated a sterile environment complete with strange silver apparatuses and a field of cots. It felt…familiar. I squinted in the dim lighting.

As I propped myself up, something gave an uncomfortable tug on my inner arm. I glanced down to see tubing jammed into my vein and blood gradually flowing into my body. Blood that was draining from some sort of container riddled with the nauseating scent of mimko extract. Blood that traveled from an arm attached to a sleeping body beside me.

Kost.

All I did was stare. We were alone in what I now realized was the medical wing of Cruor, which meant he'd either found a way to magic us here in the blink of an eye, or I'd been out for several days. Since he appeared to be sleeping sounder than the dead, even with medical equipment protruding from his arm, I assumed the latter.

My brows inched together. Why…? The events of Moeras hit me in a rush, and I sank back into the cot. The Slimacks. They'd attacked, and one had managed to rake a barbed tentacle down my thigh. The image of fluorescent green bile spewing onto my wound flooded my mind, and I flinched. I should've been dead, rotting away from the inside out. My leg throbbed, but a far greater pain arced from my forearm, the one not attached to Kost. Gingerly, I held it above my head to bathe it in the warm light of the candles. A puckered, shiny wound stretched from the base of my wrist to my shoulder. It was sealed but healing slowly.

Suddenly, the stench of mimko made sense. They'd let the Slimack's poison drain from my body and replenished me with fresh blood and the cleansing herb to eradicate what was left. Something in my chest shifted as I turned my chin back to Kost. How had he managed this? What had it been like, transporting me back to Cruor never knowing if I was going to make it? Was it like before? The panic must have eaten him away. With slightly parted lips and unkempt, ruffled hair, he breathed deeply without moving. His arm was outstretched to keep the tubing in place, and his fingers dangled close to the edge of my cot.

Close enough to touch. We'd never even kissed. Of course I'd wanted to, but his shy embarrassment was both exasperating and somehow infuriatingly intoxicating. I used to love the way the tips of his ears flushed when I shamelessly flirted with him. We'd come close a time or two, certainly, but I'd lost the will to keep trying after my death. I'd lost the will for a lot of things.

Without really knowing it was happening, I'd inched my hand toward his. My pinkie ghosted along his finger. I hated how wonderfully electric the sensation was. No matter how hard I tried to deny it, my body reveled in the feel of him. Anticipation thrummed through me, and my hand started to tremble. What was I even doing? Still,

I wavered, fingers dancing above his. I studied the space between us, so small and yet so immeasurably large. My gaze slanted to the faded, graphite-colored symbol on the back of my hand. He'd done too much. *We'd* done too much.

Retracting slowly, I laid my hand flat on my bed. The sheets crinkled beneath my touch, and a soft, questioning chatter bubbled from the corner of the room. Two sets of eyes with a nocturnal sheen stared back at me.

"Okean? Rook?" Needles scratched at my throat, and I swallowed dryly. My beasts leapt to their feet and padded toward me with restrained excitement. Their tails flicked wildly, betraying their joy, but they moved carefully as if knowing I was still in a great deal of pain. A deep purr vibrated from Okean's chest, and he gently placed his head on my cot. Standing on his hind legs, Rook sniffed the healing gash on my arm and then chuffed. I drove my hands into their fur, scratching them behind their ears.

"They refused to leave."

I jolted, and the tubing in my arm gave another uncomfortable tug. Kost regarded me without moving, his arm still propped in a way to ensure steady blood flow. In the low light of the candles, shadows played across the bridge of his nose and cut of his jaw. I didn't know how long he'd been sleeping, but it wasn't enough to fully reduce the puffiness beneath his sharp green eyes. Even so, the raw intensity of his stare made it difficult for me to think.

"Hey," I finally managed. At least I could blame the gruffness of my voice on the need for water and not something else.

His gaze dipped to my throat, and he briefly turned away from me to snag a glass of water from a table to his right. After passing it to me, he propped himself against his pillows so he was sitting upright.

I drained the glass, but my throat was still raspy. I could've downed a whole well of water, but for now, I'd make do. "Thanks."

"How are you feeling?"

"Passable." I winced as I attempted to move. "I thought we were supposed to heal quickly."

"Under normal circumstances, yes." His focus momentarily shifted to the beaker between us. "Apparently Slimack poison is far from normal, though. You've been out for days."

"Yes, well," I winced as I shoved a pillow beneath my lower back and succeeded in sitting up, "I hardly think anything about dying and healing and shadows is considered normal, and yet here we are."

I'd hoped for a small smile, or some sliver of lightness to invade his probing stare. I got neither. "Why did they attack?" he asked.

I studied the empty glass between my hands, unsure of how to answer. I'd been so convinced it wasn't me, yet everything indicated I was the root source of the problem. I wasn't entirely sure how to fix it—me—either. Before I could muster up the courage to respond, footsteps sounded in the hall. The double doors to the medical wing opened shortly after, the creaking hinges giving me an excuse to look away from him. But the sight I found waiting for me was an entirely different kind of hard, and I stilled in my sheets.

Leena, Crown of the Charmers Council and queen of Lendria—but most importantly, my friend—stood in the open doorway holding a glass pitcher full of water. The rosewood symbol on her hand dominated my vision and made me itch for my gloves. A faint smile graced her lips, but it did little to hide the sadness etched into her hazel eyes. Her oak-brown hair was pulled back in a braid, and instead of the customary regal gowns she'd most likely been wearing since her coronation, she'd donned simple black breeches, a midnight-blue blouse, and a pair of boots. Travel attire, it seemed. Still, there was no missing the miniscule silver griffin—the crest of the royal family of Wilheim—embroidered on her breast pocket.

Or the bestiary resting against her sternum. She reminded me so much of home. Of everything I'd walked away from.

"Need a refill?" Her voice was soft as she strode across the tiles to fill up my glass.

I took it greedily, both to satiate my thirst and to give me time to formulate words. Water chased away the burn of unshed tears, and I attempted a timid grin. "It's been a while."

A bit of warmth flickered into her expression. "Too long. We've been worried about you." At that, she looked over her shoulder at the door. Noc glided into the room, his gaze slanting to me as he took his place by Leena's side. He was her *anam-cara*, her chosen partner for the duration of their very long lives. His tousled, shock-white hair kissed the planes of his cheekbones and framed his ice-blue eyes. As he slipped his hands into the pockets of his trousers, the unbuttoned collar of his tunic shifted to reveal the edges of a griffin tattoo on his chest.

Noc was followed by Calem and Ozias—whom I expected entirely—and then Kaori and Raven, whom I hadn't expected at all. Raven, dressed in simple, flowing trousers and a tunic with far too many buckles, folded her arms across her chest. A scowl dominated her face. Kaori's expression was impassive, but I knew better. There were cracks in her stoic demeanor. The slight twitch of her lip. The subtle flexing of her fingers at her sides. Something, or rather someone, was troubling her. Likely me.

"This is beginning to feel like an intervention," I mused as I found a space for my glass next to the blood-filled beaker. "By the way, can this be removed?" I lifted my arm.

Uma materialized from the shadows as if she'd been eavesdropping, and Kost gave her a pointed look. She said nothing, only busied herself with removing my lifeline to Kost and then pressing a thin bandage over the wound. She did the same for him, and then quickly returned to the shadows. I'd learned after living in Cruor how difficult it was to keep secrets in a house with beings who could hear through walls if they so desired.

"Slimacks?" Raven prompted, inching closer to my cot. "Docile, dirt-eating, terrified-of-everything Slimacks?"

"Yes, I'm fine, thanks for asking." I couldn't keep the bite out of my tone. No matter how many adjectives she threw at me, I was fully aware of the absurdity of a Slimack attack.

"*We* know you're fine, because *we*"—Kaori gestured between her and Raven—"were here when you showed up unconscious."

"We needed their help. None of us knew how to deal with Slimack poison." Kost stretched his arm, likely for the first time in days.

Bitterness died on my tongue as I forced myself to meet Kaori's hardened stare. "I'm sorry." She gave an imperceptible nod. She was satisfied for now, but I had a sinking feeling she'd have more to say to me later when we were alone. "I'm still not even sure how I'm alive."

"You can thank Effie for that." Ever the picture of ease, Calem leaned indolently against the doorframe. "Her life magic saved your ass."

"And then we tapped Kost for blood and flushed the poison out of your system," Raven added. The hard edge to her words were a sharp reminder that while my apology had mollified Kaori, it'd had little effect on Raven.

"We spent hours wringing your arm like a blood-soaked rag," Ozias said. "It wasn't pretty."

"It was vile." Calem shuddered. "But seems like it worked."

Leena parked her hip on my cot as if she were merely a friend instead of my leader. "What's going on with the Kitska beasts?"

I didn't know how to answer her. I was in a room with too many eyes, but I feared if I told them it wasn't my fault, they wouldn't hear my words. They'd see what they wanted, a man not wholly in control. If I were them, I wouldn't believe me, either.

"I don't know why they're acting out." I gripped the edge of my sheets and worked the fabric between my fingers.

"They've never behaved this way before." It wasn't accusatory, but Noc's words stung just the same. His gaze bored into my very soul—or rather, perhaps, he was studying the shadows that lingered there. The awful, horrendous mess living in my core that would explode without warning. After he'd peeled back every layer of my being with one simple look, he pursed his lips. "There have been more attacks."

A dull ringing sounded in my ears. "Where?"

"All over." Leena wrapped her fingers in the chain of her bestiary. "We've been getting reports from towns all along the Kitska Forest. We had to cut our trip to Rhyne short."

And now the political well-being of two freshly allied countries was my fault, too. Words refused to surface in my mind, so I opted for staring at the floor in the hopes the room would stop spinning.

"They've attacked Charmers, too. In Hireath," Kaori said softly.

"Hireath?" I jerked my head toward her and finally met her gaze. "That doesn't make any sense."

"We know." The anger in Raven's tone ebbed away only to be replaced by frustration. "We assumed that, with the barrier gone, we'd have more encounters. But nothing like this."

A headache throbbed behind my eyes. I didn't know if my presence made things better or worse. At first, I'd thought I'd offered the undead beasts some reprieve. They'd flocked to me in the days prior to our war with Varek, the former king of Lendria, and Yazmin. But since then, fewer creatures had sought me out, and clearly their behavior was becoming more erratic.

Like your shadows.

That tacit connection hung heavy in the room as we all settled into an uncomfortable silence. I didn't know how much Kost had shared with Leena, Noc, Kaori, and Raven. Maybe he didn't have to. Maybe they theorized that I was the problem, just like everyone else. I needed help. I needed someone to come to my aid, someone to tell all these people that I was trying. They had to know that I wasn't just sitting back anymore. I didn't want anyone else, beast or otherwise, to get hurt.

"Gaige is making progress with his shadows."

A current of electricity bolted through me. All gazes roved to Kost—including mine. He looked at me for a long moment, and I didn't know if it was because of my near-death experience or simply an emotion I'd missed all this time, but I saw something in his eyes I hadn't noticed before: yearning. Not romantically—at least I didn't think, couldn't hope for such a thing—but a soft desire, as if he wanted nothing more than for me to be okay. It was so counter to all his coldness, to his blunt speech and emotionless assessments, that it made it impossible for me to speak. And then he schooled his expression into one of calm surety as he turned his focus to the group. That look was just for me. Only me.

All at once I'd wished I hadn't thrown his gift against the wall in the Wooden Flower.

Leaning over, he retrieved what must have been a pair of backup glasses from his bedside table and slipped them onto the bridge of his nose. "Not great progress, but some."

All right, maybe just a gentle toss, enough to rattle the contents but not break the frame or lenses. Still... I cut a glance to Calem and Ozias, who nodded in unison. Whatever progress they saw, I didn't. All I'd done was maintain a flimsy shield for a few minutes and quicken my movements. And both times I'd sparred, I'd lost control, only for some sort of attack to occur shortly thereafter.

"We're uncertain as to whether or not that has anything to do with the Kistka beasts, but we're watching it closely." Kost kicked back the sheets covering his legs and stood. "For now, we'll continue to investigate areas where they have attacked."

"We've dispatched a number of Sentinels to a few of the towns to help with protection," Noc said. "Charmers have joined the effort as well, but we plan on visiting each location ourselves."

Sentinels. I fought the urge to squeeze my eyes shut. They were Wilheim's most elite forces, normally tasked with protecting the capital or the royal family. They hardly ever left the city's walls. Just how bad were these attacks?

"Hopefully I can help assuage any growing fears about beasts and the dangers they pose," Leena added. She unwrapped her fingers from the chain of her bestiary to lay her palms flat against her thighs. "After we visit Hireath, of course."

"You should join us," Kaori said, tilting her head toward me. "You're still part of the Council. We all are, and we're not complete without you."

My heart gave a painful shudder. How did I make them understand? The only reason Kost, Noc, Ozias, and Calem were temporarily part of the Council was because we'd needed the support of Cruor to fight Yazmin. And they'd known it, too. Their shadow magic was a stark contrast to what Charmers wielded. We weren't even sure our people would accept them, even temporarily, in a position of power. And now I was a horrific combination of those two things with no place that really felt like home.

As if hearing my thoughts, Calem frowned at Kaori. "We're not part of the Council anymore."

"Sure you are," Raven said with an exaggerated sigh. "Turns out, all Charmers really care about is good people taking the helm—not what type of people they are. And before you go freaking out about added responsibilities"—she gave a critical nod to Calem's slack jaw—"don't. Consider yourselves more...advisers, much like Kost is to Noc and Leena."

Leena placed a hand on my leg and gave it a gentle squeeze. "Come with us. After that, well, if you still want to avoid Hireath, then you'll always have a home in Wilheim."

"And here," Kost said, his soft exclamation a breathy exhale. There it was again. That moment of thinly veiled tenderness. It was almost too much to bear.

A fist wrung my heart tight. Wilheim, Cruor, Hireath...none of them really felt like home anymore. But the people around me did. And even if I didn't really know who I was or what I was capable of, I knew I didn't want to disappoint them.

"I'll go," I said.

For the first time since she barged through the doors to the medical wing, Raven smiled. "Good."

"Tomorrow, though," Kost said with a dismissive wave. "Gaige is still recovering."

"You too." Ozias said as he crossed his arms against his chest. "I know how much blood you donated. You'll heal faster than him, but you need to rest."

"Since I'm no longer needed here"—Kost gestured to the beaker and limp tubing dangling off the table—"I'll retire to my room after checking in with Emelia and the sentries."

You're needed here. That quiet, errant thought had the power to upend my world. I'd already gone down that road before, and I knew where it ended. I couldn't keep pining over something that never was. And yet... That look he'd given me, the gentle way he insinuated that I belonged here, with him... My mind was such a mess when it came to Kost. I wanted to let go. I wanted to break away and forget everything that still stirred within me at the sight of him. It was just so…hard. I didn't know how to address it, so I simply didn't. I let that damning thought solidify into something larger and just kept quiet.

When everyone left to give me a chance to sleep, I stared at the rafters of the ceiling and tracked shadows as they writhed along the beams. My body could rest, but my thoughts certainly wouldn't. And while the poison-induced sleep had thankfully kept my dreams at bay, I feared I'd fall right back to the same nightmare if I closed my eyes. And then the shadows above my head would wreak havoc on the guild, and the Kitska beasts would attack, and the small seed of confidence that had just taken root in my chest after Kost vouched for my progress would wither and die.

And I was tired of dying.

Tomorrow, we'd go to Hireath. Tomorrow, I'd confront the home I used to have and get to the bottom of these monster attacks. Maybe tomorrow, I'd make more progress with my shadows. With myself. With Kost.

FOURTEEN

KOST

"Progress? What kind of progress? What were you referring to?" Calem asked. We'd barely made it into my private study before he'd launched into a barrage of questions, and I was already exhausted. Sinking into the overstuffed armchair before my desk, I rubbed my temples. Leena, Raven, and Kaori had excused themselves for the evening, leaving me with Calem, Ozias, and Noc. I wasn't surprised when they followed me out of the medical wing to here. I'd been the first one to point out Gaige's shortcomings in recent days, so to suddenly comment on his improvement was a bit…unexpected. Even for me.

"He tamed Rook without major incident." It felt weak on my tongue, and I knew they'd see right through it.

"Without major incident?" Calem tossed his hands into the air in exasperation. "You've lost too much blood. You're not thinking clearly, because that *incident* wasn't exactly minor."

Ozias lingered by the closed door and gripped the back of his neck. "Look, I'm the first one to give encouragement, but…I dunno, Kost. After what happened with the Slimacks, I'm not so sure anymore."

Noc pressed his lips into a tight line. After a forced exhale, he pinned me to the wall with his stare. "You really think he's improved? Answer honestly."

"As if I'd ever be dishonest," I said. Still, I hesitated to answer as I braced my elbows on my meticulously organized desk. I didn't know what had brought me to react in such a way. I'd just... I knew how hard it must've been. Even if we weren't voicing our concerns, I'm sure he felt them. He was practically shriveling away, unable to carry the weight of our expectations, of what we wanted him to be. And I was the worst at thrusting my well-meaning, but perhaps harsh and unsympathetic, intentions on him. He was finally trying to control his powers, and for once, I wanted to be the one to reassure him. Not Ozias. Not Calem. Me.

Of course, none of that mattered. The issue still remained—Kitska monsters were attacking innocent people, and Gaige still had a long way to go. At this rate, it would be years before he mastered the shadows, and we couldn't afford his wild, uncontained magic to continue to agitate the beasts.

I slipped a hand beneath my glasses to pinch the bridge of my nose. "No, I don't think he's improved. Not enough to dismiss the notion that he's inexplicably linked to the growing number of attacks."

"We can't give up yet." Ozias left his post to slump into the chair across from me. "Some people take to the shadows better than others. We've never changed a Charmer before."

"You think that matters?" Calem asked. He paced along the bookshelves, dragging his fingertips aimlessly against the bindings. His brows drew together in a frown, and I studied the thin line of mercury surrounding his muted-red irises. Calem had two magics living within him; shadows and something bestial. How did he manage?

Noc tipped his head to the ceiling in thought. "Maybe. Maybe not. I only know of a few assassins who were lost to the shadow realm, and they were all just people."

"Do we keep records of that?" Ozias asked.

Noc grimaced. "No. It never happened under my watch, and I only saw the one when Talmage was guild master. All other accounts were just stories passed down over time."

Passed down over time. A strange, buoyant sensation bubbled up in my chest. I'd been around the longest when it came to my brothers, but there were a few members in Cruor who'd been around far longer. Decades longer.

Straightening in my chair, I stared at the space between Noc and Calem. "Uma, you're needed in the guild master's study."

The words had barely left my mouth when a maelstrom of shadows exploded before me. In Cruor, the walls had ears—and Uma had already proven to be listening. She stepped out of the snarling void and tipped her head in a polite bow. Her periwinkle gaze was framed by fine lines, and her silvery hair was pulled back in a neat fishtail braid. Hands clasped before her, she took a single step into the study.

"How can I help?"

"How many people have you seen lost to the realm?" I asked.

"Three." Her answer was alarmingly swift. "You don't forget something like that."

"Were they all human?" Noc dipped his chin toward her as the crease between his brows deepened.

Uma nodded. "All the ones I knew. The first person we tried to save. But…" She looked at her hands, a deeply saddened expression clouding her eyes. She curled her fingers inward. "It didn't work."

A sour taste coated the back of my tongue. Of course it hadn't worked. No one had ever been saved from the shadow realm. It was an impossible feat. We weren't entertaining the notion of rescuing anyone; we needed to prevent it from happening altogether.

"All the ones you knew..." I turned over her words, searching for answers I hoped could help Gaige. "Has anyone other than a human been raised?"

Her lips pursed, and she frowned at nothing in particular. "I suppose it's possible, but I don't recall. You've seen the bounties that come through. We're rarely put in contact with Charmers, Sentinels, mages—anything other than Lendrians, really. People with magic aren't clambering to die to get power when they already have it. Why do you ask?"

My shoulders sagged, and I pressed my back into the worn cushions of the chair. "Gaige's shadows are just different than any we've encountered before."

Calem shifted from one foot to the next. With a definitive swallow, he forced himself to look at Uma directly. "Those who were lost... Did their shadows act like Gaige's?"

I'd never feared or wanted an answer simultaneously more in my life. Tension-racked silence enveloped us in a bubble where time ceased. It was the question I'd been asking without really asking, because I didn't want to hear that Gaige was like all those who'd disappeared. I wanted him to simply be different for absolutely no reason at all. I wanted it just to be a strange reaction to the Charmer magic that had resided in his veins first. I wanted... I wanted him to be safe. I wanted him *here*.

"No," Uma said, shattering the anxiety-riddled air with one simple word. My breath left in a rush, and my body threatened to crumple just from the sheer release of adrenaline. Ozias blew out a breath as well, and Noc's gaze softened with relief. Calem briefly closed his eyes before opening them again, a slight smile teasing the corners of his lips.

I drilled my fingers on the tabletop, then cut a glance to Noc. "You called on Isla?" When we'd traveled to Rhyne to ally with their queen, we'd been questioned by a mage in the royal guard.

She'd used a tool of sorts to observe Noc's aura and discovered a trace of magic etched into his essence, which proved his intentions were honest. Rather, it'd proved he hadn't intentionally murdered the queen's sister, the princess of Rhyne, years earlier and that led to a tentative alliance against Yazmin and Wilheim.

Now, perhaps, her magic could help us learn more about Gaige. It seemed like a stretch, but we needed answers. Fast.

Ozias straightened in his chair as he fumbled for words. Finally, he managed, "Isla?"

Noc raised an amused brow at his brother before meeting my stare. "Yes. I shadow walked to Rhyne a few days ago. What happened to the other mages you knew?"

"I've lost contact with them. She's our best bet," I said.

Noc nodded. "She had to seek permission from the queen, but I haven't heard anything yet. I can search for her again and see if she's already departed."

"Please. It sounds like we might have a small sliver of hope, considering Gaige's shadows aren't adhering to the same patterns as those who've been lost."

"That doesn't mean he's in a good way." Uma's soft words threatened to douse the spark of hope igniting in my chest. Hands quivering, she fisted the fabric of her dress. "I'm less worried about how his shadows are behaving than how *he's* behaving. Because that, unfortunately, is what really worries me."

I barely found the words to respond. "What do you mean?"

A glassy sheen obscured her eyes. "I know what you're feeling. I know you want to help. But if Gaige doesn't help himself, he'll be lost, too. He needs to truly reconcile with his existence. At least, that's what I think. I can't say for certain if that's true—no one knows, of course—but...but that's what I've seen. I'm sorry I don't have more information for you."

I stilled, along with Calem and Ozias. For a moment, I forgot I was the guild master of Cruor. I forgot that I was supposed to act with a level head and rationalize the information that had been presented to me. All I wanted to do was run to Gaige and make sure he was okay, guild be damned. How many times had I advised against such actions when it came to Noc and Leena? He'd repeatedly thrown caution to the wind just for the chance to be near her, and I'd never understood.

Now, sitting here in the study with the walls closing in around me, it was all I could think about. With a shuddering breath, I forced myself to meet Uma's imploring gaze. "Thank you, Uma. That will be all."

She tipped her chin once and then turned on her heels, stepping into a plume of shadows and disappearing from the room. The empty space she left behind dominated my vision.

"Isla will have answers," Noc said, but his quiet voice barely reached my ears. The room was suddenly too warm, and my nerves were ablaze, the very feeling of my tunic scraping against my skin an unbearable sensation.

"And if she doesn't?" I couldn't bring myself to look at him.

Noc rounded the desk to place a firm hand on my shoulder. "She will."

"We just have to make Gaige believe he belongs. We can do that," Ozias said. The warmth of his tone was a gentle poke against my heightened senses, and I relished in his surety. Noc had mentioned never losing anyone to the shadows while he led Cruor, and I wondered how much of that had to do with Ozias taking over training the newly raised assassins. He never stopped caring.

Still, he'd rallied behind Gaige from the beginning, and here we sat. The four of us with our heads dipped low as we contemplated a future we could hardly fathom. Uma had said it best—no matter

FIFTEEN

GAIGE

By the time I crossed the lawns out front of Cruor the following morning, the Council was already waiting. I'd made a quick stop to check in on Boo and Rook, only to find both of my beasts playfully wrestling to the amusement of a few sentries. After breaking them up, I sent them into the woods so they could meet me at Hireath if they so desired. At the very least, I knew Rook would find his way to me, if only for a chance to see Felicks again.

Strange how you tame a beast that shares your feelings. I shivered at the thought and turned my focus back to the group. Raven and Leena's Telesávras, lizard-like creatures with the ability to summon portals, lingered by their ankles. A familiar ache simmered in my chest. My own Telesávra was forever out of my reach. I could still feel the graze of his scaled hide rubbing against my calves.

This is a bad idea. My former home would be full of creatures, full of reminders. At least at Cruor, we all shared the same fate. No one here suddenly up and lost the ability to wield their shadows, and if they did, they'd probably joyously run to the nearest town and assume a normal, happy life. Still… My gaze slanted to where Kost stood, slightly apart from the group, listening but not speaking. I hadn't expected him to stand up for me.

Shoving my dread far into the recesses of my mind, I gripped my shoulder bag and put on a smile. "Ready?"

"Whenever you are." Leena extended her hand toward me, and I locked elbows with her. Noc held her other hand, and Kost sidled up next to me. With a delicate touch, he cupped her shoulder. He only offered me the briefest of glances, but that was enough to make my chest tighten. There might as well have been a steel thread pulled taut between us, because in my peripheral I could have sworn I saw him breathe a little too deeply. His throat bobbed as he stared at Leena's back.

"Come on, we've got work to do." Raven gestured to Calem, Ozias, and Kaori, and they took up a similar position. Once everyone was situated, Leena and Raven signaled to their beasts. Each one cracked their maws open wide, detaching their jaws and summoning a sparkling, powder-white portal. They sparked and snapped like flames devouring wood, but I knew from experience that we'd teleport painlessly and instantaneously to the beasts' designated hearth point—in this case, Hireath—set by Leena and Raven.

Even though I knew Ocnolog had destroyed our sanctuary when he'd risen from his underground tomb, part of me still hoped to find Hireath intact. I longed to see the marble keep glistening under the fine spray of water from the crystal falls. Or the rows of gargantuan trees dotted with alabaster platforms and wooden buildings suspended high above the earth in the interconnected network of branches. I wanted to inhale the mineral-coated air and hold it in my lungs, drink in the sight of vibrant flowers crowding smooth pathways through the courtyard. Most of all, I longed to hear the joyous composition of competing beast calls, all different but somehow in sync.

But when I manifested on the other side of the portal, the only thing I got was a knife twisting in my gut.

Hireath was gone. My arm fell away from Leena's as I took a few steps forward. Brittle, singed grass crunched beneath my feet. Splintered trees, blackened by fire, rose in sharpened spires around what used to be the keep. A canyon cleaved through the charred earth, and deep gouges ran the length of either side where Ocnolog had clawed his way out. And all around the ruptured ground was rubble. Shattered pieces of slab and marble, mangled debris from homes, furniture broken and dismantled. Everything else was simply ash, and it coated the quiet space in a bone-colored dust.

"It was worse before," Kaori said as she moved to my side. "We've already disposed of most of the debris, but it will take time before the trees can support the weight of our buildings again."

I didn't know how it could've looked worse than this. With a thick swallow, I nodded. "I'm glad no one was hurt."

"I'm not sure it will ever be the city it was." Raven sauntered toward the muddy banks and stared out across the basin. The ever-present crash of the falls still echoed, but even that sound felt muted. Subdued. "Everyone is eager to build a temple of sorts, but many have voiced a desire to travel or live elsewhere now that Charmers are no longer at risk of being captured."

Leena joined us and leaned her head against my shoulder. "It will be smaller, like a town, but no less beautiful or welcoming than before."

My throat swelled shut at her words, and I relished the weight of her against my frame. Looping my arm around her, I gave her a gentle squeeze—more for my own sake than hers. "I'll help however I can."

She beamed up at me. "Good."

Noc cleared his throat, and we turned to meet his gaze. Until that point, none of the assassins had spoken. It was as if they were giving me a chance to react, to soak in what had happened and process it without interfering. They'd all been here before, or at least shadow walked to Hireath and witnessed the ruination for themselves. Only I had staved off returning to the place I once called my home. A savage, deep-seated guilt churned in my stomach. I should've come sooner. My own fears, my own inadequacies, were nothing compared to the devastation all around us.

"Your parents?" Noc prompted when we didn't respond.

Leena brightened. "Right. They, along with the rest of the Charmers who want to continue to live here, have started to rebuild homes up there." She pointed to the top of the falls and beckoned for us to follow. "Fortunately, Ocnolog didn't damage that area."

We picked our way across the rubble-strewn ground and strode closer to the falls as we all fell silent. Which was fine—my throat was still pained and dry, and forcing conversation felt like it would only heighten my guilt. When we passed behind the sheet of oppressive water, Leena led us along a slick, stone path. With my jaw clenched tight, I followed her. This was the fastest way to the top of the falls. The very same place where we used to build funeral pyres for our dead.

We moved single file through the damp cavern. Lanterns with blue flames dotted the rock walls, illuminating stalactites covered in crystal water droplets. The subtle drip of their descent filled the space, until we came upon a staircase carved of the same stone as the mountain. We climbed upward in a gradual spiral, and at least twice I heard Raven mumbling about needing to adjust her Telesávra's hearth point to the top of the falls.

A faint smile ghosted my lips. "You haven't done that yet?"

I could practically hear her shrug. "I haven't needed to. Coming to save your ass was the first time we'd left Hireath, so I didn't think about it."

My grin stifled. "I see."

Leena glanced over her shoulder; her brows screwed together in mock puzzlement. "I have no excuse. I usually just fly in on Onyx."

Her Myad, a winged feline beast, was certainly capable of carrying her weight and perhaps one or two others safely, but I appreciated her making the trek with us nonetheless. I'd forgotten how much I'd grown to admire her, how much I'd missed her surety and compassion. She never intended to be queen of Lendria—or Crown of the Charmers Council, for that matter—but she found purpose in her newfound roles and embraced the challenges head-on.

Maybe one day, I'd be able to do the same.

By the time we emerged at the top of the falls, midmorning sun had crested over the trees and showered the lush clearing in a resplendent, warm glow. Churning azure water cut through the fields of grass in a winding river that eventually fell over the cliff to the basin below. Saturated purple flowers bloomed in earnest along the banks, and beasts roamed freely in the open air. Houses with red cedar planks and simple pitched roofs backed the surrounding tree line, and a few larger structures were already in progress. Canopies were stretched tight between branches and protected what items had been rescued from the desolation, including a handful of books from the library and Celeste's harp.

I forced down a hard swallow. "That's all that's left?"

Raven's eyes were glassy, but her voice was steady. "Yes. We're lucky we found this much."

Charmers mingled about the new settlement, busying themselves and their beasts with tasks. A few of them caught my eyes and smiled, and suddenly I was too exposed. Too raw. Ocnolog had decimated my home, and I hadn't been able to stop it. Worse, I hadn't returned to help rebuild the place that raised me. Even now, glancing at familiar faces and taking stock of our artifacts, I could barely bring myself to face what was left. All I wanted to do was hide.

Shadows festered around my fingers, reminding me that I could do exactly that. I could simply step into the void and disappear.

"Gaige." Kost's gentle word broke over me, and I sucked in a sharp breath.

"I just need a minute." Turning away from the group, I strode toward the trees and hid in their shaded comfort. I watched as Leena, Raven, and Kaori looked after me, but with prodding from Calem, Ozias, and Noc, they let me be. No sooner had they turned their backs than they were swarmed by Charmers, eagerly greeting them with smiles that didn't make sense.

How can they be so happy amidst all this? Gripping the rough bark of the tree before me, I peered at the clearing. Kost waited alone for a single minute before he summoned a portal of shadows and stepped into darkness. I knew where he would go the moment those tendrils flocked to him. Ever since he'd vouched for me, looked at me with such…emotion, it was like there was a tether between us. Something bigger than just a shared experience. So when he sped through the shadow realm to appear at my side, I wasn't surprised. Or bothered. If anything, I was relieved.

He said nothing as he stood next to me, but his stable presence was enough. I listened to the cadence of his breath and felt my own lungs slow to match his pace. His eyes were somber, but also guarded. I never was the best at figuring out what went on his mind, but that's always what had made him so damn intriguing. He was my favorite game, the kind I'd never grow tired of playing.

When I felt strong enough to release my grip on the oak tree, I finally braved words. "I just don't feel like I belong anymore."

He cut me a sidelong glance that was worth a conversation in and of itself. "You belong wherever you want to be."

"Easy for you to say," I muttered. "You're the guild master of Cruor. You've been at this for decades."

"I think you'll find that most, if not all, were outcasts before our found family." He removed his glasses and extracted a cloth from his breast pocket. With meticulous fingers, he polished the lenses. "We all died for different reasons, but one thing is constant for all of us—we weren't wanted by the people we left behind anymore. That's not the case for you.

"Now, if you're not ready to be here because it pains you, that's understandable. But don't think for a second that both your former family and your found family don't love you." He replaced his glasses, still refusing to look me directly in the eyes. Yet, there was that unmistakable hue of pink gracing the tops of his ears, and my heart twisted at the sight.

He couldn't have meant him. Or if he did, it was amicable. He felt *responsible* for me. Nothing more.

Still, I couldn't quite quell the sudden racing pulse of blood (*his* blood) in my veins. "Thanks, Kost."

Finally, he looked at me. "You're family."

Family. Right. "We should get back."

He gave a tight nod and broke free from the shadows of the forest without a second thought. I kept pace beside him, our long gaits eating away at the grassy plains beneath our feet. "What now?"

"Raven is rounding up the Charmers who had encounters with rogue monsters. After you're settled, we'll meet with them to assess what we're dealing with."

"And everyone else?" I'd already spied a Charmer dressed in flowy, tan clothing waving at us near one of the outlying houses. Ozias and Calem were standing beside him, chatting between themselves while they waited for us to return.

"Kaori is checking in with the Charmers who'd been held in Wilheim, and Noc and Leena are making their rounds. I suspect they'll leave before nightfall to ensure they hit the nearest town with reported monster attacks." We came to an abrupt halt outside the small structure, and the scent of fresh-cut wood hit the back of my nose.

"Our inn isn't constructed yet, so you'll have to share." The Charmer bowed in apology, dipping his head low so his beard grazed his chest.

Kost waved him off. "It's more than adequate, thank you."

The Charmer beamed at us before scurrying off. Calem leapt toward the front door and swung it open. The pleasing aroma of wood was thicker indoors, and I inhaled deeply to savor the smell. The space was small, perfect for a couple who preferred the outdoors or had no desire for copious amounts of elbow room. A quaint kitchen with a round table took up most of the space, leaving a bedroom at the back and another loft-style bedroom above the shared bathroom.

"Cozy." Calem blew out a breath.

"I think it's nice." Ozias's grin was genuine, and he ran an appreciative hand along the smooth finish of the plank walls. He dropped a duffel at the foot of the stairs leading up to the loft. "We'll figure out sleeping arrangements later. Raven asked me to help her move a few things before we gathered the Charmers."

"I don't have any place to be, but I'm off anyway." Calem waved over his shoulder and slipped out the front door, leaving it open.

Kost sighed tightly. "Be back later for questioning."

"I didn't know we were interrogating anyone," Calem teased, and I rolled my lips together to keep from chuckling. Kost narrowed his eyes, but he didn't goad his brother further. Instead, he added his bag to Ozias's and moved toward the exit.

When he got to the doorframe, he paused. A tremor worked its way down the tendon of his neck. In that moment, I was convinced he had an entire conversation with himself, and gods what I wouldn't have done to be privy to those thoughts. Quietly, if not a little hopefully, he spoke over his shoulder.

"I noticed the Charmers were able to salvage some books. Maybe we could do some research. See if we're able to learn more about your powers."

"Together?" It came out in a rush and felt blunt, but it was impossible to mask my shock.

He lifted a single shoulder. "It's where I'll be until everyone is ready to meet. You're welcome to join."

And then he stepped out into the clearing as if he hadn't just shifted the world beneath my feet with his offer. For once, he wasn't commanding me to train. The way his mind immediately went to the makeshift library made me wonder... How much research had he already done? Had he been trying other methods this entire time? My throat swelled with emotion, and I steadied myself with a shaky breath before following after, cautiously optimistic about what our future might hold.

SIXTEEN

CALEM

So no, I didn't have anywhere to be, exactly, but I'd be lying if I'd said I didn't have something, or someone, in mind. Even if I didn't want to admit it, my feet did the work for me, guiding me toward an open canopy a short distance from our temporary home. At the far end of the tent, Kaori chatted with the group of Charmers we'd rescued from Wilheim.

Gods, she had been magnificent. She still was, but that day in Wilheim when she'd finally let go and shifted to her beast, I'd floundered for the first time in my life. Not because I'd been scared. The growing network of mercury veins along her arms had been so like the mercury hue in my eyes that I'd felt connected. The air around her had shimmered with a tangible power that made my very blood quiver. I'd wanted to see her—all of her—like I'd never wanted to see anyone before. So when she'd shifted into a winding, dragon-like beast that moved with the fluidity of water, I'd nearly fallen to my knees.

Granted, she'd shifted because she'd discovered the magic used to place the captive Charmers in slumber was the work of her parents, but she'd still been incredible. I never wanted to forget the sight of her wild and free charging through the halls of Wilheim. But

I seriously doubted she'd ever allow herself to slip into that state again.

I found myself at her side without really thinking, and I shot the group of rescued Charmers a blazing grin. "How's everyone holding up?"

A woman stood to greet me, and I was instantly hit with a wave of recognition. It was impossible not to see Leena in the shape of Sabine's face. Walnut-colored hair spilled over her shoulders, and she shared the same cheekbones as her daughter. She clasped her hands before her and returned my smile.

"Hi, Calem. I was wondering when you would pop up." There was something mischievous in her stare that reminded me too much of myself, and I fumbled to find the right words to answer.

"Well, I'm here now."

She chuckled at my lackluster response. Verlin, her husband and Leena's father, wrapped a gentle arm around her waist. His hazel eyes, so like his daughter's, flickered to his wife before landing on me. "We're doing just fine. Happy to help restore our homelands."

"And the others?" Kaori prompted, glancing past them to the small cluster of Charmers gathered around a bowl of grapes. We'd discovered twenty or so people hidden in an earthy crypt beneath Wilheim the day we battled Yazmin. Green vines with mysterious, glowing veins had crowned their heads, tethering them to the land. Fortunately, once the war was over, Kaori was able to decipher enough of her parents left behind instructions to safely remove the delicate plants. She still wasn't convinced she'd done everything correctly, though. With her people safely and happily sitting before her, she studied their frames with the kind of intensity Kost reserved for solving puzzles.

"Everyone is fine. I promise." Sabine's smile softened to something warm and motherly, and a forgotten twinge of longing snaked through my heart. My mom had never looked at me like that. And Sabine wasn't even Kaori's parent.

Kaori nodded once, but the tightness never left her eyes. "Please let me know if anything changes." Abruptly, she turned on her heels and cut through the tent in the direction of the clearing.

"She's been tense for a while now." Verlin brushed a hand along his jaw as he tracked Kaori's progression. "We're worried about her."

There it was again. That foreign, parental concern that had eluded me for years. I didn't know what to do with it, how to process it, but I did know Kaori—and they weren't wrong. Something was bothering her.

"I'll check on her. Promise." I flashed them a grin and waved goodbye, trotting down the same path Kaori had taken. I caught up with her quickly, and when she didn't immediately tell me to leave, I took it as a good sign. Her glossy black hair was pin straight against her back, and she loosely wrapped a strand around her pointer finger. A hint of mercury had crawled down her veins to encircle her knuckles, and my jaw clenched. For me, the strange color had settled in my eyes. No one knew why. Maybe because I was different, already full of undead magic. Every other Charmer who'd tamed the same creature as Kaori—and subsequently undergone a bestial transformation—had a network of silvery veins surrounding the puncture site. Still, I knew what would happen if that hue suddenly spread across her pale skin. I just didn't know why her control was wavering when she excelled at managing her beast at every turn.

"What's going on, Kaori?" I grazed the back of her arm, and she jolted before coming to a stop. Dark, oval eyes threatened to unearth every one of my thoughts, and I pulled my hand back. I didn't—*couldn't*—acknowledge how badly I wanted to resume that touch.

She sighed, her eyes downcast, and tipped her head toward one of her shoulders. All around us, the clearing was alive with Charmers erecting buildings, planting vegetables and fruits in designated plots, bustling from one location to the next. We stood in the center of it all, the quiet eye of the boisterous storm, completely enveloped in a strained anxiety I didn't understand. But I wanted to understand. More than anything.

"I keep waiting for something to happen," she finally said. I hung on every word, giving her the chance to sort through her thoughts. She let her hand fall away from her hair. "Why do I always find myself talking to you?"

That was unexpected. A strange tingling sensation raced over my skin, and I blinked. "What? That can't possibly be what's bothering you. Me? I'm bothering you?" A nervous bubble of laughter escaped my throat, and I busied my hands by tying my hair into a bun. "Listen, I annoy a lot of people. No need to get upset about it, just tell me to fuck off."

At that, her somber expression broke and a sound I'd never thought I'd hear graced the air between us. She giggled. It was so incredibly pure and authentic that my body froze. It only lingered between us for a split second, but I wanted to relive that moment over and over again and burn that joyous trill into my mind. I was good at making people laugh. I fell back on humor whenever I got the chance. Yet in all my days, a giggle had never sounded as sweet as hers.

And it terrified me to my core.

"You don't bother me." She started walking again, giving me a chance to strong-arm my wild emotions back into place. "I don't know how you manage it, but you make things lighter somehow. Like when you comforted me after Yazmin sent Leena that package."

So much for steeling my nerves. My pulse throbbed in my

throat as I rewound to that moment. It hadn't been much—she'd been upset, and I'd held her. Sort of. I'd been in my shadow form checking in on Hireath, and Kaori was worried about her maniacal, imprisoned parents who'd experimented on Charmers. For all the control she wielded, she'd collapsed in that moment, so I did what anyone would have done. I hugged her. And even though she couldn't physically feel me and I couldn't physically feel her, I *had* felt her.

Which is why I'd left in a hurry with nothing more than a grin. The same type of grin I was wearing now. "That's my role. I'm here to please."

The mercury-tinted veins on her knuckles receded back to the small scar on her inner wrist. We'd reached a new canopy-covered table littered with artifacts, and she picked up a few heirlooms and rearranged them with delicate fingers. "Everything is done and over with. We're rebuilding our home. So, tell me why I'm not convinced of this peace? Why do I feel like my parents had something to do with this mess? They've been imprisoned for decades, and yet..."

"You think they are responsible for the monster attacks?"

"No. I don't know." She worried her bottom lip. "They did terrible things, Calem. With Gaige's shadows behaving in an abnormal fashion and the Kitska beasts acting out... It just feels like something bigger is going on. What if they found a new way to control people from afar? What if they've tapped into some new magic?"

"That prison they're in, Galvanhold, it's inescapable. Not only that, but it nullifies magic. *All* magic." Even the name of that horrendous place set my teeth on edge. Not because going there was a gruesome way to die, but because I knew *she* was in it. Now, though, was not the time to unpack that part of my past.

"I know, it's just..." She wrapped her arms around her stomach as her words faded away.

I allowed myself one simple touch. Just another soft graze along the smooth skin of her arm. More for myself than her, because I needed to alleviate the burn in my fingers that I refused to examine. "I think sometimes it's hard to accept that everything is okay when we've been fighting for so long. But everything *is* okay, Kaori."

Slowly, she turned, and my fingers dragged around her elbow. She stared at the space where we touched, and a single crease formed between her brows. Then smoothed. Her heart-shaped lips parted a fraction. Gods, she was so damn beautiful. But she was also my friend and my mentor, and I wasn't about to screw any of that up with a dalliance that could make our future painfully awkward.

Fortunately, Kost chose that exact moment to step out of the shadows. I let my hand slide away, thankful for the first time in the history of ever for his impeccable timing. "Time for interrogations?"

Kaori's eyes widened. "Interrogations? Did something happen?"

"Calem is just being insufferable," Kost said through a forced exhale. "We're going to meet with the Charmers who witnessed or experienced a Kitska beast attack. They're already gathered in the communal dining area. I just came to retrieve him."

"Insufferable." I flashed him a grin before winking at Kaori. "Another one of my glorious traits."

She relaxed and I finally got to see the smile I'd been waiting for. Turning back to the artifacts splayed out in front of her, she reached for a quill and some spare parchment. "Go on, then. I've already heard the accounts, and I need to continue cataloging these items."

"I'll come bother you later," I said with what I hoped was a nonchalant wave. But as I stepped into the shadows to follow Kost, I caught the whispered words beneath her breath and thought about running away entirely.

SEVENTEEN

KOST

The makeshift library was no more than a handful of tables laden with antiquated tomes. Still, it was more than I expected to find, given Ocnolog had razed the city with fire. The sprawling tree that had housed the former library must have offered some protection. Tomes were currently organized by condition, ranging from singed to simply coated in dirt. When Gaige and I stepped under the canopy to examine the contents, the Charmer who'd been cataloging the books was already leaving to help his brethren with a more demanding task.

"I'm not sure we'll find anything useful," Gaige said. It was the first statement he'd uttered since we'd left the small cottage.

"It doesn't hurt to try." Gingerly, I wiped one finger along the binding of a tome. *Queen of the Butterflies.* A cursory look inside the cover indicated it was a work of fiction. Perhaps a good read, but not what we were looking for.

I knew full well that the likelihood of us finding anything that could help with Gaige's shadows was next to impossible. If Cruor didn't have any information housed within its library, I doubted the remnants of Hireath's texts did, either. Still, I was driven to try. I'd been itching to ask Leena if she'd found information on a beast that could help, but because of the nature of Gaige's and my arrival—with our injuries, followed by our quick departure to Hireath—I hadn't gleaned much. She'd made mention of one idea to test but was pulled immediately away upon returning to her homeland. That anxiety of not knowing only drove me to search more. Even if it was futile.

Gaige moved around the table and selected another tome. After flipping through a few pages, he replaced it. "I suppose I was a Charmer before I was undead. Maybe there is something here."

The sliver of hope in his voice filled me with purpose, and I snagged a smaller text covered in dust. I wiped away the grime with a cloth on the table. "It's possible."

Gaige tilted his head as his gaze shifted from my face to the book in my hands. A smirk claimed his lips. "I can say with absolute certainty, however, that that book won't help us. At least not in the sense you're thinking."

I took a closer look at the title, and heat crept up the back of my neck. *Of Love and Promise.* There was even artwork decorating the covering, an embossed, abstract tangling of bodies and arms surrounding by roses. It seemed even Charmers enjoyed the escape of a romance novel.

"I do recommend it, though." Gaige's eyes were alight with something I didn't dare name. "I quite enjoyed it. There are a number of lovely scenes, if memory serves."

My pulse roared in my ears, and suddenly I was transported back to that time we'd researched Noc's curse together. Just the two of us, Gaige and me, sequestered in Cruor's library pouring over tomes. Searching for answers. He'd gotten so close. I hadn't been ready yet to accept his—or anyone's—advances. And now...

With a hard swallow, I set the book down. "I'm glad to see you haven't lost your ability to flirt."

He chuckled. "I never lost it. I just chose not to."

Somehow, that was harder to hear. A cold numbness settled over me. "It's probably for the best."

"Oh?" His smile went stilted.

"If Yazmin's beast hadn't killed you…" No, I couldn't place the blame of us never making it on him. On his circumstance. It was me. All me. "I'm not very good at relationships. Being intimate is… difficult. We wouldn't have gotten very far."

"I don't know whether to be insulted by that or not." Gaige's expression softened. Slowly, he moved to my side and parked his hip on the table, blocking me from continuing to peruse the books. "What happened to you, Kost?"

A familiar pang of fear sparked from the scar on my chest. We'd both just agreed that we never would have made it. Well, he didn't agree, but he didn't disagree, either. And that was enough. Fear shifted to pain as something fisted my heart tight. Being near Gaige *hurt*. Far beyond any physical ailment I'd ever had. Even when I'd been stabbed above my heart. Even as I sat for weeks and waited to die.

Unable to take this conversation any further, I looked past him to the clearing full of Charmers. "We'll have to tell everyone about your shadows. About their nature, about the correlation to the monster attacks. Everything."

He went completely still beside me. "Why can't you just be honest?"

I rounded my gaze back to him. "I am being honest. We can't hide what's happening."

"Not about me." His grip on the table tightened. "We're talking about *you*. Not everything has to be about my shadows." His voice rose an octave, and thin tendrils began to wrap around his feet like vipers. Their erratic movements matched the increased rhythm of his breathing, and I straightened.

"Gaige."

"No." He didn't budge. "Maybe I'm not the only one who needs help, Kost."

His shadows wreathed his legs and lashed out against the table, scattering books. They finally caught Gaige's attention, and he glanced down at what he'd unintentionally summoned. His face blanched, and suddenly he wasn't looking at me in annoyance anymore, but fear. Panic flooded his steel-blue eyes.

"It's okay." I grabbed his wrists and tried to anchor him to me. "Try to center yourself. Slow your breathing. Imagine throwing a blanket over your power."

He yanked out of my grip and stumbled away from the table. "Don't. I can't... What if..."

"You're not going to hurt anyone." I closed the distance between us. Alarm raced through his expression, but I wouldn't run from him. I needed him to know that he wasn't alone in this. He never had been. If anyone had been failing here, it'd been me.

Slowly, I brought my hands to his once more. He twitched beneath my fingers but didn't retreat. His shadows, on the other hand, began to recede. Every breath from Gaige made them dwindle further, until they were no longer crawling across the table.

"Good." I gave him a squeeze.

The tension racking his frame lessened. His eyes fluttered closed, and the chaotic tendrils quieted. Soon, they were no more than wisps ringing his ankles. And then they were simply gone.

Gaige peeled open his eyes and looked down at the space where they used to be. "They're gone."

"Yes." I still hadn't let go.

His relieved smile was a beautiful thing. Then, he gently freed one hand to cup my face.

And kissed me. Soft. Questioning.

I froze beneath his lips, unable to wrangle my thoughts. And yet, in that moment, I didn't want to. I didn't want to think. I didn't want to weigh the pros and cons, I simply wanted to act. So I did.

I let myself sag into him and felt my arms instinctively wrap around his neck. It was as if my response released something in him because he moaned in answer. His hands moved to my waist, gripping tightly for purchase as he crushed his mouth against mine. His breath was wild, his tongue hungry. Heat rushed through my bones and cooked the air around us, and all my senses narrowed to him and the tight, demanding pressure of his fingers. This was the kiss that should have happened ages ago. And I couldn't get enough of it. I wanted more. I wanted to live in this sensation. A deep groan broke free from my chest, and I hardly recognized the sound of my own voice.

Gaige's kiss consumed me, and I knew in an instant I was doing irreparable damage to my soul. It was a mistake to be so…vulnerable, but I couldn't stop it. A part of me needed to know what we could've become. What I'd have to walk away from now to save myself, save both of us, from any future pain.

Every ounce of my being revolted at the idea of breaking our embrace, but I did it. And gods, I wasn't prepared for the twisting ache of its conclusion. Even though I'd pulled back, I couldn't convince myself to leave his arms entirely. Chest heaving, I closed my eyes as I went to war with my desires and allowed cooler emotions to prevail. When I opened them again, Gaige was staring at me, his hands still entrenched on my waist.

"Kost…" His voice was deliciously heady, and it sent me reeling. Face flush and lips damp and bruised from my kiss, he was too much to behold.

I couldn't bring myself to answer. Nothing felt right. I couldn't kiss him again—not ever if I wanted to keep my sanity—but I wanted to. I wanted to risk everything to feel this…this thrill again. But I knew wants and desires had a tendency to be fleeting, and if Gaige's feelings ever shifted, I'd never survive. I was already in too deep.

So rather than try, rather than hope and see what we could be, I shut down.

"I'd appreciate it if you didn't do that again."

Something fractured inside me. They had been my words, my request, and still they cleaved at my heart. It wasn't a clean break, either. It splintered and shattered into hundreds of shards, so that my hitched breathing was riddled with the burning pain of razor-sharp cuts. I'd been lying to myself to avoid this very feeling, thinking that vocalizing my emotions would make everything worse. I was wrong. Nothing could have prepared me for this, and no amount of hiding from the truth could have prevented the ache.

Gaige looked as if I'd slapped him. He opened his mouth to say something, but I started toward the clearing with every intent of never discussing this again.

"Wait." He caught my wrist. Just like I had done to him. "You can't walk away from this."

"Why? You've done it countless times." I refused to turn around and look at him. I was afraid that if I did, I'd see something in his gaze that would make it impossible for me to leave.

An exasperated groan met my ears. "Would you just look at me?"

"Let go of my hand, Gaige." My throat bobbed, but I forced my voice to be even. Stern. "That's an order from your guild master."

He released me then, and the raw feeling of air against my skin burned. Even so, it was better this way.

This time when I walked away, he didn't try to stop me.

I barely had a few minutes to gather myself before we sat down with the Charmers. I wasn't positive I even fully absorbed the first handful of stories detailing the monster attacks. My mind was still on Gaige. Who, infuriatingly, had chosen to sit beside me. The tension rolling off him in waves was palpable, and Ozias and Calem continued to shoot him furtive glances. But as the stories went on, time softened some of the roiling emotions, and I was able to better grasp the Charmers' accounts.

We spent several hours listening to multiple retellings, and the only thing consistent about the nature of their encounters was that they were entirely unexpected. Some had been logging in the woods and were careful not to disturb existing beast habits, yet they were bombarded by monsters just the same. Others were returning home after a beast hunt and found themselves face-to-face with what they thought were passive creatures, only to be blindsided by their vicious pursuit. Round and round the conversations went as we all asked the same questions with different slants, hoping a clue would reveal itself. But as we pushed aside tin plates, once full of food from our now devoured lunches, we were no closer to finding the cause of the seemingly random attacks.

Leena had braced her elbows on the table and steepled her hands, grazing the tips of her fingers with her lips. "Tell me again about the Havra ambush."

Another bizarre incident. Havra were docile, nymphlike creatures with bark for skin and gangly limbs. They lived in trees, fed off berries and, according to Leena, were fairly easy to tame, maintaining strong bonds with Charmers. A full-scale, strategized attack—complete with sharpened staves from broken branches—made absolutely zero sense. As the Charmer in question began to recount the story for the fifth time, I removed my glasses and set them on the table.

"What do Raven and Kaori think about all this?" Ozias asked, pitching his voice low so as not to disturb the Charmer's retelling.

Gaige shifted uncomfortably beside me; one ear tipped toward the story but his body pivoted toward us. Even with the distraction of the Charmers' accounts, I was painfully aware of his every movement. That kiss had done something to me. Tuned me into him in a way that I could've never imagined. "They've already heard these tales. They're just as confused as we are."

"Should we consider moving everyone until the problem is resolved?" Noc subtly nodded to those around us.

"They won't leave." With a grimace, Gaige picked at the stitching of his glove. "They only just came back, and they're committed to rebuilding their home. Not to mention, they've always lived around these creatures, albeit in a strained sort of harmony."

Calem drilled his fingers restlessly against the wooden tabletop. "This is getting us nowhere. What about traps? Could we contain the monsters somehow?"

"We don't even know what we'd be attempting to lure," I said. "We need more to go off of."

Noc sighed. "Maybe we'll glean more information when Leena and I visit the towns bordering the forest. We're missing something."

Indeed we were. It took everything in me not to glance at Gaige as we fell into a tense silence. Despite the variety of locations, the encounters always happened within hours of Gaige's wayward shadows. I didn't want to acknowledge that, but I didn't believe in coincidences. When those dark tendrils erupted from his frame and shot out into the woods with the speed of Lendria's only train, it suddenly made the sporadic locations less confusing. A monster attack could happen virtually anywhere his shadows traveled, all within relatively the same time frame, give or take a few hours.

Gaige had to come to grips with his role in the matter. I *needed* him to because I didn't want to be against him on this. It felt wrong to be on opposing sides after we shared...*that*. And while I believed a small part of him had come to accept what was happening, he'd yet to voice it. He'd shifted his attention back to the Charmer describing the Havra attack, but his expression was guarded. How much would he have to hear before he would admit the inevitable?

As the Charmer once again detailed the darkening woods and the rush of beasts, my ears prickled at the description. He'd said it the same way five times over, and each time one glaring, minute depiction nagged at my conscious. Darkening woods. One Havra lingering at the rear of the attack. Why didn't it strike with the rest? And the Kitska Forest was *always* dark. Sunlight rarely permeated the thick network of branches, leaves, and pinesco pods, so any additional layering of darkness meant something else was blanketing out the light. Something like shadows.

I squeezed my eyes shut and blew out a breath, steeling myself for what I feared would invoke Gaige's anger. Opening my eyes, I speared the Charmer with a pointed look. "You said 'darkening woods.' Did you see shadows?"

Gaige stiffened beside me but didn't object. A small boon. The Charmer's stare nervously bounced from Leena, to Gaige, to me. "I–I don't know. It all happened so fast."

"You said the Havras were normal beasts. But the one that didn't attack… Was it undead? A Kitska beast?" I asked.

The Charmer rolled his lips together as he stared upward, seemingly in thought. "It's possible. Kitska beasts tend to have different shades to their hides than normal beasts. This one did seem like it had been bleached of color, but again, it was dark. Hard to tell."

"Like with the Slimacks," Ozias said.

I nodded. Then I loosened a breath. "There seems to be…shadows aggravating the Kitska beasts."

"My shadows." Gaige said, voice flat. "If you're not going to say it, I will."

"Are you certain?" Leena asked as she peered at her friend, brows drawn together in concern. Beside her, Kaori and Raven mirrored her expression.

Gaige nodded once. "The shadows we've seen..." He hesitated, searching for words until he finally sighed. "They don't feel like mine, but everything indicates that they are."

"You've been making progress. I'm sure these attacks will—" Ozias started, but Gaige cut him off.

"That doesn't excuse the people I've already hurt." He looked only at me. I got the feeling that he wasn't just referring to those who'd been attacked by monsters. He was talking to *me*. The weight of his stare was so obvious—so much so that everyone at the table fell silent as they glanced between us. The surrounding air was thick with renewed tension. And no matter how hard I tried to ignore it, I couldn't even breathe without inviting it in. I was still feeling too raw, too exposed, after our kiss. We needed to find answers, to help Gaige, but in that moment, I couldn't even think. Not with him so close, with so many things left unsaid.

I stood abruptly and pushed away from the table. "If you'll excuse me." I didn't bother to offer an explanation or wait and see if they would, in fact, object to me leaving. I just didn't have the mental fortitude to school my emotions any longer. I needed space to heal and regroup. I needed to find a way to compartmentalize my desires and focus on the tasks at hand. Which was proving to be difficult, considering those tasks involved Gaige and he was the very person causing my emotions to run wild.

I'd find a way—I always did—but for now I simply needed to be alone.

EIGHTEEN

GAIGE

I hated him. I hated every inch of his flawless, smooth skin, the intricate shade of his fern-green eyes. I'd hated how he'd looked at me with such unfettered want directly after our kiss. And then buried it behind an impassive mask. I hated that my fingers still burned from with the memory of his hips in my grasp. I even hated that raw, guttural sound that had loosened in his chest when we kissed. I hated the feel of his lips, the heat of his breath.

Most of all, I hated the way he walked away.

Once he'd excused himself, I'd remained behind with the Council to explain more in depth the nature of my shadows and the correlating attacks. By the end of it all, I was emotionally exhausted. I could have happily curled up in some dark corner and tried to sleep for an age, but Leena broke away from the group and steered me toward a more private space along the quiet tree line.

"Leena, I really need a moment to myself."

"I need you to come to the beast realm with me," she said as she held out her hand.

Her words took me aback, and I barely managed to respond. "What?"

"I know how much pain I'd be in if I suddenly couldn't see my beasts. And until we try, I can't guarantee anything but..." She hesitated, considering her words as she shook her head. "There might be a way for you to visit them without another Charmer's help."

At first, her words didn't fully register. The whole reason I couldn't see my beasts any longer was because my Charmer magic was dead. The emblem on the back of my hand was no more than a faded etching of what it used to be. There wasn't a beast in this realm or the next that could restore me to my former self. And yet, a quiet ringing filled my ears.

"I don't know if I can," I said, voice suddenly hoarse.

She frowned, and her hand fell to her side. "What do you mean? I've taken Noc several times. Your powers won't prevent you from entering."

"No, I know. It's just..." I forced a swallow. "I don't know if I can lose them all over again."

Sadness filled her expression. "Oh, Gaige. I can only imagine what you're feeling. I know it's a lot to risk, but I need you to trust me." She held out her hand again. "Please."

I considered it for a long moment, too scared to acknowledge the small spark of hope she'd ignited in me. If I spent too much time examining it, I'd most certainly walk away. So before I could do that, I took her hand.

The moment our fingers interlocked, the rosewood Charmer's symbol on the back of her hand bloomed into a magnificent tree. Roots wrapped around her fingers as branches and vines climbed up her arm, trailed beneath her clothing, and eventually sprung to life across her neck and cheekbones. Flowers blossomed along her temples and framed her eyes, and then a luminous white light washed over us.

Panic smothered me in a rush, and a cool sweat beaded along my hairline. "Wait, Leena. I'm not sure—"

But we were already gone. I slammed my eyes shut as a soothing warmth whispered against my skin. A gentle breeze tinged with the scent of lilac and vanilla tickled my nose, and my knees went weak. It was too much. Quick, shallow breaths racked my body, and I fell to the earth.

This was a mistake. I shouldn't have come. I can't do this.

"Gaige." Leena's voice was gentle. "Open your eyes."

Sitting back on my heels, I finally allowed myself to look. The beast realm was everything I remembered it to be. Lush, rolling fields dotted with white flowers came flush with a dense forest. Pine, oak, ash—all manners of trees grew together in harmony to suit the creatures that lived here. The soft but insistent tinkling of metal pulled at my senses, and I dragged my gaze across the clearing to find a weeping willow with dripping, pink strands. With each passing breeze, bronze keys winked at me from beneath the leaves.

Words escaped me as I drank everything in. A glistening, sparkling blue pond complete with fist-sized lily pads and tall, swaying reeds. The snowcapped mountains framed by the woods. The impossibly blue sky, completely free of clouds. A shadow formed overhead and raced across the ground at breakneck speed. A low, grating groan rumbled the earth, and she tipped her head toward the sun with a blazing smile on display.

Wind swept across the plains in a sudden gust as a dragon with stark-white scales and gleaming, ruby eyes cut through the air. He temporarily blocked out the sun as he moved overhead, and then he dove. Wings pinned to his back, he barreled toward the earth and then pulled up at the last moment possible. He sped past us, and the squall rippling off his monstrous body smacked into us in earnest. Leena only laughed as the monster who'd once wreaked havoc on our world climbed higher and higher into the sky.

A mixture of fear and awe rooted me in place, and I finally found my voice. "Is that Ocnolog?"

She raised teasing brow. "Who else would it be?" The magnificent creature roared in answer, and then he shot an unnecessary torrent of blazing ocher flames toward the sun. Leena rolled her eyes. "I never summon him. He belongs here, with Celeste."

Every fiber in my being went taut. Celeste, Goddess of Beasts. She was the reason Charmers existed, the reason we—they—could tame magical beings and create lasting, sacred bonds with creatures all over the world. If she saw me now... Dread added weight to my limbs, and I sank further into the ground. "You've met with Celeste?"

"A few times." Leena tracked a smaller shadow that had erupted from the treetops to fly alongside Ocnolog. After a breath, it peeled off and dove toward us with the same exuberant energy as the dragon. Leena threw her arms open wide and waited for her beast to land. Her legendary feline beast, Onyx, hit the ground running. Corded muscles bunched and loosened beneath his glossy, black hide, and his outstretched wings quivered with anticipation. Vibrant teal and emerald feathers like that of a peacock shimmered in the brilliant sunlight. With a happy yowl, he bounded forward, crashing his massive head into her chest. She wrapped her arms around his neck and stroked the length of his feathered mane, dawdling her fingers along the crown of gold nestled between his ears.

I crumbled in on myself in that moment. I didn't know why she'd brought me here, what she'd hope to achieve out of showing me everything I'd lost. I could never have...this. Not without her. Not without another Charmer. What on earth gave her the idea that I could? I didn't belong here. I didn't belong anywhere. I dropped my head into my hands and focused only on breathing. Everything else was too painful, so I simply let my senses fall away.

Something wet and cold ghosted my ear. I flinched but didn't look up. I couldn't bear to witness anymore of the realm, no matter how badly Onyx wanted my attention. An insistent, disgruntled chuff sounded, and wet spittle coated my skin as if the beast had forcefully sneezed.

"Please just..." Hot tears stung the back of my eyes. "Send me back to Hireath."

Leena didn't respond, but an unrelenting muzzle bruised my side, and large, flat teeth nipped at my skin. I yanked my hands away, ready to demand we go back, when my mind went blank. A stunning mare with a shimmery, ebony coat had dipped her head low to try to snag my attention. She shook her mane when I finally met her stare, and turquoise, fuchsia, and emerald auroras bled to life across her body, as if she were birthed from the galaxy itself. Nickering in earnest, she nearly speared me with the glowing, moon-white horn between her ears, and she thrust her wings open wide.

"Valda." My fingers trembled. I'd resigned myself to never seeing her again. She tossed her head back and reared up on her hind legs. With a loud, energetic whinny, she pawed at the earth. In response, the plains and woods and mountains came alive with beast calls. The ground rumbled with the stampede of approaching creatures, the heady thudding of hooves and the flapping of wings. Beasts flocked to me in a rush, shepherded my direction by none other than Okean. He let out a reassuring caterwaul before knocking his head against Onyx in a friendly hello.

A waterfall of tears cascaded down my cheeks, and I sobbed as I fell back to the earth and simply let all of my creatures ambush me. I don't know how long I lay there, crying unabashedly while wrapping my fingers in fur and stroking scales. I could've stayed there forever. But in the back of my mind, I knew no matter how powerful Leena had grown, she wouldn't be able to keep us in the beast realm forever. Soon, we'd have to return. Soon, I'd have to say goodbye. Because so far, I hadn't seen anything that proved otherwise, and I was too afraid to ask and have my suspicions confirmed.

Gently rearranging my beasts, I stood up and stroked the length of my Zavalluna's neck. Leena watched quietly, the rosewood markings along her face still bright and intact. I still had time. When they began to recede toward her hand, I'd worry about farewells.

Valda leaned into my touch with a content sigh, and I pressed my forehead to her coat. "Hey, girl."

"You never did tell me how you ended up with a Zavalluna." Leena inched toward my beast and extended her hand. Valda sniffed her knuckles twice before pawing at the ground and ducking her head in approval.

"I spent some time in Allamere before I became a Council member." I raked my fingers through Valda's fine mane.

"Some time?" Leena raised an incredulous brow as she trailed a fuchsia whorl along Valda's chest. "I thought you had to befriend a mage for several years before taming a Zavalluna was even a remote possibility."

A different kind of sorrow settled over me, and my smile turned sad. "I lived there with someone I loved very much. He made it a point to help me charm Valda as a birthday gift one year." Valda's glassy eyes found mine, as if she, too, missed the arms of my former lover. "He died suddenly."

"I'm so sorry," Leena murmured.

"Don't be. I mean it," I said. "It was a good relationship, but one I've long since mourned. I was actually just feeling like I could be with someone again before all this happened." I gestured to my body, knowing full well she'd understand what I meant.

"With Kost?" Her quiet question made me flinch, but I had no reason to lie to her.

"Yes."

She rolled her lip into her mouth, considering me with scrunched-up brows. "And now that's not possible because of what you are?"

"Yes. No. I don't know." I sighed, and Valda thrust her snout under my hand so I could rub the length of her muzzle. "Every time I think we make some progress, he does something completely asinine, and I'm reminded of why I am the way I am.

"I have no ability to care for or visit my beasts, let alone summon them. The only reason I'm even here right now is because of you." I stepped away from my beasts so I could throw my hands wide to the realm around us. It was just so…unfair. I gave my life to protect all of this, and my reward was being barred from experiencing what I loved.

Leena kept her hand on Valda, but her soft gaze was trained on me. She didn't say anything, and the silence only made it impossible for me to stay quiet. Somehow, being here had broken open a dam in me and I needed to simply let everything *out*.

"I hate myself, Leena." Tears stung the back of my eyes. "I hate what I've become. I don't even have a purpose anymore. How am I supposed to find something like that again?"

"Have you actually tried?" she asked.

I bit back a scoff. "Of *course* I've tried." Lifting my hand, I yanked off my leather glove and exposed the faded Charmer's symbol. "But this always reminds me of what I lost, and I don't know how to move beyond that." My voice broke and my veins lit with fire. How did no one understand this? How could they not see that the very thing that made me whole had been ripped from my dead fingers?

"I am *nothing* without this. You wouldn't let Noc turn you. I thought you of all people would understand." My hand fell limply by my side.

"I do." Her answer was riddled with pain, but she didn't shy away from my glare. "But I know you're more than just your power—both the one you used to have and the one you have now."

I'd done enough talking for the both of us, and I didn't feel like admitting she was right. After a minute, she blew out a breath and turned on her heels, stalking toward the pink willow tree. She snagged a single bronze key from within its strands and returned to stand before me. Jaw set tight and eyes defiant, she placed her hands on her hips.

"No one in this world knows how you feel. No Charmer, to our knowledge, has ever been changed before. You are alone in your experience, but you are not *alone*."

My already-prepared retort died on my lips.

Stance softening a touch, she held out her hand. "I can't give you back your powers. I could make you a key for every creature here, but both you and I know that wouldn't really work, either." She waited for me to nod before continuing. "But I can give you this."

With her free hand, she palmed Valda's neck and the space around her ignited in a stunning, rosewood hue. The key in her hand glowed with an inner light in response, and magic snapped through the air.

A sudden surge of adrenaline pounded through my veins. "What are you doing?"

"Valda wanted this." The rosewood glow died, and the key returned to its normal metallic hue. "You haven't been forsaken, Gaige. You just have to find your way again."

She grabbed my ungloved hand and pressed the key tight into my palm. My fingers curled around the warm metal, and Valda's bond threaded through my being to wrap itself around my heart, right next to Okean's. And then my Zavalluna tossed her head to the sky and ignited her magic. Effervescent light effused from her horn as a peculiar tingling prickled along my hand. At first, I thought it was my former bond with Valda solidifying once again, but the sensation shifted to that of a fresh burn being exposed to the sun. Wincing, I finally glanced down.

The breath in my lungs disappeared in a rush. My Charmer's emblem. Gone was the smeared, charcoal etching, and in its place was an inked black mark. The citrine hue was missing, and I got the feeling that it wasn't permanent, that it would only last as long as Valda's power. But I didn't care because I could feel my tie to the beast realm again. It pumped through my being with every heartbeat and rendered me completely motionless. Slowly, I dragged my gaze to Leena.

"Zavallunas amplify bestial power. You're not a beast, but the connection and love you still feel for your creatures is tangible. It's real, Gaige, and they experience it, too. Valda can strengthen the magic in their bonds enough to open the door." She closed her hands around mine. "You can't summon them to our world like you used to, but when you summon her, you can visit the beast realm whenever you want."

A strangled sob ratcheted through my chest. I threw my arms around Leena and buried my face in the crook of her neck. She enveloped me in a hug so warm and full that my legs threatened to give out beneath the weight of her support.

You are not alone.

"I'm sorry I didn't think of it sooner," she whispered. "Actually, you have Kost to thank for this."

"Kost?" I couldn't keep the shock from my voice, and I pulled out of her embrace. "How?"

"He came to me early on searching for answers. I don't think he's ever stopped searching, Gaige." She gave me a meaningful look. "Kost is… Well. I don't have to tell you. But he cares, and you know it. He's been trying to make things better since the moment you were raised."

The world seemed to tilt on its axis, and I steadied myself against Valda. "All this time…" Shame burned through me. "Here

I thought no one understood, that no one was capable of comprehending my pain or helping me through this.

"I was so lost in my new...existence that I didn't even bother to search for answers. I used to... I used to be so much more involved. But Kost kept going, even when I refused."

Her knowing look was more sobering than anything she could have said, and I realized in that moment what a colossal fool I'd been all that time. Still, she didn't hesitate to remind me.

"You're stubborn," she said, and I couldn't help but chuckle. She rolled her eyes as she continued on. "But you are kind and loyal and brilliant and so many other wonderful things outside of your powers. You still have purpose, I promise. That's what we've all been trying to tell you."

Some louder than others. Kost's visage flashed to the forefront of my mind, and I sighed. He was still a prick sometimes, an absolute ass, with a cold fastidiousness he wore as a shield between him and everyone else, but Leena was right—he cared. I still wasn't sure if it was enough to bridge the monstrous gap separating us from each other, but I didn't have to blame him anymore. I'd made the choice to remain in this world, and I carried the responsibility of unearthing my new place in it.

"Thank you, Leena." I undid the chain holding Okean's key and added Valda's to it. "There aren't enough words in the world to tell you how much this means to me."

"You're welcome, Gaige." She wrapped me in one last squeeze. "For now, though, we have to go. Noc is waiting for me so we can travel to the border towns."

Brushing both keys with light fingers, I nodded. "And I have to figure out how to stop my shadows from aggravating the Kistka beasts." I glanced at her, waiting for judgment or apprehension. I found none of it. "I'll train. I'll master the shadows and bring peace to the monsters."

And myself. Leena took my hand without another word, summoning her power to transport us back. I'd expected devastation. Despair. Agony. Instead, when we left behind the beast realm and my creatures with it, the only thing I felt was hope.

NINETEEN

GAIGE

We'd lost track of time in the realm, and when we manifested outside the small settlement, the waning sun was already hiding behind the trees. A dusky purple sky dotted with the beginnings of stars stretched on endlessly, and the burgeoning call of nightingales lilted from the forest. The Council was already waiting—minus Kost. I frowned at his absence but stalled briefly to bid Noc and Leena farewell.

Once she'd summoned Onyx and they took flight, I turned to Ozias. "Where's Kost?"

"In the house." Ozias shifted uncomfortably, and he gripped the back of his neck.

"We're going to eat," Calem said, gesturing to the communal table where Kaori and Raven were already seated with plates of fruit, cheeses, and bread. "Tell him to stop being an idiot, and then tell him to join us." He paused, giving me a hardened once-over. "You too."

I couldn't help but blink. "What?"

"Man, for you two being so damn smart, you're really fucking dense," Calem said as he strolled away.

Ozias gave a small shrug. "Just check on him, will ya?"

"Sure." I frowned at them as they left, but I was still too overjoyed by my time in the beast realm to care. And more importantly, I had Kost to thank for it. I wanted to run into his arms and kiss him senseless, but after this morning's incident, I wasn't sure that would be welcomed. If he didn't want that, then I'd respect his wishes. But he deserved my thanks nonetheless. I made my way to our temporary home quickly, trying to formulate an apology worthy of everything I'd done. Every tasteless jab, every half-baked assumption. I just feared he'd refuse to accept it, because I couldn't imagine an existence without him—platonic or romantic.

Pushing open the door, I entered the quiet house to find Ozias and Calem had unpacked their belongings, claiming the separate beds atop the loft area. My untouched bag was still on the small, tufted couch—likely where I'd be sleeping—which meant Kost had marked the single bedroom as his.

I knocked on the door. The sound echoed around me, and the silence that followed was grating. After a minute scraped by, I tried the handle and found it unlocked.

"Kost?" I peeked into his room. No one answered. Pushing the door open, I stepped into the small space dominated by a canopy bed. Twisted tree limbs with nimble branches arched toward each other, and a dusty-pink tulle overlay stretched above it like a cloud. A candle encased in a glass lantern had been lit, at least, and it flickered at me from the nightstand table. Kost's bag was propped up against its legs, full and unopened. I glanced to the small, poplar armoire. We might not have been staying long, but I highly doubted he wouldn't have organized the contents of his bag into the appropriate drawers.

A frustrated grunt sounded from somewhere outside, and I leaned against the windowsill to find Kost whirling in practiced patterns with a shadow rapier in hand.

Of course he was training. Still, the neatly packed bag nagged at me. Had he been running drills since the Council meeting? I knew how much I appreciated activity when my mind was restless. A thread of guilt snaked through my gut. No doubt he had a lot to think about. I exited the house and quietly moved around back, lingering in the shadows to watch him without immediately alerting him to my presence. He'd rolled the sleeves of his shirt above his elbows, and I couldn't help but study the tantalizing, corded muscles of his forearms. The top button of his tunic was undone, but his sable vest was still in place. He summoned glittering, ink-black diamonds that moved wildly without any decipherable pattern, and he swiftly struck each one with his blade.

When he vanquished the last one, he let his arm go lax by his side. The tip of his rapier nicked a single blade of grass. "What can I do for you, Gaige?"

Even with his back turned to me, he'd detected my presence. I stepped away from the sturdy wall of the house and walked toward him. "Ozias and Calem said to join them for dinner."

"I'll have to decline." He summoned more floating diamonds and poised to strike the nearest one. "I'm not hungry."

"Me neither." I tracked his precise movements with a mixture of awe and want. Our kiss had keyed me into his body with newfound longing. I'd always desired him, but now it was an ache that'd gone on for too long, and I itched to taste him again. Several times over if he'd allow it.

When I didn't leave, he let out a tight sigh. "Is there something else I can do for you? I hardly doubt you're here to practice shadow work." A single diamond remained, and he jabbed it with a furious rapidness that seemed entirely unnecessary.

"I just returned from the beast realm. Leena found a way for me to visit my beasts again. I won't be able to stay as long as I used to or summon them here, but at least I can see them." I grazed the keys hanging about my neck, unable to keep the smile from my face. "She said it was because of you."

He stilled at that. "Me?"

I took his question as permission to inch closer. "Yes, you. She said you visited her when all this started."

"You needed connection." With a quick sweep of his arm, he fashioned another annoying barrage of diamond targets. "You didn't seem to be getting it from…anyone here, so I looked for an alternative."

"Thank you." Those words hardly seemed like enough to convey the gratitude I was feeling, but he wasn't exactly making it easy.

"I'm glad it worked." He speared three targets at once. The distorted wisps fell about him in a mess before disappearing into the night. "Anything else? If not, I'd rather be alone."

I let out a wordless, frustrated exhale. "Would you just look at me, Kost?" Here I'd just shared with him news that promised to bring me joy and peace, and he hadn't even deigned me worthy of a glance. He would rather stab stupid, harmless shadows into obliteration than talk. About my newfound ability, about us… And I was fucking over it. Clenching my hands into fists, I focused on the remaining diamonds hanging about us. I thought about all our missed opportunities, our hedged words and restrained desires. It was finally time for both of us to stop circling around each other and speak plainly.

Simultaneously, the diamonds exploded in glittering black stardust. Ink-black particles gracefully descended to the earth, and Kost spun in place to finally, *finally*, look at me. Shock plastered his expression, but he masked it behind a flinty glare within seconds.

"What do you want?" he asked. I hated that it sounded like a threat instead of a question.

Frustration simmered through my voice. "A 'Thank the gods you got your beasts back' would be a nice start."

His knuckles turned white. "I *am* thankful you got your beasts back. I'm so thankful that you can finally focus on training and getting your shadows under control. I'm so thankful that, unlike the rest of us, you've now lost nothing. Maybe now I can finally stop blaming myself for your predicament."

"Lost nothing?" Part of me knew that it was dangerous to approach an undead assassin while he brandished a very deadly weapon, but I didn't care. "Kost, I still died. I lost *me*."

"And so did I!" He chucked his weapon to the side, and it clattered against stone before vanishing in a puff of smoky tendrils.

"This again? I know you died. Everyone at Cruor has died. I'm sorry I'm not like—"

"I lost *you*." His gaze cut into me with the precision of a blade. "I lost you when you died, and I lost you again when you rose because you weren't the same. And I knew that would be the case, that it would be a struggle every step of the way, and I was more than willing to face every obstacle at your side, but you refused to even *try*. You gave up, and it took all *this* to make you even willing to try, when all the rest of us were fighting so hard to—" He cut himself off and took a sharp breath before finishing, "You always say that I can't possibly comprehend what you've endured. The feeling is entirely mutual." His lip curled upward, and he jerked his gaze away.

I didn't know why it'd taken me so long to realize the depth of Kost's feelings. Leena was right—I had been stubborn. Thick, really. So wrapped up in myself, I hadn't picked up on the small pieces of Kost's past that he had given me. I didn't have all the details, but I didn't need them. Not to see his struggles with intimacy, vulnerability. The fear of abandonment. It was all at the root of whatever heartache still plagued him. He may have buried his past, but it changed who he was after death. A tingling current of electricity coursed through me as realization as Leena's words filled my mind.

He cares, and you know it.

Deeply. Truly. So much so that the thought of losing me or hurting me was a trigger for him, and he pulled away… Only to hurt us both. Much like he triggered me with his cold assessments and seemingly callous approach. But all the while he was working. Trying. And I just… I didn't see it. Yet all the while he was seeing *me* shut down, push him away. Seemingly abandoning him and starting the vicious cycle all over again.

Fuck, we were a mess, but I didn't want to toe the line any longer. Because I knew in my heart that together, we could be whole.

"Kost, I'm sorry." I was fairly certain it was the exact opposite of what he expected me to say.

His jaw clenched and unclenched. "You have nothing to apologize for."

"I do." Sighing, I tipped my head to the night sky. "I don't even know where to start. I'm just…sorry. For everything."

I swore he stopped breathing all together. "I'm sorry, too." His answer was surprisingly soft. Broken, even. Gods, did I want to make it better. I wasn't sure if I could, but I wanted to try. If he'd let me.

Slowly, I closed the space between us. He watched every move with cautious eyes, even taking a single, small step backward when I got too close. That was the distance, then. I'd respect that.

"Can we please, please talk about earlier?" I couldn't even bring myself to say the word. *Kiss.* My throat was tight and raspy, my heart cantering at an unhealthy pace against my rib cage. I needed to know if there was a chance for something more. He might have been interested before, but we'd done so much to each other since I'd been raised. Whatever path we chose now, in this moment, would be final. It had to be.

He said absolutely nothing, and the silence nearly cleaved me in two. I wondered if this was how he felt every time I insinuated that I didn't care about him. Shoulders deflating, I let out a quiet sigh and turned to go.

"I'll leave you be."

"I don't want you to leave."

It was so subdued, so hushed, that I almost mistook his response for the breeze sifting through the leaves. But when I turned around, he'd rolled his lips together as if he couldn't believe he'd allowed himself to speak his truth. This time when I closed the distance between us, he didn't retreat. His somber stare shattered my heart, and I lightly caressed the smooth line of his jaw with my ungloved hands.

Kost's eyes went wide as his gaze flickered to my hand and then to my face. He searched for something in my expression, and then he let out a ragged breath before closing his eyes. "I walked away because I don't know how to do this. I… It's been *decades*, Gaige."

"And that's reason enough not to try?"

Emotion raged in his eyes. "You don't know…"

"You're right. I don't." I let one hand fall to his waist and brought him in closer. "But whenever you're ready, I'll listen. And until then, I'll wait. I don't need to know what happened to know how badly you hurt. I can see it. I'm sorry I didn't see it sooner."

A strangled, wordless sound escaped his barely parted lips. "Gods, Gaige I want you so bad the thought of it just tears me up inside. Not having you is torture. The only thing worse would be having you and then losing you."

A thrill rang through me at his declaration. Finally, *finally*, I knew where I stood with him. We had a chance. We could try—if he'd dare to try with me.

“We can figure this out, Kost.” My voice was low. Hopeful. He shivered at its sound. “Imagine what our lives would be like if we actually worked together toward something instead of against each other.”

“Like we used to?” One corner of his mouth pulled upward ever so slightly, and the sight brought a prickling heat to the back of my eyes.

“Yeah. Like we used to.” Back before I died. Back when things were simpler, and the only reason he’d shy away was because of my flirtatious nature—not my bitterness. And even though he was the reason for my existence now—my new, undead life—that suddenly didn’t seem like a bad thing at all.

“I tried to hate you; I really did.” I laughed more at myself than him and was pleased to hear his own chuckle. I let the sound fill me up entirely, and then I tilted his chin so our foreheads were pressed together. “The truth is, Kost, I’m not sure I could live without you, either.”

He relaxed into my hold as his eyes fell to my lips, and that was all the invitation I needed. Softly, I pressed my lips to his. This time, he didn’t stiffen beneath my kiss. He melted. As he slid his arms around my neck, he pressed every inch of himself flush with me. My throat swelled with emotion, and I hugged him close. I hadn’t realized how much I truly needed him until that moment. And, apparently, how much he’d truly needed me.

When he broke our kiss, I didn’t complain. Not vocally, anyway. All I wanted was to feel him everywhere, all at once, but everything about tonight had to be Kost’s decision.

Longing swirled in his heavy-lidded gaze, but another emotion I recognized all too well threaded through his stare: fear. “I–I can’t just…” He cleared his throat. “Where do we stand, Gaige?”

“I thought we just made that pretty clear.” I trailed a finger along his jaw, down his neck, behind his ear. I reveled in the way gooseflesh followed everywhere I grazed. "Neither of us want to move forward without the other."

"I just..." He looked away, flustered. "I know it sounds silly to ask for more, but..."

I pressed my finger against his lips. "Not silly." Nothing about this was silly. I wanted him to feel safe and secure in my arms. I never wanted to see that errant fear of abandonment again. We both had emotional scars, and I had no intention of giving or receiving any more.

Slowly, I placed a kiss on his forehead, content to end our evening with that. "I'll say it however many times you need me to: I want you, Kostya. Only you. And unless you ask me to leave, I'm not going anywhere."

Kost's smile—real and precious and so damn stunning—wrecked me to my core. "Thank you." He angled my chin back down and, much to my delight, stole another kiss from my lips. And another. The slide of his tongue against mine was slow and deliberate, and it drove me absolutely wild. I found my hand slipping down his chest of its own accord. His heart thrummed rapidly against my palm, just as his hands pressed tighter against my back.

"Remind me why I didn't say anything sooner?" he murmured as I risked a soft kiss against the hollow of his throat. A quiet moan egged me on, so I trailed my lips along the length of his neck, halting just beneath his ear.

"You're not as smart as you think?"

He laughed. Loudly. "That's proving to be true." Then, he playfully nipped my bottom lip before stilling, as if the action had totally caught him by surprise. "Sorry, I..."

"Don't apologize." My voice was gruff, my breathing tight. I tried in vain to mask the want brimming to a head within me, but the way his eyes slanted to my throat told me he knew. With aching slowness, he leaned in closer. He hesitated there for a breath, no more than a sliver of air between our mouths, before lightly sucking on my bottom lip.

I held out as long as I could. I don't know how much time actually passed as I let him explore with his tongue, his teeth, but when his kiss became more demanding, I answered in kind with a bruising kiss of my own. We shuffled backward until we hit the wall of the house, and the wood creaked with our combined weight. Kost let out a startled gasp, but he didn't stop me. Instead, he wrenched his fingers in my hair and tilted his hips against me.

I abandoned his lips for his neck and dropped one hand to his waist, where I tugged at his tunic. I hadn't meant to do anything more than anchor myself to him, but his shirt came untucked from his breeches, and he stiffened.

I pulled back and gave him space to breathe. To assess. "I'm sorry."

"No, it's not that." His breathing was hard, his words full of heat. "I was just… I *liked* it."

"So you wanted me to stop?" I asked, trying to temper my puzzlement as best I could.

"Quite the opposite." A flush crawled over his cheeks and colored the tops of his ears. "If we keep going…"

"We don't have to do anything else." My body screamed at me for uttering those words. But for Kost, I would always put my desires to the side to make him feel comfortable.

"Let's just go inside." He cut a furtive glance to our surroundings. I could still hear the faraway laughter of Charmers enjoying each other's company over dinner, the trill of nightingales and occasionally snapping of twigs as beasts moved about. Truth be told, I hadn't paid much attention to anything other than him. I hadn't thought of how exposed he might feel.

I offered my hand and thankfully, he took it. Once we were safely indoors, I expected us to remain in the living room. Neutral territory, as it were, without any implications. But he tugged on my hand and guided us toward the bedroom, shutting the door quietly behind me.

"Kost." I swallowed twice.

"Can you just...lay with me?" His request was so small, so vulnerable. My heart broke for him in that moment. How long had he walled himself off? When was the last time he felt any semblance of love? Cupping his chin in my hands, I captured his lips with mine.

"Of course."

He sighed into my kiss, and we crawled into bed together. For a long time, neither of us spoke. We simply explored. He'd trail the length of my arm, the curve of my neck, the collar of my tunic. And I'd do the same, all the while coming back for kisses that grew deeper with every passing moment. Our quiet exploration was soft and tender, and I would've spent the rest of my life doing exactly this with him. He'd made me feel so many raw emotions since the day we met, but most of all he made me *happy*. I hoped I made him happy, too. I pressed my body against him, slanting my lips once again over his and molding to him so we were flush at every possible connection.

He arched into my touch as his hands roamed over my back before seeking purchase in my loose tunic. And then one hand drifted to my waistline, and a single finger ghosted the exposed skin between my shirt and trousers. A shiver raced down my spine.

"Now we're even," he murmured. "Unless..." His fingers skated along my lower abdomen.

I let out a low groan. "This hardly seems fair."

"Guess it's your turn to make us even."

My heart skipped a beat, and I shifted so my hand was once

again beneath his shirt. Smooth skin met my touch, and my breathing ratcheted up a notch. “The vest makes it hard to fully explore.”

“Take it off, then.”

Fuck, this was going to be difficult. Still, I didn’t dare deny him. I undid the buttons along his sternum as he peppered kisses down my neck, making it hard to focus. When I’d finally freed him of the thing, he brought my hand immediately back to his chest to address his tunic.

“Kost.” I fingered a button, unsure of whether or not to continue. “Are you sure?”

“Just be slow.” And then he started on my tunic. When I got to the bare skin of his chest, I let my fingers wander across the planes of his body, the defined cuts of his torso and stomach. The scar above his heart. I hovered there for a moment, and a tremor of uncertainty, of pain, filled his eyes. I wanted to know everything about him, even the things he despised. But for now, just being with him was enough. When he decided to tell me about his past, I wanted it to be his choice alone.

Gently, I kissed the scar once before moving on. I took my time removing every article of his clothing. With each piece of fabric that fell to the floor, I paused and lavished the freshly exposed skin with kisses. I wanted to appreciate every inch of him with my hands, my mouth, my eyes. I didn’t want him to doubt for a moment that I wanted to be here. I couldn’t fathom being anywhere else. And I willed him to feel that truth with every bruising kiss, every caress from my tongue, every purposeful look as I delighted in the feel of his body.

The last thing I removed was his glasses. It felt fitting, somehow, to save them until the end. “You know, I bought you a replacement pair in Moeras.”

He blinked. “When?”

"That's why I was late to dinner." I let my fingers dawdle along his temple where the wire frames normally sat. "It was supposed to be an olive branch of sorts."

"What happened to them?"

I bit my lip to keep my smile somewhat in check. "I threw them against the wall."

He chuckled. "Of course you did."

I caught the tail end of his laugh with my lips. "Gods, do I love that sound."

Kost sighed and dragged his fingers down my chest, halting at the waistband of my trousers. It was the one thing he had yet to take off. My breath hitched as his eyes met mine, and then his fingers tugged at buttons. I felt them come undone at the same time Kost's breath quickened against my neck.

I opened my mouth to speak, but he stopped me in my tracks. "I want this. Do you?"

The question sent a tremor of panic racing through his stare, and his fingers paused.

I rolled over so I was positioned on top of him, arms braced on either side of his head. "Yes. Gods, Kost, I want it. I want to feel every inch of you."

Heat and lust filled Kost's gaze as he looked up at me from his back, and he pulled my face to his. My lips parted for his demanding tongue, and I gave in to the sensation of him entirely. His hands racing down my back and then anchoring into my hips. The insistent need swelling between us as our bodies instinctively ground against each other. The broken, breathy exhales and moans. The taste of salt—of him—on my tongue as I peppered his neck and collarbone with kisses. I only paused long enough to fully remove my pants so that there was nothing left between us. *Nothing at all.* No clothes. No unspoken truths. No fears. Just us. My breath hitched at the visceral intensity of his stare. I'd never seen anything like it in my entire life. And that look was solely for me. I slanted my lips over his so as not to say something too disastrous too soon. We'd pent up so many feelings for so long I wasn't sure what was right and what was wrong. Still, I knew in my soul that I'd fallen in love with him ages ago—and never fell out of it.

For now, though, this was enough.

Breaking our kiss, I explored his chest and stomach with my tongue. His quiet, strangled groans filled me with want, and I paused at his strained cock. A bead of moisture had pearled at the tip, and I ghosted my fingers along its length.

He twitched in response. "Fuck."

His rare, breathy curse only made my arousal more intense. But just as my slow perusal of his body, I wanted him to feel my devotion with every touch. This wouldn't be a one-time thing. This was a forever thing. Slowly, I ran my tongue along him until I reached the tip. And then I took him fully inside my mouth.

With another delicious curse, he bucked into me and I was forced to pin his waist in place with my arm. I sucked deeply, moving without really thinking. And he watched it all with hazy, wanton eyes and parted lips. The sight undid me, and I dropped a hand to my cock. Already slick with my own desire, I stroked in time with the thrusts of his hips.

"Gaige," he gasped as he snaked his hands through my hair, "I want..."

I pulled away for a moment, and my mind cursed at me for abandoning the sensation of his hardened length in my mouth. "Tell me."

He propped himself up on his elbows, the light of the candle catching on the glistening beads of sweat across his chest. A sinful blush colored his cheeks. I knew he struggled with intimacy, and voicing this carnal want would be hard. But I wouldn't proceed without it. I wanted to know that he was comfortable. Secure. Anything less, and I'd pull back. We had an eternity to figure this out together.

"I want you inside me."

My heart hammered in my throat. "Okay."

"It's…it's been a while." His blush deepened, and I reached up to brush my thumb along his cheek.

"We can wait."

He chewed on his lip. The action was so out of character for him, so unbelievably vulnerable and honest. I knew that I'd never have the strength to deny his request when he wanted me so earnestly, and seeing his reaction only deepened the insatiable throb in my groin.

"Hold on."

I left him strewn on the bed in all his naked glory and stole a throw blanket from the basket by the dresser. Wrapping it around my waist, I poked my head out of the door to thankfully find the house quiet and made a beeline for my bag on the couch. Digging around in the smallest pocket, I extracted a small jar of lubricant and hurried back to the bedroom.

I stilled in the doorway, unable to get enough of the sight of Kost naked. It was torture to wait when I knew he wanted me inside him, but I was committed to searing this magnificent image of him into my mind forever.

When I could hold out no longer, I strode across the room to clamber over him. All at once my mouth was on him again, my hands traveling the length of his body as if the mere minutes we'd spent apart had been an eternity. Kost responded the same, and he gave a forceful tug on my hair to expose my neck. He nipped at my skin before dragging his mouth to mine and snaring my bottom lip.

I struggled to keep my desires in check. A deep ache filled me to the brim as he repositioned himself with his back to my chest. Yet, as much as he clearly wanted it, I knew we'd need to be slow. Gentle. Leaning over, I started by kissing the space where his neck and shoulder met. Then, down the length of his spine. Minutes dragged by in time to his blissful exhales of pleasure. When I reached his hips, I lathered two fingers into the slick lubricant and teased his crease. He shivered in response, so I lingered there for a moment while continuing to worship his body with my tongue. He pressed into my dawdling fingers, and I allowed one small touch. One soft circle of his rim. His sinful moan almost did me in.

"Please." It was a breathless question full of lust, and I didn't have the strength to deny him. Nor did I want to. I slipped my other hand around his waist to grasp his cock as I slid one finger in. Kost tensed around me, and I waited for him to adjust. I didn't care if it took us all night. Just watching him twist and tremble beneath me, hearing his raw and carnal reactions, was pleasure enough. When he began to rock into me, I resumed the steady pump of my fist over his cock. We moved like that for minutes, hours, I didn't know. I'd coax another finger in, allow for him to relax, and then start up again. It was torturous. It was wondrous. It was perfect.

At one point, Kost settled into my fingers and arced his back, glancing over his shoulder and spearing me with a heated look. He dragged his fingers over my lips before cupping the back of my neck and pulling me in for a kiss.

He whispered against my lips, "I want you, Gaige. I'm ready."

With a shuddering breath of anticipation, I removed my fingers and positioned myself against his crease. Want throbbed through me, the evidence of my own arousal already beading from the tip. Gently, I nudged his hole. He tensed in anticipation, and I slowly inched my way in.

"Fuck." He keeled forward and gripped the branches of the headboard for purchase, the muscles along his back corded and downright seductive. Just like before, I took my time. The sensation of him drawing me in, little by little, was delicious agony. Everything narrowed to where we were connected. The tight pressure of him surrounding me, enveloping me completely, sent me into a state of pure bliss. Each ragged breath that passed between us only served to strengthen our passion. I knew we'd come undone together, and there was no better arousal than the anticipation of that moment.

My throat dried at the sight of me fully seated in him. I dug my fingers into his waist, anchoring myself there, as I fought for control. So badly did I want to lose myself completely in him.

"Gods, Kost. I..." Words escaped me. How could I even begin to explain everything I was feeling? All of my repressed desires, my nights of longing for the man arching his back beneath me, surfaced in my mind. I bent my head to the space between his shoulders and nicked his skin with my teeth. "You're too much. I can hardly stand it."

"So don't." His voice was thick with something more than want. Something deeper and heady and bigger than this moment. "Lose yourself with me. Completely."

Then, he rocked into me once. Twice. He relaxed completely and let out a guttural, pleased groan.

The last of my control snapped. Pure, unbridled lust coursed through me, and I began moving with abandon. I stroked his cock in tandem with my thrusts, and he pushed into me, the two of us joined together in perfect unison. The sight of him consumed me. The corded muscles of his back trembling in ratcheting levels of desire. The way he peeked over his shoulder to hold my gaze as he moaned. The space where I lost myself in him. He was so fucking stunning, and I was lucky enough to call him my partner.

Something dangerous brewed in my chest. Maybe it was the same thing that filled Kost's voice with emotion. What was happening between us... It wasn't just sex. I knew it from the moment we became one. It was so obvious to me that it was impossible not to name it.

We were making love.

"Gaige," Kost moaned. Chills raced over my skin. He had to feel it, too.

I didn't dare utter those words. Not yet. They were too raw, too real, and we'd only just started down the path to figuring us out. Instead, I let myself fall completely into him. I stopped thinking, stopped trying to name things we weren't ready to face, and simply reveled in him. Our movements were synced as if we'd been partners for ages. The subtle shifts to deepen my thrusts, the demanding way we sought out each other's lips. When he tipped his head back and exposed the tantalizing curve of his neck, I greedily pressed bruising kisses beneath his ear.

"Yes." He dragged out that single word with a heated breath, and my own desires came to a head. Need coiled tight in my groin, just begging to be released. My grip on his cock tightened as I increased my speed.

"Kost. I need you to come, baby. I need..."

A wondrous, heady moan burst from Kost's lips as his orgasm spilled over my fingers. The sensation drove me over the edge, and that twisting desire seated within my groin shattered as my own climax racked my body. Shudders of pleasure raced over my skin, and I buried myself deep as I pressed my forehead to his back. Kost went limp in my arms, and I held him tight against my chest, unwilling to lose the feeling of his skin against mine.

I didn't know how long we stayed like that, lost in the afterglow of something beautiful and long overdue. But when Kost turned so he could capture my lips with his, my body finally relented, and I pulled him under the sheets with me. Tucking him against my side, I placed a feathery kiss on his shoulder.

"That was..."

"Incredible," Kost murmured.

I chuckled. "Yes. Yes it was."

The beginnings of sleep tugged on my senses, and I hugged him closer. He shifted without complaint, and within minutes the subtle rise and fall of his chest turned heavy. I couldn't recall the last time I'd felt such happiness, even before I'd died. But now I had my beasts back. I had a family to help me through any obstacle I faced. And I had Kost. His presence gave me peace, and I let myself succumb to slumber without fear of what my dreams would hold.

TWENTY

KOST

Gaige was magnificent to behold.

He'd fallen asleep on his stomach with his arms tucked beneath his pillow, and the linen sheets were bunched around his waist. Buttery-yellow light from the morning sun slanted through the windows, highlighting the smooth skin of his back. My gaze roved along the length of his spine and the dip above his waist. I'd never allowed myself to study his backside before, but now it was impossible not to fantasize about the round, muscular shape of his ass or the thickness of his thighs. A tingling flushed over my skin as desire thrummed through my body.

"You've been staring at my rump for five minutes now."

I jolted as heat ravaged my cheeks. A mischievous glint flickered through Gaige's steel-blue eyes, and he smirked.

"I thought you were sleeping," I said.

"Don't stop ogling on my account. I quite enjoy it." His voice was more like a deep purr, and blood raced toward my groin. Hickory curls fell across his cheekbones, and my fingers burned with the desire to bury themselves once again in his hair. Or trace the faint stubble along his jawline. A shiver crawled down my spine at the thought.

Gaige reached over with delicate fingers and trailed along the curve of my neck, as if he were tracking the rampant gooseflesh betraying my desires. "Of course, I'd be more than willing to let you explore with something other than your eyes."

My face went impossibly hot. It was completely illogical for me to feel so...exposed. I'd already bared myself to him in a way I hadn't with anyone since Jude. And yet, the thought of being vulnerable again in the soft light of morning had me reddening as if it were our first time together.

Something hungry lit in Gaige's stare. "That blush of yours..." His touch wandered to my cheeks, my ears. "It makes me want to lose myself in you all over again."

Just then, a loud clatter came from the quaint kitchen outside my room, followed by a hushed admonishment from Ozias. Calem's answer—a barely quieted response full of tease and instigation—was intentionally loud enough for Gaige and me to hear without being a full-on shout.

The burn of Gaige's words was doused with reality, and I sighed. The last thing I wanted to experience was a round of incessant teasing from Calem if he happened to hear anything raucous from Gaige and me.

Turning into Gaige's touch, I placed a swift kiss on his fingers. "Later."

He relented with a heavy, strangled exhale, but rolled to his side so his glorious chest, lightly peppered with faint hair, was on full display. I allowed myself one wayward touch as I ran my fingers over the tantalizing contours of his muscles.

Catching my hand, he ran his thumb over my knuckles. "You sure about that?"

"*Later*," I reiterated, to convince both myself and him. I let him thread our fingers together, and my heart threatened to leap from my chest. His grip was so warm. Safe. It was terrifying to allow myself to feel such things after I'd spent decades barricading myself from such possibilities, but when it came to Gaige, it seemed there was no construct solid enough to keep him out.

"How did you sleep?" I asked, veering the conversation toward safer territory.

Discomfort flickered through his eyes. "Not particularly well. I had another nightmare, and I didn't fall back asleep after that."

I frowned. "You weren't asleep when I woke up?"

"I was *pretending* to be asleep." A mischievous grin tugged at his lips. "I didn't want to interrupt your viewing experience."

A tingling sensation swept up the back of my neck, no doubt resulting in another round of pink ears. "Yes, well, tell me about your dream."

He flopped onto his back and pressed his head deeply into the pillow as he gazed at the ceiling. "It's the same one I've had for days now. I'm in a grayed-out world until I come to a beach and meet a twisted version of myself cloaked in shadows. Nothing really happens, and in typical dream fashion, he speaks in riddles that make absolutely no sense." He paused as he fingered the sheets and then turned his head toward me. "All I know is that after I meet him, I'm filled with this horrible sense of fear and dread."

Propping myself up on one elbow, I studied the tired, puffy bags beneath his eyes. I'd missed them earlier because of my own lust. But now, I could see the aftermath of days without solid sleep. His heavy eyelids threatening to close, but too hesitant to do so. The slow, almost laborious way he tugged at the sheets. I'd passed it off as being satiated from sex, but it was something else entirely.

And it frightened me to my core. "I didn't notice any shadows in the night."

"There haven't been since that first time you woke me up in Cruor."

A cool wave of relief washed over me. "That's good. Perhaps you have more control than either of us realized. We just need to find a new way of harnessing it."

His long, burnished lashes nearly covered his somber stare. "You've been right this whole time. About the attacks. If I'd done something sooner..."

For the first time in my life, I didn't want to be right. I hated the way he collapsed in on himself at his words, the look of total defeat marring his beautiful face. He'd been through enough. I didn't feel vindicated by his acknowledgment. In that moment, the only thing I could think about was finding a way to bring that charming smile back to his face.

Leaning over him, I slanted my lips across his. He relaxed beneath me, his soft exhale a release of all he'd been feeling for gods only knew how long. I didn't know the answer yet, but I'd always been proficient at strategizing new paths forward and finding solutions where others fell short. Together, we'd find a way to stabilize his shadows and quell the Kitska monsters.

Breaking our kiss, I brushed my nose against his. "We'll figure it out."

An obnoxiously loud knock sounded from the door. "Are we taking the day off?"

"For the love of the gods, Calem." Ozias's words were muffled, as if he'd palmed his face in exasperation. Indeed, it was the same emotion I experienced—that and an unruly amount of irritation—and my whole body tensed.

"I will be with you momentarily," I seethed.

There was a quiet pause, followed by a snicker. "You mean *we* will be with you momentarily?"

A sharp yelp crested through the otherwise quiet house and then thundering footsteps. Calem shouted a slew of vulgarities as he let out a strangled grunt.

"We'll be outside. Training," Ozias said loudly. The heavy shuffling of their feet lasted all of a minute as Ozias likely dragged Calem outside by the collar of his tunic, and then the house was once again blissfully silent.

"I despise him," I hissed beneath my breath as I rolled off Gaige and out of bed.

"No, you don't," Gaige said. I could feel the heat of his stare as I searched for my clothes on the floor, but I didn't dare turn around to confront his gaze lest I fell back into bed with him. And I very much wanted to do that.

"Just when I thought you knew me," I mused, finally yanking my trousers into place. I braved a look his direction, and just as I thought, I nearly returned to his arms. The sheets had been pulled to his feet in my sudden departure from bed, exposing his body entirely. He laid on his side with a knowing, lax grin and one leg propped up. One arm rested on his knee, and his other hand cupped his face. Gods, he knew what he was doing. He knew I barely stood a chance, too, because my eyes immediately roved down the trim lines of his broad chest, to his hardened abdomen, to the pleasing thickness of his thighs. And of course, to his fully erect cock. He'd tasted me last night, and I hadn't the opportunity yet to return the favor.

My mouth dried with want, but I forced myself to stare at the ceiling. "Get dressed."

"You're blushing again."

"Get. Dressed. *Later*, remember?"

"Painfully, yes."

Grabbing my pack by the nightstand, I decided it was safer

for me to ready myself in the shared bathroom. Behind me, Gaige chuckled, and I fled the room before he could lure me back in.

A small, perhaps egotistical, part of me had hoped that our night together would make it easier for Gaige to control his shadows. That effortless swagger and confidence he exuded, though, had already dispersed with the whispers of smoke around his quivering fingers. Sweat dampened curls clung to the back of his neck as he stood before Ozias, hands outstretched with palms facing skyward. We'd found a more secluded space behind our temporary abode where we could train in private in the hopes Gaige would feel more comfortable.

They'd only been at it for ten minutes, however, and I could already see his mental fortitude deteriorating.

Calem plopped to the ground beside me and set a platter of food between us. "You missed breakfast."

"One wrong word, Calem," I started coolly, "and I'll have Gaige sic Boo on you."

He placed a hand on his breast in mock astonishment. "Me? Why I'd never." Leaning forward with an easy grin, he braced his forearms on his knees. "Course, if I'd been in your shoes, I would've opted out of breakfast, too."

A muscle twitched along my temple. "Do you have a hearing problem?"

"What?" He laughed. "I'm just agreeing with your decision."

"You are an absolute pain." I braided my fingers together to keep myself from backhanding him. A few feet away, Ozias and Gaige were at it again, and thin ebony tendrils had begun to wrap themselves around Gaige's legs. They moved fluidly like a feline begging for attention. And just like a cat, they turned the moment Gaige tried to coax them into something tangible. He let out a frustrated exhale, and Ozias palmed his shoulder in reassurance.

"In all honesty, though," Calem said, momentarily shifting my attention back to him, "I do agree with your decision."

The soft, earnest tone of his voice quieted my irritation. "Decision?"

"To be with him." He nodded toward Gaige. "I'm glad you two figured it out."

I'd expected a rush of heat to claim my cheeks, neck, and ears at discussing the nature of my relationship with Gaige, but the only sensation I experienced was a sudden blooming warmth in my chest. It radiated outward through to my fingertips, and I felt—rather than forced—an involuntary smile.

"Me too."

Calem dipped his chin to look me directly in the eyes. "That doesn't mean I won't tease you, though."

"Naturally," I said. His devilish grin indicated as much.

"So, who made the first move?"

"And we're done." I stood, ignoring the peace offering of assorted fruits lying untouched on the ground. "I can only hope Kaori will impart some modicum of etiquette to you as the days go on."

Calem's smile stiffened. "I've got my beast under control. We don't need to train together anymore."

"Yet you still prowled after her yesterday. Interesting." I walked away, delighted to let him stew on my words and fight against something that was likely as obvious to me as my pining for Gaige had been to him. As I approached Ozias and Gaige, I kept a short distance to give them space to work without interfering. Eventually Calem rejoined my side, and for once he kept his thoughts to himself. Perhaps I'd struck a chord he wasn't ready to examine. My gaze cut to Gaige. I could relate all too well.

"Okay, let's go again." Ozias stood before Gaige with his legs planted wide and palms upward. He centered himself with an exaggerated deep breath and encouraged Gaige to do the same.

His eyes slipped close. "I don't think this is working."

Ozias broke his stance to place one hand on Gaige's back and the other on his chest. He straightened Gaige and then gave his arms a squeeze. "You can do this. The shadows are everywhere. You don't have to forge them out of nothing, you just have to call to them."

Instead of answering, Gaige opened his eyes and curled his fingers in a subtle beckon. Thin sable tendrils slithered through the grass from the depths of the surrounding forest and snaked around his ankles.

"Summoning them has gotten easier. But getting them to take shape..." He gestured with a cupping motion as he tried to will them into something more tangible. They only continued to slide over one another in response. "No progress."

Again, I was struck by how bestial the shadows seemed to behave. There was a frantic, wild energy to them, as if they couldn't determine whether to fight or flee. Pressing my lips together, I recalled all the previous instances of Gaige's shadow work. There were always two phases to his magic—the sudden rush and vicious attack, followed by a rapid escape.

They're beasts.

I'd raised my hand to remove my glasses and polish the lenses, but it stilled just before my nose. What if his dormant Charmer powers were affecting the nature of his shadows? We'd never turned someone like him before, not to my knowledge. When Gaige discussed the absence of his Charmer magic, it wasn't that it didn't exist anymore, it was more that it wasn't truly accessible any longer. I jerked my head toward his right hand, where I could just barely detect the edges of his Charmer's symbol. It was thin and faded, as if etched into place with graphite rather than inked into his skin, but it was still *there*.

Gaige had never wielded blades before, but he had tamed beasts. He'd done it for decades.

As expected, the curling tendrils fled after several tense moments, and Gaige tossed his hands up in exasperation. "What am I doing wrong?"

"Everything," I said, taking three quick strides to stand before him.

He looked like I'd slapped him. "Are you kidding me right now?"

"It's not you, it's your shadows." I nodded to Ozias, and he took a few steps back to stand beside Calem. Gently, I reached for Gaige's hands and rubbed my thumbs along his wrists.

His gaze was wary, but he didn't retreat from my touch. "You really need to work on your delivery."

"Never mind that." Hope had my thoughts cascading in a rush that made it difficult to focus. And, apparently, speak. We'd been going about this all wrong. Gaige was perfectly capable of controlling his shadows, we just had to approach it from a different angle.

Turning his hands over, I nodded to his faded emblem. "You're a Charmer, Gaige. That doesn't disappear just because you died. You *know* how to tame wild creatures."

His brows furrowed. "So?"

My pulse quickened, and I released his hands. "Try again. Call on the shadows."

"Okay," he said, drawing out the word as he glanced back at Ozias and Calem. They were equally perplexed, though, and simply shrugged in response. Extending his palms outward, Gaige once again summoned shadows from the surrounding woods. And just like before, they cut through the grass with the speed and efficiency of snakes to curl about his legs.

"Look at them," I urged. "What do they look like?"

He glanced to his ankles. "Shadows?"

I gave him a pointed look. "Try harder."

"I *am* trying. I just don't understand what you want from me." His hands fell to his sides as he forced himself to stare at the pool of writhing tendrils by his feet. "It looks like a snakes' nest. That better?"

I didn't even have to respond—the shadows did for me. A rush of power settled over us as the once wild, virulent forms shifted and solidified into something recognizable. Vipers. One hissed and cracked open its mouth, exposing gleaming, oily-black fangs. Another encircled Gaige's calf. More yet slithered up his thighs, wrapped around his torso, draped along his arms. His mouth had gone slack, and with a timid finger, he stroked the length of a snake curling around his forearm. It gave a pleased hiss in response before lifting its head.

"Holy fuck," Calem whispered.

"Honestly the coolest thing I've seen in my entire existence," Ozias said a breath behind him.

"You don't need control, Gaige. You've had it all along." Something warm and full threatened to burst in my chest. "You just needed to remember who you are."

A glassy sheen obscured his steel-blue stare, and he let out a throaty laugh that shifted to something louder and deeper. Without a word, the snakes raced off him and coalesced together in another snarling mess, only to take the shape of a monstrous feline—Okean. It wasn't his beast, not really, but it looked exactly like the legendary feline, and it bounded through the clearing with a happy caterwaul that shook birds from their roosts. Gaige flicked his wrist, and the shadow beast cut into the woods. When it emerged, it'd shifted to a wolf. The beast loped through the fields before launching into the air and dissolving into hundreds of shadows that fled into the trees.

"Kost." Gaige whirled to face me, eyes alight.

"I know." My cheeks burned from the intensity of my grin, and then suddenly Gaige's hands were on either side of my face and his lips were pressed tightly against mine. I froze at the sudden public display of affection, but his unbridled joy was contagious. I chuckled against his kiss and then returned the favor by lightly draping my hands around his neck. I vaguely registered Calem and Ozias whooping, but as it had been the night before with Gaige, all sounds were muffled. I was wrapped up in him, in his happiness, and nothing else in the world mattered.

But one sound, or rather a crescendo of earsplitting screams, cut through our private cocoon. We both broke away, our gazes first jumping to a confused Ozias and Calem. And then the shrieks crested again, and all four of us took off in the direction of the settlement. When we rounded our house and came upon the communal areas, we stuttered to an abrupt halt.

Monsters were *everywhere*.

I couldn't catalog them all fast enough. The Charmers had summoned their beasts and were barely holding them at bay, but fighting monsters was nothing like battling against an army. There was no strategy to their movements, no front line to concentrate on. The monsters had wild, erratic patterns and would lunge toward one beast only to shift focus halfway through and attack a Charmer. All around them, virulent shadows licked at their heels and propelled them forward, as if coaxing them to attack.

Gaige's knees hit the earth. "I thought... This can't be happening..."

Panic had a way of ushering me into a heightened state of

awareness, and I summoned my shadow rapier and commanded thin tendrils to gather beneath my feet. We needed to be swift. We needed to be lethal. We needed to be the monsters.

"Calem." My gaze bounced from creature to creature. "Go."

Calem sprinted away, shifting into his beast as he ran. He crashed into a monster with writhing, thorn-laden tentacles and a scaled body just before it struck Kaori in the back. She called more beasts to her side as her legendary feline, Stella, joined Calem in taking the creature down.

"Ozias, summon Jax. Gather the Charmers and protect them within a dome."

"On it." Ozias touched the key hanging around his neck as he ran. With a thunderous roar, Jax manifested beside him and was erecting blazing-hot lava walls within seconds. Glittering, ink-black blades shot from Ozias's hands as he pulled the focus of the monsters, giving Jax a chance to corral the Charmers and usher them to safety.

"I thought…" Gaige mumbled again, his head in his hands.

"Gaige." I dropped to one knee, tilting my head toward him but keeping my eyes locked on the battle unraveling before me. "Get up. I need you to rein in these monsters."

"It's my fault," he croaked.

"Listen to me." I dug my fingers into his shoulder, and he finally looked up at me. "This is not your fault. You did not force these creatures to attack." It took everything in me to hide the raw devastation swirling in my stomach. We'd found a way to control his shadows, but the monsters had still attacked. They'd responded to his magic, and as much as it agonized me to admit that truth, now was not the time to crumble. "We will find a way through this. Together. I promise."

He clung to my words, offering a single, shaky nod. "Okay."

"The Charmers need you. Your *family* needs you." I pulled him to his feet, and something hard set in his expression. With one hand, he summoned Okean, and with the other, he beckoned to the shadows lingering in our peripheral vision.

Instead of snakes, a pack of wolves prowled to his side. Their muzzles were pulled back in a display of sharpened fangs, and Gaige reached down to steady the nearest one with two fingers to the crown of its head.

"Help the others," he said to Okean, his voice deadly soft. Then, to wolves, "Herd the beasts and push them out." They tipped their snouts to the sky and howled before taking off, and I didn't know whether to be impressed or horrified, knowing just moments ago he'd wielded shadows and we'd been presented with *this*. In the least, if the monsters were agitated by his magic, he could command his dogs to flee and just maybe the beasts would go with them.

Rather than air my concerns, I pressed my lips into a flat line and gripped my rapier tight. Right now, we needed to deal with the monsters. Later, when we had time to evaluate and assess what had happened, it'd be easier to discuss the truth of what we'd unearthed.

Until then, we would fight. My gaze slanted to Gaige. We would fight together, because I wasn't ever going to let him face anything like this alone again.

TWENTY-ONE

GAIGE

I strode into the fray with Kost at my side. The clearing was littered with upturned tables, splintered furniture, and scattered food as monsters charged through the new heart of Hireath. Injured Charmers cradled their wounds and barked commands to their beasts when they could, but the sheer number of what we faced was inexplicable. Everything from low-level E-Class Kitska beasts to A-Class predators swarmed the area. Fangs bared and hackles on end, they acted as if we'd encroached on their territory and were bound and determined to eradicate us from their homes. None of it made any sense.

My body was numb, but somehow I moved through the world as if guided by a puppet master. I shouted at my shadow wolves and commanded them with more ease than I could have ever expected, and still, my movements didn't feel whole. There was a gaping void in me growing larger by the second. It had already devoured my hope. I just needed to put an end to this before anyone else got hurt.

Kost had acted with the calm surety and swiftness of a skilled tactician, and Calem and Ozias were executing their roles to perfection. The Charmers were being safely deposited behind a rock wall, while Calem lunged from creature to creature, sinking his teeth into hides and gouging scaled bodies with his sharpened claws. A few monsters had fled either because of him or my wolves, but a startling number held their ground.

None of this makes sense.

A strangled shriek pulled my focus. Raven was pinned beneath the weight of a Scorpex. Beside her, her Asura had fallen to the ground with all ten of its eyes closed. She no longer had any protective dome shielding her from the monster's unrelenting attacks, and her other beasts were surrounded. Eight tongues slipped past the Scorpex's mandibles and thrashed against her body. Angling its scorpion tail high, it prepared to impale her with its barb.

"Okean!" I shouted, and he responded by unleashing a powerful torrent of water that knocked the monster off-balance. Raven scooched out from beneath it and launched to her feet. With a nod of thanks, she pressed a finger to her bestiary and prepared to summon more beasts.

Raven was far from the only one in trouble, though. Kaori's Asura only had one eye left open. One more attack and the beast's protective magic would fade, leaving Kaori exposed. She pushed on, though, urging her beasts to chase the monsters out.

Beside me, Kost jolted as his body was lifted several feet in the air. His rapier fell to the ground, and he wrenched his fingers around an invisible hold over his neck. Countless holes the sizes of pinpricks appeared across his throat and rivulets of blood rolled toward his collar. He gave a strangled exhale as his eyes bulged.

"Kost!" I spun in place as I searched for what could be hurting him. I didn't have my bestiary anymore, but I'd researched beasts long enough to commit their powers to memory—assuming I'd encountered them. He kicked something solid behind him, and his body jostled again.

Invisible. I grabbed the rapier and lunged, lancing the space behind Kost, and I was rewarded with a spurt of blood that coated the monster in a red sheen. The Iksass howled and released his grip. Kost crashed to the ground, gasping for air, leaving me to face off with the now-visible creature. Tall, slender, and faceless, the monster shivered as it grew another tentacle-like limb and lashed it against me. Heat bloomed across my side from the hit, but I refused to buckle.

"Leave!" I inched forward to give Kost a chance to recuperate. "Just leave!"

Why? The question burned through my mind as the monster refused to budge. Both in death and in life, Iksass rarely interacted with people, and they had no set territory they guarded. They fled when confronted, and yet here it was, growing another limb and preparing to strike. This time, with serrated spikes protruding from its clear skin.

It struck me and Kost at the same time, thrusting me back and into the ground beside him. Blood flowed with abandon as the serrated barbs raked our tendons and skin when the monster pulled back. Kost glanced at me from his knees, a disastrous, rage-filled glint to his eyes. "Fucking Iksass."

From across the clearing, Okean howled and spit fury against gods only knew what, but no lifesaving stream of water came our way. He was either pinned or recharging, and I desperately hoped for the latter.

Again, the Iksass reared back, but Kost was already moving. Somehow, he had the foresight to dodge before the Iksass even slid into a striking position. He sliced into the monster, and a network of shallow cuts peeled open across its body. A glimmer of relief sang through me at the sight. The wounds would heal, so long as the monster retreated now. And by all accounts it should have. Except it didn't. The damned thing only let out an earsplitting shriek and sharpened all its limbs to deadly points. Dark, wispy tendrils floated around the speared tips, and I stilled.

My shadows. A brackish taste flooded my tongue, and my stomach churned. These creatures were being pushed to the extreme because of me. And I didn't know why. They'd always come to me when I called them, like when I first tamed Boo. It made sense that they were attracted to the same darkness that now lived in my veins. But why the shift to anger? Rage?

Maybe the enraged beasts were exactly what I'd become if I didn't throttle my powers once and for all.

The Iksass angled its limbs toward our kneeling forms. The shadows spiraling around it jumped erratically as if they were streaks of lightning instead of writhing snakes. There was an undercurrent of energy I didn't recognize, something hot and burning like an electrical fire, and the dread ratcheting in my chest faltered.

These aren't mine.

I didn't get a chance to investigate further. The Iksass drove its weaponized limbs toward us at the same time a snarling, roaring mass of fur crashed into the monster. Boo. He trapped the monster between his massive paws and bellowed directly in its face, coating the Iksass with a fine spray of spittle. And then the putrid stench of death and decay filled the air, along with an unbearable sense of dread. Rook stepped out from behind Boo's mass with his three eyes focused directly on the immobilized Iksass.

Boo snarled again. Moonlight gathered between his antlers as he threatened to wipe the monster off the map permanently, and the shadows around the Iksass fled. In the span of a breath, it went from being a frenzied creature driven by bloodlust to a scared, trembling Kitska beast withering in the face of certain death.

Leaping to my feet, I rushed to Boo's side and placed a firm hand against his neck. "He's fine now. Let him go."

Boo exhaled forcefully, his gaze full of ire, but he removed his weight just enough for the Iksass to slip out. Rook broke his stare, releasing the creature from paralyzing fear, and the monster fled into the woods without a backward glance.

Kost scrambled to his feet. "What just happened?"

"They're not my shadows." I clucked my tongue, and Boo knelt to the ground in response so I could climb atop his back. A timid, fluttering sensation brewed in my chest. This wasn't my fault. I wasn't the problem. We could fix this. "Take Rook with you. We need to shock these creatures out of the shadows' hold."

A flicker of understanding coursed through his expression, and he answered with a tight nod. Together we charged into the thick of it, Kost shouting orders at Calem and Ozias while I urged Kaori and Raven to do the same. Only a few Charmers remained outside of Jax's protective rock dome, and they didn't question my new tactic, either.

We split up and targeted monsters one by one, thrusting them to the earth and cutting off their means for escape. With the power of the full moon etched onto his bone helm, Boo could eliminate any monster here—and they knew it. Once they'd been pinned beneath his paws, they caved. And just as with the Iksass, the shadows disappeared in the face of imminent death.

Little by little, their numbers diminished. Raven's legendary feline replicated itself ten times over and surrounded beast after beast, allowing for Kaori's feline to slip in and poise its deadly fangs against the jugulars of monsters. Eventually only the Scorpex remained, but Ozias corralled it with a series of shadow blades and Calem raced through the floating weapons to pounce on the monster. The Scorpex shivered and attempted to curl in on itself for protection. Wispy tendrils pooled beneath it for a moment before shooting off into the woods like bolts of lightning, and Calem stepped off the monster. It retreated as quickly as it had appeared, and the clearing was eerily quiet.

Blood had turned the earth a ruddy brown, and the dirt

squelched beneath my feet as I dismounted from Boo. Flowers were dotted in sparkling droplets of red that stood out like gemstones against their white petals. One canopy had been obliterated, but fortunately most of the homes were largely intact. I nudged aside a broken table leg as I strode toward Jax's protective dome where everyone had gathered. Calem had shifted back to his human form and quickly snagged a pair of trousers from a nearby decimated dresser. Meanwhile, Charmers were cautiously stepping out from behind the rock walls to survey the damage and tend to their wounds.

"What in the fresh hell was that?" Raven asked. She'd crouched before her beast and was inspecting a small cluster of lacerations marring the feline's pewter hide.

"Shadows were causing the beasts to act erratically." Kost folded his arms across his chest and tapped his fingers along his forearm. He glanced to me. "Gaige thinks they're someone else's."

"Whose?" Calem tied his hair in a bun atop his head as he rolled his neck, releasing the leftover tension in his shoulders from his transformation. "I highly doubt anyone from Cruor is just shooting shadows into the forest for shits and giggles. Plus, our magic never bothered the monsters before."

"True." My brows pulled together.

"Please don't take any offense to this..." Kaori edged close to me and put a hand on my arm. "Are you certain the shadows weren't yours?"

Had she asked me this question hours ago, I would have believed I was responsible. But Kost had seen something I'd missed. He'd pinpointed a unique part of my magic that was wholly mine and mine alone. My shadows behaved like beasts. These strange tendrils were something else entirely. Slanting my gaze toward him, I waited for him to interject. He was brilliant and observant. He had to have noticed the difference.

I *needed* him to notice the difference.

Removing his glasses, he rubbed his temples. "Just this morning we made incredible headway with Gaige's shadows. They elicited none of the behavior we just witnessed."

I could have kissed him senseless in that moment, but for the sake of our friends, I refrained. "I'm telling you, it isn't me. My shadows act like beasts." I nodded to the lingering forms of wolves waiting on the fringe of the meadow, their ink-black stares trained on me. And it was as if recognizing them was all it took for my body to suddenly tremble with exhaustion. The adrenaline that'd been coursing through my system was gone. With a shaky flick of the wrist, I sent them away in a puff of smoke. A cold sweat dampened my collar, and I leaned against Boo for purchase. Rook let out a worried screech as he wound around my legs, and Okean rammed his head into my thigh. Black dots bloomed across my vision as my breath turned shallow. I started to crumple, but Kost was there to catch me. Shouldering me with ease, he helped me stay on my feet.

"He needs to rest," Kost said. "He maintained shadows for far longer than any newborn assassin. The toll it took on him…" His eyes traveled over my glistening face.

"Not to mention the Slimack injury." Ozias gave me a pointed glare. "Have you been getting enough rest?"

"No." Kost's answer on my behalf was swift and felt more like a rebuke. I rolled my eyes but didn't dream of arguing when the world was already spinning.

"No rest?" Calem's drawl, accompanied by his lopsided, teasing grin, made Kost stiffen beside me. "Wonder why that is."

Before Kost could murder him with the efficiency of a Foxel, the soft clank of metal armor rose above the quiet din of the clearing. As one we turned to the yawning maw at the edge of the waterfall where the cavern stairs were hidden, and a woman with golden hair accompanied by a small handful of soldiers in jade armor stood with her mouth agape. Isla recovered quickly, striding across the clearing with powerful steps that threatened to leave canyons in her wake. Abruptly, she halted before us, but her umber gaze never stopped skipping across the aftermath of the monster attack.

"Seems like I missed the party."

Ozias took an inadvertent step toward her. "You're here."

She frowned at him, her diminutive stature doing nothing to make her less fearsome. "I was asked to come. Noc made it sound rather important, but I don't see him."

"Of course. Right." He gripped the back of his neck and tipped his head to the sky. "Noc and Leena left to take care of some things."

Raven raised a single coppery brow at Ozias before shifting to Isla. "Welcome back. We'll fill you in on what happened. Kost was just taking Gaige back to their quarters for some rest."

"Right." Her stare lingered on Ozias for a moment before she nodded and moved to Raven's side, signaling her small accompanying troop to do the same. "Need help righting the clearing?"

"Please." Raven dipped her chin in thanks, and Isla waved her soldiers into action.

The world was dangerously close to disappearing entirely at that point, and I sagged into Kost's arms. He let out a quiet grunt before saying goodbye and steering me back toward our house. A dull ringing filled my ears, and my head lolled against his shoulder.

"You believed me."

He gave my side a gentle squeeze. "You made me believe you."

I barely remembered getting through the door, but I would always recall the way he gently laid me in bed and stripped me of my shoes, only to climb in beside me and drape us in a blanket. No matter what happened next, I'd always have his body pressed against mine, his head on my chest, and a warmth in my soul.

TWENTY-TWO

OZIAS

For several hours, I worked with the Charmers and Isla's guards to clear out debris, erect new canopies, and put back together the broken mess the monsters had left behind. It was quiet, easy work that required little thought, which of course meant my mind was running wild the whole time. I'd seen Isla and panicked. It'd been weeks since we last talked, and apparently I was still a bumbling, awkward disaster in her presence. I didn't even say hello.

It was just that she was so… I didn't know the right word for it. Course I never did, but even in my private thoughts I couldn't quite figure out what Isla was. Beautiful, absolutely. Remarkable, intelligent, confident. She was a whole array of things, which is probably why I could never pick any one thing to focus on when it came to her.

Even now, she stole my attention. Her blond hair was tied back in a ponytail, her umber eyes lost in the task at hand. She was righting a table and chairs while barking orders at her soldiers to help reclaim the Charmers' artifacts strewn about the open field. Normally, she wore the clothing of the Queen's Guard in Rhyne—an olive-green coat and matching trousers—but today she wore simple travel gear. There was something about the close-fitting white blouse and tan breeches that stirred want in me. She looked like she could handle anything.

"You're staring," Calem said with a nudge, and I dropped the broken chest I'd been holding. The hinges snapped entirely as it crashed against a stone, and books tumbled into the grass. Heat flushed to my cheeks and raced across the back of my neck.

"Do you ever keep your mouth shut?" Bending down, I gathered as many tomes as I could hold.

"How long have you known me?" He picked up the rest and offered an impish grin. "Relax, Ozias. She's not that scary."

But she was, and not just because she was a mage with the ability to summon an orb of sparking magic that hit with the force of a lightning bolt. It was her demeanor. With one look, she rendered me useless. Everything she did brooked no room for argument—it was simply her way or no way at all. There wasn't a better person to lead the Queen's Guard of Rhyne, and yet I still couldn't help but wonder how she'd ended up there.

"How far away is Allamere?" I asked as we walked side by side toward the tent where lost items were being stored.

"Can't say. I've never been, but I know it's past Galvanhold, and that's weeks away on a ship." Calem unloaded his books on a table before stretching his hands above his head.

"Galvanhold..." I set my books beside him, mindful to stack them neatly and not disorganize what had already been gathered. Now I just had to find a way to repair that chest. "The prison island?"

Something dark flashed through his eyes. "Yeah."

Like he'd said, I'd known Calem for decades and there were still dark spots in his past that I wasn't privy to. This felt like one of them, and I knew better than to press. He'd just storm away and be in an inexplicably foul mood for days. When he was ready, I'd listen. For now, it was better to shift the conversation to safer territory.

Stepping out from under the tarping, I started in the direction of the broken chest. “How do you think Isla ended up here, then?”

“You know, there’s this weird thing called a question, and you could totally ask her.” All hints of discomfort had fled, and his muted-red eyes were full of mirth. I hadn’t realized how close to Isla and her troops we’d walked, and he stepped around me to holler at her with an unnecessarily loud voice. “Isla! Come here!”

I stutter-stepped awkwardly as my feet rooted to the ground. “Calem,” I warned through a low grumble.

He ignored me and continued to beckon to her. She moved toward us with that same, powerful gait that seemed to hammer anxiety into my heart with every step. When she stopped before us, she placed her hands on her hips and gave Calem a sharp look.

“What do you want?”

I was both thrilled and terrified that she didn’t immediately swoon in the presence of Calem. All the women did. He should’ve been born a Charmer given the way he attracted people, and I envied him entirely too much for the easy way he interacted with just about everyone. So yeah, it was enjoyable to see him falter under the weight of a reaction he didn’t expect. It also was horrifying because if Calem couldn’t charm her, I sure as hell couldn’t, either.

He hid his shock well, though, and offered a disarming smile that made him hard to hate. “You never told us how you ended up working for the Queen of Rhyne.”

“That’s because it’s absolutely none of your business.” A glimmer of magic ignited in her stare, like a flame sparking to life, and we were immediately reminded that she could murder us without much effort on her part.

“Aw, c’mon,” Calem tried. “We’re just curious.”

She jerked her chin toward me. “You put him up to this?”

Words caught in my throat. Gods, why was it so hard to talk

to her? To anyone? I'd managed to forge an easy relationship with Raven and Leena, but anytime it came to someone else, someone I saw in a potentially romantic light, I completely floundered. The simplest of questions always struck me off-balance, and I ended up saying nothing or saying something just plain stupid.

Don't analyze it so much. Raven's nonchalant advice rose to the forefront of my mind. When I'd first confided in Raven about my inability to speak with Isla, she'd urged me to simply be me. Of course, Raven didn't have problems speaking her mind. She was likely to bite someone's head off if they ever tried to silence her. Meanwhile, silence was what I did best. How did it help me to be me if I never said a word?

Calem drove his heel onto the top of my foot, and I jolted, blurting out the first thing that came to mind. "I have zero control over him."

Isla's gaze jumped to our feet and then back up to my face. An amused smile toyed with her lips. "I can see that."

"Fortunately, I do." Kaori had moved behind us with the fluidity and deadly quiet of an assassin, and both Calem and I flinched. With nimble fingers, she pinched Calem's arm. "I need your help with something."

"Good luck," Calem whispered beneath his breath before turning on his heels to trail after Kaori. His soft chuckle lingered far too long after he departed, and I swallowed thickly as I tried to come up with anything to fill the dead air between Isla and me.

Fortunately, she spoke first. "I suppose I could use your help as well. There's some wood we need to move."

"Course." Action gave me purpose. Give me a task and I'd go to the ends of the realm to accomplish it. Plus, there was something about physical exertion that cleared my mind and made it easier to think. I followed her without saying anything else, pausing only when we came across one of the few broken homes toward the end of the clearing. Splintered wooden planks of heavy cedar from one of the blown-out walls littered the area. An oil-rubbed dresser had tipped over and spilled garments onto the ground, along with a handful of personal items. Two Charmers were already attending to that, which left the daunting pile of broken timber for us.

"Raven asked if we could relocate this to the woodworker's tent just over there." She pointed to a gazebo open on all four sides with a slatted roof and several tables covered in wood shavings. A bench covered with saws, chisels, and a variety of tools I couldn't name was manned by a Charmer already hard at work fixing a broken table. I made a mental note to bring him the chest I'd left behind so that its owner could still use it.

Isla bent down and filled her arms with several planks of heavy lumber. Shock tugged at my lips, but I forced myself to keep them closed. Toned biceps were visible against the strained fabric of her blouse, and she carried her load with ease. It's not that I'd expected her to be weak by any means, I just hadn't expected her to be able to carry quite that much.

"You're strong," I said without thinking.

"I know," she said over her shoulder, already striding toward the tent. "Keep up."

I fumbled after her, carrying as much as my arms would allow. A comfortable silence settled over us as we worked, and the anxiety that had rushed through to my quaking fingers receded to a dull hum in my chest. She didn't seem to mind, either. I couldn't help but admire her. She never broke pace. She never complained. Even when a sheen coated her forehead, she simply wiped it away with her sleeve and kept moving. She was marvelous, and I wanted to know everything about her. I just didn't know where to start.

So of course, I said something absurd.

“So… Have you been to Galvanhold?”

She paused, her brows inching together and forming a slight crease across her forehead. “Are you asking me if I’ve gone to prison?”

“No, I just…” Heat flushed my face, and I busied my hands with the wood. “Sorry, I just assumed you’d at least seen it since it’s on the way to Allamere. And I didn’t want to ask about Allamere because you already made it clear that was none of our business. Which I totally get. Not trying to pry.” *Shut. Up.* I focused on the timber as hard as I could and pretended I hadn’t just word vomited a nonsensical train of thought.

She blinked. Slowly. And then a laugh bubbled from her. “No, I’ve never been to Galvanhold, but you’re right. I have seen it.” Her expression turned somber. “I pray I never step foot there, either. That place has an awful aura about it. Only the truly wicked end up there.”

“Why not just kill them?” I shouldered another round of cedar and started toward the woodworker’s tent. “I’ve killed far less dangerous people for just about every reason you can think of.”

Her brows shot up at that. “Have you now?”

Fuck. I didn’t exactly regret my work as an assassin, but it wasn’t a pretty job. We didn’t kill needlessly or without cause, but we did kill for bits. Some bounties netted enough gold aurics to feed our family for weeks. It was a job that had to be done, and I just happened to be the person who did it.

“Not without a bounty.” I dropped the last of the timber to the ground and dusted my hands together.

“But anyone can place a bounty. How do you know if it’s right?”

I’d been asking myself that for decades. We’d never turned down hits from the capital for fear of how the former king would’ve reacted. Blindly accepting those requests—demands—was part of the strained peace between us and the law. There were still strangers, though, who placed hits. People with horrible intentions who lied to justify their need for a bounty. Yazmin had been one such individual when she placed a hit on Leena. And I'd known from the moment we set out on our journey together that she wasn't the one we should be hunting.

Which is, of course, why we didn't make it a habit of getting to know our bounties. "We don't. We get the details, and we execute. At least, that's how it used to be. Now that Noc is king, there are new laws surrounding the placement of hits."

Isla set her splintered pieces of wood on top of mine. "Maybe they'll start sending people to Galvanhold again."

"Maybe." It'd been years since I'd heard of any criminal winding up there. Sometimes bad people ended up in the cells beneath Wilheim's castle. More often than not, they just wound up dead. The former king didn't like the idea of his collection of bits going toward sustaining lowly prisoners. But Galvanhold was another thing entirely. That kind of sentence was reserved for those who deserved fates worse than death and transporting that kind of people to that remote island was a daunting task.

Chewing on her lip, Isla placed one hand on her jutted hip and looked out over the clearing. "If Gaige can't control his power, is that where he'll end up?"

"Over Kost's dead body." I shook my head. "But no, Noc wouldn't do that."

"Even if it's the only place capable of containing him?" Something I didn't recognize swirled in her umber gaze. "There are wards and ciphers all over that place to keep magic checked. Mages built it at the behest of one of your kings centuries ago, but some of ours have found themselves imprisoned there, too."

Ah, that's what twisted through her eyes. Apprehension. Maybe sadness. "Someone you knew?"

That forlorn look was gone in a flash, and she cocked a single brow my direction. "Not everyone has a sordid past, you know."

I seriously doubted that. "Right, sorry."

"It's fine." She waved me off and then started toward the dining tent. With the clearing mostly put back in order, the Charmers Council—minus Kost and Gaige—had begun to gather around the long table. Goblets full of wine were passed between them, and they sank to the benches with obvious exhaustion.

Clearing my throat, I tried to think of some way to keep the conversation going. "Do you know how to create wards like that?"

"Nah, that's not my type of magic."

My mind whirred. Kost had said something like that when we'd first met Isla. "What type of magic do you have?"

Her booted feet slowed, then stopped. "You saw me fight against Varek and Yazmin's forces. You know what I can do."

"Right..." I stalled, thinking of how her magic had singed the grass and turned her enemies to burnt outlines in the earth. "I just was curious."

"In my experience, curiosity is just a way for people to find new ways to get what they want." Her eyes narrowed. Slowly, she studied me from top to bottom, and her gradual appraisal caused a flush of warmth to creep across my cheeks. I would have given anything to know what she was thinking in that moment. Whatever conclusion she came to, though, was kept from me.

She relented with a short sigh. "There are five classes of mages. I am a Projector. I can use the magic in my veins and shape it into raw energy, which I then shoot." Holding up her hand, she gave her wrist a tight flick, and electric blue sparks jolted from her skin. The flame in her irises ignited to a full-blown wildfire. After a breath, she let it recede.

"That's incredible," I murmured, gaze still transfixed on her eyes. "Do you prefer electricity? Can you do other things, like fire or water?"

"I do know some additional spells," she hedged.

"Can you show me?"

Her eyes went cold. "Another time, maybe." Shoulders stiff, she power walked toward the group without bothering to see if I'd follow.

I rushed after her and, without thinking, grazed the back of her arm with my fingers. "Isla, wait. I'm sorry, I didn't mean—"

She jerked out of my touch and rounded on me with fury much too great for a question that felt so small. Drawing herself to her full height, she managed to tower over me without her head rising above my clavicle.

"Look, I don't know what your angle is. You seem nice and all, but we're allies. Not friends. I'm sure we'll see each other from time to time, so I simply request that you keep the inquiries about me to a minimum. Understood?"

Eyes wide, I let my hand fall away. "Understood."

"Good." She spun around and walked back to the tent on her own. Her hair flicked behind her in time with her agitated gait, and she barked a loud order at one of her soldiers before securing her own goblet of wine and draining it in one swallow. I couldn't even begin to fathom why she'd suddenly snapped. But as I moved toward the table and replayed our conversation in my mind, one thing cut me more than I expected.

We're allies. Not friends.

My shoulders sagged. Even if a romantic relationship was out of the question, I'd at least hoped we *could* be friends. And yet one horrible conversation from me, and that was swept off the table. I'd respect her wishes if that's what she wanted. Everyone had boundaries, and the last thing I wanted to do was make her uncomfortable.

Still, as I palmed a mug of ale and watched her from a distance, I hoped that one day she could learn to trust me enough to call me a friend.

TWENTY-THREE

KOST

Night had already fallen by the time Gaige finally opened his eyes. At some point during his respite, I'd gently extricated myself from the bed and snuck out to check on things with the Council and Isla. She assured me she could wait until Gaige woke to examine his shadows and compare them to what we'd witnessed today. Fortunately, peace had settled over Rhyne, and the skirmish along their southern borders with their neighboring country had died. Between the princess coming into power with a spectacular beast at her command, and Rhyne's reestablished allegiance with Lendria, no one wanted to take their chances against that kind of might. In other words, Isla had plenty of time.

I'd snagged a book to pass the hours and slipped back into the room to occupy the single armchair tucked into the corner. The candle on the nightstand had illuminated the pages well enough without disturbing Gaige. Until now.

Gaige groaned as he rolled to face me, lids barely open. "Tell me I didn't sleep for days again."

"Not this time." I pressed my finger to the page to hold my place. "You can go back to sleep. There's no reason to rush."

"Something out there is antagonizing the monsters, and people keep getting hurt." He stifled a yawn. "There's every reason to rush."

"The Charmers have stationed some of their beasts within the woods to act as sentries. If another attack is coming, we'll be better prepared this time." I closed the book and set it on the nightstand. "You should rest."

He pulled back the sheets and swung his legs over the side. "I just want to talk to Isla. She made it a point to travel all this way, and it'll be nice to have reassurance once and for all." He clasped his hands together and stared at the floor. "I–I know I've lost control countless times. But this isn't me. It can't be."

I moved from the chair to sit on the bed beside him and brushed my knuckles along his cheek. "I know."

"Thanks," he mumbled, leaning into my touch. He pushed past my hand to rest his head in the crook of my neck. "I don't know what I would have done if you didn't believe me."

Slipping a delicate hand around his waist, I melted into him. When he'd first told me the shadows weren't his in the clearing, I'd hesitated to respond. I could see the wild desperation in his gaze, but there was also something else. Determination. A pure sense of relief. A glimmer of hope. So I'd spent the battle studying the erratic tendrils as they coursed over the monsters. There were moments where they behaved like Gaige's, which led me to believe that whatever, whomever, we were dealing with never quite got a firm grasp on their power. But Gaige had been right—there was something different about the shadows I hadn't noticed before. A frenetic sort of energy that was distinct from the fight-or-flight response I'd noticed with Gaige's power.

These shadows reeked of unbridled destruction, and they left a puzzle in their wake.

He broke my reverie with a single graze of his finger against Felicks's key. "I'm surprised you don't have him out."

"He doesn't like to share the bed," I said. "But I suppose it wouldn't be a bad idea to have him on alert. He can notify us faster than the Charmers' beasts if another attack is coming."

Gaige chuckled. "You two are close. Tell me... Are there moments where you feel like you have his power? Can see what's coming, even if he's not here?"

I stilled. "Yes. But I wasn't aware such a thing was possible."

"It's extremely rare, even for Charmers. And the effects aren't consistent." He pulled back to pin Okean's key between his forefinger and thumb. "For example, it's not like I can shoot water out of my palms just because I have a unique bond with Okean. However, I do feel a sense of peace near bodies of water, and I can hold my breath almost as long as him."

"That's incredible," I murmured. A gentle warmth throbbed from Felicks's key. He'd given me so much. I was honored to call him my beast, and I willed him to feel every ounce of love and devotion that I held for him.

"Come on," Gaige said, freeing himself from my embrace to stand. "I want to check in with the others."

Sighing, I put aside the newfound knowledge Gaige had shared with me and got back to matters at hand. "Fine. But keep it short."

"I promise we'll both return to bed within the hour."

I raised a brow at him. "Really, now?"

"No sense in hiding it." He paused. "Unless you prefer it that way."

The tops of my ears burned. "I'm not entirely sure how to act."

Gaige crouched before me and clasped my hands in his. "I'd love to run through the streets of Wilheim and tell everyone that you are mine and mine alone. But I'll follow your lead, Kost. Whatever makes you comfortable."

Heat ravaged my cheeks and neck, but I refused to break his

gaze. I'd never witnessed a more beautiful color than that of his eyes, and now, magnified by the raw intensity of his declaration, I wished I were a painter so I could capture the hue. I wanted to coat the walls in my room with it and surround myself with him entirely. Always.

Gaige dipped his head just slightly, lowering his voice. "I plan on courting you, Kost. And then one day, I plan on naming you my *anam-cara*. I might be undead, but that custom is still very important to me."

"Gaige…" My voice was raw with unspoken emotion. Gods, I loved him. I loved him so much it hurt but I couldn't bring myself to say it. I wanted him to know what he meant to me, how he made me feel, but there was still a sliver of my old self pulling on the reins. I'd been burned badly by Jude. I'd taken a blade for him, given my life for him, only to be abandoned. If I gave Gaige my love, what would he do?

"I…" The words just wouldn't come. "It's been a long time. A really long time. All of this is so…difficult for me." It shouldn't have been. Everything with Gaige felt honest and real. But I'd felt like that with Jude, too. How was I supposed to know that it wouldn't happen again?

Small dimples burrowed into Gaige's cheek as he smiled. "Don't worry, Kost. You don't have to do or say anything. Let's just let it be, yeah? We'll figure it out in time."

My throat bobbed and I nodded. "Right."

Gaige's grin deepened. "Though you are quite eloquent when you want to be. I expect a full-hearted confession one day. I want flowers and chocolates and wine and a sinful display of this." He dragged his fingers down my chest and then gently caressed my inner thigh. Of course, I swelled at his touch and his sultry words.

As his fingers wandered over my growing erection, I bit back a moan. "Are we leaving this room or not?"

He leaned in and pressed his lips to the shelf of my ear. "We can resume later."

"Or we can sleep like you're supposed to," I countered, despite the fact everything in my body rebelled at the idea.

Gaige chuckled. "We'll see where the evening takes us." He pulled away, and the sudden absence of him against me invoked immense displeasure. Shifting uncomfortably, I stood and followed him out the bedroom door. Once we exited the house, the crisp air helped to dull my lust, and I breathed easier.

The midnight-blue sky was dotted with hundreds of burning-white stars that competed for brilliance with the pregnant alabaster moon. Its glow negated the need for lanterns and candles, but a group of people still sat before a small fire in the center of the settlement. While the days were tepid, the breeze brought an undeniable chill, and the heat of the fire chased away the nip of bitter wind.

The Council had arranged chairs for each of us and Isla around the fire. Anyone else who was still awake gave us a wide berth so we could conduct our business in some semblance of privacy. Gaige and I sat in the two remaining chairs next to Isla and mumbled quiet hellos as we accepted goblets of honeysuckle wine.

"This isn't bad," Calem said, swirling his cup. "I don't normally drink this stuff."

"First time for everything," Raven mused. We'd barely sat when she pivoted in her chair toward us. "How are you feeling, Gaige?"

His lips quirked into a smile. "I appreciate you asking me first instead of launching right into an assault."

She gave him a flippant wave. "Didn't want you getting all pissy again."

"I'm *fine*, thank you." He took a long sip. "Now, ask what you really want to ask."

The words were barely out of his mouth before she spoke. "Were those your shadows affecting the beasts?"

Ozias dragged a slow hand over his face as he side-eyed Raven. "You're almost as bad as Kost."

"No, they were not." Gaige picked at one of the jewels encrusted into the polished metal of his goblet. "Though to be absolutely certain, I'd like Isla to inspect them."

She set her glass on the ground and angled herself toward him. "I'll look, but I'm not exactly sure what I'm looking for. I wish I'd arrived in time to witness the attack so I'd have something to compare them to."

I rolled the stem of my cup between my forefinger and thumb. "In Rhyne, you used a magical artifact to detect the presence of forbidden magic in Noc. You said it leaves a permanent mark, even if it's no longer affecting the body."

"Yes." She frowned at me. "What does that have to do with this?"

"Since you couldn't witness the attack, what if you examined the aftermath and compared it to Gaige's shadows? Say, a wound?"

She blinked. Pursed her lips and then nodded once. "No harm in trying."

"I have a wound you could examine," Kaori said quietly. She stood without meeting anyone's gaze but Isla's.

"You didn't tell me you were hurt," Calem said, voice dangerously low.

She didn't face him. "It's nothing. I'll heal fine." As she moved around the fire to stand beside the mage, she lifted the hem of her blouse to reveal a bandaged area on her side. The innermost scraps of linens were already tinted a ruddy pink, and she peeled them away to unveil a puncture wound the size of a child's fist. It was packed with moss and herbs and slathered in a thick layer of salve, but the surrounding skin was enflamed and angry.

Calem shot to his feet. "Kaori, that is not nothing. What the fuck happened?"

She lifted a tight shoulder. "The Scorpex got me once before you arrived. Fortunately, their poison is painful, but not incurable. We already had the necessary ingredients to treat it."

Rage burned in Calem's stare, and the mercury thread around his irises flooded his gaze entirely. His hands curled into white-knuckled fists, and he jerked his head away from the sight. Ozias was at his side in seconds, guiding him away from the fire to regain control.

Isla stared after the pair for a moment before examining Kaori's wound. "This shouldn't hurt." With deft fingers, she snuck a quartz crystal orb from her trouser pocket. No larger than a river stone, it glinted in the flickering light of the flames. She extended her hand toward Kaori, and the spherical gem lifted into the air. It hovered above Isla's palm for a moment before gently gliding toward Kaori's stomach. It hung there for what felt like an eternity—long enough for Ozias and Calem to return to their seats and stare at it as intently as the rest of us did.

Doubt festered in my mind like an untreated wound. The tendrils had looked different than Gaige's. But what if... What if that was due to his recent progress? What if his newfound control shepherded the monsters even faster than before? They'd attacked within minutes of his bestial shadows dispersing into the woods. The monsters could have been lurking nearby, drawn here because of Gaige's presence and then agitated by his power. There wasn't a barrier around Hireath anymore, and we were surrounded by the Kitska Forest. With his unexpected developments came an unexpected attack of similar magnitude. It couldn't be true, and yet...

Finally, a sickly black shade filled the quartz, and relief slammed into me harder than a gale-force wind. I sagged into my chair and took a heavy pull from my wine.

"Dark magic," I said as I pulled the glass away.

She glared at the stone. "Yes. I..." Her words cut off abruptly as she snatched the stone from midair. Her body froze, eyes growing impossibly wide. Miniscule electrical currents erupted to life around her fingers and encircled her wrists and arms. The air snapped with energy and the flyaway hairs about her face stood on end. And then she dropped the stone as if it were burning metal.

This time, Ozias rushed to her side. Electricity thrashed around her as violent and unpredictable as Gaige's shadows. Ozias tracked their erratic movements, set his jaw tight, and then gripped her forearms. He cursed as the shock waves battered against him, but that must have been enough to pull Isla back. She looked first to his face, then to the space where he grasped her arms, and suddenly the electricity was gone. Ozias released her and slumped to his knees, breathing heavy.

"Are you insane?" Isla's voice was unnaturally high. "I could've stopped your heart!"

"It's fine. I heal fast." His words slurred together, and he swayed dangerously close to the fire. Raven was there to shoulder his weight, though I wasn't entirely sure that put Ozias in a safer position. She could've killed him with her glower.

"You're an idiot." She helped him sit his ass on the ground, and Calem bolted to find him some water. When he returned moments later, she shoved it into Ozias's shaky hands. "Drink, sit here, and do nothing."

He mumbled his agreement, and I was thankful that at least his eyes were clear. Once he met my gaze and offered a sheepish nod, I turned to Isla. "What happened?"

She glanced around until she spied her goblet and then drained the whole thing. "I don't need to see Gaige's shadows. I can tell you with absolute certainty they weren't his."

Kaori had righted her shirt and sunk back to her chair. "How do you know?"

"Because that lovely gash of yours has hints of tainted magic surrounding it. My magic." She eyed her empty glass. "Well, not mine specifically, but another mage's."

"What? Are you absolutely positive?" I frowned at her as I handed her my glass, and she gratefully accepted it.

"I know my own magic." She sipped my glass slowly this time, allowing herself to sink back to her chair and stare at the dying flames of the fire. "We're not supposed to mix our powers with anything else. It creates a massive unbalance in the world. That's why the stone reacted the way it did."

"And you?" Ozias asked, voice finally clear and steady.

She glanced at him, and the tension coiled tight across her shoulders softened a touch. "Yes. I'm sorry, I couldn't control it. It was a reaction to the magic. Powerful magic."

"So a mage is doing this? Why?" Calem asked. While the mercury hue in his eyes had dwindled, everything about his rigid posture still reeked of anger and frustration.

"An undead mage," Gaige whispered.

"Has that ever happened before?" Raven asked, tipping her head toward me.

"No. This is completely unheard of. We have no records of such a change happening at Cruor." I cut a glance to Isla. "Would anyone at Allamere know?"

Her eyes went cold. "I'm not in contact with anyone from Allamere."

Ozias studied her for a long minute before clearing his throat. "We can check some of our history books at Cruor, right?" He rounded on me with a fixed stare. "No harm in looking."

I heard the unspoken plea in his words, and I sighed. I'd read nearly every tome in our library ten times over, and I'd never encountered documentation like that. We didn't detail the nature of everyone we raised, only the leaders who took over Cruor when one moved on.

Removing my glasses, I held the frames and inspected the lenses. "We can look. It's possible a mage was raised when the guild was first formed."

"Right, well..." Isla stood brusquely and folded her arms across her chest. "I need to sleep."

"We all do." Raven shot both Gaige and Kaori a pointed glare. "Seriously, what is wrong with you two?" It was hardly a question, but she muttered it just the same. We all stood then and went our separate ways, and a handful of Charmers took our places by the fire.

Gaige and I walked side by side toward the house with Ozias and Calem on our heels. Initially, I'd expected them to pry and poke fun at my budding relationship with Gaige, but neither of them spoke. One cursory glance over my shoulder told me they were consumed with their own thoughts and far from interested in me. Calem's frame was still strung tight, and I highly suspected that he'd forgo sleep for several hours—if not the whole night—to burn off his rage either in his bestial form or with a series of unending shadow drills. Ozias was harder to read. He looked properly abashed, which made sense for the admonishments he'd received. But there was also a flicker of resignation in his drooped stare. Something was bothering him.

Something was bothering all of us. I peeked at Gaige in my peripheral vision. We still had no idea who this mage was or why they were acting this way, but we knew with utter certainty that he was not responsible for the monster attacks. And while he still had some training to do to fully wrangle his shadows, it seemed like he

TWENTY-FOUR

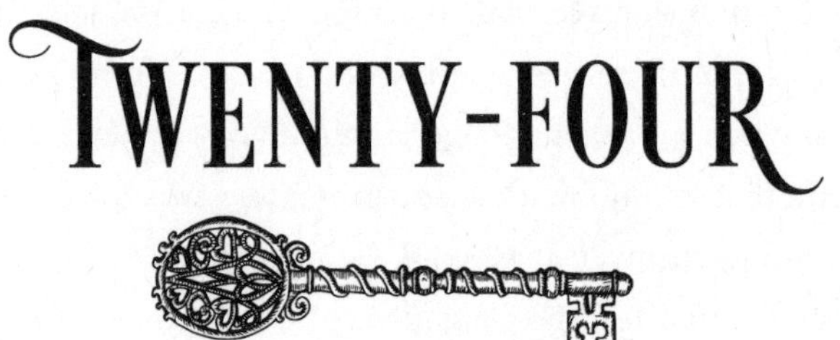

GAIGE

Gods, making love to Kost was beyond incredible. There weren't words to accurately describe every emotion, every visceral feeling, that came with seeing us joined together. We'd intended to go straight to sleep, but the moment he'd undressed, I'd found my hands on him again—and he didn't fight it. This time, he'd dropped to his knees and tasted me, and I'd nearly spilled before I even got the chance to sink myself in a different part of him.

Now, though, thoroughly sated with limbs heavier than lead, I found sleep was far from unavoidable. Kost had already drifted away beside me, and his soft snores were the perfect lullaby to welcome slumber in earnest. I'd hoped another night beside him would keep the nightmares at bay, but before I knew it, I was back in that same washed-out landscape covered in fog.

This time will be my last. I set off down the familiar, ebony path without looking back. I'd found a way to control my shadows. I'd found a way back to my beasts. I'd found Kost. There was nothing holding me back anymore. I was ready to confront this manifestation of my fears and be done with it.

Sable tendrils formed around my legs, twisting and rubbing against my calves like felines before solidifying in the shape of cats.

They prowled beside me with the kind of regal nonchalance and haughtiness specific to their nature, and I basked in it. Their confidence was mine. I would no longer be terrified of an unknown visage in a dream that had no real effect on my life. I was in charge. More shadows flung to my frame, until all manner of creatures trailed behind me. I could feel the weight of their endless eyes on my back as we walked, and I knew they would heed my command.

As the mist thinned, I sent two shadow crows ahead. "Tell him to meet me on the beach."

They cawed in response and cut through the air toward the heady crash of waves. This time, I would dictate the outcome of my dream instead of falling prey to panic. My shadows would protect me. Larger beasts gathered by my sides in response. Low snarls slipped from the backs of their throats, and they kept their eyes locked on the path before us.

When the fog peeled back to reveal the black sands of the beach and the ocean beyond, the man was already standing before a cluster of jagged boulders with his hands clasped in front of him. The crows I'd sent had landed on his shoulders, but he seemed unaffected by their presence. If anything, he only had eyes for me.

"Welcome back," he said. Even after hearing it several times over, the rasp of his voice still made the hairs on the back of my neck rise. Beside me, my beasts tensed.

"This is the last time," I said, hoping the conviction I felt would become truth.

"Oh?" He leaned forward in his stance as his lips stretched into an eerie smile. "What makes you so sure?"

"This is my dream, and it's one I'm tired of having. You are just a projection of what I used to fear." I glowered at him as I gestured to the multitude of shadow creatures around me. "But I'm better now. I will not become you." My gaze cut to his ragged appearance, to the frenzied mania that oozed from his frame and crept outward like a disease. No, I would never become that. Not now. Not ever.

"You are better now." He cocked his head. "What a boon. It's been so long since I've done this."

An unfamiliar chill settled over my skin. "Done what?"

"Collected someone." Bringing one hand to his shoulder, he beckoned for my shadow crow. It hopped into his palm and blinked up at him. "You're certainly special. I might even be able to break free with your gifts."

"This is a dream. The only one breaking free is me."

"You keep saying that, but I've told you from the start: this is no dream." A peculiar liquid sheen obscured his eyes as he brought the bird to his lips and whispered something beneath his breath. My crow shuddered, as if fighting against something invisible, and then stilled. The man whispered to the second crow. When both birds looked my way, their gazes were clouded with that same, liquid magic.

I felt my sense of surety faltering. "Who are you?"

"I am the Lost, and the Lost are me." He took a step forward, toothy grin on full display. "And you, Gaige, are lost now, too."

I backstepped into my beasts, and they darted around me to position themselves before the oncoming threat. The fear I'd suppressed hit me hard and fast. "We're in the shadow realm, aren't we?"

He nodded. "Very good."

"But how?" I scanned the environment for a sign, for a way out. "Those lost to the realm never return to the world." My eyes snagged on a jagged stone with a handful of sharpened points, and I silently commanded one of my shadows to inch toward it. As a squirrel furtively crept between the legs of my other creations, I returned my focus to the Lost. If I could keep him talking, I could injure myself badly enough to wake like I'd done previously.

"Isn't it fascinating how the truth gets lost in stories and legends?" He stroked the chest of one of my crows with a single finger. "You've left the realm before. You must know that's not true."

Or this really was still a very strange nightmare.

The squirrel snared the rock and quietly moved my direction. "Then why has no one ever made it back?"

Any second now and I'd be home free. My creature scuttled across the sand to sit by my feet, a jagged stone cradled between its paws. But just as I was about to drop to my knees and smash the damn thing against my temple, a black, endless void rimmed in moon-white sparks swallowed the creature whole. It happened so fast I hardly registered the gaping maw in the earth and its sudden disappearance, but I felt my jaw go slack and body freeze.

"Because I never let anyone," he said.

Horrifying black spires of pure night erupted from the sand all around me. My beasts scattered or were speared, and suddenly the air was coated in wispy shadows as their forms disintegrated. The rest howled and lunged in the direction of the Lost, and he stood there with open arms as they converged on his body. The gnash of fangs and rip of flesh filled my ears, but his delirious laugh rose above it all. One by one, they stopped fighting and turned to face me, eyes alight with that lustrous magic.

The Lost regained his footing and pinned me with wide, bloodshot eyes. Deep gouges marred the planes of his stomach, arms, and legs, and his tunic was nothing more than tattered pieces of stained fabric on the beach. His skin was smeared in blood and grime, but the gashes were already healing at a rapid pace.

And then all at once his appearance shifted. Gone were his—*my*—blue eyes, instead replaced by a shade of brown so deep it bordered on black. His hair shifted to an ashy blond. A jagged scar climbed up his neck in the shape of a winding river, stretching from his collarbone to his earlobe.

Mage.

"I am the apex predator here." He stalked toward me with languid ease. "I prey on the weak-minded undead. I bring them here, and I take what is mine."

"And what is it you want?"

Something dark raced through his expression. "Power."

With a brutal flick of his wrist, he summoned another round of spears from the earth, and I dodged one only to be gouged by another. The point went clean through my side, and white-hot pain arced through me as I screamed. A roar of adrenaline crested in my ears as my vision swam. This couldn't be happening to me. I'd come so far. I'd finally found my place. My home. The images of the Council, of my newfound brethren at Cruor, of Kost, flooded my mind. I wouldn't give up on them or myself.

Cursing, I force the spike out and crumpled to the earth. Sand wormed between my fingers as I steadied myself with ragged breaths. The wound would heal, but that wouldn't stop him from striking again.

"I have been waiting for you, Gaige, for a very, very long time." He circled me slowly, and the ground began to tremble. I rolled just in time to avoid another disastrous barb. "I assumed it was only a matter of time before one of your predecessors defiled the laws of magic by raising someone like you."

Scrambling toward one of my nearby beasts, I tried to will it to attack. Thin shadows formed in my palms and raced toward the creature, wrapping around its hind legs to burrow themselves in its hide. The creature's frame rippled like as if a stone had been cast upon still water, but it didn't turn on the Lost. Instead, the beast dipped its head to sniff me once and then peeled back its maw in a perilous show of teeth.

"Once I drain you of your magic, I'll finally have everything.

And then I can free myself." He dragged a hand along one of my larger beasts, rubbing its shadow fur between his fingers. A mixture of awe and hunger filled his voice. "Remarkable. I'm glad I pushed you to this."

Ice settled in my bones. "What do you mean?"

He lifted a shoulder. "I sent my shadows into the world to agitate the monsters. Every time you left here, you carried them with you." Tilting his head toward me, he inspected my body. "After that... Well, I've been with you every step of the way, waiting for you to realize your power so I could make it mine."

I had to get out. If what he said were true, then I hadn't been lost to a void of shadows. He could trap me, but I could also escape. My gaze snapped to the thin veil of mist just visible where the beach and stone path met. Maybe if I ran back the way I came, I could find a way out. Forcing myself to my feet, I winced as pain erupted from my side. Blood oozed down my leg and coated my trousers. Gingerly, I fingered the wound and shuddered. I wasn't healing nearly as fast as he had.

"Oh, yes." He eyed my injury with a knowing look. "I've been here for more lifetimes than you can imagine. The power I've collected affords me certain"—he waved his hand for effect, dragging out our conversation for the sheer pleasure of it—"benefits."

My own magic burned through my veins, and I focused on the swell of energy building in my chest. I would not die here. I would not give him anything. A pool of ink-black tendrils writhed beneath my feet, waiting to do my bidding. I widened my stance in preparation.

"But you don't have mine." As the words left my mouth, the shadows erupted and knitted together, forming a magnificent stallion. I wasted no time in vaulting onto its back. With two hands, I fisted its mane, and it bolted toward the path.

"No, I don't," he called. "Not yet."

Howls ruptured through the air and the heavy cadence of paws crashing into the earth sounded at my back. I jerked my head over my shoulder to see my shadow creatures barreling after us, with the Lost simply standing on the beach with a crazed grin.

The wolves caught up first, their fangs gnashing against the back legs of my steed. It whinnied as their teeth sank into its shadowy flesh, and I summoned more tendrils to patch the hole. Its hooves clattered against the slick stones of the path, and the harsh reverberation was amplified by the thickening curtains of mist on either side of us. Dissonant howls meshed with the racing gait of my stallion. Ears ringing, I dug my heels into its side.

"This has been fun." The Lost's voice rose from all around me. I searched for him amidst the mass of snarling shadow beasts, but he was nowhere to be found. "It's a pity it'll all be over soon."

I didn't know how long we charged into the abyss of white fog, just that my brow was drenched in sweat and my hands were trembling. My power was fading, and I could feel it in the slowing gallop of my beast. Try as I might, I couldn't find a way out. There was nothing but mist and the ebony path and the monsters at my back.

And the Lost, who'd manifested a short distance ahead of me in a plume of smoke. I flattened myself against my stallion's back, preparing to leap over him and continue on, but that dangerous sheen filled the Lost's gaze.

"Stop."

One word and my steed came to an abrupt halt. I barely kept myself from vaulting over his head, and instead slipped off the side to crumple to the earth. Slowly, as if enjoying every moment of his approach, the Lost made his way to me. He toed my chin and forced me to look up at him.

"You're mine now."

Streaks of pale-white lightning, coated in shadows, bolted down his leg and slammed into me. The last thing I heard over the heady ringing in my ears was his demented cackle, and then the world went dark.

TWENTY-FIVE

KOST

Peaceful, amber light filtered through the curtains of our room, and I wrapped the linens tighter around me. A pleasing ache still thrummed through my body from my evening with Gaige, and I wasn't ready to let go of that sensation. I wanted to remain warm in bed—and his arms—for the duration of the morning, but a prickle of awareness tingled along my back. Cracking one eye open, I turned my head expecting to find Gaige and instead discovered empty sheets. They were still wrinkled from where he'd slept, but as I ran my hand over the space, they were cool to the touch. My brows pulled together. He was certainly allowed to rise before me and do as he pleased, but I'd quite enjoyed waking up next to him. My body felt cheated by his absence.

Sighing, I got up and dressed quickly in the hopes I'd catch him for breakfast. When I exited the room, Calem was already lounging on the couch beneath the loft while Ozias shuffled about in the small kitchen area. He'd set out four ceramic mugs, and the rich aroma of coffee floated through the room.

"Morning." Calem's eyes glinted with mischief. "Your better half still sleeping?"

"No. Have you seen him? He must have awoken early." I took

the proffered mug from Ozias and blew gently over the steaming liquid.

"Nah, but he did do a lot of sleeping yesterday." Ozias walked to Calem and handed him his coffee before pouring his own. "Bet he was just ready to get moving."

"He's probably eating breakfast with the others. Gotta replenish his energy after all of yesterday's activities. And I do mean *all*." Calem smirked over the lip of his mug.

"Really unnecessary, Calem," Ozias mumbled, unable to look either of us in the eyes.

"Quite," I seethed. I took a slow drink before tilting my head toward the door. "Shall we?"

Carrying our drinks with us, we exited the house and headed toward the communal dining area. The clearing was bustling with activity as Charmers continued to rebuild after yesterday's attack. The sun hadn't been up for long, and yet they'd already managed to reconstruct one building and were almost finished with a second. As we moved under the shade of the canopy, we stopped by a long table laden with food and filled our plates before spying Raven, Kaori, and Isla. They'd taken up seats at a table nearest the clearing, and they were quietly chatting while studying the work taking place around them.

Setting my plate and drink beside Raven, I glanced around the half-empty tables. "Where's Gaige?"

"He's not with you guys?" She popped a grape in her mouth before following my gaze.

"I haven't seen him this morning," Kaori said.

"Me neither." Isla brushed crumbs from her lips with a beige cloth napkin. "Could he be visiting his beasts?"

He'd only just regained the ability to summon Valda and use her power to open the beast-realm door. Undoubtedly, he missed his companions. It wasn't a stretch to think that when he rose and we were still sleeping, he used the opportunity to slip into the beast realm.

"Or maybe he's with Boo and Rook," Ozias said, plopping to the bench beside Isla. She cut him a hard glance, but she didn't object to his presence.

Calem stiffened as his earlier mirth vanished. "Boo and Rook are in the woods. I saw them on my morning walk, but I didn't see Gaige."

Unease threaded through my gut. Was he really in the beast realm? Valda needed time to recover between activating her power, but admittedly I was unaware of what that time frame looked like.

He would have told you. With everything happening, he'd know I'd worry over his absence. Which meant, there was no way he would have disappeared without at least leaving a note.

Abandoning my breakfast, I turned on my heels and suddenly I was sprinting toward the house. Panic clawed at my throat as I tore through the front door and rushed into the bedroom. His clothes were strewn across the armchair, his bag at the foot of the bed. His scent still lingered in the room. Cedar and pears and the salt-tinged musk of us. My heart hammered against my rib cage. No note. Where was he?

The rest of the Council wasn't far behind me, and soon too many bodies were in a space that had been wholly mine and Gaige's not hours before. My throat swelled and I turned away from the sight of our mussed sheets and pushed into the main living space.

"We have to find him," I said.

Calem's face was bone-white. "Do you think…"

"Don't." I choked on my words and gripped the edge of the kitchen counter to steady myself. "Don't say it."

"He can't be lost to the shadows," Ozias whispered anyway. His words scraped against my skin, and I flinched.

"I don't understand." Raven began to pace, her booted feet pounding in time with the roar of my pulse in my ears. "I thought he'd learned how to control them."

"He did," I managed. "And...and I would've noticed. He was right *beside* me." Gods, how had I not noticed? How had I slept when he'd been stolen away by the very power I'd forced him to wield?

"We still don't know..." Calem fumbled for words, and then he looked at Kaori. "Can you go to the beast realm and search for him?"

She grimaced. "Of course I'll try, but the beast realm is massive. Unless a Charmer enters with another Charmer or is part of their family, they don't typically manifest in the same location. It could take years of searching, and he'd be more liable to return here in far less time."

"So we wait?" Ozias asked.

"We can't just sit here." I slammed my fist into the counter, fracturing the wooden surface. "He's not in the beast realm, and you know it."

"Okay." Ozias glanced between all of them before landing on me. "What do we do?"

Keep it together. But I couldn't. I didn't know how to handle this situation. Gaige was gone. I'd only had him for a handful of moments, and yet I knew in my bones the memories would stay with me for the rest of my unnaturally long life. I couldn't let him go. I wasn't ready.

I never even told him that I loved him.

"We're bringing him back." I shoved away from the counter and stalked up and down the short length of the house. "There has to be a way."

"Kost..." Ozias's words were too soft.

"Just because we haven't witnessed someone returning from the shadow realm before doesn't mean it can't be done." I answered before he could even state the obvious, trying to smother my own doubts with a conviction I didn't wholly feel. "We have to try."

"Okay, but how?" Calem shifted his weight from one foot to the next as he tracked my own agitated movements.

"A beast?" I tipped my chin toward Kaori and Raven, but they pursed their lips and shook their heads. I rounded on Isla. "A mage?"

"I wouldn't even know where to start." She wrung the hem of her tunic. "To be honest, I'm not sure a mage from any other class could do it, either." She finally met my probing stare. "We have nothing to tether the magic to."

I stopped abruptly in front of her. "But you don't know for sure. Can you contact mages with different powers? Convince them to help?"

Her stare turned flinty. "I don't know any other mages."

I threw my hands toward the ceiling and let out a wordless grunt of frustration. "You can't contact Allamere. You don't know other mages. What, *exactly*, can you do?"

Her jaw slackened for a fraction of a second, and then her sharp brows drew together as the air around her snapped with electricity. Blue currents danced across her arms. "I can wipe you off the fucking map."

"Easy," Ozias said, pushing between us. He shot me a rare glare. "Kost let his emotions get the better of him. He didn't mean anything by it."

Forcing out a tight exhale, I turned away. He was right, of course. This wasn't Isla's fault. It was mine. I'd failed Gaige. If I'd only noticed the unique bestial behavior of his shadows sooner, we wouldn't have been here. Instead, I'd indulged in my own self-pity and ignored what he needed most: love. Support. Understanding.

And now, when I'd finally figured that out and bared my heart to him, it was too late.

"I apologize for my outburst," I finally managed as I slowly straightened and met her guarded eyes.

"It's okay." She blew out a breath and her anger with it. "I'm willing to help however I can, I just wish I could've seen how it worked. Magic manifests differently for all of us."

Something clicked in the back of my mind, and the world slowed. "Someone else has witnessed it before." I jerked my chin toward Ozias. "Get Uma. Now."

He was on the couch in seconds, eyes slipping closed, with his hands clasped over his chest. The formerly quickened pace of his breaths slowed to a steady rise and fall, and then Calem and I watched as his consciousness separated from his body in the form of a shadowy apparition. He nodded once in our direction before disappearing entirely.

"He's shadow walking, right?" Raven tilted her head as she regarded his immobile form.

"Yes." Already I was pacing beside him, body itching for his return despite the fact he'd just left. "He'll be back shortly."

With her face pinched in curiosity, Isla inched toward him. "Is he in the shadow realm? Can't he just locate Gaige, then?"

I shook my head. "No. Shadow walking is the act of separating our conscious mind from our physical bodies so we can traverse this world in seconds, so long as we know a rough idea of where we're going."

"The shadow realm is like this world, but not." Calem slumped into the armchair as he studied his brother. "Think of it like an in-between."

"We can move through that space without affecting our surroundings and remain undetected. When our power wanes, we must return to this reality." My fingers twitched, and I removed my glasses and began polishing them to try to give my nerves some semblance of an outlet. "Gaige isn't there, either."

Isla crouched before Ozias to get a closer look at his face. "I thought you said he was lost to the shadows?"

Raven and Kaori had gone silent, but their rapt gazes were trained on me. My feet slowed until I came to a stop by Ozias's feet. They needed answers just like me. No, not answers—hope.

"We don't exactly know what happens to someone when they're lost to the shadows," I said quietly. "We don't have records. The few who've tried to search for the lost—in this world and in our parallel realm—have never been successful, either. The lost simply disappear without a trace."

"Magic always leaves a trace." Isla chewed on the inside of her cheek. Abandoning her position beside Ozias, she moved to the wall and leaned against it, tipping her head toward the ceiling as if deep in thought. "How long can you stay in the realm, give or take?"

I watched her carefully. "That depends on the person. At the risk of generalizing and greatly oversimplifying, maybe a day or two."

Calem scoffed. "If you don't move and use absolutely no power, sure."

With a wordless hum, she glanced at Kaori and Raven. "It's relatively similar for the beast realm, too, right?"

"Yes," Kaori said swiftly. She plucked at a stray thread dangling from the hemline of her sleeve and rolled it between her fingers. "There aren't many Charmers who can last more than a few hours."

"That's because all magic has limits," Isla murmured.

"What are you getting at?" I asked.

"I'm not sure." She let out a defeated sigh, but her brow remained creased. "Something just doesn't feel right, but I'm new to your type of magic. I could just be analyzing it too much."

Before I could press her more, a plume of shadows erupted in the center of the room. They writhed in indecipherable swirls until they knitted together, and Uma materialized before our eyes. Comprised of thin, sable tendrils, her form was wispy and shifted with even the slightest current, but she was very much present. She tipped her head by way of greeting just as Ozias sucked in a heavy breath and sat up from the couch.

"How can I help?" Uma asked.

All of Isla's concerns faded to the back of my mind, and I moved to stand before Uma. "Back at Cruor, you mentioned trying to save someone from the shadows."

"Once," she hedged. "It didn't work."

"Explain to me exactly what happened."

She fidgeted, and the lines of her shoulders blurred and re-formed. "I don't understand."

"Uma." I steeled myself against the burning impatience rising within me. "Gaige is gone. Please, just explain to us what happened."

Her gaze bounced from person to person until finally she stared at the floor. "I lost my pair bond to the shadows."

No one spoke. No one breathed. We all waited, giving her the chance to sift through her emotions and find the strength to carry on. Eventually, she forced herself to raise her head.

"He'd only been raised for a week, but he just never got used to it." She hugged her midsection as she spoke. "All I remember is waking up one night to find him standing in our room, but in the shadow realm. I got up and joined him so I could hold his hand. He was just…staring." Glistening, onyx tendrils streamed beneath her eyes. Her body, wherever it was resting, was crying. *She* was crying.

"I don't know how it happened. We were standing there, and then there was this awful disturbance… Shadows surged all around us, but they were different. They *felt* different." Her gaze riveted to me. "They *hurt*. And I–I let go. I didn't mean to let go. But as soon as I did, those shadows stole him away."

"Uma..." I couldn't find the words. Her pain, so much like the agony I felt in my core, was evident in the way she now stared at her upturned hands. Her faraway eyes were locked on her palms as if she could still feel the ghost of her pair bond's grasp.

Isla pushed around me to kneel on the floor in front of her. "May I?" She nodded toward Uma's trembling fingers.

"You won't be able to touch her," I said. "She's only a projection."

"I don't need to touch her." Isla pressed her lips into a thin line as she extracted the quartz stone from her pocket. Everything about her was rigid. Still, she forced the floating gem to hover above Uma's outstretched hands.

Ozias and Calem had come to my side while Kaori and Raven crept closer. I didn't know what we were waiting for, but there was no mistaking the bob of Isla's throat as she stared daggers into the magical orb. Seconds ticked by. I glanced at Ozias, but he only regarded Isla with a strained intensity that magnified the moment the quartz turned black. Hand trembling, she wrapped her fingers around it.

And just like before, miniscule electrical currents surged across her arms. She released the stone and gritted her teeth, weathering the effects of the magic much more skillfully than before. Her power fizzled out, and she used the edge of the counter to help hoist herself up.

"Show me where you last saw Gaige."

Heavy, uncontrollable ringing flooded my ears, and I nodded. I could barely formulate thoughts, let alone string together a sentence, so I led her into the bedroom without a word. The others followed, leaving Uma behind as she attempted to compose herself.

Again, Isla performed the ritual to detect trace amounts of magic in the space. And again the stone turned black and electricity coated her body. By the time she'd wrangled her power, her hair stood on end around her like a halo, and the magical sheen in her gaze had blown her irises wide. Face parchment-pale, she stood at the foot of the bed and clung to the frame.

"The shadows that took Uma's pair bond are the same shadows that affected the monsters." Her voice was raspy, and she forced a dry swallow before meeting my gaze. "They're the same shadows that took Gaige."

"What does that mean?" My words were barely a whisper, but she heard them all the same.

"It means that he's not lost in some unknown realm that may or may not be real. It means he was forcibly taken." She released the bed frame. "And it means that there's a chance we can bring him back."

TWENTY-SIX

KOST

After sending Uma home, we remained in the kitchen while Kaori brewed tea full of herbs at Isla's request. She listed off ingredients like comfrey, extract of daisies, essence of horehound, and sage. And while Kaori had always been skilled at preparing excellent drinks, even she paused at Isla's peculiar list.

"Don't worry about the flavor," she'd said with a wave. "I'm more interested in the magical properties. I'll need all the help I can get." At that, Kaori had nodded and left abruptly to ransack the herb supply near the dining tent. Ozias had gone with her and secured an assortment of fruit, nuts, and bread for Isla. They returned quickly, and Isla picked at her food while Kaori got to work. The anxiety was so thick in the air I couldn't bring myself to sit. Instead, I paced.

"This might not work," Isla said as she accepted her tea from Kaori. Gently, she blew the curling steam off the liquid before taking a sip. "I've never done anything like this before."

"I don't even understand what we're doing," Calem muttered from his perch on the couch.

"I'm going to try and rip open a portal by blending my magic with shadow magic like this other mage did." She took another drink from her cup before setting it down. For a long moment, she stared at the remaining dregs of her tea. “I just… I need you to understand something.”

“What is it?” Dread wrung my heart tight. I couldn’t take any more of this emotional whiplash. One moment Gaige was here, the next he was gone. Now there was a chance we could save him, yet there was an obvious hang-up she’d yet to voice. I would risk anything for even the smallest chance of this working. I just needed her to agree to that level of commitment, too.

“I’m not exactly the most powerful mage.” She toyed with her mug.

“I’ve seen you annihilate the front line of an army with a sparking ball of electricity.” Raven side-eyed her as she gripped the lip of the counter. “Pretty sure that makes you powerful.”

“I can perform some magic exceedingly well. I didn’t spend enough time in Allamere to learn it all, though. Other mages don’t even need this.” She gestured to her tea, and then brought it to her lips. When she set the cup down, it was empty. “But I will try. I will do everything that I can.”

“That’s all we need,” I said with a tight nod. If she could provide even a glimmer of hope, I’d find a way to navigate the rest. For Gaige, I would do anything.

“We need to move quickly.” With a definitive shove, she scooted her stool away from the counter and stood.

“Who’s all going?” Calem asked as he jumped to his feet.

“All of us,” Raven said with a hard look that dared anyone to defy her.

Fortunately, I didn’t have to. Kaori stepped beside her and placed a shaky hand on her shoulder. “I want to rush after him, too. But our powers don’t work in the shadows. What if something were to happen? The Charmers need a Council to help them rebuild.”

Raven’s lips quivered as she fought back what was likely a

biting response. She gave in with a forceful exhale and rolled her lips together, ignoring the weight of our gazes. "Just bring him back."

"I will," I said. Isla had already moved toward the bedroom, and I fell in line behind her, along with Ozias and Calem. We had no idea what we were walking into. I would have loved to utilize the Charmers' powers, but there was no arguing against Kaori's logic. I glanced over my shoulder and saw Kaori pull Raven into a one-armed hug, but her eyes were glassy with unshed tears. She nodded to me, then let her gaze slip to Calem's back before dipping her head to speak with Raven.

"The magic already worked once here before, so perhaps the veil is still thin enough for *my* magic to pierce it again," Isla said.

Ozias stood to her left and held out his hand. "Ready?"

She studied the lines of his palm and then gripped his forearm instead. "Let's go."

Shadows unfurled from the rafters and poured from the hidden crevices of the room in a flurry of movement. They blanketed us in a spectacular world of onyx, sable, and charcoal, wreathing the furniture and casting everything in darkened hues. Since my death, I'd found peace in the realm. But now, staring at the washed-out space that had been so full of life, so full of color, just the evening prior… I needed to see the flushed red of Gaige's sweat-slicked skin, the steel-blue of his eyes heated like fresh metal, dampened hickory curls plastered against the nape of his neck… Before, the shadows had been a reprieve. Now, they only served to remind me of what I'd lost.

Wide-eyed with her lips slightly parted, Isla raked her gaze over the room. "I can still feel his magic."

Hope purled in my chest. "Gaige's?"

"No, the mage's." She'd focused on the bed and raised her hand above the space where Gaige had slept. She sucked on her teeth as the hair along her arms stood on end. "This person… His magic feels…old."

"What does that mean?" Calem asked, drawing closer to the bed so we were all within arm's reach of the frame.

Her throat bobbed. "That he's very, very powerful. I don't know how he managed to blend our magics or why, but that's how he's trapped Gaige somewhere." Tipping her palm toward the ceiling, she centered herself with several breaths. "Okay, Ozias. I'm going to send an electrical current over this space, and I need you to cover me in shadows while I do it. Understood?"

"Understood." Eyes tight, he studied the space where her fingers had entrenched in his forearm. Inky tendrils began to wrap his muscular arm until his skin was obscured. They stilled near her touch, waiting for her command. She said nothing, but the swell of electricity was unmistakable even in the realm. Yet, as the sparks arced down her arms in faded-white waves, the charge felt stifled, like an uncomfortable prickle instead of a torrent of violent magic. She noticed, too, because she gave Ozias's arm a squeeze, and then his shadows enveloped her so rapidly and with such hunger that, for a moment, there was a void where her body stood.

And then the shadows jolted. Tiny, electrical zigzags spired off her like miniature lightning strikes, and she grunted as she forced the magic to follow the path down her arm. Sweat broke out along her forehead and her muscles strained as she braced against Ozias. Electric shadows lashed against his skin and left visible wounds, but he didn't flinch. He braced her with two steady hands, feeding more shadows to her currents until her eyes rolled to the back of her head.

Her power left in a rush as a thunderous clap shook the realm, followed by a sickening rip. A gash hung in the space above the bed, and through the rip in the veil, I saw a world of gray mist and a path laden with ebony stones.

I'm in a grayed-out world until I come to a beach and meet a man cloaked in shadows.

Gaige's recollection of his dream slammed into me, and my breath caught in my chest. He'd been dreaming about this place—visiting this place—for days on end. That first time... Back in Cruor... It hadn't just been a dream. I'd witnessed him being stolen away and ripped him back from the clutches of this dangerous mage without even knowing.

And now that I knew, I would most certainly do it again. "Let's go."

"I don't think Isla can make it," Ozias said, cradling her tense body against his chest. Her eyes moved rapidly beneath her closed lids, and quiet, mumbled words spilled out of her parted lips.

"Fracture. The fracture. Don't..." A violent shake ran through her body and then all at once she went limp, save the shallow rise and fall of her chest. Ozias's grip on her tightened.

"Take her back. Quickly," I said.

"What about you two?" Ozias asked. He glanced between Calem and me, but he was already commanding the shadows by his feet to pull back so he could return to the corporeal world.

"We'll figure it out." I tipped my chin toward Calem, and his single nod was the only confirmation I needed.

"Be safe." He tucked Isla closer to his chest and backstepped out the realm. Unwilling to wait any longer, I leapt into the fracture—for indeed she had managed to split the shadow realm to reveal this hidden sphere—and landed quietly with Calem a breath behind me.

With the jerk of his thumb, he indicated to the gash behind us. "How long you think that'll last?"

"Without Isla..." I started to jog. "Not long enough."

Our long strides ate away at the river-stone path beneath our feet, but the misty, gray expanse never shifted. We were cocooned in a world of fog and dew with little to no visibility beyond our own wingspan. Our footfalls were muffled, as if being passed through a cloth filter, and there was little else to decipher except the path laid out before us. A weak breeze whispered through the air.

Minutes crept by as our breaths quickened in time with our pace. Shadows manifested beneath our feet, and we pushed harder, faster, rounding a bend until finally the mist began to thin. The outlines of trees took shape, but they never fully came into focus. Somewhere, an owl hooted.

Calem slowed beside me. The mercury in his eyes had blown wide to douse his irises entirely, but he shuddered as he tried to summon more of his beast to the forefront. When nothing happened, he glowered at the widening path now interspersed with grains of black sand.

"I can't shift."

Unease stirred in my abdomen. "Not entirely unexpected. Charmers can't use their magic in the shadows, and beasts can't enter our realm." I thought back to the time I'd snuck through the bowels of Wilheim's castle with Leena at my side. We'd nearly stumbled upon Yazmin, and I'd been forced to wrap her in the shadows with me. Her beast had been left on the outside. He'd safely camouflaged himself, but it was explanation enough for why Calem's power had been stifled.

"This doesn't feel right," he muttered. Shadow blades formed by his hands, and I was viscerally reminded of just how deadly Calem had been before he'd been granted a second power. His bloodlust already rivaled that of a beast. This mage might have had old magic, but I had my brother by my side. I had my shadows. And both of us would go to the end of this realm and the next to save our family.

"No, it doesn't." Willing tendrils to gather in my palm, I fashioned a rapier and gripped the hilt tightly. The air was thick with dread. Indecipherable shadows, like that of fleeing beasts, darted through the mist on either side of the path. As we stepped out onto the beach and left the fog behind us, we froze.

Horror filled the marrow of my bones. The ground was *writhing*. Hundreds upon hundreds of shadows coated the beach in a serpents' nest. They swirled tirelessly without any real direction, converging upon each other. The dull breeze from earlier had shifted to full-on wind, and if not for its rippling effect on the choppy waves, I wouldn't have been able to decipher where the shadows ended and the ocean began. White spray shot into the air as seawater slammed into a barrier of rocky boulders. A lustrous moon—tinged a faded daffodil around the edges—showered the entire scene in an ominous light.

"Where the hell are we?" Calem's hushed words were barely audible over the waves.

"I'm not certain." I braved a single step onto the shadow-infested beach, and the tendrils I'd stepped on streaked away into the fog in the direction we came. Slowly, I took another step, and more shadows fled. "I think we're all right to continue on."

"To where, though?"

I didn't know. To our left, an empty beach. To our right, the same. We couldn't go back the way we came—we'd already traversed that path and found no sign of Gaige or the mage. Crouching, I waved my hand through the mess of interlocking shadows. They recoiled from my touch and raced away, peeling back to reveal more beach and the occasional rough stone. While most of the tendrils had fled at my gesture, a few had remained behind to hungrily lick at a damp spot in the sand.

With two fingers, I scooped up the wet grains and rubbed them against my thumb. "I don't understand. Why are they..."

My voice died as the grains fell away and left my fingers stained a deep red. Slowly, I once again inspected the beach. The shadows weren't moving aimlessly. They were collapsing in distinct spots and violently snaking around each other to devour whatever lay beneath.

Blood. It was blood. And I had a horrifying idea of who it belonged to.

Launching to my feet, I sprinted along the beach and swiped my rapier through the snarling mess of shadows. Darkened blood spots bloomed to life and created a new path for us to follow. Calem caught on to what I was doing, and he sprinted nearby, releasing countless thin blades of his own to skewer through the tendrils and send them rocketing away. Adrenaline roared in my ears.

Gaige's blood. We were too late. We had to be. There was so much. And the further we ran, the more apparent the tracks became. At the beginning, they'd just been small blemishes against the already dark sand. Now, there were rivers cutting canyons into the soft ground and rough trenches, as if he'd been dragged through the muck. Fear did dangerous things to my senses, and I think for the first time in my existence I understood why Calem often fell prey to his wild emotions.

Because in that moment, fury was all I felt. I wanted to kill the person who hurt Gaige this badly, and I didn't want to worry about remorse, about right or wrong. I wanted him to feel the same pain Gaige had felt when he'd experienced *this*. Bile soured my tongue, and I pushed forward until there was a noticeable drop in the number of shadows.

In the distance, a motionless body laid in the sand. Alone.

I knew I should have waited. I should've taken stock of my surroundings and strategized an approach. We had no idea where we were or what lurked in this foreign environment. But the moment I saw him, draped in ravenous shadows with smeared blood painted against his too-pale skin, all rational thought fled. My heart roared in my ears as I sprinted across the beach, and the remaining inky tendrils scattered.

Sliding to my knees, I ran my hands over Gaige's exposed body.

Uneven, jagged lacerations stretched from the base of his collarbone to his abdomen, and the shreds of skin had failed to restitch as blood continued to pool beneath him. Grains of sand coated his feet and calves, caked into place by a hardened layer of dried blood. His eyes were closed, lips barely parted, and a clammy sheen covered his brow. I gently wiped my thumbs across his forehead, but he didn't react to my touch.

Calem rushed to my side. "Is he…?"

I found the vein along his neck, and a feeble, dull pulse thudded against my fingers. "He's alive. Barely."

"Let's grab him and go." Calem crouched beside me and prepared to slip his arms beneath Gaige's legs when a miniscule shadow raced from under his thighs and shot through the sand. I glared at the wry tendril as it slunk away, only to slither around the bare foot of a man. My body went cold.

"Calem."

He looked up and stiffened beside me. The mage. It had to be. The shadows about him exuded a raw and violent energy as they snapped about his frame, lashing away at his skin. His curled hair was matted and tangled in places with his unkempt beard. Tattered clothes limply hung about his frame and were stained with dirt. His face was gaunt, but there was an undeniable intensity teeming in his black-brown eyes.

"Hello." The grating rasp of his voice sent a chill racing down my spine. "I wasn't expecting visitors."

My grip on my rapier tightened. "What have you done to him?"

"Taken his blood." He shrugged as if it were the most obvious answer, and he continued forward until he was only a few feet away. "I needed it."

My blade was against his throat in an instant, and I relished in the ruby rivulet that swelled and dribbled down the central ridge. I could kill him if I had to. "Not another step."

"Fine, fine." He raised his hands in a feeble show of surrender. The amused cock of his brows and quivering corners of his lips contradicted the action entirely.

"Who are you?" I asked.

"I am the Lost, and the Lost are me." His smile twisted. "And you are in my domain."

Domain? I refused to break his probing stare. There was something about him that didn't feel quite whole. Isla had mentioned he'd be powerful, but then why the rags? Why the sallow cheeks and depleted figure, as if he hadn't eaten a proper meal in months? Years, even.

"Why did you need Gaige?" I asked.

The muscle above his brow twitched. "The lost become me, and he was lost."

"He'd found a way to control his shadows." Barely constrained anger surged through to my fingertips, but I held my weapon steady. "He wasn't lost."

"I have claimed many." He leaned into my blade, not caring that it drove the tip deeper into his flesh. "I decide who is lost, and I take what is mine."

Beside me, Calem summoned his own volley of inky blades. They hovered by his body and waited to do his bidding, steady despite Calem's twitching fingers. Again, the mercury ring around his irises flooded his stare until only that disastrous hue was visible. Even if he couldn't shift, his body reacted to the rage Calem must've felt.

"Enough riddles." Calem's words were a deadly whisper. "Give me one reason why I shouldn't kill you now for what you did to our friend."

The mage's focus snapped to him. The smile on his face erupted into a full-blown grin. "You're different, too. I had no idea. How could I have missed you?"

Calem didn't take the bait. "Let's kill him."

A strange hunger tugged at the Lost's expression, and the shadows about his frame jumped with a visceral, frenetic energy. "Who are you? What power do you possess?"

I pressed the point of my blade deeper, and more blood trickled down my weapon. This time, the undead mage dragged his gaze to the sight and stilled, as if realizing that I did, in fact, pose a threat.

"This is your final warning," I said. "We will kill you."

He looked at me directly, and for the first time I noticed a ring of crimson around the brown-black of his irises. It seemed to throb with power, and a dark chuckle slipped from his chapped lips. The blood on my blade—his blood—vaporized into a curl of wispy, black steam as he leaned back and batted my rapier away.

"You couldn't kill me if you tried. And I'd very much like to see you try."

He lunged. Not for me, but for Calem, and the shadows that had been spiraling from his frame arced toward us like lightning. They struck with the same force, ricocheting off our bodies and searing the sands, turning the ground into heated, black glass. We were thrust back into a pair of jagged boulders, and the force of the hit had spots blooming across my vision. The roar of the ocean waves coalesced with the rush of adrenaline in my ears, and I braced myself against the rock. Beside me, Calem cursed and spat blood at his feet.

"My turn," he hissed. Without a second thought, he bolted toward the mage. I made a move to join him when a single shadow in my peripheral vision snagged my focus. It'd streaked forward the moment Calem had abandoned his position, and it licked at the frothy, red-tinged spit he'd left behind. My gaze snapped back to Gaige and the ravenous shadows that had resumed their meal.

"Calem!" I screamed, but I was too late. The mage was all too eager to welcome Calem's rage-filled assault, and he stood with his arms thrust wide open as if expecting an embrace instead of a blade to the heart. Calem's shadows flung to him like armor, and he commanded his weapons to fly right at the Lost's center mass. He didn't even bother to dodge. His shadows were too fast, and they cut through Calem's attack and pierced him clean through his shoulders. Calem shrieked as the mage's shadows pinned him to the ground. More tendrils raced over him in a flurry, drinking the blood pooling beneath his body.

The Lost shuddered as visible gooseflesh covered his skin. Eyes alight, he stared at his prize. "You bury so much. I can taste it." He dragged an absent finger along his lips and held it there. "You could have been *great*."

We needed to get back to the portal. Now.

My gaze cut to Gaige's crumpled form. He was still breathing but otherwise unconscious. I needed to free Calem first, and then we had to find a way to carry Gaige and escape the Lost's grasp. I just didn't know how. I couldn't analyze the mage's motives. First he wanted Gaige, and now Calem? The only thing that stuck out was the Lost clearly had no interest in me.

A familiar prickling sensation crawled through my mind. Felicks.

My focus narrowed on the Lost. Images began to flood down the bond I shared with my beast as the world around me slowed. I was surprised his powers worked here, but then again, he wasn't here. These small flashes of the future were because of our bond. Because of how much time we spent together, learning from each other, loving each other, training together.

That connection surpassed realms. And I would use it to save my family.

Focusing all my energy on the bond I shared with Felicks, I summoned more shadows to my being until another rapier took shape in my left hand. I rotated them in a large, sweeping arc before rocketing toward the Lost. Shadows gathered beneath my feet and guided me toward my target with unnatural speed, and the mage only glanced my direction when I was already upon him. I raised both swords high and prepared to drive them down through his chest, but the shadows that'd pinned Calem released their grip to form a barricade before the Lost. My blades shattered the mage's shadows, and they streaked outward in a circle before petering out and dissolving to nothing.

The Lost backstepped and turned his fury on me. "You." His gaze shifted to the space where I used to be, as if calculating the distance and my movements. Then, he stormed toward me. "How?"

Without looking over my shoulder, I barked an order to Calem. "Take Gaige and go!"

"Like fucking hell I'm leaving you," Calem growled.

"Don't worry. I won't let that happen." The Lost summoned shadows from the ground itself, and they burst through the sands in monstrous spires that nearly gutted us. Calem had rolled just in time and landed a few feet from Gaige. He scrambled toward Gaige's motionless body and hoisted him up, but the Lost's shadows were already poised to strike at them again. More premonitions bloomed in my mind, and I darted toward the forming spears and cut them at the base before he could command them.

He snarled in frustration and summoned more. "I can do this forever."

All magic has limits. Isla's words whispered through my mind, and I gritted my teeth as I again cut through the barrage of daggerlike shadows. The Lost couldn't possibly maintain this level of power forever. His magic would eventually ebb away. I just needed to keep utilizing this precognition to stay one step ahead. The only downfall was that I had no idea how long I'd be able to hold on to Felicks's power.

"Go, Calem!" I needed to buy them time. Gaige still wasn't healing. Maybe if they got closer to the rift, closer to the real shadow realm, his restorative powers would strengthen.

"I already told you—"

"NOW!" I roared. "That's an order from your guild master."

The Lost shot more shadows soaring through the air, and while I deflected a few, a handful still found their targets. In the soft flesh of Gaige's thigh. Calem's shoulder and calf. He howled—in rage, frustration, pain, or some combination of all three—and glared at the Lost before finally, finally, dragging Gaige toward the ebony path.

I wasn't sure if I'd ever see Calem and Gaige again, but at least I could give them a chance to live.

Turning my back on them and hoping Calem would, for once in his stubborn existence, escape, I gripped the hilts of my swords with renewed vigor. More tendrils knit around me in a shimmery armor, and I took a step forward.

"I will not let you have them."

And with that, I lunged headlong into a swarm of writhing shadows.

Twenty-Seven

Gaige

When I managed to finally open my eyes, I thought I was still lost in the fog of my subconscious. All around me was a wet, milky-white mist that settled like a cold blanket against my skin. I couldn't see anything else, but my body ached as if I'd endured yet another Slimack attack. I wanted to fall back into a deeper state of unconsciousness, but awareness flickered in my mind like a ripple on a pond. It was quiet at first. I couldn't quite place the sound, but as it grew closer, louder, I realized it was scream.

Kost. I bolted upright as my memories slammed into me. That wasn't my subconscious—I was physically surrounded by fog, which meant I was still in the mysterious realm where the Lost resided. I jerked my head around in search of Kost, but he was nowhere to be found. There was nothing but gray-on-gray, and the feel of smooth stones beneath me. Pain blossomed from my abdomen as I stood, and I gnashed my teeth together. Wincing, I grazed the healing, reddish-pink wounds puckered against my midsection.

On the beach, my body had refused to heal. I'd fallen unconscious in a pool of my own blood, my hands going limp over wounds that refused to close. But here… I glanced around. I still wasn't entirely sure how I'd ended up in this place, but I knew I entered it *somewhere*. And that somewhere was close. The real shadow realm was close. It was feeding my powers, making it easier for my body to heal.

That still didn't explain how I'd escaped, though. The last thing I remembered was being buried alive by shadows, and now this. I couldn't even see the path anymore. Somehow, I'd made it back into the foggy abyss. Somehow...

Another scream, closer this time, shattered the too-quiet surroundings, and a blurry outline whizzed past me. I barely glimpsed it at first, but it crashed into the ground nearby and a plume of mist furled outward at the sudden disturbance. A body covered in lacerations similar to my own appeared.

"Kost." I ran toward him, ignoring the heat and stickiness of blood as one of my gashes reopened.

A dangerous growl, more feral than human, simmered from a chest too broad to be Kost's. I skidded to a halt and waved away the mist above his head. Loose blond hair streaked with blood fell about wide shoulders, and Calem jerked his head toward me. Awareness clicked in his mercury-filled glare, and his brows smoothed a fraction.

"Thank fuck you're finally awake. We need to move."

"How did you get here?" I offered him my hand and pulled him to his feet. He didn't meet my gaze, instead tracking invisible threats in the mist and settling lower into his stance.

"I'll explain later. Right now, we're being hunted." As if responding to his words, a shadow wolf of my own making lunged from the fog and slammed into Calem with brutal efficiency. Fangs tore at his bicep, and blood spurted across the ebony stones at our feet. He summoned a blade in his other hand and drove it into the shadow beast's heart. It exploded in a flurry of wispy tendrils as more eerie howls echoed through the mist.

Eyes lit with that dreadful, magical sheen bloomed to life all around us. Calem pressed his back against mine and cursed. "Can you do anything about this?"

"The mage turned them against me." My gaze flitted from one indecipherable shape to the next.

"Fucking prick," Calem hissed. "I hope Kost kills him."

I went stock-still. "Kost is fighting him?"

"He's the only reason we're alive." Shadows curled around us as Calem called them close. Hundreds of blades formed a sphere around our bodies, and they hung perfectly equidistant from one another as they waited for the beasts to strike.

But all I could think about was Kost fighting against the mage alone. I knew I was weak. I hadn't trained enough to hold a candle to the mage. Kost, though, had spent decades finessing his magic. He'd never settle for anything less than a perfect execution of his power.

And I still knew in my gut that he wouldn't survive. He didn't stand a chance against the Lost. A different kind of pain speared my chest, and my breathing hit hard. I didn't know how he'd managed to come here, but he'd risked everything to save me. I'd be damned if I was going to leave him here to die.

"We have to go back."

Calem braved a quick look over his shoulder at me. "Trust me, I didn't want to run, either. But it's what he wanted."

"Screw what he wanted." My hands fisted by my sides, and shadows crept through the mist to converge at my feet. A few of the beasts in the fog whined. "Do you really think he'll survive without us?"

Calem flinched. "No."

"Then do we even have a choice?"

All around us the beasts edged closer, drawing near enough that I could pick out their snarling muzzles and flattened ears. There were too many of them for Calem's blades. He could release his weapons now and decimate the first wave of creatures, but there were endless rows of glowing eyes waiting in the mist. Another wolf dared to fully emerge from the fog. With its hackles standing on end, it drew its snout close to the blades. A shiver coursed through its wispy hide. There was a glimmer of recognition in its magicked gaze as the shadows I'd summoned curled in my hands.

If I could charm a Kitksa monster with a shadow lure, then certainly I could charm a beast of my own making. Slipping my eyes closed, I drew in three slow breaths and cupped my hands before me. With each inhale, I willed the shadows to do my bidding, and with each exhale I thrust out all my doubts. I had the power to save my friends. I had been given a second chance at life. I wasn't a burden. And I alone was responsible for my fate.

When my eyes flew open, a magnificent sphere the size of a freestanding globe hovered before my torso. Its polished, sable surface was completely smooth and perfectly intact. Each shadow had woven together in perfect harmony, and when I gazed into its reflective sheen, the only thing I saw was me.

"Come back to me," I whispered, and the orb erupted in hundreds of beautiful threads eager to carry my command. They shot like arrows through every shadow beast before returning to flood into my center. The cool blast of power was followed by a deep sense of knowing, as each beast shook off the Lost's control and fell back onto their haunches. I felt their bonds now, attached to my magic and my soul. This was *my* power. It didn't belong to the Lost; it lived within me. It was part of me in a way that had once been terrifying, but now... Now I would sooner die than let anyone take it away. The shadow beasts shuddered in recognition, and I knew they would not fall prey to the mage's control again.

Slack jawed and unmoving, Calem watched it all. "I really wish you'd done that sooner."

"Me too." I grimaced as a sharp twinge spurred in my side.

Between my wounds and the sheer amount of power I was attempting to maintain, I wasn't sure how long I had. "Come on."

Calem called off his blades as two shadow steeds trotted to our sides. They bent to their knees and allowed us to climb atop their backs. The moment we'd wrenched our fists in their manes, they took off. They didn't need the ebony stone path to navigate this world, and instead cut directly through the dense mist. And my beasts followed. The scrape of their claws, the clatter of hooves, the earsplitting howls, and wet snarls—they pounded through me with the effectiveness of a battle drum calling soldiers to war. It reverberated through my bones and dulled all my pains, my fears, until all I had was one overriding certainty.

I would protect Kost with my life.

The roar of crashing waves met my ears as the mist began to thin. So did the sharp scrape of metal on metal. *Kost.* My heart pounded in my throat. At least he still wielded his rapier. So long as he had that, then he couldn't be too badly injured. He had to be...

Time slowed as we broke through the veil of fog. The Lost floated above Kost in a maelstrom of lashing shadows. He was the center of the storm, and he ceaselessly battered against Kost's weakening form. With two rapiers crossed before him, Kost held off the brunt of the Lost's attack, but countless more streaks cut around his barricade and sliced into his already weeping skin. His tunic was gone, shredded and discarded about the beach. His glasses were missing, and his whole body trembled as if it were on the verge of giving out. I knew his skin was pale, but I couldn't see it beneath the thick sheen of blood covering him from chin to waistline. Worse, I could no longer detect the solid ridges and hard lines of his chest and abdomen. There were too many open wounds and layers of skin cut down to the bone.

It was the most horrific thing I'd ever seen in my life, and it filled me with such rage that I hardly recognized myself. Fury burned through me with a fire that would rival any mage's, and it sped down the shadow bonds to my creatures and filled them with a similar animalistic rage. Beside me, scales raced over Calem's shaking arms, but his beast never came. The unbridled fury in his mercury gaze, though, was something that no manner of magic or shadow realm could repress.

Just then, Kost crumpled to one knee and his rapiers fell to the ground. His chest heaved as blood splattered against the sand before him. Hand trembling, he tried to grasp his nearest sword, but one of the Lost's shadows smashed it into oblivion.

A deep, rumbling laugh shook the air as the Lost summoned one disastrously long lance twice the length of his body. He held his arm high, guiding the weapon into the air and poising it like the guillotine it was right above Kost's head.

"You never stood a chance."

I moved without rational thought. Heels driving into my steed's sides, I urged it to run with godly speed fueled by panic and rage. Its muscles writhed beneath my legs as it heeded my call and drove us between the Lost's rapidly descending weapon and Kost. He looked up at me, a dawning look of both relief and panic filling his expression, and he raised a limp hand. I snagged his wrist and yanked him up behind me without stopping, and the lance impaled the space where he used to be.

"You came back." His voice was hoarse and so dangerously soft, but I took solace in the weight of him against my spine, in the loose wrap of his arms around my waist.

"I will always come back for you." I jerked my steed around until I was staring down the Lost. Calem and my beasts thundered to my side. For a moment, the mage did nothing. With his lips peeled back in a tight grimace, he simply stared. His virulent shadows, however, never tired. They continued to lash out aimlessly, striking the ground before us with the force of lightning and turning small spots in the sand into glimmering, onyx glass.

"You regained control of your powers." The Lost's tight gaze flickered to the army of beasts. "I knew you were extraordinary."

"We're leaving." I still wasn't sure we could beat him, but I prayed my heightened power was enough to convince him to let us go. Once we were healed and could find a way to bring the full force of the Council, we'd end the Lost. We had to, because I knew from the deranged look in his tight stare that he would never give up. He'd already tasted my blood, and he was far from satisfied. He wanted everything I had to offer, and I had no intention of giving it to him.

He sighed—a bored, annoyed thing. "No, you're not."

"Then you'll die." Glittering, ink-black blades formed around Calem in the same, heated fashion he'd displayed in the mist. Scales continued to appear and recede along his arms, never fully taking shape but not disappearing, either.

A horrifying, too-wide grin split the Lost's face as he targeted Calem. "That's it. Try harder. Show me your power so I can take it."

"We have to run," Kost croaked against my back. "The rip in the realm..." His voice died off as he slumped against me. My throat tightened with worry, and I forced a single, shadow snake to slither up the saddle and constrict around us. If he slipped off now, I feared the Lost would kill him without a second thought.

But the Lost had gone impossibly still. "What did you say?"

"I don't know what he's talking about," I called. Because I didn't. But I also didn't like how Calem stiffened with awareness beside me. His lips twitched.

"Do you trust me?" Calem asked.

"So long as you're not about to ask me to leave you behind, then yes." My steed shifted impatiently beneath me, responding to the anxiety pulsing through my body.

"Run." And for the first time in my life, and quite possibly the last, I witnessed Calem flee from the promise of battle. He dug in his heels, ushering his stallion into a dead sprint toward the stone path just past the Lost.

The mage lunged. Bolts of shadows rained down from the sky and struck around Calem. Sand erupted in a volatile shower of black grains as he guided his steed left and right, dodging most of the Lost's assault. One bolt slammed into his shoulder and he winced, just as another tendril speared the flank of his mount. Shadows dispersed at the point of contact, and before I realized I'd done it, I'd sent a wave of my own tendrils across the beach to reseal the wound and keep his stallion moving.

I charged after him with my beasts at my side, and the Lost roared. "You cannot escape me!"

Again, we raced down the stone path, and the mage pursued us. Kost's head bobbled against the space between my shoulders, but I could still feel the shaky skate of his breath against my neck. Alive. I had to keep it that way.

The Lost's shadows carried him at a breakneck speed, and he flew beside us through the gray expanse. His erratic tendrils, charged with a foreign magic more powerful than any I'd ever encountered, shocked the very mist around us. Thousands of tiny, pale-white volts arced through the air and slammed into our bodies. A scream pushed its way through my lips as red-hot welts formed against my skin. When the charge subsided, so too did the mist, revealing a tumultuous, rocky expanse dotted with barren trees. The earth was covered in a layer of dew, and pale light reflected harshly off the glistening surfaces.

"Hurry!" Calem shouted over his shoulder.

The Lost shrieked and sent a volley of lances toward Calem. Toward my brother. *Brother.* For that's what he was. Both Calem and Ozias had stayed by my side throughout this mess, and I would forever consider them family. And Kost… He would one day be my *anam-cara*—the other half of myself—if we made it out of this.

When we made it out of this.

Focusing on the threads of power connecting me to my shadow creatures, I commanded them to peel off and attack. A flock of angry crows slammed into each other, their shadows unstitching and rethreading to form a dragon with a wingspan twice as long as my body.

With a heady roar, it reared itself up and extended its wings wide, taking every hit intended for Calem. The final spear was too much for my power, and it dispersed in a fragmented wisp of smoke, but it'd done its job. Calem was safe.

And the Lost was furious.

He rained another series of shadow bolts down upon us, and again my beasts merged to protect us. But their numbers were waning, and so was my power. A cold sweat had broken out along my hairline, and I could feel the clamminess of my own skin against my collar. Blood oozed from my wounds as all my magic was focused on attacking rather than healing, and a quiet, dangerous ringing had started in my ears.

I couldn't hold on much longer, and I had no idea where we were going. There was nothing in front of us save the endless path crowded by tumultuous, jagged terrain.

And then my gaze caught on a peculiar glint of silver a short distance away. There, hanging in the air where the path came to a sudden and abrupt end, was a rip in the sky. And in that rip, I could just glimpse a familiar realm. The real shadow realm, the one every undead had access to. Not this awful hellscape we'd known nothing about.

Hope crested in me, and I pushed my mount faster. If we could get back to the shadow realm, we could get back to our world. We could escape the Lost. We could save Kost.

A shadow bolt struck me through the abdomen, and I keeled over against my steed. Stars bloomed behind my eyes and the world swam. If not for the serpent tightened around Kost's and my waists, I would've fallen to the earth. Calem shouted something I couldn't decipher, and then a volley of shadow blades soared through the air above my head.

"Gaige!" He'd pulled back on his stallion to ride beside me.

Everything blurred and my stomach knotted. Clenching my jaw tight, I forced myself to meet his gaze. I couldn't speak. My tongue had swollen, and my throat had dried, and one by one I felt the cords snap between my shadow beasts and me. As quickly as my muddled brain would allow, I found the threads to mine and Calem's mounts and gripped them with everything I had. They pulled taut against my consciousness but held, and some of the nausea passed.

The Lost snarled, and then his head snapped to the rip in the realm. Something shifted in his power, and I caught sight of claws pushing through his hands and wings emerging from his back. They beat furiously against the shadows and moved him even faster, pushing him ahead of us.

"What in the actual fuck?" Calem shouted.

The Lost landed before us with such force that the realm trembled. Black tendrils spiderwebbed across the ground from the impact, snaking out from his feet and lancing into the earth to create canyons in the rocks. A shock wave slammed into us, and all at once the ties to my steeds snapped. My shadows fled, and the three of us crashed into the ground. The force of the hit jostled Kost awake, and he moaned as he managed to pull himself to his knees. Looping his arm over my shoulders, I slowly helped him stand. Calem was already on his feet, and with one quick motion, he summoned a wall of shadow blades. They quivered with anticipation as Calem stared down the Lost.

But the mage was far from fazed.

"You will not leave. I have not claimed what is mine." Brutal tendrils lashed at the space between us and him, measuring the distance.

Calem didn't bother to respond. He released his hold on the blades and they sang through the air, speeding toward their target with impeccable accuracy. Their sheer numbers gave me hope. At least *one* of them had to make it. I wasn't sure if Kost had been able to land any blows, but neither Calem nor I had been able to do so. The Lost had always blocked our attacks with his own magic.

And yet again, he managed to do the same. As Calem's barrage of blades neared the Lost's body, columns of shadows erupted from the earth to intercept his assault. Each time one of Calem's weapons embedded itself in the Lost's defenses, both sets of shadows went up in wispy smoke. But Calem never stopped. He kept fashioning more and shooting them across the path, taking one step closer with every new advance.

The Lost moved furiously, thrusting his arms this way and that with mind-numbing speed to construct more defenses, only for Calem to tear them down. Kost and I inched along a breath behind our brother. I wanted to help, but my body was already screaming as I shouldered Kost's weight. A heady ache had settled behind my eyes, and it was all I could do to keep moving.

A scream ruptured through the whoosh of shadows, and my gaze snapped to the Lost. A single blade of Calem's had slipped through the mage's flurry of columns and struck him in the side. Relief lit a fire beneath the small dose of hope I'd been harboring since we caught sight of the rip in the realm. We could do this. We just had to slow him down. We... My brows drew together at the same time Calem sucked in a breath.

The Lost didn't bleed. Shadows pooled out of him like writhing insects and dropped to his feet. He clamped his hand over the wound in an attempt to slow the spray of darkness, but tendrils leaked through his fumbling fingers and crawled down his legs.

"But I saw him bleed." Shock brought my voice back, but the words still burned my vocal cords, and I rubbed my throat. Kost had stiffened in my hold, but he said nothing as he watched the Lost with narrowed eyes.

"More magic," Calem grumbled. "Come on!" He summoned more blades and fired them off. Then, he grabbed my wrist and jerked Kost and me in the direction of the rip. We picked up the pace, Kost finally releasing his grip on me to hobble along with us. Still, his jaw was set tight, and he scoured the area as if searching for something none of us could see.

And then the Lost disappeared in a sudden vacuum of darkness, leaving the path to the rip dangerously free and clear. At first, we didn't move. Ears straining, I listened for anything. It was deafeningly quiet, so much so that my heartbeat was maddeningly loud and my ratcheting breaths reminiscent of a howling wind. Without saying anything, we met each other's gazes and instinctively knew—moving was the absolute worst idea possible.

Except a single, haunting sound, like the gentle slide of a needle stitching thread, destroyed that plan entirely.

The rip was resealing.

"Go!" Calem shouted, and we ran. We ran as if we hadn't just been beat to a pulp by a murderous, rampaging mage. We ran like this was our only opportunity for survival, because it was. If we remained here, we knew we'd die. We couldn't stand up to the Lost forever—he'd already proven that. My pulse roared in my ears as we shortened the space between us and safety. Ten more strides... Five...

The Lost appeared above us in a vortex of lethal tendrils. He pinned the three of us with ease. Shadows wrapped our bodies and embedded themselves in the ground, creating unbreakable chains that eliminated all possibility of escape. Descending slowly with the help of his shadows, he finally touched down at our feet and glowered our direction.

"I think I'll kill you here, where you can see your home but not quite reach it. You can't imagine what that feels like." Something dangerous flickered through his burning stare. The wings at his back stretched and shuddered, as if they hadn't truly graced the skies in years. "I wish I could do it slowly, so you could fully comprehend the pain."

Another stitch pulled at the seams of the realm. We weren't going to make it.

"I'll use all of my power to do it. You've earned that." His smile turned wicked, and his biceps bulged, as if he'd somehow doubled the layers of muscles beneath his skin. That same, disastrous sheen obscured his eyes, though I doubted we needed any level of manipulation to succumb to death. Except, for some reason I couldn't grasp, the shadows dripping out of his shoulder from Calem's wound suddenly looked like blood again.

Had that been the case all along? I had no idea what was real anymore. And I think that was the point. He was too powerful to overcome, and he'd torture our minds and our bodies to prove it.

Pressing my cheek against the ground, I angled my gaze toward Kost. If I was going to die, I wanted him to be the last thing I saw. But he wasn't looking at me. He was focused on the sudden display of ruby blood, and his lips were peeled back in a grimace. His fingers twitched against the ground, and I saw the beginnings of a shadow curling beneath his palm.

What are you doing? I wanted to inch toward him, but the Lost's hold was unyielding. The thick bands across my abdomen and chest pressed tightly into my body, deepening with every passing breath and slowly cutting off circulation to my limbs. A dull tingling had already started in my fingers, but I didn't have any magic left to try to escape. Not like Kost.

"I used to be able to do so much more." The Lost spat at the ground. "I was *grand*."

"And now you're delirious," Calem chuckled through a mouthful of blood. His own stare was still full of mercury, but his labored breathing and sweat-slicked skin was revealing enough. Like me, he had emptied his reserves.

Again, that subtle whisper of thread tugging through fabric drifted over us.

"I hope that beast in your veins defies the will of magic like it's been trying to do since you arrived." He raised his hand and poised his daggerlike claws directly above Calem's sternum. "I desperately need it to."

Cocking his elbow back, he prepared to strike. Just as he released the tension in his muscles and began driving his claws toward Calem, a thin onyx blade cut through the air and sliced off the Lost's arm. It happened so fast I barely caught it. So wrapped up in Calem's banter and his own bloodlust, the Lost hadn't noticed the final shadow Kost had willed to life. The Lost stared in horror at his appendage on Calem's chest, and then all at once shadows erupted from the severed limb and the mage's body. They fled over the rocky expanse and darted away from their master, leaving him screaming as he tried to regain his power.

With the sudden release of his shadows, our holds dissipated.

"Run!" Kost shouted.

We leapt to our feet and tore toward the rip. The Lost screamed at our backs and the world began to tremble as an endless sea of shadows seemed to unravel from everywhere. The ground slipped out from under us, spinning away like water down a drain. Calem lunged and managed to anchor himself with one arm and leg in the shadow realm, and he reached back in time to snag Kost.

"Gaige!" Kost shouted. Our fingers met. Slipped. The darkness threatened to swallow me whole. I couldn't decipher left from right, up from down, just the howling snarling mess of tendrils collapsing on each other and the Lost's rage-filled scream. There was a glimmer of gray, a small slip of silver where the seam between our worlds waited. And then Kost's hand found mine, and he clamped my wrist so tightly I swore my bone cracked. Sharp pain spiraled from his touch, but I dug my fingers into his forearm with the same force. With a yank, he dragged me into the familiar shadow realm.

Our room came into focus, grayed-out and layered in varying shades of black, but undeniably the very same room I'd slept in with Kost just the night before. My heart trembled in my chest, and slowly, we called off the shadows and prepared to find solid footing back in Hireath.

I'd never really paid attention to the intricate way the shadows receded as we left the realm. It was like watching brushstrokes paint the world in color, and my eyes ached at the sight of emerald greens, pastel blues, polished browns—all of it.

A smile pulled at my lips. "Thank the gods that's—"

An explosion of oil and ink blacked out our world and shot into the room. The walls shattered in a spray of wood and debris, the furniture obliterated along with the foundation of the building. We were thrust out into the clearing, and my back cracked against the earth as I stared into the burning light of high noon. Terrified, confused screams crested around us. Rolling to my side, I blinked away the red afterimage left by the sun's rays and froze. Thousands upon thousands of wretched tendrils had wrenched through the rip, forced their way through the shadow realm, and followed us out.

And in the middle of the abyss was the Lost. He gripped his missing arm, but otherwise showed no signs of pain.

His crazed smile deepened as he peered at us from the dark. "I'm not done with you."

Shadows streaked like lightning across the settlement, cracking into buildings with the same force. Raven, Kaori, Isla, and Ozias had rushed toward us the moment we appeared, and they were now frozen in horror. Face ghost-white, Isla fell to her knees and clamped her hands over her mouth. Her own magic crackled around her in response, and the Lost shifted his focus to her.

"Weak." He flicked his wrist and a dark bolt arced through the air to strike her in the chest.

Ozias roared and charged toward the Lost with murder in his eyes. Blades sprung up around him as he ran, and he sent them flying without a second thought. Raven was right there with him, summoning her legendary feline and screaming at the top of her lungs as she charged alongside her friend. Kaori had sent a wave of her own beasts into battle with them, but her body shuddered as mercury veins covered her arms and face.

"No," Calem barked, his words a harsh rasp. He stared at Kaori and reached for her with a weak, trembling hand. "Don't let him see."

But it was too late. Her eyes had taken on that same, mercury hue as Calem's, and the air was charged with power as she prepared to shift. The Lost's attention snapped to her.

"He's not real," Kost whispered, dragging his battered body closer to me. His limbs were crooked at odd angles, and a bone punctured the already damaged skin of his leg. I hadn't seen how he landed after being expelled from the shadow realm, but one thing was clear: several of his limbs were broken. He winced as he fought against the weight of his unusable legs, desperately trying to inch his way forward.

"What are you talking about?" Everything hurt. My bones. My skin. The very breath I needed to survive. But somehow, I managed to pull myself up. Somehow, I craned my neck toward the Lost.

"He's a shadow projection. Whatever blood you saw... It wasn't real. You just need to make him disperse."

Terror wound through me as the Lost struck Ozias down. Then Raven. Kaori was only moments away from shifting, and I feared if she got too close, he'd simply steal her away and kill her safely in the confines of his realm. I tried to pull on my reserves, to summon shadows from the depths of my soul, but nothing came. I'd expended everything on the Lost, and now, when my family needed me most, all I could do was watch. Raven's beasts had been cast to the side with the same quickness she'd suffered, and I wasn't sure there was a creature in this realm that could do anything to help us now.

But maybe a monster. Adrenaline filled my limbs and roared through my ears, ushering in a small wave of energy. I clambered to my feet and took one shaky step forward. And then another. Ozias had returned to the fray and was distracting the Lost with another onslaught of blades, much like the attack Calem had used to first injure the mage. But it wouldn't be enough.

I just need one shot. Forcing myself to ignore the screaming burn in my legs, I picked up my pace and whistled sharply. Boo and Rook barreled out of the forest to meet me midstride. Boo immediately fell to his knees, and I crawled atop his back. We were moving again in seconds, and I gripped his hackles tight. The full moon etching on his helm was a welcome warning.

"Charge," I said. Magic thrummed from his center and purled like a heat wave toward his head. Beautiful droplets of moonlight gathered between his antlers. I just needed to give him a chance to fully amass his power.

Dropping my gaze to Rook, I jerked my chin in the direction

of the Lost. “Paralyze him but avoid his shadows. I don’t know how well your power will work on him.” Rook barked in answer and peeled off, darting behind debris to position himself in the Lost’s eyesight. Death rolled through the clearing with the scent of mothballs and the frigid kiss of ice. The Lost hesitated as he scoured the open meadows for the source of the magic.

Ozias used the opportunity to strike, and a blade found its home in the Lost’s shoulder, the same spot Calem had marked before. A high-pitched howl escaped from the mage’s chest, and the rest of his arm fell into the thick blanket of writhing shadows. Wild, furious eyes tracked Ozias as he ran.

Boo continued to charge as we skirted around the exterior of the battle. His body cooked with the unbridled power now coursing through his muscles. The moon blooming between his antlers was almost complete, but I had to be certain. I’d only have one chance to shoot off a beam of pure moonlight and obliterate the Lost’s shadows. Boo wouldn’t be able to summon that kind of power again until the next full moon.

A sharp cry snared my focus. The Lost had pinned Ozias and was preparing to strike.

And then Rook leapt forward, positioning himself in the wild mess of shadows and turning the full force of his power on the Lost.

Time slowed to a halt. The air was thick with the presence of death, and even though I wasn’t the recipient of Rook’s magic, a shiver crawled down my spine. The Lost had gone stock-still, but his shadows still snapped about him and threatened to crack down on my beast. Rook refused to budge. A tremor worked its way through the Lost’s body. Then, a grimace. Rook’s hold wouldn’t last.

“Now!” We shot from the fringe of the woods and rocketed toward the Lost. All I could see was him. His world of darkness and terror that blanketed out the sun. His deranged smile and bulging eyes. His writhing shadows where his arm should have been. I didn't know what he wanted or why he'd thought I was the answer, but I would never let him take me or anything, anyone, I loved.

I screamed as loud as my lungs would let me as Boo roared. A beam of blinding moonlight shot from his antlers and blasted directly into the Lost's chest. His shadows tried to knit together and form a shield around their host. But Boo's magic was unrelenting, and they began to evaporate like steam. The angry hiss of their departure filled the clearing, and then all that was left was the Lost. Moonlight slammed into his body, and he shrieked loud enough to rattle the leaves. His limbs began to unfurl first. The form he'd somehow created was losing shape, and black tendrils wildly flailed in the wake of Boo's power until they withered and dispersed like dust. First his fingers. Then his arms. Then the center of his body was a snarling void that seemed to collapse in on itself until it too was nothing more than a wisp. The only thing left was the haunting apparition of his eyes. And then they too disappeared. The last threads of darkness dispersed, and Boo's moonlight carried straight through into the shadow realm. The presence of light destroyed the remnants of the Lost's power, and the rip quickly resealed.

Slumping against Boo's neck, I hugged him tight. "You did great."

He chuffed gently before plopping to the ground. His muscles quivered with exhaustion, and I slipped off him so he could recover without my added weight. With the Lost gone, though, my own adrenaline left in a rush, and exhaustion hit with the same force as Boo's attack. I sank to my knees and gripped the earth to try to steady the swaying ground. The shouts of Charmers, of Ozias and Raven and everyone else, were muffled. But as I let out a steady breath and tilted my chin up, I caught Kost's loving, green eyes.

And I was more than happy to fall asleep to the sight of that.

TWENTY-EIGHT

KOST

I didn't quite recall what it felt like to be raised from death, but I imagined my current predicament wasn't too far off. I wasn't in pain, but there was a heavy blanket wrapped around my mind that muddled my thoughts. I was vaguely aware that I was lying in a bed, draped in linen sheets with a soft pillow beneath my head. When enough awareness prickled through to my fingers and toes, I braved opening my eyes. Each blink scraped like rough parchment, and I winced. Slowly, the abrasion dulled, and I shifted in bed to try to place my surroundings. My body protested at the movement, resulting in an undignified slump as my arms gave out.

"The healing draught will wear off soon enough," a faintly amused voice murmured from the corner, and I spied Noc sitting in an armchair. With one brow raised and a slight curl to his lips, he leaned on one elbow and regarded me intently.

"Noc? What are you doing here?" This time, I managed to prop myself up against the pillows and not crumble. I quickly scanned the room, and while I didn't recognize the space, the cedar-plank walls and simple furnishings were of the same fashion as the house that had been destroyed by the Lost. Another dwelling in Hireath, perhaps.

"Ozias shadow walked to us and told us everything. We came back as quickly as we could." The easy expression on his face tightened. "Though I'm not sure what to make of it all."

"Me neither. All I know is, Gaige..." My pulse kicked up a notch. "Is he all right? Where is he?"

"He's fine." The tension in Noc's frame released, and he leaned forward to brace his elbows on his knees as he braided his fingers together. "He's with Leena, Raven, and Kaori, and he'll be absolutely pissed that I didn't come get him the moment you woke up. He's hardly left your room."

Warmth gathered in my chest and filled the marrow of my bones. "What about everyone else? Calem? Isla?"

"Isla is fine, but she hasn't said much. She is scheduled to return to Rhyne today. She asked about you. I'm guessing she wants to discuss what you witnessed." Noc's lips thinned. After a tight exhale, he continued to speak. "Calem is still sleeping. You two suffered serious injuries. Kaori gave you draughts to aid with the healing process."

My fingers skated along my bare torso, searching for any one of the multitude of wounds the Lost had inflicted, but I came up empty. Thankfully. "The Lost... He's an undead mage."

Noc nodded tightly. "He must have been raised before our time. Uma is the oldest member of the guild, and she doesn't recall him, either."

"Where has he been all this time? Why show himself now?" I leaned across the bed to retrieve my glasses, but I stalled at the empty nightstand. I'd forgotten the Lost had destroyed my spectacles during our battle. Instead, I gripped the hem of the sheets and prepared to pull them off when the door to the bedroom swung open.

Gaige stood in the opening, one hand still on the handle and the other gripping a small parcel. He looked so...alive. Gods, if the sight of him didn't do wondrous things to my heart. The collar of his tunic was unbuttoned to reveal the first smatterings of chest hair, and the deep, ocean blue perfectly accentuated the hue of his eyes. His trousers pulled tightly against his thighs and tapered down his calves, where they tucked into worn, leather boots. Damp locks, as if he'd freshly bathed, framed his face and grazed his neck, and I found myself drawn to the sharp cut of his jaw and the bob of his throat. When he'd registered that I'd awoken, he released the iron knob and took three quick strides to the bedside. With mock irritation—or perhaps it was more real than he let on—he speared Noc with a frown.

"You were supposed to get me when he woke up."

Mirth filled my brother's eyes, and his lips twisted into a grin. "Sorry. You were next on my list, I promise."

"Well, now that I'm here..." He let his words fall off without breaking Noc's gaze.

I didn't think it was possible for Noc's smile to stretch further, but it did. It was genuine, though, full of happiness and relief that seemed to fill every inch of his being. When his gaze slipped back to me, it was soft and full and warm. Without saying anything at all, I knew what his expression meant.

I'm happy for you. He turned back to Gaige. "I'll go check on Calem. The others will want to speak with Kost, soon, though."

"They can wait." Gaige only looked at me. Heat filled his steel-blue stare, and a delicious tingle crept over my skin. Neither of us said a word until the door clicked closed behind Noc and we were finally, blissfully, alone.

Something freed Gaige, and he dropped his parcel on the nightstand and crawled on top of me to crush his lips against mine. I let out a startled groan, but quickly brought my hands to either side of his face to hold him there. I wanted to relish the velvety feel of his lips forever. The intricate slide of his tongue against mine. In the heat of his breath, the scrape of his teeth against my skin as he tasted my neck. After he placed a bruising kiss where my jaw and throat met, he dragged his heated gaze to meet mine.

"You're okay," he murmured.

"Of course I am." I couldn't help but frown.

With a dimpled grin, he rolled his eyes. "Of course you are." Then, gently, he ran his knuckles along the side of my face. "I was worried."

"So was I." I leaned into his touch as I remembered his crumpled body, motionless, on the beach. There had been so much blood. Too much for my mind to properly strategize an attack when it came to the Lost. All I'd wanted was to let my emotions run wild and fight without care. And then, when the Lost's world collapsed and the shadows were dragging Gaige under, I'd just barely managed to grab hold of his wrist.

I'd almost lost him twice, and I still hadn't been honest about my feelings.

"Gaige..." I swallowed thickly. A familiar fear stirred in my gut, but it was nothing compared to what I'd just endured. It certainly wouldn't compare to the agony I'd feel if I never got the chance to tell him again.

He pulled away so he was sitting on the ledge of the bed, and his gaze roved over my face, searching. "Yes?"

"I..." My throat tightened. Gods, why was this so difficult?

Gaige's expression softened, as if reading my thoughts. He reached over and brushed his thumb across my lips. "When you're ready, Kostya. Not a moment sooner."

His response only made me love him more. Emotion filled my eyes as tears threatened to spill over, and I pushed his hand away. I couldn't sit still. All those unspoken fears and words filled my limbs, and I needed to move. Pulling the sheets aside, I jumped to my feet and paced. Gaige tracked each step with guarded eyes as he clasped his hands.

"Kost..." He began when I'd passed him for the fifth time over. "It's okay."

My feet rooted to the floor. Slowly, I forced myself to meet his stare. His shoulders were slightly rolled forward, his head tilted to the side. He looked up at me through the tops of his lashes, and his lips were pressed together in a thin line. Something sad flickered through his eyes, and my heart twisted painfully.

"Here," he said as a breath loosened from his chest. He snagged the parcel and handed to me. "I got you something."

Quietly, I undid the thick parchment to reveal an oblong, polished, mahogany box. I unclasped the golden toggle at the center and flipped it open. A pair of rimless, silver spectacles sat pristinely atop a bed of mulberry silk. Gently, I ghosted a finger along the thin frames.

"I still owed you some after Moeras. If you don't like them, we'll find a different pair." His words were so incredibly soft, so full of that damn unspoken emotion waiting to be named.

I stared at the liquid sheen of the glasses, unable to take my eyes off their perfection. Off *his* perfection. I'd spent lifetimes waiting for someone like him. And here he was, baring his heart to me with this immensely honest and heartwarming gesture, and I was still afraid. I was afraid of losing him, one way or another. I was afraid of what that would do to me if it happened.

And he still had no idea why. I owed him that, at least.

"I was in love once before." I saw him stiffen in my peripheral vision, but I forced myself to keep going. "His name was Jude, and we lived together in Moeras. I saved his life, but in turn..." I touched the bone-white scar above my heart and felt his gaze shift to the same spot. "I died. Not right away. The local healer managed to stitch me up and fill me with herbal remedies, and while the wound healed, the underlying infection never dissipated. It was slow. Painful.

"About that time, an assassin had come through town to complete a bounty, and Jude convinced him to take me back to Cruor and have me raised." I removed the glasses and set the box on the nightstand, still unable to let go of the gift Gaige had given me. "Jude wasn't prepared, I suppose, for what that would entail. He found the shadows...revolting. After years together, after what I gave up for him, he simply left.

"And then there was Noc." I didn't know where the words were coming from, why they were finally flowing, but I didn't dare stop. "I loved him, too, but it was...different. Deliberate. Because of his curse, his inability to love, I knew he was safe. He *couldn't* love me, so he couldn't hurt me. Not the way Jude had.

"But you, Gaige." I forced a hard swallow. "You were someone I could actually be with. And therefore someone who could actually break me. I put up a wall because it was the only way to protect myself from that heartache."

"Kost..." For a moment, that was all he said. Even now, I savored the way my name sounded coming from his lips. "Thank you for sharing that with me. You didn't have to; I would've waited just the same."

Gingerly, I slid the spectacles up the bridge of my nose. "I know."

Gaige stared at me long enough to stir a quiet heat beneath my skin. "You still haven't told me if you like them."

"I love them." Something fractured in my chest. Something beautiful and wonderful and terrifying, but it was such an intense feeling that I never wanted to let it go. Nothing had ever felt more real in my life.

Gaige remained perfectly still. “Good. I’m glad.”

“I love *you.*” A tear finally slipped down my cheek, but I didn’t dare brush it away. I wanted him to see. I held his gaze and watched as every muscle in his body tensed. As his breath caught and his eyes widened.

“I love you so much it terrifies me.” Slowly, I walked toward him. “And I have for quite some time now. I was so afraid of what would happen if I said it out loud and still lost you somehow.” I dropped to my knees and grabbed his hands. I stole his strength, his compassion, and his way with words as I pressed my lips to his knuckles and allowed all my emotions to keep flowing. “I can’t endure something like that again. So if you’re going to love me, too, it needs to last forever.”

In one swift movement, he snaked his arms beneath my shoulders and yanked me into his lap. Once I was pressed tight against his broad chest, he slanted his trembling lips across mine. I tasted salt and thought that errant tear had finally made its way to my mouth, but when we broke away to breathe, I noticed a wet sheen beneath his eyes.

He pressed his forehead to mine. “I suppose this means I lied to you.”

“How so?” A flicker of panic shivered through me.

“I planned on courting you before calling you my *anam-cara.*” A wry smile claimed his face. “But you caved after one small gift. I must be good.”

Anam-cara. That one phrase completely eliminated my fears, and warmth infused my body, straight through to my soul. He wanted forever with me. He *picked* me. And I’d picked him. I’d choose him every single day of my life, good and bad, so long as he’d have me.

I couldn’t keep myself from grinning—and I didn’t want to. “I suppose I failed you as well.”

“Dare I ask how?”

My fingers trailed over his collarbone. "You asked for a full-hearted confession, complete with flowers, chocolate, and I believe wine."

His baritone laugh, so deep and sultry, shook me to my core. When it quieted, he rounded on me with soft eyes full of love. "This is enough. *You* are enough."

Pure euphoria surged through to my fingertips, and I pressed my lips to his. He answered with a groan and pulled me closer, pressing our bodies together so that all I could feel was him. When he broke away, his eyes burned like molten steel as he toyed with the waistband of my trousers.

"I think I also asked for a sinful display of *this*."

"I can accommodate that," I said.

Pushing his back against the bed, I undid the buttons of his tunic and discarded it to the side. I ran my hands over his chest, exploring the tantalizing shape of his muscles. Gods, he was beautiful. I brought my lips to his skin so I could taste every inch of him, from the base of his throat down to his navel. He moaned as I neared his trousers and dragged a single finger along the outline of his swollen cock. He twitched against me, and I smiled.

"I feel like you're taking an unnecessarily long time to get to the *display*." Gaige rolled his hips into my hand for effect, ensuring I palmed him in entirety.

"You didn't set any parameters to begin with." I undid the buttons holding his trousers in place, and then curled my fingers along the waistband. "That feels like an oversight on your part, and entirely not my problem."

"It's about to be your problem." He arched into my touch and bit his lip, swallowing whatever complaints were still waiting on his tongue. I removed his trousers and stroked the length of his impressive cock, pleased with his string of heated curse words.

"Indeed it is." I went to remove my glasses when he stopped me with one heated look.

"Leave them."

Nothing in this world or the next could have pried them from my face.

When I placed my mouth on his length, his language grew even more colorful. I reveled in the velvet slide of him, in the unique scent that was a mixture of lust and something unique to Gaige. I got lost in it, wrapped in the scent of us and our future, and it wasn't until he forcibly pulled me up his chest that I was able to stop myself.

"Something wrong?" I murmured, my lips wet and swollen and eager for more. He stared at them with such hunger that my insides nearly exploded with desire.

"I want to feel every inch of you," he growled. "I want to look over my shoulder and watch you lose control."

I nearly did just at the mere thought of burying myself in him. His heated words gave me vigor, and I pressed a bruising kiss to his mouth before breaking away to remove my trousers. He didn't even give me the chance to keep tasting him. The moment I withdrew, he rolled to his stomach and exposed his glorious backside, and my mouth went dry. Nothing was more pleasing than the path of his spine leading to the dip just above his hips, the roundness of his ass.

I paused only for a moment to rummage through the nearby nightstand drawer. Fortunately, a collection of ointments and balms had been left behind, and I found a suitable lubricant among the glass jars. Gaige watched with rapt hunger as I screwed off the lid and coated myself. When I teased his rim, he groaned with anticipation.

"I need you inside me now. You promised a display. Now, give it to me."

Heat flushed to my cheeks. I'd enjoyed the fullness of him twice already, but I'd yet to feel his body wrap around my length. I couldn't deny him. I didn't want to deny him. But I did want to make him writhe. Pivoting my hips so my cock was no longer poised to enter him, I watched closely as he rolled his eyes in annoyance. When he opened his mouth to complain, I snuck between his gloriously firm ass and brought my tongue to his rim.

The resulting curse was by far my favorite reaction, and I continued to lave his entrance as he ground into me. When I was satisfied with my work, I lifted my head to find he'd skewered the pillow with his teeth and fisted the sheets. Several beads of moisture had already pearled from my tip, and I slid my hand along my length once before adding more lubricant to his rim. I positioned myself against his crease.

"Watch," I murmured.

One simple request full of heat and lust, and Gaige's eyes flew open. Lips parted in unrepentant want, he stared as I lined up and thrust inside. A deep groan simmered from the back of his throat as his eyes fluttered. There was only a smidge of resistance, and then he relaxed, drawing me in and wringing my nerves unbearably tight. I needed release as much as he did, so I wound my arm around his waist and found his cock.

He cursed again at my touch, and I shivered as I started to move in earnest. "Such a wicked, dirty mouth you have."

"Only for you." He never stopped looking at me. Not when I kissed the length of his sweat-slicked spine. Not when I anchored my free hand into his hip to set an unyielding pace. Pleasure drove us wild. He ground against my hand in time with my thrusts, and I got completely lost in everything that was him. In the salt-tinged scent of cedar and pears. In his heated moans barely muffled by his pillow. In the glorious sight of us joined together as one.

My release wound impossibly tighter, pulsing through my abdomen and begging me to find completion. Pulling Gaige against my chest, I spoke into the shelf of his ear. "I love you, Gaige."

He let out a cry as he coated my hand and trembled in my arms. "I love you, Kost. My *anam-cara.*"

Those words carried me into blissful oblivion, and I lost myself inside him. My orgasm shattered me entirely, and I held onto his broad body far longer than necessary simply to steady myself. As tension finally fled my frame, I eased my way out of him and collapsed to the bed with Gaige by my side.

He placed gentle kisses along my shoulder. My neck. My jaw. "That was quite the display."

"I'm glad you approve," I mumbled, still riding the high of adrenaline pumping through my veins. We lay together without saying anything at all for minutes, maybe hours... I didn't care to find out. I was wrapped up in the feel of his fingers tracing whorls along my abdomen, in the slight tickle of his chest hair against my back. If we'd never left that bed, that room, it would've been quite all right by me. But eventually, there was a knock at the door, followed by a quiet inquiry from Kaori.

"Isla is preparing to depart. Are you able to meet with her before she leaves?"

A grumbling sigh pushed its way out of my chest. "Yes. We'll convene at the dining tent shortly."

"All right. I'll gather everyone." The sound of her quiet feet padding against the wooden floorboards signaled her departure, and I sank further into Gaige's arms.

"Why did you agree to that?" I could feel his wry smile against my shoulder, so I turned over to capture it with my lips. He exhaled deeply and palmed my cheek.

Begrudgingly, I forced myself to pull away. "The Lost isn't dead. We'll need to discuss what that means for all of us. Isla seemed particularly flustered by his appearance."

Gaige's brows drew together. "She did."

"Come on." My body and mind protested greatly at those words, but I willed myself out of bed and began to dress. "We need to see her off. She's the reason I was able to get back to you."

Gaige yanked on his trousers. "*You're* the reason you were able to get back to me."

"Yes, well…" I buttoned my shirt and moved to the door, pausing for a moment to check my reflection in the mirror and smooth the mussed pieces of my hair. "Agree to disagree, I suppose."

Gaige sauntered behind me and draped one arm around my waist. "I have a feeling there will be a lot of that between us for years to come."

"Indeed." I turned to steal a quick kiss and then led us out the door, Gaige hot on my heels. When we emerged from the quaint cottage and broke out onto the lawn, he didn't hesitate to take my hand and thread his fingers with mine. The action sent a jolt through my body, and I stutter-stepped before recovering. There was no denying the heat racing up the back of my neck and most certainly tingeing my ears a damning pink. I doubt I'd ever grow weary of the feel of his bare, ungloved hand in mine.

"This makes you blush?" Gaige said with a squeeze of my hand, confirming my suspicions. "Gods, I cannot wait to see what else I can do to make that hue cover your whole body."

In that moment, he achieved just that. "Behave."

He answered with a devilish chuckle that must've turned my blush from pallid pink to vibrant red.

When we arrived beneath the stretched canopy of the dining tent, Isla, the Council, Leena, and Noc were already seated. The area was clear of Charmers, and a few glasses of water had been placed around the table for each of us. Midmorning sunlight settled low over the quiet clearing, reminding me I must have been out for at least a day. My gaze immediately went to Calem, and I was relieved to see him relaxed as ever with his chair reclined on two legs and his hands cradling the back of his head. There was a slight sallowness to his eyes, a hint of exhaustion he had yet to shake, but his impish grin still deepened at the sight of Gaige's and my intertwined hands.

"Welcome back," he said. "Seems like you've recovered fully."

"You as well." I dropped into the first available chair, with Gaige following suit on my left.

"I'm glad everyone is all right," Leena said. She sat at the head of the table with Noc beside her, and she toyed with the stem of her water glass as she looked over us. "We've heard snippets of what happened, but I'd appreciate the full story." Her hazel eyes bounced between Gaige and me.

Letting out a tired breath, I retold the series of events that led to the attack on Hireath. I explained Gaige's disappearance, and he interjected with details of his own and how he'd been snatched by the Lost. We recounted the horrid landscape we'd happened upon, Gaige's broken body, the Lost's strange obsession with Gaige's magic. No one spoke as Gaige and I traded off recounting one of the most horrific events of my life. We were safe here in the clearing, but I couldn't stop my heart from reacting to the mage's name. The Lost. It sent a flurry of panic racing through my bones. He was still alive. We had no idea if—when—he would attack again.

Isla drained her water and set it on the table before her, studying the diamond pattern etched into the glass. "I tried to warn you."

"I know," I said, letting my hand find Gaige's thigh beneath the table. "We had no other choice."

"That's not what I meant." Her umber eyes were hollow. "I knew you would go in after Gaige. I just meant I tried to warn you about *him*. The Lost, or whatever he's calling himself."

"You know him?" From the seat beside her, Ozias tipped his head her direction.

"No." She pursed her lips. "I just know he's old. He's Unfractured."

Raven narrowed her eyes as she regarded Isla. "What does that mean?"

She picked at a stray, splintered piece of wood until it broke from the table. "Mages are awful, horrible people. They're selfish and power hungry and entitled." She finally looked at each one of us, as if needing to remind herself that she was here in Hireath and not lost in Allamere. "Mages used to have immeasurable power. The goddess Luminessa granted us the ability to harness the energy that teemed from the world itself, and we could do wondrous things.

"But like I said, mages are awful. Our greed turned Luminessa against us, and she fractured the power we'd been granted, splitting us into five factions." She held up her hand and ticked off each finger one by one in time with her words. "Projectors. Manipulators. Transmutators. Enhancers. Creators. We all possess a unique type of magic the other factions can't master. But if the Lost lived and died before the Fracture, he would still have access to all the magic Luminessa stripped from her children."

The Fracture. Her weak warning rattled through my mind as I rewound the events of her ripping into the Lost's universe. I'd thought she'd been referring to the chasm she created, not the person lying in wait.

"Why Gaige, then?" Noc asked. Everyone's gazes rounded on my lover, and I squeezed his knee tighter. He dropped his hand to mine and brushed his thumb along my wrist.

"I don't know. He never said." Gaige's brows drew together sharply. "He just wanted power."

Isla glowered at her glass. "Typical mage."

"He wanted me, too." Calem ceased his reclining and settled his chair on all four feet. "He took our blood."

"You let him?" Isla rounded on him with wild eyes.

Calem glared at her. "I didn't *let* him do anything. We were transported to an entirely different realm, and he was the only one who had the magic, the *ability*, to do anything." Tension snapped from his frame as the mercury hue around his irises threatened to encroach upon his muted-red shade, but Kaori placed a gentle hand on his arm. He didn't visibly react to her touch, not at first. Eventually, though, he once again leaned back in his chair and tipped his head to the off-white canopy.

"About this realm," Noc said, bringing our focus back to him. Jaw tight, he stared first at some indistinct spot on the table, then me. "You think we've been wrong all these years."

"Yes." I adjusted my glasses, and the action settled me. Partially because of habit, but more likely because they were a precious gift from Gaige. "After considering Uma's own personal history with losing someone, the Lost's rambling, and the realm itself, I believe we've been led astray."

Ozias frowned as he crossed his arms over his chest. "How so?"

"We've always been told that control of the shadows was necessary. And it is." I cut a quick glance to Gaige, and he rolled his eyes. "But I believe the risks associated with lack of training were incorrectly deduced. If the Lost is as old as we think, he could have lived, and possibly died, during the same time as Zane."

"No shit," Calem whispered. Indeed, it would have been incredible if that were the case. Zane was the fallen son of the First King—the first undead assassin who started Cruor. The power to raise the dead and wield the shadows started with him.

Still, that was centuries ago, and this was now.

"We don't know what happened to the Lost. Not in the slightest. I do believe, however, that anyone who was 'lost' after him was actually taken. His misguided search for power resulted in him preying on his own kind to amass more magic. Why, though, I can't fathom."

Kaori pressed her back stiffly against the carved frame of her chair. "Some people are fixated on things like that."

Calem's eyes were on her before she could finish speaking, and he stilled his precarious rocking without bringing his chair's feet back to the ground.

Isla sighed. "No one more so than mages."

Aside from her initial questioning, Leena had remained silent throughout the conversation. But I'd noticed the worry lines caving across her forehead and the way she'd wrapped her fingers in the chain of her bestiary. She chewed on the inside of her cheek as she studied Kaori, then Isla.

She eventually shifted her focus to me. "Why now? If he's as old as you say, where has he been all this time?"

"To our knowledge, Gaige is the first Charmer assassin. There was no need to strike until the Lost discovered Gaige's power. As to where he's hiding..." I tried to hide my frustration, but Gaige's grip on my hand tightened. I didn't like not having the answer. I didn't like that being in the dark essentially meant putting my family in danger. Because I'd witnessed the Lost's power, but more terrifying yet was his drive. He would come back for us. For Gaige. For Calem.

My eyes drifted to Kaori. Possibly for her, too.

Raven shifted uncomfortably in her seat before palming her glass. "What's to keep him from coming back now?"

For the first time since I'd glimpsed her at the table, Isla relaxed. A glimmer of life reanimated her dull umber stare. "Magic takes a toll. That world he created, the one where he was apparently not even really there... That takes an immense amount of power even for an Unfractured. He'll need to recuperate. It's probably why he takes so long between choosing his victims."

"We need answers," Noc said. His hand found Leena's on the table, and the two of them shared a knowing look before he once again met our waiting gazes. "And it sounds like we might have some time. Leena and I still have a kingdom to run, but we'll comb through the libraries in Wilheim to see what we can find out about this mage."

Leena nodded in agreement, and then tilted her head toward Isla. "Can you contact anyone in Allamere? We need to know what we're dealing with."

She flinched. "It's not for lack of want. I simply don't know anyone in Allamere."

Guilt wormed through my gut. I'd more or less insinuated she was useless, and she'd proven to be the exact opposite. Without her, I never would have been able to get to Gaige. Without her... I might never have been able to express just how much I loved him or learned that he felt the same way.

"I'll see if I can regain contact with Eryx." Gaige followed my tight stare to Isla. "I still have that parcel he left with me. If I threaten to damage it, I'm sure he'll turn up." Relief washed over Isla, and she straightened against her chair. Though after our last encounter with Eryx, I wasn't certain her relief was warranted. We had been desperately trying to break an ironclad magical contract, that, if reneged, would have resulted in Noc's death. Eryx had been unable to help, yet he'd still demanded Gaige still do something for him in return. In exchange for absolutely nothing—his time, I suppose—Eryx had given Gaige some scrolls and insisted he keep them safe in return.

Gaige had never spoken of them again. Likely because Eryx had insinuated that examining the contents would result in Gaige losing his vision. Given the strength of Eryx's magic, I was inclined to believe his threat. His power was different from Isla's. A peculiar luster had filled his gaze, and with one simple command, he'd rooted Calem to his seat after one of his typical outbursts.

The same luster as the Lost's. My stomach churned. The sheen that had obscured the mage's eyes and the eyes of Gaige's shadow beasts... He'd been manipulating them just like Eryx had manipulated Calem.

The Lost truly was Unfractured, and that meant on top of the shadows, he wielded five unique types of magic that even a goddess thought were too much for humankind.

Leena stood and offered a defiant, resolute nod. "Let's plan to meet in Wilheim in two weeks. Until then, research. Try every contact to see what we can learn."

"I think I can manage two weeks. Of course, everything will need to be cleared by my queen," Isla said.

Kaori glanced out over the clearing. Her gaze lingered on a few of the homes that were midrepair. "We'll do whatever is necessary to protect what's left of our home."

"You two have a kingdom to run." I tilted my chin to regard Leena and Noc. "Leave the research and inquiries to us."

The tension racking Leena's shoulders dissipated as her lips curled into a small smile. Instead of responding to me directly, she glanced up at Noc. "Wasn't he supposed to be our royal adviser?"

He grinned. "He was."

"But he isn't. Should we consider his advice valid, then?"

I grimaced as Calem and Ozias chuckled. "We can discuss my future once we've dealt with this rogue, undead mage. I feel like adviser or not, that's something we can all agree on."

"I always thought it was strange you didn't stay in Wilheim," Gaige mused, a hint of mirth skating through his eyes. "Seems like a nice place to for us to call home. Lots of libraries."

"Your tailor lives there, too," Calem added, his mocking grin on full display. "Imagine having all the clothes your heart desires only a short walk away."

The banter continued as Ozias and Raven even joined in, but

it was all din in my ears. *A place for us to call home.* Us. Not me alone. He and I, together. Forever. Accepting the role as guild master of Cruor had been a natural progression, but it'd been born out of a sense of duty. I wanted Noc to know that the home he'd left behind would be cared for. More than that, I wanted the assassins to have a place where no one feared them. I didn't want them to experience what I had. But maybe now, with Noc and Leena shaping our world for the better, perhaps there was a chance for us to be something more. All of us. It would take time, but… My gaze slanted to Gaige, and a knowing smile—authentic and warm and stunning—graced his face.

"My home, Kostya, is wherever you are," he whispered against my ear, and gooseflesh rippled down my neck.

Turning quickly, I placed a chaste kiss on his lips before my blush could completely ravage my face. "The feeling is entirely mutual, Gaige."

With the laughter of my family bubbling around us and the promise of a future—our future—unfolding right before my eyes, I knew I'd finally found my sliver of happiness. My forever. And no one, not even the Lost, could take it from me.

EPILOGUE

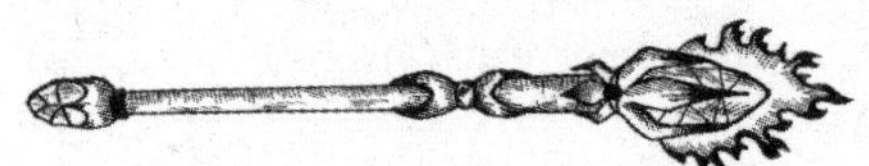

THE LOST

I'd long since grown used to the wails reverberating against the cavern walls. The incessant moaning of lesser minds unable to fathom a way out of this nightmare. Water dripped from pointed stalactites reaching from the ceiling like jagged fingers. We were all crones because of them. Broken backs bent at odd angles. Knees that creaked when we moved. The musty air was thick with the scent of shit and body odor. Nothing about this place was pleasant. And yet, the most damning thing about this prison was the glyphs on the walls. They were glowing reminders of the magic seeped deep into the stone. A barrier far stronger than the iron bars preventing me from roaming through the maze known as Galvanhold.

The lucky ones died. But I was already dead and still I remained.

A heavy slam shook water from the ceiling and pulled my focus to the entrance of my cell. The warden glowered at me, arms crossed, and face twisted in a mixture of disgust and pleasure. Eyes the color of faded bricks looked down at me.

"You're a mess, Zexus," she drawled.

"That's not my name." Maybe it was. I couldn't recall. It didn't matter what they called me, though. I would tear this place down just the same.

"I'll call you whatever I want." She dragged her painted nails along the bars, and the hair-raising scrape echoed through my cell. "Some of the prisoners have been acting strange lately. You wouldn't happen to know anything about that, would you?"

"No." Yes. My plans were my own, though, and I'd never share them with her.

"I see." She studied me for a long moment and then let out an exaggerated sigh. "I'll bring in the dogs again, Zexus."

I went stock-still, my body teetering on the edge of fear and rage. "That won't be necessary."

"Then cut it out. Whatever you're planning, don't." Her grin sharpened to something feral. It was hard to believe she'd ever been human. I didn't say anything else as she strolled away, callously taunting other inmates as she went. Only when her footfalls disappeared did I dare to move toward the back of my cell. We weren't given beds, and the linens were absolutely vile, but they were good for one thing—hiding. Peeling back a corner of the sheet, I brushed aside a blend of moss and mud until I spied the wavering glyph. A long scratch marred it from top to bottom, and the internal glow flickered more like a dying ember. It'd taken me years to dig deep enough to disturb it. I'd never eliminate it with brute force alone, but I'd weakened it. I'd created a soft spot in Galvanhold's armor. A space where I could project my power to the outside world.

"Did you get it?" a raspy voice called.

"Yes." With trembling fingers, I held my hand over the glyph. A thin shadow, so weak and strangled by the magic, emerged like a vine and formed a miniscule basin. But it'd done its job. A small sampling of blood churned in the bowl.

A dry cackle rose from the chamber across from me, and two bodies shuffled to the edge of their cell. Their dark eyes were wild and hungry, and they stared at my prize with rapt focus. The man gripped the iron bars, and his sable Charmer's emblem glistened like oil in the light of the surrounding glyphs.

The woman leaned against him, her smile wicked. "Go on. Drink it."

I didn't need their prompting. I'd been hunting for far longer than they'd been alive, but ever since these two Charmers were placed in the chamber across mine, I'd felt a sort of sick kinship between us. We all wanted to see the world burn. And they'd slowly been destroying glyphs along with me.

I licked my lips. "We're almost there." And then I downed the proffered blood as my shadow dispersed. Power slammed into me with such ferocity that I keeled over. Two very different, distinct flavors of raw magic—one filled with rage and bestial strength, and the other with the beauty of creation. Control.

A laugh bubbled from somewhere deep in my chest and my body shook.

Soon, these wards would fall. And no one could stop me.

Bestiary

Asura

Pronunciation: *ah-sur-ah*

Rank: B-Class

Description: An Asura is the size of a small child, with an upright humanlike torso, cow legs, and a cow head. Its body is covered in tan hide, and it sports six humanlike arms. It also has ten milky-white eyes, which correspond to the number of hits that can be absorbed by its shield. When activating its impenetrable defensive shield, the Asura holds two hands palm up toward the heavens, two flat and parallel to the earth, and two pressed firmly against the ground. The invisible, bubble-like dome this creates can withstand any attack for up to ten hits. The number of closed eyes indicates the number of hits sustained at any point during the battle. Asura are slow to move and incapable of physical attacks. Their shields will remain intact if they travel with their Charmer, but since movement requires them to remove their lower two hands from the earth, this weakens the shield.

Taming: Taming an Asura takes considerable time. The Charmer must sit cross-legged before the beast, with arms extended outward, and activate charm. This position must be held for several hours while the Asura chews on wheatgrass and evaluates the Charmer's power. If it finds the Charmer unsuitable, the Asura will walk away and become untamable for seven days.

Azad

Pronunciation: *a-zad*

Rank: C-Class

Description: Azad are small, mouse-like beasts with porcelain-colored fur and pearl-like eyes. They primarily reside in frozen landscapes, where food is scarce, and they will use their treasure-tracking powers to find their prize—grubs and grass. Their claws are incredibly sharp, and they can dig easily into frozen earth in search of food and to hibernate between feeds. Once tamed, Charmers can use their power to seek treasure of other types by communicating their desires to the beast.

Taming: Azads are incredibly hard to find, and only surface under the light of a full moon. While they're used to eating grubs and grass, they're particularly fond of fruit. Due to the frozen landscape in which they live, they rarely get to enjoy this treat. As such, if a Charmer wishes to tame an Azad, the easiest way to do so is to lure one out with fruit and wait under a full moon. Eventually, the scent will attract the beast. Initiate charm once it has started in on its meal.

Bone Katua

Pronunciation: *bone cat-ew-ah*

Rank: A-Class

Description: The Bone Katua is one of the ten legendary feline beasts and is russet-brown in color with bone spikes protruding along its spine. Its devil-red eyes have the potential to cause paralysis in prey, making it a supreme hunter. Since the Bone Katua can heal itself by rubbing its fur against trees, it's difficult to kill. Its yellow fangs stretch past its maw and can pierce thick hides with ease.

Taming: Bone Katua are difficult to locate, often living reclusive lives in mountains populated by dense forests. The Charmer must discover the Bone Katua's den and take up residence near it, demonstrating a willingness to live fully with nature by eating and drinking only enough to survive and maintaining no contact with the outside world. After several months, the Bone Katua will approach and paralyze the Charmer with its stare. It will then sniff and lick them from head to toe, determining whether they've truly dedicated themselves to nature. If it believes the Charmer has, it will sit before them until the paralysis wears off and then allow them to tame it. If it feels the Charmer does not value nature, or has contacted another human or indulged beyond what's necessary during those few months, it will kill them.

Boxismus

Pronunciation: *box-is-mus*

Rank: B-Class

Description: Nimble and fast, Boxismus swiftly move through jungle trees with ease. They're covered in orange fur with silver plates protruding from their shoulders and knees and along the backs of their hands and knuckles. They live in large groups together and are known to be extremely territorial, with the strongest Boxismus becoming the leader of the family and responsible for all members' safety. If a Boxismus considers a Charmer part of their family, it will go to any length to protect them.

Taming: To charm this beast, the Charmer must locate a family and challenge a Boxismus to fight in physical combat. However, entering directly into a fighting match with this beast will always result in serious injury or death, as the Boxismus has incredible power and stamina. To counteract this, set up a series of heavy sandbags and lure the Boxismus to them with fruit. The Boxismus will punch each one until they split. After five or so bags, they will have spent enough stamina for the Charmer to safely enter a fighting match without risking loss of life. Injuries will likely still happen, but once the Boxismus tires, initiate charm.

Canepine

Pronunciation: *cane-pine*

Rank: C-Class

Description: Canepine are wolf-like beasts with ivy-green fur and powder-blue eyes. Male Canepine have small white flowers that grow naturally along the undersides of their bellies, neck, and around their faces, while females have indigo flowers. They live in packs deep within the woods and are peaceful in nature. They have excellent tracking abilities, making them sought after by Charmers who frequent beast hunts. In addition, they can purify any water source, making it safe for consumption.

Taming: Taming a Canepine largely depends on whether or not the beast is attached to its pack. It is impossible to convince a Canepine to leave if it has already mated or birthed pups. Therefore, it's easier to tame youngsters than adults. Once a Charmer has caught the attention of a Canepine, they must play fetch for as long as the beast desires. Once the Canepine is satisfied, it will take an item off the Charmer and run away, returning sometime later. At that point, the Charmer must find the missing item. If they're able to track it down, the Canepine will allow itself to be tamed. If not, the Canepine will leave.

Dosha

Pronunciation: *doh-sha*

Rank: D-Class

Description: Dosha are no bigger than teacups and have exceptionally long tails and large hands. They're generally tawny-colored, with slight coat variations between males and females. While all Dosha have three eyes, female eye color is blue and male eye color is green. The adhesive secreted from their palms is so strong that a single finger attached to a branch could keep them from falling. When they wish to unstick themselves, a secondary dissolvent secretion is released from their hands, granting just enough movement for them to dislodge themselves. They live high in the treetops to avoid predators and eat a variety of leaves and fruit to sustain themselves. Thanks to a special lining in their digestive system, they're immune to any poison they might consume. As such, they're useful for detecting whether or not food is safe for human consumption.

Taming: Dosha never leave their treetop homes. To tame one, the Charmer must climb as high as the tree will allow and present the beast with a ripe coconut. If the Dosha accepts, it will glue itself to the Charmer's body while consuming the fruit. Once the Dosha is finished eating, the Charmer should initiate charm.

Dreagle

Pronunciation: *dree-gul*

Rank: B-Class

Description: Dreagles live in flocks atop mountain peaks and form deep bonds with their family. As the seasons change, the coats of their deer-like bodies adapt to match the environment—dirt brown and black during the warmer months and snow-white during the winter. With powerful, eagle-like wings, they can fly for hours without tiring. They use their antlers and sharp talons to catch small game or unearth grubs. Their incredible eyesight cannot be fooled by magic, and they're able to detect threats from great distances.

Taming: Dreagles have a unique relationship with Charmers. So long as high peaks are provided for them to stand guard—as well as more secluded mountaintop perches to nest and birth young—they'll watch over a designated area without needing to be tamed. They can be tamed with standard charm, but it's generally not recommended to separate a Dreagle from its flock, due to their highly social natures.

Drevtok

Pronunciation: *drev-tock*

Rank: B-Class

Description: Drevtoks are no bigger than a toddler with two spheres that make up their body. The bottom, larger sphere is hollow with branch-like bars that display an empty cage if the beast has not recently gathered food. The smaller, bulbous sphere is its head. Endless vines erupt from its center mass to snare its fruit and protect itself from potential threats. Drevtoks can open and close their lower sphere, and once tamed, store both people and belongings safely within their bodies.

Taming: Drevtoks are solitary creatures that live near orchards or locations with a large amount of fruit, which is their preferred food source. They only eat when hungry and the rest of the time protect their fruit from other threats by ensnaring them with vines. To tame a Drevtok, a Charmer has to successfully steal a piece of fruit. When the Drevtok attacks, the Charmer must bypass the endless vines without harming the beast in order to make it amicable to taming. If the beast is harmed, it will immediately flee.

Effreft

Pronunciation: *eff-reft*

Rank: B-Class

Description: Effrefts are roughly the size of small dogs, with falcon heads, long, feathered tails, and wings. Their mint-green coloring and pink eyes make them easy to spot during the day, so they typically hunt at night. They can shower the space beneath their wingspan with magic, encouraging plants to reach maturity in seconds, and the soil left behind is regarded as the most fertile in the world.

Taming: The Charmer should find an open field on a moonlit night and prepare a cornucopia. After overflowing it with a variety of food, they must initiate charm and wait. A successful taming may take several days, because Effrefts have unknown migratory patterns and might not be present. More sightings have occurred in the south, as they seem to prefer warmer wind currents.

Fabric Spinner

Pronunciation: *fabric spinner*

Rank: B-Class

Description: Fabric Spinners are reclusive beasts that live deep in caves far from civilization. While they're skittish in nature, they've been known to attack anything that strays into their territory. They wrap their prey in a web and slowly devour its organs over a period of time. They have humanoid heads with insect features, and human torsos that end in bulbous abdomens reminiscent of arachnids. With eight hairy legs, two pincers at the space where the torso transitions to abdomen, and two spiny, human-like arms, they're exceptionally talented at snaring prey. The ducts on their inner wrists shoot an endless supply of near-unbreakable silken thread. Their fingers are coated in tiny, retractable barbs that allow them to slit their webs if need be. The spinner that protrudes from the beast's rear produces a single thread that tethers the Fabric Spinner to its lair. If it senses danger or wants to return after a successful hunt, it will retract that thread and be pulled at immense speed back to safety. Given they're solitary creatures and rarely mate—females often attempt to eat males after copulation—not many Charmers own this beast. Those who do own the beast are often tailors, using the silk threads to craft immensely sturdy clothing or other sought-after materials, such as fishing line.

Taming: After finding the lair of a Fabric Spinner, the Charmer must bring several buckets of fresh organs to present to the beast. It will examine each offering one by one, and if it finds the organ appealing, it will wrap them in webbing for later consumption. If one of the organs has gone foul, the Fabric Spinner will become enraged and attack. Assuming all organs are satisfactory, the beast will then weave an intricate web. The Charmer must willingly ensnare themselves and wait patiently while the Fabric Spinner eats the provided organs, symbolizing the patience the beast exudes while hunting. The Charmer must remain completely still for the entire duration of the meal, otherwise the Fabric Spinner will attack. Once the beast has finished eating, it will cut the Charmer down from the web and allow itself to be tamed.

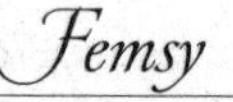

Pronunciation: *fem-zee*

Rank: D-Class

Description: Like the sparrow, the Femsy are small and flighty. They travel in flocks and rarely hold still, making it difficult to snag one's attention long enough to charm it. They're steel gray in color with violet breasts. When one is tamed, a yellow film slides over its three black eyes, marking it as owned. After a successful taming, the Charmer can tap into the bird's eyesight for short intervals by concentrating on the bond. Because there are no distance limitations to shared sight, the Femsy is often used for reconnaissance. However, the act is quite draining on the bird and can only be used three times before it must be sent back to the beast realm to recover.

Taming: No additional taming requirements are needed aside from standard charm.

Foxel

Pronunciation: *fox-elle*

Rank: B-Class

Description: There are only two reasons the Foxel is not considered an A-Class beast: they don't hunt people, and they only interact with those who have a connection to a Poi. Otherwise, this beast will live its days out in solitude, shying away from conflict at all costs unless its den is damaged. A Foxel is the size of a large hound with the body of a fox and an owl-like head. They have large antlers and ears, and three eyes. Their thick hides are feathery and resistant to water. A Foxel hunts by locking its gaze with its prey and initiating a magic that summons unparalleled terror. In people, this manifests as horrifying thoughts that become visceral and all-consuming, immobilizing the person in fear. This magic is preceded by the scent of mothballs and a cold chill.

Taming: The only way to tame a Foxel is to have formed a legitimate bond with a Poi. Foxels have a special relationship with Poi, often forming lifelong friendships and refusing to harm Poi under any circumstances. As such, the taming is simple, so long as the Charmer in question has a Poi and the Foxel in question has not bonded with another Poi. After finding a Foxel's den, the Charmer must summon a Poi and lure the Foxel out with small game. Because the Poi is in the vicinity, the Foxel will refuse to initiate its magic. It will then judge the bond between the Poi and its master, and if it finds it suitable, the Foxel will agree to be tamed. If the Foxel in question has already formed a bond with a different Poi, it will simply leave, refusing to be tamed but not harming the Charmer or the Charmer's Poi.

Graveltot

Pronunciation: *grah-vul-tot*

Rank: D-Class

Description: The Graveltot is a small, spherical beast covered in slate and rocks. It moves by rolling across the ground, only popping out its head and feet when prompted to activate its power. When its hooves meet the earth, it manipulates the force of gravity in a perfect circle around it, making it impossible for anyone caught in its trap to move. It only lasts for fifteen minutes, and the Graveltot must rest for several hours before it can use its power again.

Taming: No additional taming requirements are needed aside from standard charm.

Groober

Pronunciation: *groo-ber*

Rank: E-Class

Description: Groobers are round, fluffy beasts with white fur softer than a rabbit's fluff. They have stubby arms and legs and circular eyes. When squeezed tightly, Groobers emit a mixture of lavender and valerian to aid with sleep.

Taming: No additional taming requirements are needed aside from standard charm.

Gyss

Pronunciation: *giss*

Rank: C-Class

Description: Gyss are the size of coffee mugs, with human torsos and misty, wisp-like tails for the lower half of their bodies. They can only be found in sacred sites and often adorn their hair with flowers or leaves. Their sharp, pointed teeth are used to crack nuts, one of their preferred food sources. Exceptionally cunning and mischievous, they like to talk in riddles and are the only known beast with an active relationship with the gods. Male Gyss have been spotted but not tamed. Gyss have the ability to grant one wish every six months. There are no limitations, so long as payment is met. However, the breadth

of their ability is dependent on the master's power and intelligence. While Gyss can use their relationship with the gods to argue for less severe payments, they often don't, as they take joy in using their power to the fullest extent of their abilities. As such, they are rarely, if ever, called upon. Many Charmers feel Gyss should be ranked higher, but their restricted conditions for wish-granting caused the Council to rank them as C-Class beasts.

Taming: Gyss can only be found at sacred sites and require utter stillness to tame. Otherwise, standard charm is all that's needed.

Havra

Pronunciation: *Hav-rah*

Rank: E-Class

Description: Havra are small and slender in stature with gangly limbs and knobby fingers. They have long faces with four deer-like eyes. They are solitary creatures who live in forests and survive off berries. While holding their breath, they are able to materialize through objects. Because of this and their bark-like skin, they were initially thought to be tree spirits.

Taming: Havra can only be found in dense wood. The Charmer should place a basket of fresh berries at the base of a tree and wait. Once a Havra is spotted, the Charmer must hold their breath and initiate charm.

Iksass

Pronunciation: *ik-sass*

Rank: B-Class

Description: The Iksass alters its constitution to suit its master's needs. Generally, though, they appear to be tall and slender and take human shape, but are faceless. Despite that, they have excellent senses. Limbs appear and disappear on a whim, and they prefer invisibility, making them difficult to locate. They lurk unseen and hunt small game or steal food from wandering travelers. Needing vast amounts of sleep to power their ability, they can only be called upon for one two-hour stint during a day once tamed. Many Charmers use Iksass for protection, as their shape-shifting abilities make them formidable opponents.

Taming: The key to taming an Iksass is locating it. Without a known preferred habitat, the only way to tame one is for the Charmer to catch it picking their pocket in search of food. When this happens, immediately activate charm to keep the beast from fleeing, and maintain it for two hours or until the beast tires.

Kaiku

Pronunciation: *keye-kew*

Rank: C-Class

Description: Kaiku are small, pale-blue beasts with jelly-like bodies and four stubby tentacles. They're found in shallow ocean waters (not on any Lendrian coast). Females have an aquamarine gem embedded in their centers, whereas males have a ruby. When its power is activated, the Kaiku can, without fault, guide the Charmer to any location they desire. Their gem glows as they determine the location, and then they direct accordingly with their limbs.

Taming: After discovering the Kaiku's habitat and noting its sex, the Charmer must acquire at least twenty matching gemstones and offer them to the beast. If the beast finds a stone that is shinier than the one embedded in its body, it will shed the old gem and replace it with the new one. Then, charm can be initiated. If the Kaiku does not find a suitable replacement, it will flee and taming will be unsuccessful.

Kestral

Pronunciation: *kes-tral*

Rank: Unknown

Description: The Kestral is an untamable beast that magically appeared when Wilheimians forced Charmers to flee after the First War. The Kestral emerged and created an unbreakable border around Hireath to keep the dark magic of the Kitska Forest out. The beast maintains the threshold at all times, only allowing Charmers and those it deems fit to cross. It has incredibly long tail feathers, a large wingspan, and a slender, paper-white body with blue eyes.

Taming: Not possible. Trying results in the beast casting the Charmer across the threshold, only allowing them to return after an undetermined length of time.

Krik

Pronunciation: *crick*

Rank: D-Class

Description: Krik are pear-shaped birds with tiny green feathers. They have small, trumpet-like beaks that emit a staticky, dissonant sound known to steadily drive those who hear it insane. The Krik's lungs operate independently of each other, allowing the bird to inhale fresh air while still exhaling to maintain its call.

Taming: No additional taming requirements are needed aside from standard charm.

Laharock

Pronunciation: *la-ha-rock*

Rank: A-Class

Description: Larger than an elephant and built like a wingless dragon, the Laharock is one of the largest beasts in Lendria. It uses its thick claws to traverse the rough volcanic terrain of its preferred habitat and is surprisingly nimble. The bone mane around its crown acts as an extra layer of protection for the head, and large, pupil-less white eyes glow with the intensity of fire. Red scales rimmed in gold cover the Laharock's spine, neck, and legs, making the underbelly the only unprotected portion of its hide. These scales are easily corroded by salt water, which can cause damage to the Laharock. If the Laharock grows up in the wild without threat or human interference, it will develop magic that allows it to summon scalding fires and intense heat. Offspring, on the other hand, are empathic metamorphs, susceptible to an outside trigger that could alter their power. Once the trigger event occurs, the power solidifies.

Taming: Laharock absorb minerals from the volcanoes on which they live. Charmers will need to seek out an active volcano and bring a freshly caught marlin. Once the Laharock spots the Charmer, they should leave the fish on a slab and take several steps back. While the Laharock is eating, the Charmer should insert ear plugs, then summon a

Songbloom and use its lullaby to put the Laharock in a stupor. The Charmer must remember to approach slowly and find sure footing along the mountain, because one loose rock or loud noise can break the trance and enrage the Laharock. Regardless, the Laharock will produce an intense aura of heat as a means of protection. Being burned is unavoidable. To avoid severe damage, Charmers should immediately summon a Poi afterward to tend to their skin. Once upon the Laharock, Charmers must place a hand on its snout and initiate charm.

Alternative method (discovered by Leena Edenfrell): Find a Laharock with her recently birthed young. Separate the mother from the child. Carefully approach the offspring and tame it first (no additional requirements outside of standard charm). Be careful not to spook it, as that might cause a flood of unstable powers to occur. Once the offspring is tamed, the mother will call off her pursuit and willingly allow herself to be charmed in order to stay with her young.

Mistari

Pronunciation: *mis-tar-ee*

Rank: A-Class

Description: The Mistari is one of the ten legendary feline beasts and has a white coat and scaled crystal plates over its chest. Four wings sprout from each of its ankles, resembling jagged pieces of precious gems. They enable the Mistari to propel itself forward, even gliding over short distances. The crystal feathers are highly valuable and, when dropped, can be broken and embedded in the skin of two people, granting them the ability to share thoughts. Mistari live in small prides scattered throughout the plains. Due to their wings and speed, they are difficult to track.

Taming: Charmers should approach with caution and begin the following sequence: first, encircle the Mistari with a mixture of highly valuable gems and stones while half crouched and chuffing to symbolize deference. Then, lie facedown on the ground and remain completely still. If the Mistari does not approve of the Charmer's offering, they should run. Taming will not be successful and could result in death. If the beast does approve, it will pick the Charmer up by the scruff (Charmers should wear thick clothing to prevent injury) and bring them into the circle. Charmers should stay limp until the beast begins to lick them, then initiate charm.

Myad

Pronunciation: *my-ad*

Rank: A-Class

Description: The Myad is the largest of the ten legendary feline beasts, with a panther-like build, black fur, and a mane comprised of peacock feathers. The same vibrant teal and emerald feathers travel the length of its spine and tail, as well as onto its wings. Gold casings protect the weak points of its ankles and appear around the crown of its head. When the Myad is about

to take flight, blue magic streams from its feet and eyes. The Myad has the unique ability to place its prey in a stupor while prying into their deepest memories. The person in question is then forced to face the horrors of their past, which often results in insanity. If the Myad finds them unworthy, the person's mind is burned to ash, leaving them in a comatose state for the rest of their lives. Because Myads are carnivorous, they are likely to consume their helpless and unfeeling prey.

Taming: Taming a Myad is a dangerous three-step process. First, the Charmer must acquire the blood of a murderer, freely given, and present it to the beast. Second, they must offer a token of loyalty with high personal value. And finally, they must allow the beast to bite them, thus spurring a connection that enables the Myad to review memories and determine worth. Throughout the entire process, the Charmer must not scream, because that will break the Myad's concentration, causing it to either flee or attack. If the Charmer can survive the evaluation of their past, the Myad will grant permission to tame.

Nagakori

Pronunciation: *na-ga-kor-ee*

Rank: B-Class

Description: Nagakori mate for life at a young age and, as such, are always found in pairs. They are twin serpents that float in the air with dragon-like heads and whiskers that trail the length of their bodies. Females are electric-blue in coloring and can spew water from their unhinged jaws, while males are snow-white and shoot frost. When tamed, they must both be summoned at the same time, as they refuse to be separated.

Taming: Pairs can be found in cold areas near bodies of water. They're attracted to pleasant sounds, so Charmers should lure them out with a musical instrument or by singing. While maintaining the music, the Charmer must then perform a ribbon dance. The Nagakori will begin to mimic the flourishes of the ribbons, eventually surrounding the Charmer and allowing charm to be initiated. The Charmer cannot falter with the music, as this will cause the Nagakori to freeze them and flee.

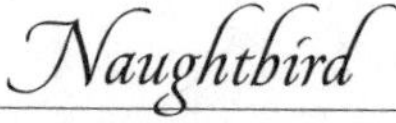

Naughtbird

Pronunciation: *nawt-bird*

Rank: C-Class

Description: These small, sparrow-like creatures have hundreds of tiny iridescent feathers. When they're in flight, their wings move so fast they're hard to pinpoint, and their tail feathers resemble that of a boat's rudder, angling from left to right to help steer. They have long, needle-shaped beaks that can pierce nearly any hide. When that happens, their saliva infiltrates the target's system and places them in deep slumber.

Taming: Naughtbirds live in hives. To lure one out, create a trail of flower petals that lead to a small bowl of nectar. If interested, the Naughtbird will follow the trail and drink from the bowl. Once the nectar is gone, initiate charm.

Neytmar

Pronunciation: *nite-mar*

Rank: C-Class

Description: Neytmars are the size of large wolves with humped backs and bony, protruding spines that end in arrowhead tails. They have bat-like heads and whiskers that trail from large, pointed ears. They are almost entirely blind, but have an incredible sense of smell and otherworldly hearing, and their whiskers are used to feel out their surroundings. They tend to form packs and have strong bonds with one another, but they rarely interact with humans and prefer to hunt rabbits.

Taming: Neytmars prefer to bask in open fields under the light of a full moon, and as such, this is the most opportune time to tame one. Slowly approach the beast with at least three hares and lay them at the Neytmar's feet. If the Neytmar has recently returned from a hunt, it will refuse the offering and the taming will fail. If the Neytmar accepts one hare, chances of taming are slim but not impossible. The more hares the Neytmar accepts, the greater the odds of a successful taming. During the duration of the Neytmar's meal, the Charmer must remain still and allow the beast's whiskers to roam over their body without flinching. If the Neytmar finds the meal satisfactory, and the Charmer maintains composure, initiate charm.

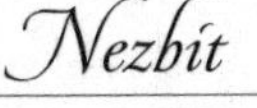

Nezbit

Pronunciation: *nez-bit*

Rank: C-Class

Description: Nezbits are small, have rabbit-like builds with brown fur, and are coated with teal feathers. Exceptionally rare, they're near impossible to find because of their low numbers and their preference for living underground. They form small colonies and create large networks beneath the soil, only poking their wing-like ears up once every few days to absorb nutrients from the sun. Their ears can hear sounds from miles away, and they track reverberations in the earth to avoid danger. When tamed, they're used to listen to people's hearts

and determine lies from truth. Their opal eyes flash green for truth and red for lies.

Taming: As they live underground, the Nezbits have no known preferred environment. Finding a colony involves luck and careful examination of the earth, because Nezbits leave behind small mounds after sticking their ears up from the ground. Once a possible mound has been sighted, the Charmer should remain still for several days until the ears appear. The Charmer should then quickly yank the beast up from the dirt and immediately initiate charm. It's important to note that the mounds in question are extremely similar to those left by prairie dogs, and because of that, reports of colonies are often inaccurate.

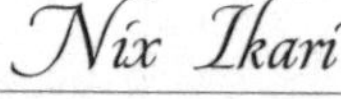

Nix Ikari

Pronunciation: *nix ih-car-ee*

Rank: A-Class

Description: One of the large legendary feline beasts, Nix Ikari are known as supreme hunters given their ability to completely mask their presence and teleport. They have snow-colored fur covered with dark, royal-blue spots with indigo inlays. When their power activates, glowing orchid light streams from their eyes and the spots, indicating they're about to teleport. They have elongated canines, twin curling horns behind their ears, and a thick, bushy tail twice the length of their bodies. They can travel great distances, though they normally only teleport in short bursts when hunting. The greater the distance required for teleporting, the longer it takes the Nix Ikari to recover.

Taming: Nix Ikari are fierce predators and will not be tamed without first deciding whether or not the Charmer in question is willing to fight. As such, very few Charmers have ever tamed this beast. After a Nix Ikari has marked a Charmer for a potential master, it will follow them unseen, judging their actions for an undetermined period of time. Once the decision has been made, the beast will appear and either kill the Charmer or allow itself to be tamed. Nix Ikari live in cold, near-inhospitable climates, and to start the taming process, the Charmer must provide prey, encircle it in the Charmer's blood, and decorate the area with fire opals.

Ossilix

Pronunciation: *oss-eh-lix*

Rank: A-Class

Description: While Ossilix are the smallest of the legendary feline beasts, they exude a calm fury and are lethal, using size to their advantage to outmaneuver prey. Slightly larger than an ocelot, they have lithe bodies coated in metal, giving the appearance of silver and making their hide near impenetrable. They're known to be incredibly intelligent, displaying exceptional tactical thinking and striking only when they see the possibility of a killing blow. Ossilix saliva is a potent healing balm with the capability of bringing someone back from the brink of death. However, accepting this gift requires the recipient to sacrifice a sliver of humanity in exchange. The effects vary from person to person, but largely involve a physical transformation to that of a beast.

Taming: After finding an Ossilix, the Charmer must allow it to inflict a life-threatening injury and then accept its healing balm. If the Charmer does not accept, it will kill them quickly. If they do accept, the Ossilix will retreat and watch from a distance as their humanity slips away and they transform into a beast. This transformation represents the constant fury the Ossilix feels and, as such, is incredibly difficult to control. The Ossilix will study the Charmer's behavior, killing them if they're unable to withstand the burning rage, or accepting them as its master if they're able to revert back to human form.

Poi

Pronunciation: *poy*

Rank: B-Class

Description: Poi are solitary creatures that often establish territories over small clearings in the woods. They have fox-like bodies with white fur and a single black stripe running the length of their spines. Their most identifiable feature is the jewel-like amethyst orb nestled between their ears, which turns cloudy when a prediction is brewing and clears once the future has been set. Poi bites are venomous and will slowly kill, but the poison can be removed by the beast if tamed. Their saliva can close minor wounds and alleviate burns, though their true power lies in their ability to predict outcomes two minutes into the future. When tamed, the Poi can share its visions with its master.

Taming: No additional requirements are needed outside of standard charm, but the Charmer must hold their charm for several minutes while making no sudden movements, allowing the Poi to perform a series of predictions and determine the outcome of being tamed.

Quolint

Pronunciation: *qoh-lint*

Rank: D-Class

Description: These small, frog-like beasts are the size of one's finger, with bright-green skin and red spots. They have tiny, see-through wings, allowing them to glide short distances while hunting for flies. Their skin secretes a viscous poison that has memory-altering powers. In the wild, this acts as a defense mechanism, causing a predator to pause and forget its actions if the poison touches its mouth. When tamed, Charmers can wear gloves to safely siphon some of the secretion and brew memory-altering concoctions that are tasteless.

Taming: No additional requirements are needed for taming other than to initiate charm, but it's important to note that the Charmer must not touch the Quolint during the process. While ingesting the poison will cause more lasting memory loss, touch can still cause temporary amnesia. Thus, if the Charmer grazes the Quolint while taming, they will forget why they're there, and the beast will escape.

Scorpex

Pronunciation: *scor-pex*

Rank: B-Class

Description: The Scorpex is a dangerous beast that can grow to roughly thirty feet in length. Its wormlike body is plated in thick orange scales and coated with a shimmery mucus. It has four legs, each ending in hooked fingers, and a barbed tail with a stinger like that of a scorpion. Its poison is painful but not incurable. With six eyes, three on either side of its mandibles, the Scorpex is difficult to catch off guard. It is carnivorous and uses its eight tongues to strip carcasses down to the bones in a matter of minutes.

Taming: Scorpex are rarely owned, because taming one requires collecting carcasses for weeks to accumulate enough food to entice the beast. The smell alone dissuades most Charmers, not to mention the danger of the Scorpex itself. After presenting the pile of carcasses, the Charmer should wait until the beast has finished eating to initiate charm. If the Charmer has not provided enough to satiate the Scorpex's hunger, it will strike. A relatively "safe" number of carcasses to present is somewhere in the high twenties.

Slimack

Pronunciation: *sly-mack*

Rank: D-Class

Description: Slimacks are solitary creatures with salmon-colored, worm-like bodies. Their skin is coated in mucous, and they have four, squatty legs that they press flush to their bodies when moving through the earth. Each end of the Slimack's body has an open maw with barbed tentacles in place of teeth for ingesting earth, and they produce a toxic bile that can disintegrate virtually anything. They prefer to live underground and have formed a symbiotic relationship with people, eating waste surrounding farmlands and fertilizing the earth with their excrement. The soil produced by this process is the most nutrient-dense earth found to date.

Taming: Offer the Slimack a heaping pile of filth and then initiate charm.

Songbloom

Pronunciation: *song-bloom*

Rank: D-Class

Description: The Songbloom is a relatively harmless beast found in rosebushes in remote parts of Lendria. The lower half of their bodies mimic the petals of a flower, and their human-like torsos bloom out of the center of the bulb. They can detach and float from plant to plant, reattaching via miniscule roots at the base of the petals that allow them to pull nutrients from the plant. Male Songbloom are ivy-colored and camouflage with the leaves, whereas females take after the actual roses. Both male and female Songbloom spend their days singing in an unknown language. There are a variety of tunes, and each one has a unique effect on the listener, ranging from feelings of elation to causing temporary slumber. Charmers frequently use Songbloom to elicit feelings of joy and love during ceremonies between mates.

Taming: Find a Songbloom colony by listening for their voices while searching through rosebushes. Once found, the Charmer must seat themselves before the beast and listen to a song of the Songbloom's choosing. Once the tune is complete, they should offer applause and then initiate charm. If the Songbloom elects to perform a sleeping tune, the Charmer will fall into slumber and be unable to offer applause, and the taming will fail. As the effects should only last a few minutes, the Charmer is free to try again once waking, assuming the Songbloom has not fled.

Telesávra

Description: *tell-eh-sav-rah*

Rank: D-Class

Description: The Telesávra is a lizard the size of a small boulder and has a rocky hide. It can detach its jaw to suck in air and summon a flickering white portal that will transport any beast or person with Charmer's blood to a designated location, referred to as a hearth point. The Telesávra can only remember one hearth point at a time. Many Charmers set Hireath as their hearth point for efficient and safe travel home.

Taming: No additional taming requirements are needed aside from standard charm.

Uloox

Description: *oo-locks*

Rank: C-Class

Description: The Uloox is a black snake found in caves with yellow eyes and three fangs. It can eat prey up to five times larger than its body size, thanks to its unhinging jaw and fast-acting digestive system. Tiny ducts are found along the roof of its mouth, just behind its fangs. Uloox venom is dangerous, and is known to cloud the mind and cause hallucinations, as well as weaken the body. Muscles will seize and become nearly immobile until the venom fades. Very few Charmers own one, as they're known to be temperamental and find little joy in being summoned from the beast realm.

Taming: To tame an Uloox, a Charmer must allow themselves to be bitten as many times as the beast deems fit. This is highly dangerous, as multiple bites can result in death. Once the Uloox is satisfied that the Charmer has become immobile, it will wait until its venom has cycled out of the Charmer's system. Only then will it allow itself to be tamed. However, if the beast becomes hungry during the taming process, it will slowly devour parts of the Charmer, such as fingers or toes, until it is either full or the Charmer is able to move. It's recommend that several field mice are brought along to the taming to prevent this.

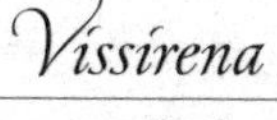

Vissirena

Pronunciation: *vis-sy-reen-ah*

Rank: B-Class

Description: Vissirena have human torsos and fishlike lower bodies that end in long, colorful tails. Iridescent scales varying in color cover the entirety of their figure, and their hair is a mixture of seaweed and tentacles. Their faces also share similar structures to those of fish, and additional fins often develop along the forearms. Vissirena live in schools in the waters to the west of Hireath. The fleshy voids on their palms can open and close, altering currents to bring prey in their direction. When tamed, they can channel powerful streams of water with immense force. Vissirena can only be summoned in bodies of water.

Taming: Do not attempt to charm a Vissirena underwater. At the first hint of danger, they will send the threat to the bottom of the ocean via an unforgiving current until drowning has occurred. Likewise, do not attempt to catch from a boat, as they'll simply destroy the ship. Instead, a Charmer should fish for one from the shore. Only a magically reinforced pole, coupled with fishing line made from Fabric Spinner silk, will hold the Vissirena's weight. Preferred bait is tuna wrapped in orange peel. Once the Vissirena is hooked, the Charmer should prepare for a fight that could last several days. After the Charmer has reeled one in, they should initiate charm.

Vrees

Pronunciation: *vrees*

Rank: S-Class

Description: As one of the five known S-Class beasts, the Vrees's power exceeds that of all A-Class beasts. Normally, the beast is massive in size with burning, white eyes. It has a fox-like head with the body of a wolf and three foxtails. Its form is more like a sieve with cutouts and negative space that mist passes through. In its center, a ball of blue electricity sparks and summons lightning. Weapons cannot scathe its hide, and only the right type of magic can harm this beast. When summoning a bolt of lightning, it takes a few minutes to charge prior to striking. When there are no threats around, the Vrees will shrink in size, reaching about midthigh in height.

Taming: The exact number of Vrees in the wild and their breeding habits are entirely unknown, as they are thought to live in storm clouds. Tracking this creature takes years and can span many continents, as they have no set home. To start, the Charmer must first find a lightning storm and look for a storm cloud in the shape of a wolf. Then, they must follow the storm until the clouds reach a sandy area. If it strikes, the lightning will petrify, creating an object that looks similar to a tree branch. Once cooled, collect the petrified lightning. If the bolt came from a cloud other than the wolf-shaped one, it won't work. If the Charmer is lucky enough to collect petrified lightning from the wolf-shaped cloud, they must then wait again for the storm to reappear, sometimes years later in an entirely different location. When this happens, the Charmer must present the petrified lightning. The Vrees will sense the offering and strike it, shattering the object and manifesting before the Charmer. It will then strike the Charmer with a bolt of lightning, and if they survive, allow itself to be tamed.

Whet

Pronunciation: *wet*

Rank: B-Class

Description: Whets are owl beasts that lead solitary lives and can only be found in high treetops at night. They have three gleaming ocher eyes, bark-colored feathers, and twin branch-like horns that stretch outward on either side of their head. In the wild, these horns embed themselves into trees and telegraph information to the Whet about where their prey are, making them expert hunters. Once tamed, they can be used to record information into tomes based off what they hear.

Taming: Whets are extremely difficult to locate, as they can sense when another being is in their territory and will flee. However, if they have recently eaten and are sated, they're less likely to fly away and will instead survey the approaching Charmer. The Charmer must then sit on the forest floor and read to the Whet for hours. As the Whet will likely get hungry during this process, it's necessary to bring small game to keep them in place. Once the Charmer has finished reading at least a minimum of three hundred pages, the Whet will be open to taming. Initiate charm.

Xifos

Pronunciation: *zy-fos*

Rank: A-Class

Description: Because of its replication magic, the Xifos is regarded as one of the most difficult legendary feline beasts to tame. It has a slender, slate-gray body with twin tails that form sharp arrowheads. When the Xifos is activating its power, all the hair on its body stands on end, solidifying into fine needles, and then it shudders, creating an exact replica of itself. The number of copies one Xifos can maintain varies, though the recorded high is two hundred and three. Each copy can attack with the full strength and force of the original. If a copy is injured or otherwise incapacitated, it will dissolve into smoke. Xifos are solitary, yet they usually have a pack of copies flanking them for protection.

Taming: A Xifos will only bond with a master cunning enough to separate the original from the copies. Simply approaching the beast and initiating charm will cause the beast to activate its power, surrounding the Charmer with copies. After the copies have shuffled, the Xifos will wait until the Charmer touches the one they believe is real. If they're wrong, the copy disappears, and all remaining forms attack. No one has ever guessed correctly via this method. Instead, after locating a Xifos, the Charmer should study it for several months to ensure they have the original version pegged. Charmers should find a cavern that can be used as a den, and construct an elaborate display of mirrors. They should then lure the Xifos to the cavern with the mating call of a pheasant, their preferred prey. If arranged correctly, the mirrors will trick the Xifos into thinking it has already summoned copies of itself. While it's searching for the pheasant, the Charmer should slowly approach. Thinking the Charmer is already surrounded by copies, the beast will sit and wait for them to choose. Touch the original Xifos, and initiate charm.

Yimlet

Pronunciation: *yim-lit*

Rank: B-Class

Description: Yimlets are beetle beasts with iridescent orange hides, barbed horns, and pincers larger than their heads. The size of a small dog, these beasts are surprisingly fast and can fly short distances, making it easy to snare their prey. When they bite their target, a toxin secretes from their mouths, deteriorating the skin of their prey immediately upon impact. The toxin will spread, eventually killing the target and allowing for the Yimlet to eat in peace. They can ingest up to five times their body weight in one sitting.

Taming: The only way to tame a Yimlet is to capture it with a net made of Fabric Spinner thread. Any other material will dissolve with the Yimlet's venom, and they will attack the Charmer in a rage. Because Yimlets eat so frequently, they will soon become hungry after capture and allow for the Charmer to tame them, simply so they can be sent to the beast realm to hunt.

Zavalluna

Pronunciation: *zah-val-loo-nah*

Rank: A-Class

Description: Zavallunas are incredibly rare horse-like beasts found only in foreign lands near places of highly concentrated magic. Auroras of varying colors, ranging from emerald to fuchsia to turquoise appear across their ink-black hides as they move. They have large feathered wings and a single blade-like horn that glows white. When their power is activated, they produce a dome of magic in a small radius that amplifies the abilities of any beast. This can only be done for a short amount of time, though, as extended use may cause permanent damage to the Zavallunas' horns.

Taming: Zavallunas are extremely selective when it comes to choosing a Charmer. As such, many become family beasts that are passed down from one generation to the next. To tame a wild Zavalluna, the Charmer must first travel to mage lands and partner with a mage in order to summon the beast. Once the beast has appeared, the mage must make a case on behalf of the Charmer, attesting to their magical prowess and kindness. Zavallunas will only agree to a taming if the mage and Charmer have been true friends for several years. The stronger their relationship, the more likely the taming will be a success.

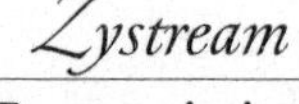

Zystream

Pronunciation: *zy-stream*

Rank: A-Class

Description: The Zystream is the only legendary feline beast that prefers water to land, though it's capable of breathing in both environments. Liquid-blue, its coat is a mixture of water-resistant fur and scales. It has a long tail that ends in fins, as well as finned whiskers lining its jaw and throat. Fluid in nature, it's nearly impossible to pin and can shoot immensely powerful jet streams from its mouth. It's stronger in water and can summon small rain clouds to follow it when on land.

Taming: The Zystream can be found in fresh or salt water during the warmest month of summer. A Charmer must approach while the beast is swimming, where it will assess the Charmer by circling them several times. At some point, it will dive beneath the surface and snare the Charmer's foot, dragging them into deep water. It's imperative that a Charmer does not resist. If they do, the beast will become irritated and either kill them or release them and flee. If the Charmer remains calm, it will continue to swim until it senses the Charmer's lungs giving out. At that point, it will leap out of the water and place the Charmer on the bank. Then, it will press its snout to their chest and use magic to coax any water from their lungs and encourage them to breathe. Now that the Charmer has become one with the water in its eyes, the Zystream is ready to be tamed.

The People of Lendria & Beyond

Kost

Pronunciation: *kawst*

Alias: Kostya

Role: Guild master of Cruor, member of the Charmers Council, undead assassin

Family: Gaige (partner)

Description: Tall, slender build with a faded scar over his heart; fair-skinned with light-brown hair perpetually styled in a pompadour; wears spectacles and favors bespoke attire; green eyes

Likes: Fine clothing, coffee, books

Dislikes: Clutter, pine nuts

Gaige

Pronunciation: *gage*

Alias: none

Role: Undead Charmer, member of the Charmers Council

Family: Kost (partner)

Description: Average build with broad shoulders and an ashen Charmer's emblem on the back of his hand; fair-skinned with dark-brown hair that falls in loose curls and a trimmed beard; blue eyes

Likes: All beasts, architecture, libraries

Dislikes: Small spaces

Noc

Pronunciation: *nock*

Alias: Aleksander Nocsis Feyreigner

Role: King of Lendria, former guild master of Cruor, undead assassin

Family: Leena (partner)

Description: Tall, lean and athletic build; fair-skinned with a crescent-moon scar above left cheekbone, griffin tattoo on chest; shock-white, tousled hair and blue eyes

Likes: Evenings, stiff drinks, puzzles

Dislikes: Most fish

Leena

Pronunciation: *lee-na*

Alias: Leena Edenfrell

Role: Queen of Lendria, Crown of the Charmers Council

Family: Noc (partner), Sabine Edenfrell (mother), Verlin Edenfrell (father)

Description: Average height, slender build; fair-skinned with oak-brown hair and a rosewood Charmer's emblem on the back of her hand; hazel eyes

Likes: All beasts, chocolate, traveling

Dislikes: Bitter beer, cold feet

Calem

Pronunciation: *kay-lum*

Alias: none

Role: Undead assassin, member of the Charmers Council

Family: none

Description: Bronze skin, shoulder-length blond hair often kept in a bun; muted-red eyes with a ring of mercury around the irises; broad build; tall

Likes: Competition, sparring

Dislikes: Bats, losing

Ozias

Pronunciation: *o-zi-us*

Alias: none

Role: Undead assassin, member of the Charmers Council

Family: none

Description: Dark skin with deep-brown eyes; cropped hair and large hands; broad body with a large, muscular build; average height

Likes: Family life, cooking

Dislikes: Bugs

Kaori

Pronunciation: *kay-or-ee*

Alias: none

Role: Member or the Charmers Council

Family: Unnamed mother and father, imprisoned

Description: Smooth, pale skin with dark eyes and lashes; long, sable hair; slender build with sharp features; sapphire Charmer's symbol on the back of her hand; mercury veins lining the underside of one wrist; short-to-medium height

Likes: Tea, beasts, crafting

Dislikes: Liars, tight clothing

Raven

Pronunciation: *ray-ven*

Alias: none

Role: Member of the Charmers Council

Family: none

Description: Tawny skin with inked forearms, reddish-purple Charmer's emblem on her hand; wavy, copper-colored hair and yellow eyes; lean build, average height

Likes: Fighting, trying new foods

Dislikes: Dancing

Isla

Pronunciation: *eye-lah*

Alias: none

Role: Captain of the Queen's Guard (Rhyne), mage

Family: none

Description: Beige skin with blonde hair and umber eyes; relatively short but strong build with definitive muscles; powerful gait and presence; magic typically resembles electricity

Likes: The outdoors, stiff drinks

Dislikes: Mages, fish

Uma

Pronunciation: *oo-mah*

Alias: none

Role: Undead assassin, resident healer of Cruor

Family: none

Description: Short stature with periwinkle-blue eyes; fine lines and wrinkles that hint at age; silver hair often pulled back in a braid

Likes: Herbs, spices, tea

Dislikes: Traveling

Sabine

Pronunciation: *sah-bine*

Alias: none

Role: Charmer

Family: Verlin Edenfrell (partner), Leena Edenfrell (daughter)

Description: Fair-skinned, medium-height woman of average build; angular cheekbones that mirror her daughter's; walnut-colored hair

Likes: Coffee, quiet evenings

Dislikes: Early mornings

Verlin

Pronunciation: *ver-lin*

Alias: none

Role: Charmer

Family: Sabine Edenfrell (partner), Leena Edenfrell (daughter)

Description: Tall, medium build with fair skin and black hair; hazel eyes that mirror his daughter's; freckles across his long nose

Likes: Running, hiking

Dislikes: Sedentary activities

Emelia

Pronunciation: *eh-me-lee-uh*

Alias: none

Role: Undead assassin, lead sentry at Cruor

Family: Iov (brother)

Description: Medium height, athletic build; black hair often braided, widow's peak; dark eyes; sepia-toned skin; twin to Iov

Likes: Training, physical activities

Dislikes: Reading

Iov

Pronunciation: *ee-ov*

Alias: none

Role: Undead assassin

Family: Emelia (sister)

Description: Medium-to-tall height, athletic build; black hair with widow's peak; dark eyes; sepia-toned skin; twin to Emelia

Likes: Practical jokes, beasts

Dislikes: Board games

Astrid

Pronunciation: *as-trid*

Alias: none

Role: Undead assassin

Family: none

Description: Small, lean build with wiry muscles; short-to-medium height; short, spiky hair

Likes: Competition, physical sports

Dislikes: Cooking

The Lost

Pronunciation: *lost*

Alias: Zexus

Role: Undead mage

Family: None

Description: Tall, medium build with broad chest; brown-black eyes with a ring of crimson around the irises; lanky, ash-blond hair; jagged scar running from his collarbone to his earlobe

Likes: Power

Dislikes: Mages

Acknowledgments

Shadows of the Lost was a labor of love. I couldn't have been more excited to finally pen Kost and Gaige's story, and while I was thrilled to give them their happily ever after, there was a part of me that agonized over Gaige's predicament. He was so uncomfortable in his skin, and that feeling was something I recognized in myself.

Let me be abundantly clear: Gaige (and Kost) have always been, and always will be, comfortable with their identities. Until recently, I wasn't. Gaige's struggle to reconcile with his shadows, to embrace who he was fully, was mine. And I believe it's a struggle many of us have experienced in some fashion or another. The beauty of it all was Kost's ability—and Ozias's, and Calem's, and Noc's, and Leena's… everyone's—to go on that journey with Gaige and support him as he stepped into his whole self.

So I have to thank the people who helped me step into me, without fear of judgement, with open arms and open hearts. Sarah McMillan, Chaz Martineau, and of course, my husband Jacob. I love you all more than words can ever express.

I also have to thank my writer besties, Alexa Martin and Lindsay Landgraff Hess, for always being a phone call away when I needed to vent, laugh, or cry (or sometimes all three). You're my rocks.

And of course, my eternal gratitude goes out to my agent, Cate Hart, and my editor, Mary Altman. These two are the real champs. They both do so much to bring this series to life—thank you.

About the Author

Maxym M. Martineau is an article and social media writer by day and a fantasy author by night. When she's not getting heated over broken hearts, she enjoys playing video games, sipping a well-made margarita, competing in just about any sport, and, of course, reading. She earned her bachelor's degree in English literature from Arizona State University and lives with her family in Arizona. Connect with her at MaxymMartineau.com or through Twitter and Instagram @ maxymmckay.

Discover Maxym M. Martineau's

BEAST CHARMER SERIES

with

KINGDOM of EXILES

THE FROZEN PRINCE

THE SHATTERED CROWN

ART BY
Therese Andreasen

I will not fall. I will not flee. I will not break.

I will fight—for her, for all of us—until
I have nothing left to give.

I am their Crown. Their Queen. Their Chosen.
Their Martyr.